# HOOKED

ALSO BY ASAKO YUZUKI

*Butter*

# HOOKED

*A Novel of Obsession*

## ASAKO YUZUKI

*Translation by Polly Barton*

ecco
An Imprint of HarperCollins*Publishers*

Without limiting the exclusive rights of any author, contributor or the publisher of this publication, any unauthorized use of this publication to train generative artificial intelligence (AI) technologies is expressly prohibited. HarperCollins also exercise their rights under Article 4(3) of the Digital Single Market Directive 2019/790 and expressly reserve this publication from the text and data mining exception.

This is a work of fiction. Names, characters, places, and incidents are products of the author's imagination or are used fictitiously and are not to be construed as real. Any resemblance to actual events, locales, organizations, or persons, living or dead, is entirely coincidental.

HOOKED. Copyright © 2015 by Asako Yuzuki. English translation copyright © 2026 by Polly Barton. All rights reserved. No part of this book may be used or reproduced in any manner whatsoever without written permission except in the case of brief quotations embodied in critical articles and reviews. For information, address HarperCollins Publishers, 195 Broadway, New York, NY 10007.

HarperCollins books may be purchased for educational, business, or sales promotional use. For information, please email the Special Markets Department at SPsales@harpercollins.com.

Ecco® and HarperCollins® are trademarks of HarperCollins Publishers.

hc.com

First published in the Japanese language as *Nile Perch No Joshikai* in Tokyo in 2015 by Bungeishunju Ltd.

English translation originally published in Great Britain in 2026 by 4th Estate, an imprint of HarperCollins Publishers.

English language translation rights in North America reserved by Ecco under the license granted by Asako Yuzuki, arranged with Bungeishunju Ltd. through The English Agency (Japan) Ltd. and Rogers, Coleridge and White Ltd.

FIRST U.S. EDITION

Library of Congress Cataloging-in-Publication Data has been applied for.

ISBN 978-0-06-344241-2

Printed in the United States of America.

26 27 28 29 30  LBC  6 5 4 3 2

# CHAPTER ONE

*I want to swim* – so went the urge that overtook Eriko in that moment.

She imagined letting her shirt, her skirt and her underwear fall to the floor, and then feeling the softness of the water and the refracted light against her bare skin as she swam on and on, endlessly, through soundless space. As her skin grew accustomed to the temperature of the water, the boundaries between herself and the outside world would grow hazy, and trappings such as her age, her weight and her gender lost their significance. If she attempted to speak, her words became tiny bubbles, rising up and up to merge with that distant white before disappearing entirely. But why did she feel this craving so powerfully, when the hottest season of the year was drawing to a close?

Then the answer hit her. It was because the early morning office spreading out in front of her so closely resembled a deserted indoor pool.

The desks set out in neat rows as if broken up by lane dividers; the silent, pale blue space that recalled the water's surface. In the way that they both seemed to bring memories flooding back, the smells of chlorine and toner ink were not at all dissimilar. Eriko's search for a place and a time when she could be utterly alone, so as to work uninterrupted, had eventually led her to this very office where she spent the majority of her days. Mostly it was a space where she felt the pressure to show herself at her most capable, and yet right now, she could have yelled whatever nonsense she wanted at the top of her lungs, or broken into some bizarre dance routine, without any consequences whatsoever. Of course, she didn't actually do any such thing. Eriko was not the type to yell or to do zany dances, whatever the circumstances.

Between 6 and 7 a.m., the food sales division that subsumed half of the eighteenth floor of the head offices of Nakamaru, Japan's largest trading company, was entirely devoid of people. Broadly speaking, the division's remit was a classic one for a Japanese trading company: importing food products from overseas, and selling them to domestic companies.

The fresh, untainted air spreading out before her calmed Eriko Shimura's mind and body, both of which were perpetually seeking out a conclusion. It was the task of whoever arrived first in the office to switch on the clocking-in machine. She crouched down, stuck the plug into the dusty socket and flicked the switch. Removing the card with her name on from the box on the wall, she inserted it into the machine. A clunk resonated through the silent office space, and another 6 a.m. time stamp was added to the row on her card.

Ever since she'd been a young girl, Eriko had liked being ahead of other people. Her father, who had worked at this same company many years before her, had impressed upon her that *getting in there first* was a crucial skill in a successful businessperson. Certainly Eriko's parents, with whom she lived in an apartment in Setagaya, weren't delighted by the fact that their only daughter ate breakfast apart from them, but now that she was in her eighth year at the company they no longer complained about it.

Even at the age of thirty, Eriko had no intention of leaving home. She knew that without her mother's support, there was no way she'd be able to work this hard, while also remaining this immaculately presented and healthy. Besides, she thought, if she were to leave home, her mother would soon feel stifled by a life spent with only her taciturn father for company.

However early Eriko got to the office, though, the most she would have to herself was a meagre forty minutes. Most of her colleagues arrived an hour ahead of the official start time of 8.30, checking their emails with one hand as they chowed down breakfasts purchased from the convenience store with the other. Weaving her way between the fifty or more desks filling the office in the Tod's high heels that her mother had polished so thoroughly that they reflected the lights of the ceiling, Eriko made a beeline for her desk. Half of the staff in her division were permanent employees of the company, but of those, the only woman other than Eriko was Sayako Yoshiba, a sales director ten years Eriko's senior. The temps and those on temporary contracts were all women, but they arrived just in time to begin work at 8.30.

The convenience store bag containing Eriko's breakfast and a copy of today's *Nikkei* newspaper rustled against her beige pleated skirt. She sat down at her desk and switched on her computer. The deep boom of the start-up noise resonated at her feet, tracing invisible arcs in the air as it spread through her surroundings. This moment, and this moment only, was time given to her when it was acceptable to think and do nothing whatsoever. It was quite possibly the most at peace that she felt throughout the entire day. Eriko savoured this little scrap of freedom, which lasted until her neatly organised desktop materialised on the screen in front of her. Now that her salary easily surpassed ten million yen, Eriko could say with confidence that the most valuable resource in this world was time. You could make a go of most things, if you only had time. Today, with everybody rushing around so frenetically, the mere understanding that an abundant amount of time had been spent on a certain project, product or artwork served to increase its value. The high status afforded to such things as light, natural-looking makeup, food cooked in the traditional way, and letters spanning over three sheets of paper and starting out with genteel references to the changing seasons reflected people's reverence for the time spent in creating them.

To clear a space for her breakfast, Eriko first cleaned the squeaky surface of her desk with disinfectant wipes, making sure not to overlook the cracks in her keyboard and her phone receiver. She understood that this was a finicky habit, but she also knew that if she didn't undertake this ritual, this portion of space that had been allocated to her wouldn't feel like her own. She made her way through the office circulars that had accumulated in a pile on her desk, skimming her eyes over each in turn. At this time of day, she could accomplish everything at several times the speed at which she worked during business hours, when people were forever coming and going around her, and the phone rang incessantly. You could create time, if you only used a bit of inventiveness – that was something she'd learned from her first-ever boss. When, a few minutes later, she reached the bottom of the pile, Eriko internally rubbed her hands in glee as she moved the convenience store bag to the centre of her desk.

From the bag, she took out a small carton of café au lait, shortly followed by the main article: a Karintō Melon Bun, resplendent in its plastic wrapping. This morning, she'd searched two convenience stores near her house for it, but it had been sold out in both. She'd finally managed to locate the brand-new product in a convenience store inside the subway station. She knew full well that the baked item, which brought the sweet, deep-fried crunch of karintō together with the classic melon bun, was not going to be healthy, and yet still she flipped it over to check the ingredients. Quite possibly this was an occupational disorder. Mitsuzaki, the name of the bread manufacturer written on the packaging, was a client of the cereals division. Even at this age, eating food laced with artificial sweeteners, preservatives and colourings – the kind of food that her mother, who liked everything to be natural, so vehemently abhorred – was enough to give Eriko a sneaky thrill. All that excitement, for a mere 918 yen! Hadn't her classmates back at high school used to buy sweet buns like these from the school store? As much as she'd appreciated her mother's home-cooked bento boxes, she remembered feeling terribly envious of those huge sweet buns with their garish colours. It had seemed to her as though the bodies of the girls of her age that were so readily and joyfully filled up by those cheery confectionery items concealed temperaments that were laid-back and unrestrained.

She opened her bookmark list, hovered the cursor over the URL of her favourite blog, and then, with a single click of the mouse, dived into a pool of time that was hers and hers alone. As her eyes ran over the lines of text, she took a bite of the melon bun, which was nearly as large as her face. The thick cookie dough encrusting its surface broke open with a crunch, and out spilled the aroma of butter and brown sugar, and the unmistakable taste of melon. Yes, it was exactly like she'd described. The combination of saltiness and sweetness wasn't bad, but the overall flavour was hardly sophisticated. Savouring it alongside the words flowing down the screen, though, its deliciousness seemed to percolate through her body.

*The idea of combining karintō and the trusty melon bun is, of course, totally stupid. Honestly, I burst out laughing when I saw it there in the convenience store. But here's the thing: when you bite into that greasy, crunchy coating with its hint of soy sauce not unlike mitarashi dumplings, it's like emerging from a tunnel into the light, with the bright, fresh green flavour of melon fanning out all around you. I have to report that I'm now totally addicted. A stupid taste. A stupid price. But you know what, getting by on 'stupid food' actually makes things very easy. It's kind of soothing to feel like you've found a way to cheat at life. I don't know if I'd recommend it per se, but hey …*

*Found a way to cheat at life* – that struck her as a neat phrase. For Eriko, life so far had been something to take deadly seriously, to grapple with as earnestly as one could. As she was sitting there, a faint sense of achievement washing through her as the heaviness of stale oil in her chest lulled her into a light daze, she heard a voice from somewhere above her.

'Wow, that's such a schoolgirl breakfast choice, Shimura. You'll get fat if you keep eating stuff like that, you know?'

Yasuyuki Sugishita was a fellow member of the seafood team. His modus operandi in any given situation was to act in such a way as to make his conversational partner worry that they were out of line in some way – and then, as they were engrossed in checking their own behaviour, Sugishita would forge on ahead to gain the lead. This strategy apparently rendered him immune to criticism too, because despite his being far from a perfectionist, Eriko had never seen him being cautioned or told off by a superior. In the sales section, where jock types were the norm, Sugishita's skinny physique and his pretty, longish face with its narrow jaw and pale, colourless lips stood out from the pack.

Somewhat unusually, he had joined the company fresh out of an architecture degree, which meant he was two years older than Eriko, despite being part of the same cohort of university leavers.

'Morning! You mean this bun? There was an article about it on a blog that I read regularly. I finally managed to get hold of one.'

Even as the unhappy realisation that her alone time had been cut shorter than she'd anticipated resonated through her body, Eriko gestured to her computer screen. Sugishita rested his hands on her desk and he leaned right in. Wow, that's very close, Eriko thought, but she didn't pull back. The scent of Sugishita's hair product filled her nostrils.

'Woah, is this like a wife blog?! What does a single girl like you get out of reading something like this?'

For two years now, Eriko had been reading a blog entitled *The Diary of Hallie B, The World's Worst Wife* practically every day. The website design was pretty basic, the long entries featured few line breaks, and the shoddy photographs were clearly taken on a smartphone. And still, it was a permanent fixture in the list of the 30 Most Popular Homemaker Blogs, as featured on an influential website. Perhaps one of the things that made it unique was that it didn't attract any of the trolls that were a staple of the other homemaker blogs.

'It is, but it's a bit different to the others. She doesn't go on about being a wife all the time – in fact, she's surprisingly slapdash about things. She's fairly lax when it comes to food and domestic tasks, without it ever feeling overly sloppy. We're the same age, as well, which makes me feel close to her.'

Hallie B lived with her husband, a supermarket manager, in a Tokyo apartment. They apparently had no intention of having children at present. They didn't seem to be particularly wealthy, but there was no indication that Hallie did any part-time work, either. Despite being a full-time homemaker, she didn't always cook; often she would meet her husband in a family restaurant or a conveyor-belt sushi place for dinner. Her husband didn't seem to criticise her for this, and in general, they appeared to get along very well – yet neither was there any bragging about how perfectly blissful their marriage was. Eriko liked how, instead of calling her husband 'hubby' or using his real name, Hallie had a special title for him on the blog: 'The Demon King.'

> *I want kids, but somehow we never get to the making-them stage … I guess sex isn't so bad once you get started, but it's the lead-up that I struggle with. It always seems like such a massive effort! Hey, Demon King, are you reading this?*

Hallie would come out with faintly shocking pronouncements like this in a nonchalant manner. Eriko found it unspeakably refreshing to read Hallie stating flat out that she never bothered using coupons or collecting up points from supermarkets or pharmacies – that was the type of wife she was, and she was fine with it.

> *I just think those people who concoct this points nonsense are stealing our precious time >;-( You save up all this money to get a discount of a piddly 500 yen or whatever. Once you've factored in the faff of scrabbling around to find your points card and take it out of your wallet every time you're at the cash register, it's frankly not worth it. I bet if you added up all the time that an average person spends on all that palaver over the course of a lifetime, it'd easily be ten hours or more. I'm hardly rich, and it's possible that I'm missing a trick here, but I kind of don't care? Let's tell it like it is: it's a pain! I tossed all of my point cards in*

*the bin and lo and behold, my wallet was suddenly so light! Not to mention my spirits …*

Eriko had always hated how her mother's wallet was so bloated with points cards and coupons. With her father becoming president of one of Nakamaru's subsidiary companies quite early on in his career, they'd lived quite affluently; Eriko found it dispiriting, nonetheless, that her mother was toyed about with by the whims of the retailers in a bid to save a paltry 100 or 200 yen here and there. On first impressions her mother seemed easy-going, but there was also a dogged, persistent quality to her personality. She refused to throw anything away, insisting on holding on to everything just in case it came in handy one day. Maybe Eriko resented this impulse in her mother in part because it wasn't dissimilar to her own. Hallie B seemed to instinctually know that time was more important than money. That was what enabled her to exist so spaciously, so without constraint.

'I don't see the appeal. What's a diary like this got to do with your life? It's so … domestic?!'

Pushing back an inexplicable sense of hurt that Sugishita didn't seem remotely impressed by the blog, Eriko began to talk faster.

'I like how real she is. You don't get a sense she's making an effort to dress up her life in any way. It's cute – she's cute. And the prose has a nice pace to it. It's like you can sense the expanse of time on her hands.'

'Oh, I get it! You think it's fun to look down on stay-at-home women with nothing to do with themselves, huh? Man, women are mean! You really love seeking out women of a lower status so as to feel better about yourself, eh …'

Eriko was accustomed to the male employees at work coming out with these kinds of lines, but that didn't mean that it didn't grate on her. When she'd first joined the company, the extent to which overt misogyny went unpunished shocked her, but by this point she'd resigned herself to it. The trick was to let it wash over you. The men didn't mean it maliciously – there was a surprising absence of any thought behind these casual utterances – so it was a mistake to take them to heart. The only one to feel ashamed if she went calling this and that out would be her. So long as someone like Eriko, an immaculately presented permanent employee with the backing of her father, worked as hard as the men, then she was treated equally. There was no point in spinning out about it. Eriko refused to break her good-tempered attitude for something of this ilk.

'No, it's not that ... You know how wife blogs often have this show-off quality about them? As if they're trying to impress on everyone how incredibly happy they are, how talented at cooking, how pristine their houses, and so on. It's as if you can sense their desperation for other people to recognise that. But with her—'

The phone on Eriko's desk rang, cutting through the pair's conversation. Eriko picked up the receiver to find someone from a California tuna company on the other end of the line. The phone calls that came in at this time of day were predominantly from the States.

'May I take your name, please? When shall I have him return your call?'

After dealing with the call in her best English, Eriko turned once again to look at Sugishita.

It was frustrating, to find herself this incapable of explaining herself. She liked the way that Hallie didn't put on airs and played a touch dumb, if anything, while actually being sharp in her thinking. She selected her words gently, yet in a way that conveyed a certain intelligence, and she was never hurtful to others. She lived a pretty idle life but didn't seem ashamed of that fact, nor did she try to force any meaning onto it. Above all, her blog was dotted with nice turns of phrase that lingered with Eriko and uncontrived ideas that she found herself wanting to imitate.

For instance: on muggy summer days, doing the housework in one's swimming costume, then slinging a dress over the top and heading down to the local pool for a swim. Getting a whole bunch of easy-reading non-fiction books out of the library. Ordering in pizza and watching Hollywood films on TV. Going around numerous convenience stores in search of a particular corn chowder-flavoured ice lolly.

Eriko was drawn to this approach to life: not immersing oneself in one particular thing all day long or searching for something to give everything else meaning, but remaining without plans and living according to one's whims, a bit like a cat. When was the last time that Eriko had spent time in that way? She couldn't even recall. Simply by reading Hallie's blog, she felt her nerves, frazzled from nightly work dinners and endless market research, loosening a little.

Eriko was forever attempting to avoid wasting time. When she wasn't at work, she would pour her attention into beauty treatments, personal research and study, while of course also prioritising rest and sleep. She could say with confidence that everything she did produced some benefit and felt no doubt that today's Eriko was superior to the Eriko of yesterday. At some point, though, perhaps around the time she'd turned thirty, she'd started to experience painful twinges that began behind her nose. Suddenly, she'd feel as if she didn't have enough oxygen, as if she were unable to reach out and touch anything, however much she flapped and flailed. When one of these episodes struck, she'd take a huge breath, tell herself that she was okay, and then enumerate her strengths, the various ways in which she'd improved, and all the ways in which she was contributing to the company. When this didn't succeed in calming her, she would begin acting unnecessarily modestly towards the people around her, so as to elicit praise from others, which would unfailingly restore her to a state of normality. And yet, however much she fought the sensation, she felt with each close of a passing day, each dawn of a new morning, that the possibilities available to her had been subtly shaved away and the course corrections she tried to implement were becoming less and less effective. Was this an age-related panic? Would she get used to it in a few years' time? When she caught a glimpse of this urgency in those of a similar life-stage around her, she couldn't prevent a sense of relief and twisted joy from seeping through her.

For Eriko, the real clincher when it came to Hallie B's blog was that the only character to appear consistently, other than Hallie herself, was her husband – there was no mention whatsoever of female friends. This was a key difference from the other homemaker bloggers, who were inclined to boast relentlessly about their broad social network. Eriko harboured the secret hope that this woman knew the trick to managing the issues that she herself struggled with.

She felt lifted by the fact that even someone like Hallie had no friends. Even someone with the type of character that, thanks to some miraculous balance of qualities, didn't put other people off might find themselves incapable of making friends, through simple bad timing or similar. Maybe not having friends wasn't such a terrible, embarrassing flaw after all. Maybe it wasn't even a flaw at all, but one of the many variables that existed among the diversity of humankind.

> *I'm a 30-year-old stay-at-home wife, living in a crummy apartment in central Tokyo with my husband. My favourite food is the engawa from my local 98-yen-a-plate revolving sushi place bar, Smile Sushi.*

It was when Sugishita read Hallie's profile that his look of disinterest finally cracked, and a touch of excitement crept into his tone.

'Engawa is her favourite food, huh? You know that those cheap conveyor-belt sushi places make their engawa with halibut? I wonder whether "Hallie B" isn't a veiled reference to that. If so, that's a pretty niche sense of humour she's got there.'

The sushi known as engawa was a specific cut of fish, from the muscular section beside the fins. The traditional, expensive version was made with olive flounder, but one olive flounder only contained enough engawa meat for four nigiri. A halibut, on the other hand, could exceed 200 kilos and grow up to three metres long, thereby generating far more engawa meat. Halibut put up a vigorous struggle when you tried to haul them out of the water, to the extent that it was standard practice in Alaska to kill them with a shotgun to pacify them. Feeling as though she herself had been complimented, Eriko puffed out her chest in pride. As she did, a certain thought occurred to her. 'Come to think of it, you were handling the Russian halibut account last year, weren't you? Didn't you say you'd done a deal with Centre Village Holdings?'

This was the enormous restaurant chain that owned Smile Sushi. Seeing Sugishita grin in assent, Eriko clapped her hands together. 'That's incredible!' she exclaimed. 'We're all connected. Hallie B's favourite food turns out to be part of your professional remit …'

As a feeling of wonderment ran through her, Eriko surveyed the office floor, which still only contained the two of them. She adored those moments when the dissemination of a product or a particular pattern of numbers would suddenly make the world seem small enough to grasp in her hand. Day had dawned, without her realising it, and the late-August sunlight cascaded in through the windows. The carpet, which frequent cleaning had left with a fluffy white top layer, began to emanate a warm smell. Working in a product trading company, you began to see unexpected depths within everyday scenes. This café au lait, this melon bun, this newspaper, for instance – it was impossible to look at them on her desk this morning without thinking about which country the raw materials used to make them had come from, their means of distribution and the processing that had led to their being here in this form. You only had to hold them in your gaze to feel their individual stories unfolding before you. This form of clairvoyance was something that had been instilled in both Eriko and Sugishita over the years.

Japan consumed around 6,520,000 tonnes of seafood annually, and 40 per cent of that was imported. Many of these imports were 'nameless fish' – in other words, types of fish commonly mislabelled or used as substitutes. Since moving to the seafood team, Eriko had developed the ability to identify any fish by taste, regardless of how it had been labelled or processed.

'Don't you feel bad for the consumers when you think about it? Although I suppose engawa is the name of the part of the fish, so it's not a bona fide deception.'

'If you think about it rationally, though, there's no way in hell you'd be able to eat righteye or olive flounder for under a hundred yen a pop. I'm sure the consumers must be vaguely aware.'

'It's like they're being fed alien meat or something … It's kind of scary.'

'But when that alien meat is cut up and perched on top of their nigiri, everyone gobbles it down and says how delicious it is. Think about things like "fish burgers" and "white fish à la meunière" – if you started interrogating each and every bit of fish that you consumed, there'd be no end to it. This world is full of information that you're better off not knowing.'

Sugishita was in the habit of making these detached proclamations, but when it came to business negotiations, he would reveal an extraordinarily charming, smooth-talking persona. While he could initially come across as slightly twitchy, he had in fact been born into a family that owned a clothing company in the exclusive Mitsukoshi department store, which went back for generations.

'You're in charge of the Nile perch account from this month, right? Someone as keen on family restaurants and conveyor-belt sushi as Hallie B is bound to ingest the fish you've traded sooner or later, no?'

At these words, Eriko reached out and absent-mindedly flicked through the file of documents that had been passed on by her predecessor. Nile perch was a species of freshwater fish, in the family *Centropomidae* of order Perciformes. It grew up to two metres long and weighed up to 200 kilos. Native to the African subcontinent, it lived in lakes and rivers. It was a carnivorous fish, with a ferocity of nature that seemed utterly at odds with the clean, light taste of its white meat. Since its introduction into Lake Victoria, it had wiped out 200 different resident species of cichlid, such as tilapia. Its mild flavour appealed to the sensitive Japanese palate, and in the nineties it had even been passed off as sea bass, but of late, 90 per cent of stock was exported to Europe and America, and it was rarely seen in Japan. Eriko had spent these last few months preparing to open up an import route to Japan once again, and to equip the local producers with the facilities to make this long-distance export possible. The more she found out about the Nile perch, the more she was irresistibly drawn to it.

'Yes, there's no rivalling the Nile perch when it comes to vitality!'

'It's carnivorous, right? Who knows what it goes around eating! Scary stuff. You should check out that documentary – *Darwin's Nightmare*, I think it's called. Apparently it shows how the Nile perch totally desecrates any surrounding ecosystem it enters.'

'It's on my radar, but I haven't got round to it yet. Besides, I feel like it might be best to hold off until I've tied up the deal. You know, if the Nile perch hadn't been released by humans into that lake, it might have gone its whole life without ever realising the ferocity in its own nature. I feel bad for the poor creature. I've heard it's a popular choice for commercial aquariums as well. It's silver, and very beautiful. With this sort of sad-looking face …'

'Apparently, they've got a couple in that new aquarium in Shinjuku. Shall we go take a look some time?'

But Eriko offered neither a clear yes nor no in response to this mumbled invitation, pretending instead to be engrossed in the blog once again. She was fully aware that Sugishita had something of a soft spot for her. He seemed to have imposed on himself the rule that verbalising his feelings constituted a sign of weakness, and a troubled expression, which appeared to be a combination of longing and embarrassment, now floated across his features. This whole barrage about the blog that he'd decided to subject her to was also, surely, a manifestation of his affection. Perhaps not wanting to admit to himself that she'd sidestepped his invitation, he reverted to their former topic with alarming speed.

'Maybe it's fine if you're just reading her blog. It's not like there's any hope of you two hitting it off in real life, anyway.'

'I don't think that's true! I reckon Hallie and I could be good friends.'

'Oh yeah? Despite the fact you don't have a single female friend?'

Eriko felt the heat receding from her fingertips. Even when she made as much effort as she did, still she gave off the aura of someone without any friends. Her heart pounded noisily in her chest at being confronted by this unshakeable truth. Meanwhile, Sugishita's words wore a slick, suggestive sheen. She knew that men were vaguely turned on by women who couldn't hit it off with other women. He even oozed a certain pride, as if he'd managed to locate a major flaw in the opposing team without even having to get his hands dirty. Pretending not to notice, Eriko affected a perfectly indifferent tone.

'I guess that's true. I've pretty much fallen out of touch with my university girlfriends since starting work. It's not like I've got the time for girls' get-togethers, even when I am invited …'

This was a negotiation trick she'd learned: conceding an adversary's point as a way to maintain a superior position overall. No such group of university friends existed, and she'd not once been asked along to a 'girls' get-together'. The slyness, the childishness of women of a certain age still referring to themselves as 'girls' sometimes seemed stunning to Eriko.

'But I mean, you don't go to lunch with the temps or women from other sections, do you?'

He had never come out and said it, but rumour had it that Sugishita was dating a temp called Maori Tagasugi on the sly. Maybe that was why he was so well informed about the social lives of the female employees.

'No … The timing of my lunch break doesn't match up with the people from other sections, and it's difficult to go out to lunch with the temps. Lots of them are trying to eat out for under 1000 yen, you know, which makes it hard to ask them along on the spur of the moment …' Eriko did her best to maintain a cheery tone of voice, deliberately neglecting to add that, of course, they never invited her. 'It's true that I've never been particularly good at female friendships. I've always been the upright A-grade student type, you know? I know you're not supposed to say that about yourself, but it's true. Back at school I was always being asked to be class rep and so I got used to being set apart from other people. I don't really get all those unspoken rules that exist for women, and I end up sticking out, without realising it.' Eriko was aware that she was speaking extraordinarily quickly. Internally, she intoned a prayer: *Please, please, please don't ask me anything else.* Anything further in from here was uncharted territory. She had no faith that she would be able to keep from revealing her true self.

'Envy probably plays a part too. A stunning girl like you who aces everything without even having to try – of course other women are going to resent you. Female jealousy is a scary thing, eh?' Sugishita screwed his eyes up affectionately. He seemed to think that he was praising her. Most likely, he was comparing her to Maori – pudgy, talkative Maori who was incompetent at her job. Eriko felt certain that he was stringing Maori along. And yet, she was perpetually surrounded by a cluster of other female employees, in a way that Eriko envied intensely.

*Without even having to try*, he'd said. Sugishita had likely never thought about the amount of time and money that had been poured into achieving this flawless skin, this glossy hair. What toner did Hallie B use, Eriko suddenly wondered. It was likely some cheap one that she'd found on sale at the drug store – or was she an unexpected organic cosmetics devotee? Whichever it was, Eriko wanted to try using the same one. Now, as she was scrolling back through the past blog entries, she found her lips moving.

'And it seems like she lives close to me.'

'Seriously?'

'See this Gisele, the organic café she's featured here? It's one station away from where I live. I know it well because my mum was helping out there when it was first set up. And then I've noticed that all of her favourite fast-food restaurants and chain stores that she mentions are clustered outside my nearest station. Although I guess they're places you can find anywhere ...'

'Isn't it a bit extreme to know all that? From where she's coming from, you're not far off being a stalker, surely?'

Startled by this word, which had never even come to her mind before, Eriko turned around and stared wide-eyed at Sugishita.

'What!? I'm only reading her blog! I happened to notice that her house is close to mine. Through sheer coincidence.'

'I dunno, Shimura. You're imitating what she's eating, reading about how she spends her days, and you just so happen to live close by ... Even if you've no bad intentions, she's bound to find it a bit creepy. Just take things easy, okay?'

With this, Sugishita turned on his heels and headed for his desk. Other employees were beginning to arrive. Had he got into work this early specifically to be alone with her, out of Maori's sight? Was it conceited of Eriko to think that? It was a year since she'd broken up with her last boyfriend, but she didn't yet feel lonely by herself. It was her intention to get married at some point, but right now, moving between her parents' house and the company took up every scrap of her energy.

Had Hallie ever thought to imagine that somewhere out there, there was a woman working in an office, munching on the same melon bun as her, as she read through her blog? Eriko couldn't help but feel that Hallie must somehow sense her presence. Her attitude might seem utterly unaffected, but she was quite possibly sending out a secret message to the masses. The message went: *You're fine just as you are. You can relax a bit. It's okay to be alone.* Eriko read through Hallie's diary entry again, as if repeating affirmations to herself in the mirror.

# CHAPTER TWO

The fingers that were moving across her phone screen busily updating her blog now fell still, and Shōko Maruo lifted her gaze.

A pair of jeans hung out to dry on the balcony of an apartment across the street were flapping in the breeze and caught her eye. They seemed in danger of flying away at any moment. Jeans that skinny had to belong to someone young, Shōko thought. Now that she was in her thirties, there was no way she could get away with wearing anything like that. She remembered how, back when she was working in the department store, she'd stand around in pants so tight they cut off her circulation. It hadn't been unusual for her to stand for ten hours a day back then, and sometimes she only had two days off a month. What would the Shōko from back then have to say about her current lifestyle, she found herself wondering. She'd probably be quite envious.

She'd got here a bit too early, Shōko now realised. The organic café Gisele was a favourite spot of hers, just fifteen minutes' walk from her flat. It being a Saturday, there were several solo women diners. The large plate set down on the table in front of Shōko was crowded with an assortment of riches – konnyaku and chicken liver salad with karashi mayonnaise, coleslaw with bitter melon, brown rice balls with sesame and red perilla, and slices of rolled omelette with sea lettuce – and yet Shōko had polished it off at a pace stunning even to herself. It was a while since she'd eaten a meal this well balanced, this replete with vegetables, and nor had she served any such meals to Kensuke. What a useless wife I am, she thought to herself yet again. Tonight, she resolved, she'd make sure at least to boil some hijiki to go with their dinner. Yet the truth was that even the idea of doing so sent a wave of intolerable weariness washing over her. Maybe she'd buy something here at Gisele to take back for him. She really couldn't be bothered to do the washing-up tonight. Of all the household tasks, Shōko disliked those involving water the most.

She'd met her husband, Kensuke, the manager of a supermarket specialising in selling imported foodstuffs, while she had been working part-time at the same store, and they'd tied the knot three years ago. In essence, she did her best to economise in order that the two of them could get by on his income alone, but she didn't want this to result in an overly sanctimonious approach to life. When it came to little indulgences, she dipped into the savings that she had from her single days. Recently, she was also earning a small income from the affiliate ads on her blog. She and Kensuke hadn't had a wedding ceremony, he hadn't bought her a ring, and they hadn't been on an overseas honeymoon. Needless to say, they hadn't bought a house either. In place of these large-scale extravagances, they had taken the decision not to scrimp on the little things. If they were going to argue about the washing-up at home, it was better to eat out at a cheap restaurant – this was the agreement they'd made between themselves at the registry office.

In truth, it would probably have been fine to make the more economical choice of a coffee chain or family restaurant today, but conscious of the fact that the person she was meeting worked in media, Shōko had suggested the most stylish place she could think of. The light wood interior here always calmed her. Now

Hashimoto, the young waiter who came to clear away her plate, suddenly crouched down beside her so his head was right beside hers.

'Thanks so much for featuring the new autumn menu on your blog, Shōko!'

'Woah, woah, that's way too close! You gave me a fright!'

Hashimoto's breath tickled her ear. At twenty-five, he was the same age as Shōko's younger brother, which was maybe part of the reason she found him easy to get along with. When she hit him in playful reproach, her fingers struck a toned bicep under his shirt, whose existence she wouldn't have predicted from his lanky frame. The firmness of his muscle, which her fingers seemed to bounce off, was a far cry from the wobbly upper arms of her husband, who had started putting on weight again.

'You know the days we're featured on your blog, we get more customers than usual.'

Shōko was a firm fan of fast-food chains and family restaurants, and Gisele was one of the few independent businesses that she frequented. Since helping out over the busy New Year period this year, she'd become friendly with the staff, and continued to stop in once or twice a month as a customer. The management had asked her if she wanted to work there on a regular basis, but she'd turned them down – she had little doubt that once it became her regular workplace, she'd no longer be able to pop in to relax.

Shōko moved her eyes back to her phone screen. When reading the comments left on her blog, she found that time flew by with an almost miraculous speed. None of the commenters criticised her for her laziness. On the contrary, the majority of the messages she received were words of encouragement: 'This is so comforting to hear!' or, 'Reading your words makes me feel better about myself.' Readers posted links to favourite products or venues. Shōko was delighted to have found a place where she felt she belonged, but the deluge of kind words left her with a sense that she was deceiving her readers. Nonetheless, the good feelings were addictive, and she could pass hours at a time reading back over the comments. It seemed to her that the sensation wasn't unlike steeping in a jacuzzi. When something was so soothing, you stopped knowing when it was time to get out.

Shōko wanted more areas of her life where she felt at ease. She didn't want this feeling to be limited entirely to the internet. But it had been eight years since she'd moved to Tokyo, and she still didn't feel as though she could properly relax here. While working, she'd been too busy to go out and enjoy herself, and after getting sick she'd stopped leaving the house entirely. The bell by the café door tinkled as a woman of forty in a suit stepped inside. Her eyes found Shōko immediately, and she strode directly over.

'You must be Hallie … I mean, Shōko Maruo. It's so nice to meet you! I'm Satoko Hanai from the Third Editing Department at Shūmeisha.'

Shōko hurriedly stood up, bowing and accepting the business card that the woman handed her. Satoko Hanai had a nice figure and a pretty face, but her dry skin and the dark circles under her eyes left a distinct impression of exhaustion.

'Gosh, this is a surprise! You're so much prettier and more charming than I was imagining, somehow!'

Shōko noticed that Satoko didn't go as far as to say 'beautiful' or 'gorgeous' – that the caution unique to the elite was at work. Feeling some sensor in her that had been dormant for a while leaping back into action, Shōko realised that she was being sized up. She was quite aware that her outfit today – a worn-out T-shirt teamed with chinos that had been Kensuke's when he was thinner, and no makeup – was hardly an appropriate look for a first meeting. It was true to say that since quitting her job at the apparel company her interest in clothes, which she had once shopped for so avidly, had thoroughly waned. But even back then, she hadn't had an appearance that caught people's attention. Her figure was without curves, her eyes were single-lidded, and her white skin was dotted with freckles. Her lips naturally curled back, and she had a complex about the way that her gums showed when she smiled.

And yet there had been some women who, as if by some prior arrangement between themselves, had found Shōko detestable.

*She flirts with all the men.*

Those were their words. It wasn't flirting, that was the thing. It was just that Shōko found it easy to show men the consideration and care that she was fairly sure women showed to one another constantly. Often, around other women, she'd find herself at a loss for what to say, while with people of the opposite sex, she instinctively knew what to do. Maybe it was in part because her parents had divorced and she'd grown up with her father and two brothers. But she definitely wasn't the tough-cookie type, and nor did she have much experience with romantic relationships. That she'd earned such a reputation simply by behaving freely around men came as a surprise. Since then, her fear of this happening again saw her behaving unnecessarily goofily in front of women.

Satoko Hanai ordered a coffee and then set about spreading an array of Shūmeisha publications across the table – magazines aimed at married women and books by wife bloggers – explaining this and that. The truth was, Shōko simply wasn't that into the idea. Just passing her eyes across the gushing prose written by wife bloggers about how happy and fulfilled their lives were left her feeling tired. Her disposition was one that sought to avoid excess hassle as much as humanly possible. Apparently oblivious to all this, Satoko was spouting forth at a tremendous pace.

'These days, the homemaker blogging sphere is sufficiently large that it's divided into all kinds of sub-categories, and within that ecosystem, I feel that your USP is how natural you are. I love how your blog is so refreshingly free of shoulds and musts. In the current climate, when Japanese society is accepting of so many different ways of living, lots of housewives find themselves feeling quite lost, quite torn. I think your laid-back stance will resonate with lots of people, and I'm not only talking about other housewives either. Your undogmatic approach means your message could really appeal to single working women as well.'

'Yeah ... I'm just struggling to believe that anybody would read a diary like that as a book, you know?'

'Yes, well, so I was thinking that we could absolutely take those diary entries as a base, but reorganise them into essays. I think it would be great if you could write a manifesto for your way of living as a real woman, who doesn't try too hard.'

Shōko felt an itchy sensation spread across her shoulders and down her back. This, she thought – this was why she didn't like these intellectual types. Until now, she'd never written anything that she'd given serious thought to – not once. She objected to having this grand significance foisted on her, objected to being pigeonholed like this.

It was undeniably true that ever since her blog had hit the most popular blog ranking, she'd found a new enthusiasm for writing. Yet when the message about making the blog into a book had arrived from the editor at Shūmeisha – a major publishing company that everybody had heard of – it had taken her so by surprise that she'd barely known how to respond.

That she was here at this meeting at all was down to her husband's encouragement.

'It's maybe about time you thought about re-entering society, isn't it?' he'd said. 'With talent like yours, it'd be a waste if you didn't.'

And then, 'How incredible is it that an editor would get in touch out of the blue like that?! It's like a modern Cinderella story. It's so cool that they want to release a book of yours!'

The interaction made Shōko think back to her days working part-time in the supermarket. As a manager, Kensuke had been a bit slipshod, hardly the ultra-competent type, but his total disinterest in hogging the limelight, and the way that he genuinely rejoiced in other people's successes, meant that all the staff liked him, and, overall, the working atmosphere had been pleasant. She remembered how amusing it had been to observe his astonishment at her customer service skills, which had been instilled in her during her department store days. Kensuke was shorter than Shōko, and got a little rounder with every passing year, but she felt more comfortable around him than with anyone she'd dated before.

'Have a think about it, and then be in touch? I'm confident that it would do very well.'

After pressing several blog books on Shōko, Satoko left, leaving her barely touched coffee behind on the table. For a moment, Shōko stared off into space and let her shoulders drop. She was struggling to process all the information that had just been rattled off at her. She felt like she needed a cigarette – although the café was non-smoking.

'Excuse me, um—'

Taken aback by someone addressing her unexpectedly, Shōko lifted her face in the direction that the voice was coming from. A woman as flawlessly beautiful as any doll was standing beside her table. Her skin was perfectly clear, the black hair slinking down to her shoulders lustrous. She wore a short-sleeved knitted top with a diamond pendant. It was hard to gauge her age, but from the faint creases by her eyes, Shōko imagined she must be in her thirties.

'I was wondering … are you Hallie B, by any chance?'

Not knowing what to say, Shōko shot the woman an ambiguous smile. The woman's eyes lit up.

'I'm so sorry for being so rude, I happened to overhear your conversation … Also, you mentioned this place in your blog once, didn't you? I'm a big fan of yours!'

As Shōko was fumbling around for how to reply, the woman handed her a business card. The angle, the speed at which she held out the card seemed to Shōko far straighter and faster than that of Satoko.

It was later that evening, in their one-bedroom apartment, which they found plentifully spacious for the two of them – located in the middle of a shopping arcade – that Shōko told Kensuke about what had happened in Gisele. As he drank his cheap beer along with the Thai curry that she had heated from a can, he adopted the kind of suspicious expression that it was rare to see him make.

'And you're sure she's legit?'

'The editor? Or the woman from the manufacturing company?'

'The woman from the manufacturing company. I mean, she's a total stranger, right?'

Shōko pressed mute on the TV, sat up straight and turned to face Kensuke.

'You'd understand if you met her. She's incredibly pretty, gorgeous actually, and so young-looking, like you'd never guess we were the same age. She was dressed really classy, in the way you can just tell everything she's got on is high quality. After all that time working in department stores, I came to understand that you can trust people like that.'

The company where Eriko Shimura worked was Japan's best-known general manufacturing firm. Even more reassuringly, she also seemed to know Hashimoto and the other staff at Gisele. It turned out that her mother was a friend of the owner.

'It's clear that she is who she says she is, and she told me where she lives as well. You know those expensive-looking apartments opposite the post office?'

'What? But you said she's single, no? Does she own one by herself?'

'It sounds like she's living with her parents.'

'A-ha, the pampered princess type! I guess there are a lot of rich people in this area.'

It irked Shōko slightly to see relief spread across her husband's face at this information.

'I don't know that many people in Tokyo, you know? I want to have the kinds of friends who I can meet up with easily, for a coffee or whatever. Of course I know I've got to keep an eye out for dodgy types too.'

Shōko had only chatted with Eriko for ten minutes or so in Gisele, but she'd been left with the feeling that she wanted to see her again. What Eriko had said about being an avid reader of her blog appeared to be the truth, for she'd gone on to enthuse about aspects of it that Shōko herself had never even thought about. In the manner of a true salesperson, she'd kept up a smile throughout their chat, and displayed a subtle sense of consideration for others. In all honesty, she had made a markedly better impression than Satoko. Maybe more than anything else, Shōko found herself enticed by the knowledge that Eriko had grown up in this part of town. Becoming close with Eriko might help her finally shake off the ever-pervasive sense of being an outsider that she felt living here.

'That's a very cautious statement by your standards.'

'Yeah, I just think I need to be careful. I've been getting these creepy messages recently on the blog.'

'Creepy how?'

Unsure of whether or not to say it, Shōko grabbed Kensuke's beer and took a swig, then looked him directly in the eye.

'I know where you live, and you live right by so-and-so station don't you? That kind of stuff.'

'Jeez … That's pretty stalkerish, isn't it? You need to be careful. Although you've got me, so you'll be okay.' Even as Kensuke screwed up his face in distaste at this new information, he didn't stop moving his food to his mouth.

'I'm thinking it might be best to give up the blog, you know? It started out as a hobby and now it's suddenly becoming this big thing … I don't know if I can be bothered with it. We can get by fine on your salary. I don't want to force it, you know?'

'You're weirdly lacking in ambition, eh? I guess that's just who you are, and part of what drew me to you. At the end of the day, you have to play it how you want to.'

'Hey, what do you say we have sex tonight?'

The exertion of meeting multiple new people for the first time in a while had left Shōko feeling stiff and achey. It was at times like these that she wanted him to take her, hard. To let all the tension ebb away, and then fall into a deep sleep. Of late, although Kensuke would agree to have sex with her if she asked, he never initiated it. But Shōko didn't mind that so much. It wasn't like she had a particularly high sex drive to begin with.

'I dunno, I was on the early shift today and my back's killing me. What if we do it in a way that's not tiring?'

'Aw, no, not *that* position again ... I can barely feel a thing.'

'In that case let's leave it until the day before my next day off. We'll do it then. I promise.'

Pouting sulkily, Shōko booted up the Mac that she shared with her husband. She would write about Eriko on her blog, she decided. She was sure Eriko would be pleased, and she somehow wanted to create a record of the day.

> *On a visit to one of my favourite cafés, I met a girl who reads my blog! She was absolutely \*stunning\*, and seemed to have a good brain on her too. I felt guilty that someone so impressive was reading this absolute dog's dinner of a blog ...*

As she wrote, Shōko mused on whether it was permissible to call someone over thirty a 'girl', but then decided to leave the entry as it was. She knew that neither she nor Eriko were young, per se – but when women were together, weren't they always girls, whatever their age?

# CHAPTER THREE

The message from Hallie a.k.a. Shōko, who lived just across the railway tracks from her, had come three days before. Eriko had barely been able to believe it. Ever since their encounter in the café, her heart had been aflutter at the idea that it was possible to meet someone so casually, so freely. Now, she got off the train at the station by her house and headed directly for the family restaurant located under the train tracks.

Shōko had been even more charming in person than Eriko had imagined. It was hard to believe that she was the same age as Eriko. Her skin was freckled and her hair had a tint of golden brown to it, like a young girl from overseas. The simple, faded T-shirt in which her slim frame was attired spoke of effortless style. To top it all, she'd written about Eriko in her blog that very night. Finding herself appearing in a blog that she read regularly was a slightly strange feeling, but it had left her with a warm, fuzzy feeling in her chest.

Sure, it did feel a bit odd to be referred to as a 'girl' at her age, but given that people in their sixties still referred to all-female meet-ups as 'girls' get-togethers', maybe it was okay.

\* \* \*

Tonight, she and Shōko had arranged to meet in a Denny's, one of the all-night family restaurant chains beloved not only by families with children but school-kids and students too. Something about the plan made Eriko's heart race, as if she'd finally become a popular high-school girl. Usually when she got together with other working people, they would inevitably meet in a sought-after city-centre restaurant or a hip bar that served trendy nibbles. That was why the atmosphere always felt so tense, Eriko thought – why those kinds of relationships didn't last. She felt amazed by the simplicity and ease of meeting in one of the chains you could find anywhere, at a location close to where they both lived.

She glanced down at her watch to see it was past eleven. Pushing open the door, she spotted Shōko sitting in an armchair by the window, smoking a cigarette while looking at her phone. Eriko ran over.

'I'm so sorry! I was with some clients and couldn't get away. I can't believe it's this late. Does your husband not mind you being out at this time?'

'Oh, no, he's fine. He's at home playing *Dragon Quest*.'

Shōko stubbed out her cigarette and pushed her phone away, then handed Eriko the menu. Eriko ordered black tea and leaned back in the armchair. She would now have to come up with an entertaining topic of conversation, she realised, and she felt a nervous tension begin to sink its talons into her. Luckily, Shōko pre-empted her.

'You work in sales, right? You must be so busy. Were you working overtime?'

'It was drinks with clients. They don't like us to stay late at the office.'

After the workers' union had demanded a review of working conditions at Nakamaru in light of the high numbers of employees suffering from depression in the last few years, it had become frowned upon to work overtime or go in on days off. However, the issue remained that employees' workloads could not be accomplished within their working hours alone. After a data-leak incident, employees now needed to fill out a complicated form in order to take work home. It was for that reason that most of the employees came in early in the morning. When Eriko explained this, Shōko replied, 'That's so messed up, though! You can't forbid people from working late but then not reduce their amount of work. And prevent them from taking it home on top of that! It doesn't make any sense.'

'Exactly,' said Eriko, nodding deeply.

Shōko slowly drew her mobile back towards her.

'I've got this editor who keeps emailing me. She wants me to turn my blog into a book, but I'm not convinced it's a good idea.'

'Really? Why not? It seems like a waste to turn a proposal like that down, no? If you wrote a book I'd totally buy it.' Eriko found herself surprised by the casualness with which this response came slipping out. Shōko shrugged.

'But I don't want it to turn into an obligation, you know? Really I want to keep posting this stuff more or less unnoticed. As someone who in theory falls into the category of "homemaker blogger", I think suddenly having all these proper homemakers who are all over their housework and childcare reading it would be a lot. And then once it's out, I'll have to do discussions with other wife bloggers for magazines and stuff. I just don't think I've got it in me.'

It was true that the thought of Hallie B artfully navigating her way through a crowd of other homemakers felt somehow off-brand.

'I get it. Groups of women can be a real pain. I struggle with that too.' Before she knew it, a frown had formed across Eriko's forehead. Shōko leaned in with sudden enthusiasm.

'Right!? Other women have always had a problem with me, for some reason.'

'Seriously? That surprises me. You're so frank and open – I always think those are the qualities that other women take to.'

There was no element of a lie in what she was saying. Chatting with Shōko like this, it struck Eriko as positively bizarre that there were no mentions of female friends on her blog. She felt exhilarated by the idea that women this cheerful, this enjoyable to be around, could also find themselves on their own.

'I think it's rare to encounter people as easy to be around as you are,' Shōko now said.

'Easy to be around? Me?'

'Yeah! I mean you're gorgeous, and you have this super-impressive job, and yet … Maybe because you've got it all, you're operating on a different level to other people? There's a bit of a goofiness about you. I just feel really at ease around you.'

At that moment, a train went thundering above their heads. This was the first time Eriko had ever been spoken about in this way, and the assessment left her almost dizzy. All her past relationships had ended not long after her boyfriends had started to tell her that she was 'tiring' to be around and that her perfectionism was 'exhausting'.

'I moved to Tokyo straight after graduating, and was working for a brand called Bloom. Have you heard of it?'

'Wow, yes. I've got one of their sweaters. That's incredible!'

'The thing about apparel, though, is that the whole industry revolves around these messy, catty relationships between women. A whole beehive full of queens.'

'Oh, that figures. I know exactly what you mean.'

Formulating these kinds of responses to Shōko brought Eriko a strange joy. That they were communicating successfully with each other, managing to have a conversation, appearing to be on each other's wavelength, seemed close to miraculous.

'The stress of it broke me in the end, and I got sick. I quit after four years.'

'Are you not going to go back?'

'Nope. For a while I got by on a string of part-time jobs, but I knew I couldn't go on like that forever. Then, as I was wondering what my next step should be, I met my husband. From then on, things have been as they are now. I guess in the eyes of a high-achiever like you it's a "dropout" sort of life.'

'Not at all. I don't necessarily feel everyone should go out to work. That my mum's at home is a huge help to me. Although I do feel bad that I'm the reason she gave up work in the first place …'

Eriko thought back to when her mother stepped away from Gisele: her concerned gaze, her hands red and raw from the extra washing-up and cleaning that she'd been doing on top of her domestic tasks. Eriko had enjoyed seeing her mother having fun running the café with her friends, and it had felt heart-wrenching that she had to stop.

'How nice that you get on well enough with your parents to live with them, though. Ever since my dad got remarried, I've struggled going back home …'

'It's not as idyllic as it sounds. Since my dad retired he's basically given up speaking entirely. Unless I'm talking, the house is deathly silent. I feel like I'm surrounded by tension, at home as well as at work. It's not good for the nerves. I sometimes feel tempted to cut loose and be by myself.'

Eriko was surprised to hear the words coming from her mouth. It was the first time she'd admitted to herself that she found the situation at home stressful. Had she been suppressing her feelings all this time? Being with Shōko, she felt a sense of liberation washing over her. She blew gently on the tea that the server had brought over.

'You can always call me when you feel that way, you know? If you ever need to vent, I don't mind listening. We live so close after all.'

These casually uttered words struck something deep in Eriko. She hadn't thought that making new friends was a possibility at this age – not to mention this effortlessly.

'You must be so popular with men!' Shōko exclaimed.

'I wouldn't say so. The beginning part is fine, but I always end up getting dumped. Maybe because I live with my parents, or maybe because I'm getting on okay in life being single, I don't feel any urgency to get married …'

'Wow, I really get that. If I hadn't been on my own in Tokyo and living such a precarious existence where I was never sure how I was going to get by week to week, I'm not sure whether I'd have married the Demon King.'

Eriko liked it when Shōko came out with these kinds of stark statements, which managed to seem neither self-deprecating nor insincere. She guessed that she could say these sorts of things precisely because she had actually built a good relationship with her husband.

'I don't see any need for you to get married, at all, but if you do end up becoming a stay-at-home wife, let's laze around together?'

'That sounds so fun. Actually, now you put it like that, marriage suddenly seems like a more appealing prospect …'

The two paid up and left the restaurant. Shōko crouched down by the railing outside and unfastened her bike chain. It was a man's bike, the same one that Eriko had seen photos of on the blog. She faintly recalled that Shōko shared it with her husband. They walked along slowly together, Shōko pushing her bike.

'This breeze feels so good. It still has that faint smell of summer. Honestly, I've been so busy with work this year that now the summer's over before I've had the chance to do anything at all summery.'

'What are you saying? September's still summer! It's not too late! You could go for a swim in the pool, or the sea? It's funny, walking along pushing a bike like this makes me feel like I'm young again. Like I'm coming home from school or something.'

The word 'school' snagged in Eriko's chest. The never-ending row of concrete pillars towered above them, so that it seemed as if they were moving through a temple. Thinking back to the time before the overpass was built here, when there had been no trace of these concrete columns, she felt as though she'd been struck physically by the weight of the months and years that had passed since, and averted her eyes.

'I actually never cycled to school,' Eriko said. 'My school forbade us from cycling in, for some reason, so I took the train. Even though it was a girls' school not far from here, in the same ward of Tokyo! If you look on a map it's so close, but going by train I ended up going all around the houses to get there. It drove me mad.'

'Wow, you really are an inner-city kid! While you were commuting in, I was thundering along the river on my bike.'

'Did you ever get lifts on the backs of the bikes of boys you liked?'

'I sure did!'

'Argh, I'm so envious,' Eriko said with a sigh, and Shōko's eyes glinted.

'Do you wanna get on the back of mine, now? You live in those apartments in front of the post office, right? That's on my way home anyway. Go on, I'll give you a backie.'

Eriko hesitated at first, but then sat herself down sideways on the luggage rack at the back of Shōko's bike and wrapped her hands around Shōko's surprisingly slender waist. The bike began to move. The last train came into view on the tracks beside them, then passed them by. The inside of the carriage was sufficiently bright that Eriko could make out the expressions of the people inside, juddering like a series of stop-motion photographs. Eriko found tears coming to her eyes. The scent of fabric softener emanated from Shōko's top – the very fabric softener she'd mentioned on her blog: *It's made in America and smells just like cotton candy*. Eriko had read and reread the blog until she practically knew it by heart, and there was now very little about Shōko that she wasn't aquainted with. Her skirt billowed out in the breeze. The bike cut past the front of the station, and they passed the convenience stores, coffee shops, drug stores along the street. This scenery she knew so well suddenly seemed different and became a ribbon of light streaming in front of her eyes.

'I've never lived anywhere other than this.' Though it was past midnight, Eriko found herself shouting to make herself heard over the headwind.

'You're a true-blood Tokyoite. I'm jealous!'

'There's nothing to be jealous of, I promise you. Sometimes I get depressed about how limited my worldview is. Besides, these days there's not much difference between Tokyo and the provincial cities. Just look at it! It's all chains. Places shut early, and the only place you can go for a cup of tea late at night is a family restaurant. In a few years' time, everywhere in Japan will look exactly the same.'

Eriko had never thought she would get to have these kinds of conversations with someone.

The sensation of making a new friend, which she hadn't experienced for decades, came flooding back to her. It wasn't dissimilar to that sense you had when you were falling in love that the world was opening out in front of you, but it was also distinct from that feeling. With a new friend, the world around you seemed subtly different. You discovered a new side to yourself. The change was only a minor one, and yet it set your heart singing. Now I've found her, Eriko thought, I'm not going to lose her. Having a female friend clarified her own contours and colours, gave her a feeling of confidence in herself. Before she knew it, she was squeezing her arms tight around Shōko's waist.

'And here we are!'

The realisation that she had arrived outside her own apartment block brought with it a sudden clench of loneliness, like waking from a dream and noticing her cheeks were streaked with tears. She wanted to ride on Shōko's bike longer, chatting as they went. She said her thanks, and waved her new friend goodbye. As if sensing Eriko's reluctance for this to be the end, Shōko said, 'Shall we meet at Smile Sushi next time?'

So there would be a next time – Eriko felt like doing a little dance. From now on, she could meet Shōko whenever she wanted.

'That sounds great. I've never been to that kind of place.'

'It's amazing, honestly. Conveyor-belt sushi places these days are so high-tech. You order everything through a touch screen, and the plates have location technology built in, so they can track them as they emerge from the kitchen. An old woman like me can barely keep up.'

'Hah! You know, now you mention it, I think you wrote about it on the blog.'

When Eriko turned back at the entrance to her building, Shōko was looking in her direction, smiling so broadly that she could see it even in the dark. Eriko stood waving until Shōko pedalled off. She opened the entrance door with a spring in her step and headed for the elevator. It was then that she glimpsed the figure in the corner of her vision.

Keiko was leaning against the railing by the ground-floor apartments, smoking. She wore a tracksuit that was mostly indistinguishable from a pair of pyjamas, and her frizzy hair was flapping about in the night breeze. Eriko felt her whole body tense. This was not part of the plan. She hadn't wanted to be seen, not right now. As she stood there, frozen, Keiko spoke.

'Was that person out there your friend?'

Finding it hard to process the encounter, Eriko opened her eyes wide. The unflinching look in Keiko's rabbit-like eyes, from which one felt no animosity at all, was utterly unchanged from when they were fifteen. There were any number of things that Eriko wanted to say in response, but the words refused to come out.

*Yes, and it's hardly anything to be surprised about! Do you realise how many years have passed since all of that stuff? I've made a proper friend. She's a famous wife blogger, who lives nearby. She's amazing. She wrote about me on her blog. Yep, that's right: I've managed to develop the skills needed to make friends outside of work and school. So don't treat me like an idiot, okay?*

'Good for you! I have to say, I didn't think someone incapable of giving other people any space would ever manage to build a proper friendship.'

Not wanting to hear any more, Eriko turned her back on Keiko mid-speech and hurried over to the elevator, pressing the button twice.

'You don't have to be so twitchy. Are you running away from me? Hah! Anyone would think that I was the perpetrator in all this …'

In the darkness, Keiko's gloating laughter came chasing after her.

# CHAPTER FOUR

The ancient vacuum cleaner was a bit like the corpse of a large bird, thought Shōko. It was as though she was clinging onto its neck and dragging its torso around the floor. Her lower back felt achy, and it was a nuisance to have to unplug the vacuum and plug it in again in each room she went into. When she was done vacuuming, she had to run the washing machine, clean the windows, wipe down the verandah, and then start preparing dinner. This list of basic domestic duties seemed to her like a never-ending journey lying ahead of her, and she found herself crouching down despondently alongside the vacuum cleaner. Her breathing was shallow, most likely on account of all the dust. The resin from her father's cigarette smoke had stained the whole house, and although she herself was a smoker, it left her feeling nauseous.

Were they really basic domestic duties, though? A regular part of everyday life that one was expected to undertake as a housewife? Shōko found it impossible to view them as anything but a terrible punishment, which ground down the body and soul. They struck her as unreasonable, bitterly hard, sometimes even imbued with a terrifying darkness.

Back when she was Shōko's age, her mother had performed these tasks day in, day out. Her mother now lived far away from here with her new family, and Shōko hadn't seen her in years, but her thoughts flew to her now. In her daily life back in her apartment in Tokyo, Shōko didn't use a vacuum cleaner. Two or three times a week, she'd wipe the floor with floor wipes, and leave it at that. If she found a stain, she'd quickly wipe it up with her floor-mopping slippers. Hers was just a small apartment with parquet flooring, and she found that this sufficed. Musing that her father's partner, Urumi, had her work cut out for her using this unwieldy vacuum cleaner all the time, she felt a burst of sympathy towards her.

How long had it been since she'd been back here? Looking around at the house where she'd grown up, Shōko let out a heavy sigh. For starters, it was far too big for the number of people now living here. Exposed beams, dark ceiling with sunken panels, spacious living room – it was a traditional Japanese-style house, which made it a rarity even in these rural surroundings. The maintenance of the surrounding farmland had long been entrusted to other people, and of late there was very little for Shōko's father to do, other than organize memorial services for the deceased family members and carry out little administrative tasks. Today he had been out from early in the morning, playing pachinko. The idea of giving his daughter a hand with the cleaning didn't even occur to him.

Beyond the verandah, the large river glinted in the distance, and the September sun shone into the room, illuminating its interior. The wooden shutters grew harder and harder to close with every passing year, but nobody had bothered to fix them, so they now remained permanently open, even at night and during bad weather. Over the years, the sunlight had left the dust-coated tatami thoroughly faded, while age had frayed it. Urumi was unbothered by details like this. The time was approaching to replace the tatami entirely, but Shōko felt that involving herself by making this suggestion would be to play right into her dad's and brother's hands. She was convinced that her father would be better off selling the place, but knowing that this would inevitably entail her becoming embroiled in the negotiations and admin, she resisted raising the issue. Her intention was to fulfil her daughterly duty by cleaning the place as briskly as possible, and then leave. That was enough. Excessive concern would only end up in her wringing her own neck. Shōko got reluctantly to her feet and resumed vacuuming.

As she dragged the heavy machine behind her, her thoughts turned to when her mother had walked out on them, leaving her father for another man.

Shōko had been in high school. Before she'd had time to resent her mother for leaving, she had found herself lumped with the entirety of the housework. It had spun her right off her feet. For a while she made a brave attempt to keep up with it all, but it wasn't long before she threw in the towel. In her guilt about this, Shōko did her utmost not to return home. Instead, she would walk between the houses of boys her age, waiting for their mothers to invite her to have dinner with them. Without Shōko doing the housework, the family naturally dissolved. Her brother, who had just begun university, ate out all the time, and her younger brother, still in primary school, got by on bento boxes from the convenience store. Her father either sat drinking wordlessly in the house, or went out to bars. It wasn't all Shōko's fault, of course. The people in her family were fundamentally lacking in accountability. Eventually, when her aunt started coming over occasionally to clean or bring food, some semblance of their daily life began to return. It was then that Shōko learned the operating principle of their household: the one who caves first, loses.

Four days previously, Shōko had heard the news from her younger brother Yōhei that their stepmother, Urumi, had walked out again.

'It seems like this time might be for real. It's been three weeks. The house is in a total state, and Dad seems dazed. I'm worried about him. Will you come and see?'

*You're twenty-five years old, can't you do something about it yourself?* – these words had been on the verge of slipping from Shōko's lips. After quitting technical school, Yōhei's plan had been to go into business with his friends, but he'd given up on that idea somewhere down the line and was still living at home, doing part-time jobs. Of all Shōko's family members, he was the least reliable. He had a sweet, charming side to him, but he was also fundamentally lacking in consideration for others, the type of person who failed to notice that he was driving everyone around him mad.

'It's been a while since you've seen your dad or Yōhei, no? You should go down for a few days, have a change of scene.'

Kensuke had been very positive about the whole trip, but Shōko's reluctance to go meant she'd made laborious work of her packing, and taken several detours before finally arriving at Tokyo station. It was two years or so since she'd got on the bullet train – and then she had to change to another train line to get to her hometown. The instant she laid eyes on her house, she knew that she couldn't wait to leave. That sensation endured now. She felt as if her entire self was being wiped out by the stagnant, grey time of this place.

Her eyes fell on the Buddhist altar where the pictures of her grandparents were displayed. The stems of the chrysanthemums left in their vase had turned brown in the water, and the flowers were withered. Moving closer, she detected a funny smell. Shōko knew that she was lazy, but her father was on another level. How was it possible for someone to slack off this much from the tasks of daily living – to slack off from life itself? In the three weeks since Urumi had left, everything in the fridge had gone off, and the rubbish bin was spilling over onto the floor. Shōko wasn't entirely without sympathy for him, but when she thought it through, he was only sixty-five, and still in good health. There were politicians far older than her father out there who would speak with the media as they received a bashing from across the country – why, then, this total lack of vitality? He'd always been this way, since Shōko was a child.

Someone who'd never make the first move …

Instead, he'd hold his breath and wait for someone else to act on his behalf. Things had been the same back when her mother had still been around, and now, when Urumi left him, he never went to get her back, never went out looking for her. He stayed here with a faint smile glued to his face, slumped in front of the TV as he transmitted his resentment into the distance. In all likelihood, Urumi would somehow sense his performance of solitude, and be drawn back to him. Although she seemed cheerful and frank on first impressions, she was actually quite timorous. That was doubtless why her father had pinned his sights on her.

Her father had met Urumi, who was currently in her mid-fifties, when she was working at a bar that he frequented. She had moved in when Shōko had begun studying at the local women's university. By that point Shōko barely came home, and so had little real interaction with her father's new partner, but still felt a sense of gratitude towards her. Urumi was a busybody, and generally quite careless, but having her around brought the house back to life.

The one who suffered the most when Urumi didn't come home was Shōko. In that sense, Urumi was her sole lifeline.

Without Urumi, it was Shōko, as the daughter, upon whom the responsibility for looking after her father fell. This knowledge was forever weighing on her. Yōhei was useless in that regard, as he'd amply demonstrated, and since vehemently opposing her father's remarriage, her elder brother had more or less no contact with him.

Quite possibly, holing himself up in this dusty house was her father's way of exacting revenge on his girlfriend for running away. Feeling this wordless protestation drifting through the air around her, Shōko felt stifled. What was it that her father was so set on proving that he was willing to sacrifice his own life into the bargain? Or was she reading too much into this? He was merely an ageing man, who no longer had any ambitions whatsoever. This was how it always was here. Just being around him, she found herself running around second-guessing this and that, so that before she knew it she was utterly worn out. She had a powerful urge to go home to Kensuke right now. Next to him, she could breathe with ease.

Craving a cigarette, Shōko cast her eyes restlessly around her. Was it possible that her stash from her uni days remained?

In the drawer of her bedroom desk, she found a pack of the Camels that she used to smoke as a student, along with a lighter. She lit one, and fell backwards onto her bed. A layer of fine dust rose up from her duvet cover. The smoke formed a spiral, drifting slowly towards the ceiling.

This was her childhood bedroom, where on paper at least she'd lived until leaving university, and yet being here didn't bring her any comfort. The various items adorning the room, which had once been oh-so-trendy, now pinned her with a confronting gaze: the *Trainspotting* poster; the back issues of *Dazed* magazine; the rows of big-format comics. She wanted to shudder with embarrassment. What thoroughly mediocre tastes she'd had! All these supposedly fashionable items were things that she'd bought after they'd been given the stamp of approval by some famous person given the role of tastemaker. She couldn't feel in the least bit nostalgic for that part of her past, when she'd been so desperate to be seen as 'unique'. She wanted, if at all possible, to forget about that section of her life, from age fifteen to twenty-two, when her entire personality was a breathing mass of self-consciousness. Of her repeated rebellions, nothing had stuck – now here she was, a thoroughly ordinary thirty-year-old.

If her blog was made into a book, Shōko thought, friends from that period of her life would be sure to see it – that was the most terrifying part of the whole thing. She didn't want anyone here to know that the girl who'd talked big about how much she hated this town and couldn't wait to get out, about how she wanted to work in fashion and live an exciting life in Tokyo, had ended up having a very mediocre marriage and living a mediocre, laid-back sort of life.

She envied Eriko Shimura. There was no way that Eriko would have a past that she wished she could rid herself of. She'd confessed a touch bashfully to how she'd never set a foot outside of Setagaya. Shōko knew what that meant: that her life had been spent building layer upon perfect layer from that flawless foundation, like an exquisite mille-feuille. The more that she knew she would never match up to her, the greater her admiration for Eriko grew. She was dying to see her again. They'd said that they'd meet next time at the conveyor-belt sushi place. It was an informal plan, but in this moment it felt like something precious to cling onto.

There was a knock and then the sliding door opened to reveal her brother, Yōhei. 'Hey,' he said, lifting a hand in greeting. In the time she hadn't seen him he'd grown rounder, she thought, and his cheeks had become ruddy. 'Sounds like you've been working hard.'

'You could at least give me a hand if you're in!' she said, pouting, and Yōhei cackled. He looked alarmingly like her young father, as he existed in Shōko's memory.

'Yeah, sorry. When it gets this bad, I've no idea where to make a start, you know?'

'I can't do any more, I'm exhausted. I give up. Hey, what about asking a professional cleaning firm?'

'I guess that's a possibility. You know how much Dad hates letting strangers into the house, though.'

'Yeah, that's exactly the problem. Is there anything he doesn't hate, I wonder?'

'Still, you've got to feel sorry for him in a way. Tied to this land that his parents left him. He's like the last victim of the "you've got to protect the family house at all costs" school of thought.'

Why did the two of them tiptoe round their father like this, Shōko found herself thinking. If he was content with his life as it was, then there was no call for them to feel this level of concern. The whole thing suddenly seemed ridiculous.

'It'll be okay. Urumi will be back soon, I'm sure of it. The longest she's ever away for is a month. Although I haven't really spoken to her recently.'

Saying this, Yōhei sat himself down on the bed. A layer of dust rose up once again. Considering how he'd summoned her, in a manner deliberately designed to rouse her anxiety, he seemed completely unconcerned by the whole situation.

'I haven't been around much. I've been staying at my girlfriend's place. I'm thinking about moving in with her.'

Shōko was tempted to give him a talking-to, but then she remembered that she herself had been exactly the same, and shut her mouth. She'd spent as much time as she could away from home during school and university, and then had run away to Tokyo as soon as it was time to get a job.

'It's hard to be here, isn't it?' Shōko said, in place of reproaching her brother. 'Without Urumi, it's like a deserted island.' She looked up at the ceiling. There was no way she could live here, she thought once again. The thought that her and Yōhei's laziness was something they'd inherited from her father made her mood bleaker.

'I've been reading your blog. Kensuke told me about it. It's amazing that there are strangers out there reading that stuff. And it's quite high up the rankings, right?'

'What!? Why the hell are you reading it?'

'It's funny. The contrast between all the other housewife bloggers out there who are so glamorous and well put-together, and then your days spent lazing around on your arse.'

It stung to hear this, but Shōko knew it was true. Other popular housewife bloggers all described their meticulously crafted lifestyles, filled with bright smiles, innovative ideas and delicious meals, 365 days a year. It was as if the business of daily life was unspeakably enjoyable for them. Surely, everyone's lives included the less enticing days: the days when you had to clean your parents' house in silence, or deal with family members you found difficult, or apologise for things your children had got up to. What did those bloggers do on days like those? Did they just not post? Or did they search hard until they found one glittering moment, which they plucked out from the surrounding mire for the entertainment of their readers?

Whatever the answer, Shōko knew this way of being to be beyond her. It was people like Eriko Shimura who should be writing blogs – people born into wealthy households, flawlessly stylish in their attire, who could write about their days working in Japan's largest manufacturing company. A life like that would surely look good however you sliced it. It was ironic that people like that, whose lives were so rich and fulfilled, had no time for writing blogs.

'But you haven't posted for a couple of days now. Is it okay to just leave it like that?'

'I forgot my mobile at home.'

'For real? Hah! Call yourself a blogger? Shall I lend you my computer?'

'That's okay. I can't be bothered.'

Yōhei bummed a cigarette, then left the room.

It seemed conceivable to Shōko that she'd forgotten her phone accidentally on purpose. She could talk with Kensuke on the landline, so not having it wasn't a problem. The blog wasn't yet her job and being in this place hardly put her in the writing mood, anyway.

Disconnected from the internet, she began to realise quite how much time there was in a day, and a darkness spread through her chest. She thought of her life in Tokyo as full, but was it simply that she spent her entire time online? If that was the case, she could do that anywhere, even here, she thought to herself in despair.

What an idle life she led, she thought. It wasn't that different to that of her dad, whose sole pleasures were booze, TV and pachinko. Maybe I'll go back to work, she tried thinking to herself, but the thought alone sent the acid rising up from her stomach. Her experience of quitting the apparel firm after developing stress-induced stomach ulcers came back to her with alarming rapidity. Belonging to a specific group and keeping in step with those around her, doing her makeup and then heading into work

– all those things that she used to do so unthinkingly were elements of a world that now seemed incredibly distant to her.

The screen door slid open again – her father had returned without her hearing him. Her first thought upon seeing him was how much he looked like her. Single-lidded eyelids, lips curled back to reveal yellowing teeth. He wore a grubby tracksuit, his hair was peppered with grey, and his face was covered in stubble. There was a faint white patch on his jumper, presumably where he'd spilt something on it. He seemed to have shrunk since she'd last seen him. With every passing year, he paid less attention to his appearance. If she'd passed him in the street as a stranger, she'd doubtless think of him as an unhygienic old man. She felt a pang of guilt for assessing him so coldly.

'How's it going, Shōko? It's fine to take a break if you're tired. It's not like we get visitors, so it doesn't matter if the place is a mess.'

Her dad smiled down at her as she lay there on the bed. She couldn't stand the inexplicably imposing air he commanded, when on the surface he seemed so laid-back, even jokey. In his cheerful, reddened face she sensed something you couldn't pass off as mere laziness, something approaching mania. Was it odd to be diagnosing her own father like this? *He acts like he's some kind of king* – every time she'd complained in this way to her friends as a youngster, the response had been the same.

'Really? But he seems so fun and nice.'

Shōko hadn't known what to say in response to their confused expressions. Kensuke had taken a similar line, saying, 'He's just awkward, he doesn't know how to be with people. On the inside he's lonely.'

He'd meant well, but she knew that there was no way that someone like him, who'd grown up in a well-balanced household, could understand. Thinking of her mother- and father-in-law living in Ōsaki, their reasonable conversations and their unremarkable yet contented lives, Shōko was struck by a pang of envy.

She smiled now at her dad.

'I'm okay. It's the first time in a while that I've properly cleaned, so it's tired me out. Have you thought about maybe taking on a cleaner?'

'Ah, I can't be bothered. What shall we do for dinner tonight?'

'I'll rustle something up. But it won't be right away. Sorry.'

'That's okay, take your time.'

Maybe he really was as considerate of other people's feelings as his peaceable tone seemed to make out, Shōko thought now, and for a moment she despaired of her own vexation. As a youngster, she'd adored her father. She used to offer to clip his nails and clean his ears. She could still remember the scratchy feel of his freshly shaven cheek when he rubbed his chin up against her. She'd felt proud of him, the father who everyone in the neighbourhood adored. Even now, it wasn't as if she didn't love him. He hadn't done anything terrible to her. He always gave her plenty of money. As it happened, they'd never had a real argument of any kind. Why, then, did she find his presence so suffocating? It didn't make any sense to her.

'You don't have to worry about the cleaning, love. If you're tired, just don't do it. You should take it easy.'

At these words, a burst of hatred flared up in her towards her father, who was once again smiling down at her. *Don't play the good guy*, she thought. *If I don't do it, who else will?* Shōko's suspicion that what had driven her mother away wasn't, in fact, her father but rather Shōko herself had never left her. If she'd only helped out more around the house, as useless as she may have been at domestic tasks – or at the very least, been there for her mother when she needed someone to talk to. Her mother had been the kind to do everything by hand, drying fresh sour plums to make umeboshi and making her own miso. She organised immaculate celebrations for all the family's birthdays, ran around the whole year attending memorial services for this and that person, and entertaining visitors warmly. She was always smiling, always talkative, and yet Shōko knew that she was constantly monitoring her father's mood. Her mother had corralled this group of lazy individuals into a family, all on her own.

The ultimate proof of this was how, as soon as her mother left, everyone had disappeared from the house.

Shōko felt grateful for her childhood, where she had never wanted for anything, but she had no wish to become a martyr like her mother. She wanted to be free in all that she did. Letting the family home and the family meals eat away at your soul, your lifeforce, was putting the cart before the horse. Was there any greater contradiction than making yourself unhappy over the very tasks meant to make life enjoyable?

Shōko had a vivid memory of the Girls' Day party that they'd thrown at home back when she was in primary school.

'I can't eat this.' Those were the words her father had spat out the moment he dug his chopsticks into the chirashi-zushi that her mother had woken early to make. With that, he'd stood up from the table and flung himself down in front of the TV. Her friends, who had been laughing with one another until that point, all froze. Shōko felt all the blood in her body rush to her head. She couldn't believe that the father she'd been joking with seconds before and the man with his back now turned to her were one and the same person. When, afterwards, her mother had hesitantly enquired what he hadn't liked, he'd replied, in a perfectly ordinary tone, 'It was a bit sweet.' He'd eaten her mother's chirashi-zushi any number of times before; Shōko still couldn't understand why, on that particular occasion, he'd chosen to criticise it. It was made according to a recipe her mother had learned in the house she'd grown up in. The rice was stirred through with pieces of slow-simmered gourd and dried shiitake, and even the pink fish powder sprinkled across the top was handmade – altogether, it was a time-consuming dish.

'I think I'll do either stew or curry tonight. Does that sound okay?'

'Anything at all. Anything you cook is good with me,' her father said with a smile, and went off, leaving the screen door open. She guessed that he'd never ask after Kensuke, or how married life was going for her.

Shōko lit another cigarette. When the smoke finally reached the squares in the latticed ceiling, it split into two strands before disappearing entirely.

# CHAPTER FIVE

As Eriko's eyes blinked open, they fell on her mobile, which she was clutching in her right hand. The screen still displayed the top page of *The Diary of Hallie B, The World's Worst Wife*. Her sleepiness immediately lifted.

Four days had now elapsed since the last post. This year, Shōko had updated the blog practically every day, so this was a highly unusual occurrence. As someone who knew Shōko personally, Eriko resolved that she had to find out what was going on. She felt spurred on by the number of worried messages that had accumulated in the comments section: she wasn't the only one who was concerned.

She could think of a few possible reasons why Shōko might not be updating her blog – her laptop had broken, or she'd got sick – but the fact that she was also not replying to texts caused Eriko dismay. Again and again, she recalled the words that Shōko had let slip that night in Denny's: 'I sometimes get strange messages on the blog … These days, the administrator deletes them automatically, but in the past there was some quite creepy stuff …'

Shōko had gone on to explain that she'd received messages along the lines of *I know where you live* and *Don't get too full of yourself, or there's no telling what will happen to you*. Was it possible that even while Eriko lay here in bed, Shōko had been abducted by some stalker? The thought sent a shiver down her spine. Shōko was married, but that didn't necessarily mean she was impervious to such a fate. She acted so unconcerned, so free – that was, of course, one of the attractive aspects to her, but it was nonetheless true that Hallie B was fast becoming a celebrity online. It would be little surprise if she had become a magnet for people's resentment, hatred and other twisted emotions. Eriko wished that she'd impressed on her friend the need to take better care. Would it be possible to work out where Shōko lived from the details on her blog? To answer this question, Eriko realised, she needed to reset her mind, and read the diary through the eyes of a criminal. That was how she'd come to fall asleep last night while making her way through the two years' worth of blog entries.

There was no avoiding the conclusion to be drawn from her investigation: Shōko was incautious. These days, even a middle-school student would have been able to work out what area of Tokyo and what part of Setagaya she was living in simply by looking at the photographs from near her house and her notes about favourite restaurants. The photos taken inside her apartment also contained several crucial clues.

But, if nothing had happened to Shōko, then why wasn't she replying to Eriko's messages? Eriko had taken care to make her texts sound casual, so that Shōko wouldn't think about them too much. And yet, none of the ten texts she'd sent over these last four days had elicited a response. As a result, when Eriko was video-calling with people in the Tanzania branch, as she was conducting sales talks with a client from a big fast-food chain, there was some part of her mind that was always fixed on Shōko. She now found herself resorting to checking Shōko's blog even during working hours.

'What are you looking at, Shimura? Save that for when you're at home, will you?'

So absorbed had Eriko been in scrolling that she hadn't noticed her boss coming up right behind her. Hearing him admonish her in his low voice, she'd broken into a cold sweat. Was she losing a grip on herself? She knew there was a reason that she was falling so head over heels into all this: the situation echoed one she'd been in fifteen years previously. The intolerable feeling of the panic she'd felt back then returned to her.

*Did I do something wrong?*
*Why are you ignoring me? I thought we were friends!*
*Will you at least tell me why you're avoiding me?*
*Please, just say something.*

If this was how she was going to react, then, for the sake of her concentration at work, she needed to make sure that Shōko was safe before going into the office. If she couldn't work out her whereabouts on her own, maybe she was best off contacting the police. Jumping up from her bed, Eriko quickly donned the thin sweater, skirt and sheer tights she'd laid out the previous evening. She put on a light face of makeup and then clipped back her meticulously blow-dried hair. Taking care as usual not to wake her parents, she stole silently out of the house.

The moist dawn air that enveloped her body with its scent of fresh grass was so chilly that it was hard to believe that the cicadas had been singing only a few days previously. Stepping away from the apartment block, she noticed a figure standing in front of her, shrouded by the morning mist.

It was Keiko. She stood there stock still in her pyjamas. Keiko, the childhood friend whom she'd known for twenty-four years, and who still lived in the same apartment block. Keiko, the only girl who knew her from the beginning of primary school through to the end of high school. Eriko would have far preferred not to have to interact with her, but bumping into her like this, it was hardly possible to ignore her.

'Morning,' Keiko said, turning to face Eriko straight on. Her face was perfectly impassive. Hesitantly, Eriko surveyed this person who she had once regarded as her best friend, now illuminated by the early morning light. Her makeup-free skin was flaky and dry, and there were deep lines etched at the corners of her eyes. Her complexion looked aged and tired, quite at odds with the childishness of her movements as she scratched her cheek with the fingers poking out of the sweatshirt sleeve. Her hair looked like it hadn't been washed in a long time, and was plastered greasily to her forehead and neck.

'What are you doing? The station's in the other direction. Aren't you going to work?'

Keiko was the last person that Eriko wanted observing her movements, so she replied with deliberate ambiguity.

'I've got an errand to run in the arcade. What are you doing up this early, is surely a better question.'

'Nothing in particular. Just a little morning stroll. In a while I'll go and walk in the opposite direction to all the office workers heading to the station. It's fun doing that. It feels like time is rewinding itself.'

Keiko's soft, mumbling way of speaking was utterly unchanged from when she was fifteen. As she talked, she narrowed her eyes and gazed off into the distance.

This was how she was, Eriko remembered. The unusual statements or turns of phrase that had her listener repeating them back to her, a sensibility slightly different to everyone else's – back then, these features had been so impressive to Eriko. Now, as a thirty-year-old woman, these idiosyncrasies simply made Keiko seem a touch unwell.

'I've got to go. Bye.'

Promptly turning her back, Eriko strode off in the direction of the arcade. She glanced behind her after a while to see Keiko still standing in front of the apartment block, staring fixedly after her. Eriko understood what was going on well enough: this was Keiko's version of revenge. By refusing to move away or to find her place in the world, by instead drifting about in this way, Keiko was mounting an appeal to the other residents, to Eriko, and to her parents: *Thanks to Eriko Shimura, I've been left incapable of living a normal life.*

It had been fifteen years already. Of course, Eriko knew that she had been at fault, but the blame didn't lie exclusively with her – some of it belonged to Keiko too. The teachers, even Keiko's own parents, had admitted as much. In continuing to blame Eriko, Keiko was attempting to flee her own life, to remain squarely in her comfort zone. Saying these words to herself, Eriko felt her heart rate slow slightly. She crossed beneath the overpass and entered the shopping arcade.

*An old block of flats with plaster walls, behind the rice shop* – recalling Shōko's words, Eriko pressed on. She thought of the photo Shōko had uploaded to her blog, showing the view from her flat window. There had been an electricity pole, and a red-brick apartment block – yes, here they were! And directly opposite them, a white building with a stippled plaster exterior.

She'd found it! Her chest lightened by a sense of accomplishment, Eriko stepped inside the building entrance. It didn't take her long to find a letterbox with a nameplate reading 'Maruo'. Flat 303. The letterbox didn't appear to be overflowing. Eriko went to open it, only to find that it was, naturally, locked. It was just then that she heard a voice behind her.

'Eriko?'

Shōko was standing behind her, her eyes wide with surprise.

'Shōko!' In her relief, Eriko felt all the power draining from her body. Thank heavens, she thought. The short, plump man standing next to Shōko had to be her husband. Wow, Shōko was way out of his league, Eriko thought fleetingly, but that wasn't important right now. Ignoring him, she turned to Shōko, barely resisting the impulse to throw her arms around her in relief.

'I got worried because I couldn't get in touch with you! I started thinking something bad had happened. You know how you were saying that people had been leaving alarming messages on your blog …? And you'd told me that you lived around here, so I came to check if you were all right.'

'Did I tell you where my flat was?' Shōko smiled, but her face looked strained.

Vexed by the shallowness of Shōko's memory, Eriko found herself adopting a reprimanding tone of voice.

'Yeah, you did! You said it was in the arcade, just past the rice shop! And there's a photo of a red-brick building on your blog, so I figured it must be this one. You should stop posting pictures like that, you know. It makes it too easy for people to figure out where you live.'

For a little while Shōko said nothing, before eventually starting in on a series of what sounded like excuses.

'I'm sorry. My father wasn't well, so I went back home for a couple of days. I accidentally left my phone here, and I only got back last night. Oh, this is my husband.'

The man standing behind her finally bobbed his head in greeting.

'He's got the day off work today, so we stayed up all night and binge-watched an entire drama series. The cut-off point for DVD returns at Tsutaya is 10 a.m., so we thought we'd take it back before we went to bed.'

As relieved as Eriko was to see Shōko smiling as if she didn't have a care in the world, she simultaneously felt anger welling up inside her. Nothing terrible had happened to Shōko, after all. Even if she'd only got back recently, she'd had any number of occasions to send Eriko a text. Giving herself over to her feelings, she began to speak.

'Okay, but you could at least have sent me a text? You must have known I'd worry. Your readers are worried too. I could barely sleep! We're supposed to be friends, but you—'

With a shock, Eriko tuned into the words spilling from her lips. This was the exact same line that she'd come out with all those years ago – back in the spring of her first year at high school, to Keiko. Eriko raised a hand to her mouth.

It was in that moment that the thing she feared most of all happened. As Eriko watched the faces of Shōko and her husband, the same look surfaced there that had appeared on Keiko's face years ago. Some mixture of terror and fascination, as though they'd discovered that the fish they ate on a regular basis was, in fact, a ferocious carnivore. A clear boundary line had now been drawn between them and her. No, no, no, Eriko thought, this wouldn't do. She had to find a way to take back what she'd said. A thick cord of sweat began to run down her back. The knowledge pressed in on her: they were looking at her like she was unhinged.

'Ah, sorry! Am I being weird? Haha.' She aimed for a jokey tone, but her voice came out high-pitched and tinny. The unsettled expressions on the couple's faces remained unaltered.

\* \* \*

At her desk later that day, Eriko found that the morning's debacle had rendered her incapable of getting stuck into her work as usual. Before she knew it, she'd ended up accepting one of Sugishita's invitations that she standardly ignored. By 8 p.m. that evening, the two of them were standing alongside one another at the counter of a British-style pub inside the Shinmaru building.

Eriko deliberately avoided speaking about her private life. Instead, she filled him in on her progress at work, taking care to maintain a distance between them and preserve an atmosphere that was an extension of how they behaved at the office. She shared the news that she'd been asked to go out to Tanzania to inspect local facilities and begin Nile perch trade negotiations. For once, her boss's eyes had been filled with expectation as he clapped his hand on her shoulder.

The idea that she'd finally broken through the first obstacle brought with it a surge of emotion. In order to start importing Nile perch into Japan again, they would need to install freezing facilities into a Mwanza processing plant. This required an investment of several tens of millions of yen, meaning that it hadn't been an easy proposal to get past the board, but thanks to the tenacity of Eriko's persuasive tactics, and the track record of agreements she'd reached with several major clients, it seemed as though they were finally moving in the right direction.

Before it was transported, the fish had to be filleted, skinned, frozen, and then packaged. The reason that Japanese imports of Nile perch had mostly dried up was that the laboriousness of this procedure, together with the month-long shipping period during which the funds would be held, meant it didn't present a particularly tempting offer for the sellers. European buyers on the other hand, who now made up the large majority of Nile perch sales, could simply fly the fish chilled across the Mediterranean, greatly reducing the need for processing.

The Japanese market wanted to cook and eat fish from overseas in a similar way to fish from its own waters. This was markedly different to the approach in Europe, where if consumers liked the taste of an unknown fish, they'd welcome its idiosyncrasies on its own terms. The more that Eriko learned about the respective preferences of different consumers, the more it seemed to her as though the Nile perch had themselves taken the decision about where to go.

'Wow … So you'll be going to Tanzania all by yourself? How amazing that the boss singled you out specifically. Though I'd expect nothing less, of course, from the ace of the division …'

Thinking that she noticed Sugishita's lower eyelid twitching, Eriko wondered with a slight chill if she'd taken her triumph too far. It was Saeko Yotsuba, her senior and the only other woman in the sales team, who had taught her that a man's envy was ten times more frightening than a woman's. Stroking the egos of men that she wasn't even into wasn't part of Eriko's skillset. She did prefer, however, to be liked by all people, regardless of their gender, and so she now smiled broadly at Sugishita.

'Hardly! They only asked me because they're short of hands. Speaking of which, it seems like it's hellish for the temp girls at the moment, eh? I heard they axed another handful.'

'They're hardly "girls"! Have you seen them? Besides, I don't think it's on us to worry about anyone other than the permanent employees.'

Sugishita made no attempt to disguise his look of distaste. It was rich to take such a scathing attitude to the temps when he was secretly dating one of them, Eriko thought, cocking her head.

'I know everyone says that manufacturing companies are on the way out, but I honestly think there's still plenty of room for expansion. Surely the whole essence of our job is to discover new resources and untapped markets? I'm thinking I want to go abroad more – as much as possible, even.'

As nervous as the prospect made her, Eriko was itching to see more of the world. She wanted to open up new markets, under her own steam. That was the feeling that had taken hold of her since her trip to Tanzania had been decided. What would she see if she put Setagaya behind her, escaped the grasp of her parents, and ventured forth bravely for once? It even seemed plausible to her that, if she were to be offered the chance to move to an overseas branch right now, she'd jump at it. Indeed, it sometimes occurred to her that that was the life she was suited for. All the skills that you needed to decipher the atmosphere in those tension-laden spaces unique to Japan, to carefully navigate the subtle, complex relationships between people – were they really necessary? Maybe Eriko didn't need friends; maybe she was fine without. Talking this way made it seem as though the humiliation from earlier that morning was all a dream.

'You're a teacher's pet through and through, aren't you? I like that about you, though. You've got your own goals, and you're committed to them in a way that's refreshing to see. You're not needy, like other girls.'

Eriko had wanted to carry on talking about her plans within the company, but this pronouncement by Sugishita, his eyes narrowed in affection, brought an end to their conversation.

'You take care in Tanzania, okay?' he said, and patted her head. The gesture irritated her, but it also made her feel fragile, breakable, in a way that was faintly pleasurable. It was a long time since she'd been touched by a member of the opposite sex. 'A girl like you can't be too careful.'

What the hell? Sugishita had pulled her up for using the word girl before, but it was apparently okay for him to use it about her. She rolled her eyes, and he looked baffled.

Well, she thought, thanks to him and the Irish whiskey, she at least felt confident she'd get a good sleep that night.

# CHAPTER SIX

The gentle sound of running water drifted over from the kitchen where her husband was standing. To think that having someone else doing the housework for you could feel this comforting! Shōko thought she could sense the fatigue that had built up at her father's house ebbing away.

Sipping her coffee, Shōko sat in front of her laptop, running her eyes down the huge number of comments she'd received.

*There haven't been any updates for three days and I'm worried about you. Are you okay, Hallie?*

*I was so worried about you that I couldn't get any work done! If you're going to take a break, it would be nice if you could let us know.*

It had never even occurred to Shōko that this many people would be so affected by the fact that a housewife they didn't even know hadn't updated their blog for a few days. Satoko's criticism had been formulated more directly:

*Your blog is no longer something that belongs to you alone, so if there's a reason why you're not updating it, then you need to communicate that. Please ensure that you are reachable at all times. You didn't reply to my messages, and I was concerned for you.*

But I haven't even agreed to work with you, Shōko protested internally when she first read it, but then thought that she should perhaps take this as an indication of how serious, how committed Satoko was. That Shōko had caused her to worry, at least, seemed beyond doubt. In which case, maybe Eriko's behaviour wasn't that out of the ordinary, either.

However many times she reiterated that to herself, though, she still couldn't shake off the shock of that morning. With no warning whatsoever, Eriko had been standing there, slap bang in the middle of that most familiar scenery. Shōko had felt as though the fabric of the everyday world had been ripped open, and she'd been afforded a glimpse of something shocking lying beneath, garish in its brightness. Eriko's way of speaking had been fevered, as if something had taken hold of her. When Shōko had checked afterwards, she'd been stunned by the number of messages that Eriko had sent. Even if she hadn't been replying, that level of worry was excessive.

They'd still only ever met three times.

Shōko didn't want to go off Eriko so soon. Now that she'd found a friend, she didn't want to lose her over something like this. She'd finally grown accustomed to this city, finally got to the stage where she could make female friends, like other people managed to. Though she knew it seemed over-dramatic, she felt as if letting Eriko go meant missing out on her chance to become a real person forever.

The blame lies with me – it was always healthier, psychologically speaking, to think like that. Eriko was doubtless a very upright, meticulous person. Besides, anyone was bound to feel anxious if they couldn't get in touch with someone they knew personally. Shōko had herself experienced this exact situation with her father. Although he didn't often leave the house, he was prone to occasionally disappearing without telling anybody where he was going. As everyone was going out of their minds with worry, he'd come padding back home as though nothing had happened. It always made her feel stupid for having fretted in the first place.

Her brother had texted to say that as Shōko had set out back for Tokyo, Urumi had returned. Reading his message, Shōko let out a long, deep sigh. Now, there would be a period of reprieve, when she didn't need to think about that house. As a powerful sense of liberation rippled through her, making her want to cry out in relief, she also felt disgust towards herself flaring up too. Didn't this make Urumi a kind of human sacrifice? Shōko had urgently wanted her stepmother to come back, but, like her father, she'd made no attempt to look for her. She'd kept on hoping she'd return. Although Shōko didn't want to admit it, she and her father were extremely similar.

Kensuke's voice, accompanied by the fresh scent of coriander, hauled her out of the mire of these dark thoughts.

'What's with the glum face? Here you go! Vietnamese-style brothless Sapporo Ichiban ramen!'

Shōko peered down at the bowl that Kensuke set on the table with a clunk. The thin white noodles were adorned with plentiful sprigs of coriander, one of her most beloved ingredients. She picked up her chopsticks eagerly.

'We've got a Vietnam fair going on in-store right now,' Kensuke said, 'and the staff are all obsessed with making this.'

'Ken-chan, you're a genius!'

The evenly seasoned noodles slid down smoothly into her stomach. The quantities of the ingredients – the lime, the Nam Pla, the minced garlic, the white and black sesame seeds, the tom yum powder, the sakura shrimp – were all perfectly judged. The balance between the sourness and the spice was so delicious, Shōko could feel it radiating through her whole body.

'Listen, about that Eriko woman,' began Kensuke, who'd sat down across the table from her.

'What's up?'

'I just think you should be a bit careful with her.'

So it was niggling at him too, Shōko thought to herself as she affected a nonchalant tone. 'You mean because of what happened this morning? She was just worried, I think. It's my fault for not letting her know what was going on.'

'Hmm, maybe. But even if you were truly concerned about someone, would you go seeking out their house? It seems quite extreme.'

'That's true. But I think she's like this pampered, goodie-goodie type, who's naturally a bit of a worrier. She doesn't mean any harm.'

'You're too trusting sometimes, Shō-chan. Think it through, a bit. You know how clingy and frightening women can get. She's clearly envious of you and your life.'

For a second, Shōko doubted her ears. The idea that Eriko might be envious of her had not once occurred to her. Her eyes widened and the hand holding her chopsticks fell still.

'I mean, you're married, and your blog's a huge success. From where she's standing, you're on the winning team. My guess is that she feels inferior to you. She's single, right?'

At this, Kensuke laughed through his nose, and then shrugged, as if to say, see? There was something unpleasant about these gestures, which instantly sapped Shōko's appetite. The words rose as far as her throat – *aren't you the one that feels inferior?* Knowing full well that if she voiced them the peaceful mood between them would be decisively shattered, she bit them back. All of the issues she'd struggled not to think about now went parading round her head.

Shōko was fairly sure that Eriko's salary was more than double Kensuke's. She flew overseas, concluding sales deals that determined what appeared on Japanese dinner tables, and traded with the kinds of manufacturers that were household names. Her intellectual capacity was fundamentally different from that of Kensuke, who had graduated from a small, third-rate university. Then there was her flawless appearance, her affluent family ... The truth was that whatever aspect you considered, Shōko's new friend outran her husband.

What on earth was he saying, then? How could he believe that someone like Eriko would envy the indolent lifestyle of people like them? Shōko felt herself to be content, but the habit of internally scoffing at her own way of life in this way shook her. If only she hadn't met Eriko, this would have been a day when she could have wallowed in the comfort of her own home. The thought left her faintly irritated.

'Well, in any case, it won't happen again. Urumi's back now, and everything's sorted,' Shōko said. She made a show of throwing back her noodles with great momentum, yet inside she didn't feel so carefree.

There was no certainty that Urumi wouldn't one day be overcome by stress and leave, just as her mother had done. Oh, it was all so ridiculous, Shōko thought. Keeping up that huge empty house, which nobody wanted to visit; the memorial services that were only about going through the motions; the blog photos that were only there to impress other people – all of it was so dumb and pointless. Surely there were more authentic forms of connecting with people out there that should be the priority?

Suddenly a thought came to Shōko, and she sat up with a jolt. If, in detailing her life as the sort of homemaker who was consistently slacking off, she was providing a release valve for the pressure imposed on all those women like her mother, then maybe her blog did have a meaning after all. If she could actually be of service to people, then surely all the time she'd frittered away up until now would be wiped from her record? Without processing what she was doing, Shōko set down her bowl and started up her laptop. An elation of a kind she'd not experienced before raced through her.

'Are you not going to eat any more?' Kensuke asked, a note of disapproval in his voice.

# CHAPTER SEVEN

'Irasshaimase! Welcome to Smile Sushi!' the staff bellowed in unison as Eriko walked in the door, and she found herself shrinking reflexively into herself. The place was crowded, but her eyes immediately found Shōko at one side of the counter, hunched over a glass of chilled sake. A constant stream of announcements over the tannoy enumerated the new sushi items being placed on the belt.

'Sorry to keep you waiting.' Placing her bag down on the counter, Eriko settled herself beside Shōko.

It was already ten days since the morning she'd navigated her way to Shōko's apartment building. Since then, the pair had exchanged a few messages back and forth, and it seemed as though the tension between them had dissolved: Eriko had apologised for coming to Shōko's home unannounced, and Shōko had apologised for leaving Tokyo without telling Eriko.

'That's okay. I made a start already.'

'Is it okay to leave your husband on his own?'

'Yeah, I told you before, it's fine. He's at home playing *Dragon Quest*, as usual.' Shōko seemed irritable. Was it because Eriko had kept her waiting half an hour? Eriko was so tired that she was dying to be horizontal, and this treatment left her feeling peeved. Shōko seemed utterly inconsiderate of the fact that she'd been working all day and was exhausted. On the train ride here, Eriko had read the blog that Shōko had been updating without fail since her absence, so she knew that Shōko's day had consisted of going back to bed after seeing her husband off to work, sleeping until after lunchtime, watching reruns of dramas on TV, and reading magazines in the library. Sometimes too much knowledge could cause its own problems, she reflected. And yet her desire not to lash out at her friend won out. She wanted to return to that close, warm feeling that had existed between them that night in Denny's. Seeing Eriko looking down at the floor in silence, Shōko's tone softened slightly.

'Sorry for being cranky. I'm wound up because I've been getting these weird messages. It's not your fault for being late.'

'What, again? Are you okay?'

'It's all this "I know which area you live in," and "I know you go shopping at such-and-such a place," that kind of stuff. Whoever it is seems to know that there's talk of my blog becoming a book, because there was also one that said, "You think you're all important now, because you've been offered a book deal? Don't get ahead of yourself." It's odd, because there's only a handful of people who know about that: my husband, the editor, you ...'

Shōko took a teacup, scooped in some powdered matcha and pressed the button for hot water, then handed it to Eriko. Eriko felt as though the plates on the conveyor belt had suddenly sped up. How did the diners ever manage to retrieve them when they were circulating at such a pace? It was a struggle to ensure her voice didn't tremble when she spoke.

'Are you saying that because you're worried that it's me?'

'What?! No, of course not! You're overthinking this.' Shōko opened her eyes overly wide and waved her hand to brush the idea away. Eriko reached for her teacup and winced at the rush of heat on her fingertips. She wouldn't be able to drink it for a while. Next to her, Shōko let out a big sigh.

'But it's scary, you know, having your personal life exposed to the general public like that. I think I've got to be more careful with the blog. If I decide to continue with it at all, that is.'

With that, the pair fell into silence. Who did she think she was, playing the victim at this stage of the proceedings, Eriko couldn't help but think. For a thirty-year-old, Shōko was overly naive about the workings of the world. Eriko felt the same brand of irritation that she felt towards the temps who complained all the time despite failing to do their jobs properly, or her classmates back at school who never really lifted a finger. Yet she also found this tension between her and Shōko unbearable. Attempting to bring some harmony to the mood, she looked over towards the wooden boards listing the various kinds of nigiri toppings, which were plastered across the walls.

'Ah, they've got Japanese sea bass! Did you know that what they called Japanese sea bass in places like these used to actually be Nile perch? Although now that restrictions have tightened up on false descriptions, they can't do that any more.'

'Nile perch …? What's that?'

'It's a type of fish that I'm in charge of importing at work. I'm going out to Tanzania soon, which is where it comes from.' This was the first time that Eriko had explained anything about her work to Shōko. She found that her words instantly came out smoother. 'It's a light-tasting, white-fleshed fish, so it can be used in all kinds of dishes. You know how sometimes on restaurant menus it will just say "white fish", without specifying what fish it is? For a while, a large proportion of that unidentified "white fish" was Nile perch, imported from Africa. It's not so common now, but in 1998 and again in 1999 there were bans on importing it in

Europe, and so a boatload of it came to Japan. The bans were because of a cholera outbreak, and a pesticide incident. You and I will definitely have eaten it at some point, but we'll have no idea when or where, and we won't remember what it tastes like. That's the fascinating part – the idea that we've encountered it without realising. That's Nile perch for you. It's the same as how the engawa that you like isn't made of righteye or olive flounder, but halibut, right? Or "Hallie B", as some people call it, haha. Nile perch and halibut are alike in that they're similarly ferocious. Nile perch are carnivorous and totally desecrated the ecosystem of Lake Victoria, while halibut are so vicious that the people fishing them have to use a shotgun to stop them thrashing around.'

As Eriko went on speaking, she noticed that Shōko's expression had grown strained. Eriko cocked her head, wondering if she'd said something off. Was it just the lighting, or did Shōko look a touch pale?

'Is that really true? About the engawa being made of halibut?'

'Did you not know? I always assumed you'd given yourself the pen name Hallie B because you're such a big engawa fan.'

'Hallie B is the nickname that my male friends all called me in high school! Because I was like a "big happy-go-lucky baby", they said, and somehow it got shortened ... I'd never even thought about it being similar to halibut.'

'Are you serious? I was convinced that was what it was a reference to ...'

Feeling flustered, Eriko picked up a clump of sushi ginger with the serving tongs. Shōko was looking at her, her lips twisted into a scowl. It seemed there was no preventing tension building between them.

The unpleasant thought flashed through Eriko's mind that she had overestimated Shōko. She had invested the tranquil days that

Shōko wrote about with too much meaning. This was a long-standing pattern of hers. The second date, the second kiss, her second time sleeping with someone: because she'd been so euphoric the first time, had let her hopes balloon to such a crazy extent, she'd countless times found herself feeling thoroughly let down when time number two rolled around. But it was best not to think dispiriting thoughts like that now. Finally, Shōko's expression relaxed slightly, and she smiled.

'I don't really need to hear that stuff, you know? It only spoils the taste of this sushi I'm paying good money for. So long as I don't know anything about pesticides and shotguns and ecosystems and carnivorous fishes and stuff, it tastes good. I'm very happy not knowing.'

'Sorry, in that case.'

Eriko felt immensely irritated at herself for apologising reflexively, when she didn't actually feel she was remotely in the wrong. It was this type of excruciating exchange between women that she couldn't stand. It made her feel as though her skills were being put to the test; even now, at the age of thirty, she couldn't get used to it.

'There's no need to apologise. I just – I just didn't need to know that.'

Saying this, Shōko grinned, then reached out an arm towards one of the plates of melon drifting her way. Eriko followed suit. She wanted something to refresh her palate, and melon seemed like the most trustworthy ingredient in a place like this. Yet the speed of the belt was so fast that her timing was off, and she failed to catch it. This place was a war zone, she thought. How many of these slivers of raw fish whizzing past her eye line were actually what they pretended to be?

It gradually dawned on Eriko that the misery she felt was as if she had been told that she herself was a fake. Sitting there at the counter, she was performing a wealth of worldly experience, but internally she was terrified that Shōko's affection towards her was already fading. She didn't even understand this conveyor-belt system. Alongside someone of the same gender, she realised that she was no more than a child, frantically trying to keep up the appearance of understanding how the world worked.

All of a sudden, Shōko seemed quite arrogant to her eyes. She seemed to think that it was natural that she would be able to eat all kinds of high-quality fish here, despite paying only 98 yen a plate; she said that she wanted more female friends, but as soon as anyone came too close, she pushed them away.

Surely it didn't matter if the fish she was eating was halibut or Nile perch or anything else? None of the fish conceived of themselves as substitutes or fakes, and went around feeling humbled as a result. It was humans who had assigned them certain roles, based on their own selfish criteria.

'If they hadn't been released into the lake …'

'What are you saying? I can't hear you.'

'I was saying that if they hadn't been released into the lake, the Nile perch would have gone their whole lives without realising how ferocious they were …'

But as she spoke, Eriko's words were drowned out by a message over the tannoy announcing that fresh rolled omelette nigiri was making its way onto the conveyor belt.

That night, as the three of them sat down for their nightly cup of tea, her mother set a plate of sliced Japanese pears and figs on the table. Of everything that Eriko ate, it was only her mother's food that imbued her daily life with any sense of the passing seasons.

'Keiko's quit her job again. Apparently she's just hanging around at home. Her mother seems practically despairing. Mrs Yamazaki from the second floor was telling me.'

Eriko's jaw, ready to bite into a segment of Japanese pear, stopped abruptly at this news. It was roughly three times a year that the name of her former best friend would get mentioned in the Shimura household. Her mother's behaviour was like that of a police detective seeking to test her, she thought. Her father pretended to be absorbed by the TV, but she could tell that he was monitoring her reaction. Eriko suspected that neither her father nor her mother believed the account that she'd given them at the age of fifteen. The complex nature of her relationship with her friend was not something that she'd have been capable of putting into words back then, and so she'd stayed resolute in her assertion that it was all down to a big misunderstanding on Keiko's part. Still, she did her utmost to affect a casual tone as she replied,

Hah! That sounds like Keiko sure enough! She never could see anything through. If anything, sticking it out for three months is good going for her. Where was it this time, again? A manga café?'

'Yes, exactly. How old was she when she got married, again? Twenty-five? And then got divorced not long after, and came back home, and she's not had a lasting job ever since. What's the matter with her, I wonder?'

Her mother darted a glance in Eriko's direction, implying that she knew all too well where the issue lay, but Eriko pretended not to notice.

'Such a waste of time! But then she's always been a slacker. She moves at a slower speed to other people. It's not like she's not bright, so it's a real shame. All those talents gone to seed.'

Eriko took a bath, and then, once alone in her room, found herself reading Hallie B's blog once more. How many hours of her day were used up in perusing this site? Several times she made to leave a comment but stopped herself. The two of them had only just parted, but she was already thinking about Shōko again. Over an hour they'd been in each other's company that evening, yet Eriko didn't feel like they'd truly seen one another.

Eriko switched off the ceiling light, and read on in the glow of her desk lamp alone.

She couldn't put out of her head how uptight Shōko had seemed in the sushi place. She felt that there was a good probability that Shōko had misconstrued her as some kind of stalker. Even if not, there was no doubting that she'd been marked out as someone to be wary of. The thought made it hard to breathe. Ah, this horrible feeling was too much to bear. Taken by the urge to lie down, Eriko slumped her upper body down on the desk.

At this rate, things were going to end the same way as they had before, all those years ago. She had to resolve this misunderstanding somehow ... But even as she thought this, an awful suspicion rose up in her, filling her chest with a heavy darkness. Was it possible that she really was a thoroughly off-putting person, and she had no awareness of it? That, unbeknown to her, she was acting in ways that frightened other people? Yet, as much as she scoured her body, she could find no trace of malice there. All she'd ever wanted was to be friends with Shōko ... The very idea that, at thirty, she was still incapable of making a single friend left her feeling utterly desperate.

The next thing she knew, Eriko's fingers were buried in her hair, tugging at it. This was a bad habit of hers that she'd quit with great difficulty at the age of sixteen, but doing it again now she felt that familiar comfort come surging back. With something approaching nostalgia, she gazed down at the single hair now lying in her palm. She liked the raw sensation on her scalp, and she knew that once she'd pulled out one, it was impossible to stop. The sight of the glistening root brought on a shudder: a mixture of excitement and horror. On she went, pulling out one hair after another, until a pile like a faint black shadow had formed on top of her desk.

As she pulled, the humiliation and the shame of that time as a teenager when she'd been branded a perpetrator came flooding back to her, ebbing its way into every corner of her body.

But it was also true that it was only once she'd lost everything that her life as the Eriko she was today had begun. Yes, Eriko had died once, fifteen years previously. To resurrect herself, she'd had to mobilise all her effort. Before, she'd been someone who lived somewhat in a world of her own, but she began taking care to pay attention to those around her, choosing her words carefully and adopting a modest attitude that wouldn't rub people up the wrong way. To distance herself from the gruelling relationship issues at her girls' school, she aimed for the most well-known mixed universities in the country, forgoing sleep so as to study for the entrance exams. She had eventually got into her first-choice university, and subsequently entered the same manufacturing company as her father, which also happened to be the largest in the country.

She wasn't the same as back then, she thought to herself now, and it followed that she wouldn't make the same slip-ups as back then. Her biggest mistake was never getting to the heart of the misunderstanding, and instead letting the rumours spread.

She would use her words, use her wisdom. Everyone thought her competent, didn't they? She would write more messages to Shōko, to help her understand who she was as a person. Or maybe hand-written letters would be better? She could do her utmost to bump into Shōko at the sushi place, the family restaurant, and at

Gisele, making out like it was a coincidence. By now, she had a good enough grasp of the places that Shōko frequented. If that didn't work, then she'd visit her at home again.

Eriko wasn't a stalker: of that she felt certain. Stalkers were more isolated, people not recognised by society. They lacked imagination and consideration for others. She had to get Shōko to understand that, and she wasn't too fussed if that entailed drawing on methods that might take her by surprise somewhat.

Sensing something swaying about on the ceiling, Eriko looked up with a start. For a second, it seemed like the shadow of an enormous fish. It took her a moment to realise it was the silhouette of her own torso, slumped over the computer, wavering from time to time.

# CHAPTER EIGHT

After seeing Kensuke off, Shōko cleaned up their breakfast things – although that was probably a grandiose way of putting it. Of late, she'd begun just serving him a banana in the morning, as recommended by a health trend a little while back, so all she really had to do was wash the coffee cups and throw the banana skins in the bin. When that was done, Shōko made a beeline for the sofa positioned at a right angle to the balcony, pushed aside the pile of laundry she'd brought in and dumped there yesterday, and laid herself out sleepily. Usually, she would fall back to sleep again, enveloped in the smell of her favourite fabric softener as the sunlight filtering through the window warmed her stomach, but today she took her smartphone out of her pocket. In that pool of light, the screen seemed very dark, and she found herself squinting.

Scrolling back through her messages, she found her stomach tensing. Her breath tasted sour to her – was that something to do with the consommé-flavoured potato chips she'd eaten in place of proper dinner yesterday? Her inbox showed the same name, over and over: Eriko Shimura. It hadn't yet been forty-eight hours since they'd met at the conveyor-belt sushi place, and yet in that time, Shōko had received over twenty messages from Eriko. The texts said mostly the same thing. Feeling overwhelmed by both their volume and the avalanche-like pace at which they arrived, she had no sense of how to reply:

*I want to tell you that it's not me that's writing those messages on your blog. I'm not a stalker. But I'm very sorry if I did anything to give you the impression that I might be.*

*If there's a misunderstanding between us, it's best that we meet and talk it through. When would be good for you? I can meet you any time. I'll adapt to your schedule. I'm sorry to ask when I know you're busy.*

*When we met before, I think I was a bit distracted because the conveyor-belt system was new to me and I didn't understand it. I'm sorry if that somehow tainted the atmosphere between us.*

*I'm sorry for being late to our meeting, things were just so busy at work that day. So you see, I don't have the time to be a stalker! Haha.*

*I want to apologise if what I said about the falsely labelled fish upset you. You'd told me before that you liked it, so I should have pretended not to know and said nothing.*

Why was it that when apologies came this thick and fast, Shōko began to feel that it was her that was being blamed?

Unable to gauge Eriko's true intentions, Shōko let the arm holding her phone drop heavily to her side and shut her eyes. She'd barely lifted a finger, and yet her body felt heavy and exhausted. She didn't think that her behaviour to Eriko that night at the restaurant had been that cold. She'd waited for her to finish work, and then the two of them had sat there side by side eating sushi, and parted ways outside. What on earth was there to get this worked up about?

Shōko guessed that, although the two of them had ostensibly been looking at the same scenery, it had appeared very differently to Eriko. Shōko fast-forwarded now through her hazy memories: the circulating sushi plates, the scent of sushi vinegar, the pale hands of the chefs working busily on the other side of the counter, the tower of plastic dishes, the shrill tannoy announcements, the bland conversation they'd kept up throughout ... The footage that was now replayed on her internal screen didn't contain so much as a single murky patch. How was it possible to have formed such a catastrophic interpretation of these events?

Eriko insisted that she wasn't a stalker, but the persistence and ghastly urgency of her protestations were hard to term anything but stalkerish in nature. Shōko had never once called Eriko a stalker – she had no memory of even using the word in front of her. She'd only spoken about the unwanted messages she was getting on her blog.

Shōko had the same thought now as she'd had when Eriko had found her way inside her apartment building, namely that Eriko had a tendency to let her assumptions run away with her. Rather than considering the state that the other person might be in, she rushed in headlong with her whipped-up feelings. Although Shōko didn't want to be entertaining thoughts of this ilk, she had started to wonder whether Eriko might be a bit emotionally unstable. She knew that Eriko wasn't a bad person, and she certainly seemed to live an extremely busy life, so maybe the stress was to blame. She'd told Shōko that her romantic relationships didn't tend to last, so it was possible she was dragging around the wounds of multiple heartbreaks. It was, after all, quite odd that there was no sign of a man in the life of someone that attractive.

And there was I thinking we could be friends …

Bringing to mind her positive first impression of Eriko, that warm feeling of the first night they'd met at Denny's, a profound melancholy crept over Shōko. Sure, she had been somewhat dazzled by Eriko, but Eriko had also been that rare person whom Shōko had warmed to from the first moment, in quite a simple, uncomplicated way. Now that she'd found out about this side of Eriko, though, there was almost certainly no going back. She recalled them riding together on her bike – the smell of Eriko's hair, the ticklish sensation of her slender arms wrapped around her waist – as though it were a memory from the distant past.

It was exactly like Kensuke had said: she'd been careless to try to befriend a stranger who declared herself a fan of the blog. The unfamiliar sense of regret made her stomach feel even heavier. She burped, and tasted yesterday's oil.

Slowly sitting upright, Shōko gazed out at the block of flats facing her. The wisest plan would be to distance herself from Eriko gradually. If she were to block her or whatever now, it was very possible that Eriko would come storming into her apartment again. Now that Eriko knew where she lived, it wouldn't be easy to sever their ties completely. She would have to just move slowly, without hurrying things. Thank goodness that Eriko was as busy as she was, Shōko thought. If she could only succeed in putting a bit of space between them, then hopefully Eriko would get swept up in the content of her days, and forget about Shōko. Still, the prospect of gradually tapering out their friendship seemed like such a pain to Shōko that it made her vision spin. Her eyes fell back to her phone screen.

You have nothing to be frightened of, Shōko tried telling herself in a bid to calm herself down. If worst came to worst, she could file a complaint at the company where Eriko worked. But no, that would be too mean. Maybe the smartest approach would be to talk with the owner of Gisele, and issue a warning to Eriko that way: through her parents. That would be the absolute last resort, though. If at all possible, Shōko wanted to avoid escalating the situation. As soon as third parties got involved there was the need for evidence, and it would become clear that Shōko hadn't acted perfectly herself.

What would she do if it got out that in fact there hadn't been any sinister messages to her blog, for instance?

From where Shōko was coming from, it was a bit of harmless fantasy. Whoever she told the lie to would show concern for her wellbeing and treat her nicely – Kensuke included. This was decidedly not the case otherwise; nobody worried about a childless housewife who whiled away her days in her neighbourhood, doing exactly as she pleased. The creepy messages fantasy also had the benefit of implying, very subtly, to her listener how popular her blog was. This type of lie would never get out, and never hurt anybody. Who on earth could blame her for it?

The absence of any trolls was one of the strengths of Shōko's blog, but it was also proof that nobody envied her and her life. Shōko knew this better than anybody. People were entertained and charmed by her frivolous, unproductive days and her laid-back lifestyle peppered with junk food, but they didn't go around thinking that they wanted to be like her. She imagined that a big factor in the blog's success was the relief that readers felt at seeing a depiction of a way of living even less polished than their own. She had no doubt that having people attacking her online would hurt, but encountering no jealousy or resistance whatsoever was lonely in its own way.

That evening, as she'd come running in late to the sushi restaurant, Eriko had seemed tired, but she'd also had that sparkle unique to people living a fulfilled life. Her disarrayed hair, her heavy breathing and her faded lipstick had all seemed to Shōko to accentuate her femininity. It wasn't just a question of appearance, either; Shōko had felt confronted by the fact that Eriko was way, way more distinguished than she was. The other men at the counter had stared at her the whole time. It seemed to have been Eriko's first time to visit a cheap revolving sushi place of that kind, and Shōko had been slightly exasperated by the way that she kept glancing around her anxiously, like some sheltered maiden who'd never left the house before. The idea that Eriko must think her to be satisfied by the cheap, indolent life that she had led filled her with the desire to illustrate her power to her friend. She wanted the woman sitting in front of her to know that she was in a position that other people found enviable. The moment she'd mentioned the messages on the blog, Eriko's expression had clouded over, and she'd shot Shōko a look of genuine concern.

This was quite possibly the first time that a lie Shōko had told had come true.

The tendency to invent things had been with her for a long time. Back in high school, she'd pretended not to understand a simple maths problem so as to persuade the boy she fancied into helping her. After studying for the upcoming test together, they'd ended up dating. As an adult, she'd called up a different crush late at night to tell him that she felt like she was being followed, and succeeded in luring him over to her apartment. She didn't feel guilty about these deceptions. Being neither beautiful nor having any outstanding talents, she needed some hook in order to attract people's interest. It was something that everyone did, to a greater or lesser degree.

Suddenly, her phone began vibrating so violently that the bones of her fingers shook. It was Satoko. In her relief, Shōko pressed the phone tight against her face.

'Good morning. Are you okay to talk now? Listen, *Melanie* is holding a tasting session for a new product, and I wondered if you might like to attend. It's next Monday, at a meeting room in our offices. The product is a new brand of ready-to-serve soup …'

*Melanie* was a women's magazine released by Satoko's publishing company. Several popular homemaker bloggers wrote for it regularly, and the fashion pages and round-table discussions all featured readers – although all the readers were so gorgeous and glamorous, it was very hard to believe they weren't professional models. Shōko had no confidence that she could integrate among people like that.

'I'm so grateful for the invitation, of course, but I'm not sure about going public …'

'Oh, that's okay, I understand. In which case, why don't you come along as an observer? It would be very instructive for us to hear your opinion. I think your views might shift if you made friends with other bloggers. We can give you lots of samples to take home, and there'll be a demonstration with a professional chef. Everyone loves our tasting sessions.'

Shōko found herself a touch taken aback that Satoko didn't push the issue of her revealing her identity. Why was she being so understanding, when Shōko still hadn't agreed to the book?

'Would that really be okay? Just to observe?'

'Of course! I understand your reservations about showing your face. It's a frightening age we're living in. Our relationship with you is valuable to us, and we absolutely won't pressure you into doing anything you don't feel comfortable with. If and when you decide to publish something with us, we'll support you in all the ways we can.'

Since their first meeting, Shōko had struggled with the feeling that Satoko was trying to steamroll her into something, so she found herself softening at this display of consideration. Oh, yeah, she thought – this is what editors are for. She decided, on the spur of the moment, to confide in Satoko.

'Thank you … As it happens, there is something that I wanted to discuss with you. You know the café where we met that time? Well, almost immediately after you left that day, this woman approached me. She introduced herself as a reader of the blog, who lived in the neighbourhood, and we got to know each other a bit. But I think there's something a bit off about her. She knows people I know, so it's not like she's pretending to be someone she isn't, and for a while I figured that meant she must be okay, but she's started bombarding me with messages, and one time she even came round to my house …'

Satoko left a small pause, and then began in a serious tone, 'I see … It definitely sounds like you'd better be careful. If anything happens, it might be best for me to intervene. Through working closely with several homemaker bloggers, it's become clear to me how harmful other women's jealousy and envy can be.'

On the other end of the line, Satoko let out a deep sigh, conveying her exhaustion with this state of affairs. When making these kinds of 'women can be scary' pronouncements, women would always heave a big sigh, as if to testify that they themselves were the exception. The same went for Shōko herself, she realised, and before she knew it she was murmuring, 'Envy, you say …?'

'Sorry?' Down the line, Shōko could hear the hubbub of what she assumed to be the editing department in the background, advancing and receding like a wave. An image of overlapping shades of grey, like a winter ocean, drifted into Shōko's head.

'The thing is, this woman has got it all. She's gorgeous, she's rich, she went to a prestigious university, she works in a top-tier company, and was raised in Tokyo by her parents, who she gets on well with. It should be me who's the envious one …'

'But it's always the ones who appear the most flawless that have some issue. I'm guessing that this woman is single?'

Shōko was surprised to hear this woman with a hotshot media job coming out with almost the exact same response as Kensuke. 'Well, yes … But—'

'Are you wondering whether I'm the same? I'm actually married with two daughters,' Satoko said in a deliberately businesslike tone. Then, promising to send over the details for the new product tasting session in an email, she put down the phone. It took Shōko a short while to realise that she'd effectively consented to attending the session.

In a bid to pull herself together, she began sorting the mound of laundry on the sofa, but soon gave up. Just the act of folding a towel into four somehow induced a feeling of revulsion in her. What need was there to fold each and every one of these and put them away on the shelf? Surely it was fine if she and Kensuke plucked what they needed from the pile, and eliminated the heap that way? She was aware that her laziness had grown more pronounced since coming home from her father's house. It was as though that two-day deep clean had worn away at something inside her.

If Eriko was envious of her, as Satoko had said, then maybe the issue was a surprisingly simple one. Shōko was beginning to understand that at the root of Eriko's extreme behaviour lay a desperate scream, emanating straight from her heart. Maybe she wanted Shōko to understand her. She clearly *really* liked Shōko, and that was why she was so consumed by what had happened between them. She simply wanted, with everything she had, to be closer to her. Conceptualising things this way was somehow even more off-putting to Shōko. She felt herself on the verge of being sucked in by the fathomless depression and loneliness that caused Eriko's intense neediness. If Eriko remained this dissatisfied, despite her myriad blessings, she must have some real issues. Once again, it hit Shōko that what she'd been drawn to in Eriko was her status, all her superficial aspects. Alongside a woman like this, she'd felt, she would be carried off to glamorous, sunny places. She'd be able to get used to Tokyo, in all its smooth sophistication. She wanted Eriko to share with her the shiny, intelligent world to which she belonged. Of course she understood that when you shared fun times with someone, your souls would end up colliding, and you would eventually come to share in their heavier feelings too, but she'd felt that was a long way off in the distance. It wasn't something she'd wished for immediately.

And who could blame her for that? Was there anyone out there ready to accept the murkiest parts of a woman they'd only just met? She was quite sure that Eriko herself had been drawn by the best features of Shōko, as she presented on her blog. The person that Eriko liked was the happy-go-lucky, funny, popular homemaker blogger Hallie B, not the Shōko who was still haunted by the guilt she felt towards her mother, and who lived in fear of the long, dark shadow cast by her father's house.

It would be easy enough to send Eriko a message oozing with care and consideration, but Shōko knew that even one such message would mean she'd never get away from her again. She'd be stuck playing the 'good friend' for the rest of her life. The thing about same-sex friendships was that, unlike with relationships between men and women, it was extremely difficult to bring them to a definitive end. If she were to acknowledge the darkness in Eriko, she would have to continue hearing her out until she was done.

*Ugh, what a pain* – her father's catchphrase floated up in her mind. She found it ironic that she, as someone with all this time on her hands, couldn't be bothered to get involved in other people's problems, while the ever-busy Eriko was the one chasing her. She pulled out a very bobbled fleece from the laundry pile, put it on, and decided to step outside. The scent of fabric softener like cotton candy rose up from its fabric. That alone was enough to make Shōko feel she was doing a decent job at life, and so she let herself, ever so easily, off the hook.

# CHAPTER NINE

At nine in the evening, the Denny's contained only a scattered handful of customers. Eriko settled herself down into an armchair by the window, ordered a cup of green buckwheat tea and spread the cashmere scarf she was wearing over her knees.

What am I doing here again …? The question brought her floating gently back to herself. Why wasn't she making her way home to her apartment, so close to here? By this point of the evening she should, by rights, have been smiling at her parents as they welcomed her home, sitting at the dinner table with them, getting herself prepared for tomorrow. Instead she was giving up her own precious private time, when she had no assurance that Shōko would even turn up here. Maybe there really was something wrong with her.

Finishing up her work for the day, Eriko had rushed to the station. Inside the train carriage, she'd made a beeline for the priority seat, where she sat and read the latest instalment of *The Diary of Hallie B, The World's Worst Wife*. Arriving at her station, she'd stormed through the ticket gates and headed straight here. With her Tanzania trip approaching, there were any number of tasks that she should have been seeing to – reading over the materials, doing research, and so on – but she found herself putting them off, telling herself that she could make up for it by going into work early in the morning. Eriko herself had an awareness that her bad habits were getting the better of her. Of late she was arriving at work progressively earlier, so that she could spend all the time that she wanted reading Shōko's blog.

> *The Demon King's got work drinks tonight and will be home late, and I can't be bothered to make dinner for one … I'm sitting here in the study room at the library, thinking through my options. They've got charging points here, which I'm always fighting the students for. I should let the young people with bright futures ahead of them have priority, you say? Yeah, yeah …*

It wasn't like she'd drawn up statistics or anything, but Eriko knew by now that on the nights Shōko's husband was out late, she usually either ate at this family restaurant, or had a sandwich at the chain coffee place in front of the station. She also knew that when Shōko had been to that particular coffee place two days ago, she'd complained that she was 'getting a bit sick of this soup and basil chicken sandwich', so the probability she'd opt for this place tonight seemed high.

When Eriko had visited before with Shōko, the restaurant had seemed light, airy, and generally so pleasant that she regretted she'd never been in there before, but now she was on her own, it struck her as stuffy and rather sad. Men and women in their thirties, apparently on their way out of work like her, sat playing with their phones or staring dazedly into the space above their glasses of wine. At first glance they appeared relaxed, but looking again, one saw that they were all shrouded in a haze of longing, putting off their return home in the hopes that something interesting might happen to them. Closer inspection revealed how stained the floors and tables were. The middle-aged server who stood slumped languidly against the wall was gazing vacantly into the darkness outside the window. Aside from when the trains were passing overhead, the restaurant positioned under the overpass was so quiet that you were inclined to forget you were in the heart of the metropolis.

With a sense of helplessness creeping over her, Eriko chose to think over the conversation she'd had with Maori Takasugi that morning. The truth was that she felt so weak and overwhelmed that it was only in clinging to such small wins as this that she felt okay. Even as she turned the episode over in her mind, her eyes remained pinned on the restaurant door.

Though she knew it to be a bit extreme, Eriko had caught the first train into work that morning, which got her to the office at five-thirty. As usual, she'd sorted through the documents on her desk, and had just finished the sweet pastry recently featured on Hallie's blog when, to her surprise, her eyes had alighted on Maori the temp, still in her regular clothes.

'Wow, you're in already!' Maori had said. 'You high-achievers are something else!'

Electing not to mention that it wasn't for work that she was coming in this early, Eriko smiled ambiguously at Maori. As it happened, she'd woken up early with the sudden brainwave that she could write to Shōko from her work email account. Surely even someone like Shōko was bound to take an email with a signature from a company everyone had heard of a bit more seriously? Eriko didn't care what lengths she had to go to – she was dying to put an end to this fruitless one-way communication pattern they'd fallen into, and as soon as possible. She felt so disheartened, she didn't know what to do with herself. Now, although Eriko hadn't asked her a thing, Maori took out her pink-cased mobile as if handling something extremely precious, and launched into a breathless explanation.

'I was having dinner with my friend yesterday evening when I realised that I'd left my mobile in the changing room at work. I knew that it wasn't worth going back and getting it, but then it played on my mind so much that I couldn't sleep. I kept thinking, like, what if I've got messages from my boyfriend and stuff, so I ended up getting up really early and coming in to get it.'

'When you say your "boyfriend", do you mean Sugishita?' Eriko let the words slip out her mouth without meaning to, and Maori instantly flushed.

'Oh, you noticed? Please, please don't tell anybody else about it, will you?'

'Of course not. These men in sales are so preoccupied by their reputation. My dad was the same, so I understand. I've known plenty of couples who had to break up because the rumours got out, even though things were going perfectly fine between them. I won't tell a soul, I promise.'

'Ah, I knew I could trust you! You've got like this experienced older-sister vibe about you. I bet all your friends say the same! I've never been able to pluck up the courage to talk to you because you're so stunning, and you seem so superhuman almost, but you're actually really kind! I'll come and find you next time I need someone to confide in.'

Maori, who was only twenty-three years old, clasped her plump white hands together and looked up innocently at Eriko. It was a long time since anyone of the same gender had been this affectionate towards her, and it filled her with pleasure. She hoped the time would come when she could help Maori out. If she was needed and relied upon by people younger than her, then Shōko avoiding her and perceiving her as dangerous had to be a big mistake. A mistake that she had to set right.

The door opened with the tinkle of a bell, and Eriko looked up. Unable to contain her joy and excitement, she found herself standing instantly to her feet, and calling out, 'Oh my gosh, you really came!'

She waved frantically to Shōko, who was standing stock still in the doorway. Eriko tried to pretend she hadn't seen the look of displeasure that surfaced on Shōko's face. Shōko drew towards her slowly, looking unimpressed. She took the seat opposite Eriko and stared at her silently. When she showed no sign of speaking, Eriko quickly offered an explanation.

'I thought if I waited here then you might come.'

Shōko hunched her shoulders slightly and pursed her lips. Trying to lighten the atmosphere, Eriko smiled brightly.

'You know I'm going to Tanzania next week? So I wanted to see you before then. To tell you that this is all one big misunderstanding.'

Shōko ordered a coffee from the server who brought over Eriko's green buckwheat tea, and then, finally, spoke.

'How did you know that I'd come here?'

'I mean … You said on your blog post at four that your husband was going out for drinks tonight, right? And most nights when he's out you come here for gratin and wine. It was the same on the twentieth of August, and the fourteenth of September, and the twenty-sixth too. So I was pretty sure that if I waited here, you'd show up.'

'Listen, Eriko …' Shōko looked up hesitantly at her. 'Do you not have any awareness that what you're doing is a bit extreme?'

Eriko returned Shōko's gaze. Maybe it wasn't unreasonable for Shōko to misunderstand in this way, but she herself wasn't in the wrong. She needed Shōko to see that.

'Extreme? Me? You've got it wrong, I'm telling you. The reason I've been emailing you and waiting for you like this is that I'm trying to sort out our misunderstanding! The problem is that you don't want to listen.'

'Do you realise that you sound exactly like a stalker?'

So her hunch had been right. Eriko suddenly felt like she couldn't catch her breath. The idea that she would be labelled a criminal, a perpetrator – she clasped a hand to her chest and took deep breaths in a desperate attempt to regain some tranquillity. Willing her face into the imitation of a smile, she raised the corners of her mouth and narrowed her eyes.

'I'm telling you, I just want to talk.'

'But all this lying in wait for me and coming round to my house stuff? It's scary.'

'But I'm only DOING that because you're IGNORING me! I need you to …' Realising how loudly she was speaking, Eriko quickly shut her mouth. She saw that the words she was coming out with were the lines of a stalker she'd once seen in a corny thriller – almost to the letter, in fact. Thanks to Shōko's preconceptions, Eriko was being forced to play this role that she'd been cast in. Frustration ballooned inside her.

'Listen, Eriko, are there things worrying you?'

'Things … worrying me?'

'I mean, it seems like it's been a while since your last relationship, and I wonder if you're maybe a bit lonely.'

Eriko stared at Shōko, flabbergasted. It seemed as though Shōko had her down as one of those two-a-penny needy women who couldn't get by without a man.

'No! I don't have any worries! I never so much as think about my ex. I don't have any need for romance in my life right now, and I have no intentions of getting married any time soon, either.'

'Is that true, though? You don't seem very content to me. Are you sure you're not actually quite isolated?'

So this was what it felt like to be left speechless, Eriko thought to herself. She couldn't believe that these words were coming out of the mouth of cool, independent Hallie B – words that sounded like the take of someone from decades earlier. This was why you couldn't trust women who'd never had a proper job, Eriko thought, feeling outrage surging.

'I can't believe this … Do you really think that getting married is that big a deal?'

As Eriko watched, Shōko's face flushed and she stirred her coffee, apparently embarrassed.

'Sorry, I didn't explain that well. It's hard to know how to put it … It's just that you're so competent, and from where I'm standing your life seems so enviable, but the way that you're acting is off, somehow. All this sneaky checking of my blog, anticipating my next move, ambushing me like this …'

'Sneaky …?'

'You're so sneaky! Covertly checking up on me the whole time. It's like you've staked out my blog and are surveilling my private life.'

Forgetting even her shock, Eriko burst out laughing. Shōko recoiled, as if confronted by some chilling apparition.

What the hell was this woman on, Eriko thought to herself. How was it possible for someone to be this dumb? What could possibly be 'sneaky' about looking at her blog, when this was information she was deliberately broadcasting to the world? Why was she so lacking in any sense of danger, when this was the position that she'd willingly put herself in? The moment she encountered even the slightest criticism, she reached for the victim card, and beat a speedy retreat to a place where she couldn't be hurt. She spoke about how she hated the tension and cattiness between women, without ever realising the corrosive cruelty emanating from her own body.

Maybe there was no smoothing over this rift between them. If that were the case, Eriko decided internally, then she was going to drag Shōko out of the warm, comfy haven that she inhabited. The two of them had to stand on equal ground. Eriko had barely slept these last few days. Shōko could do with having her life similarly disarrayed. As a friend, it was her duty to sometimes impart things that Shōko didn't want to hear, for Shōko's own good. Otherwise, it would only be Shōko who would face humiliation in the end.

'What about this is amusing to you?'

'I was just thinking how your way of seeing the world is like a child's. You're always the heroine or the wounded victim.' As Eriko said these words, she really did find them genuinely funny, and found herself tittering. Shōko's face lost all its expression, and she grew visibly pale. These past few weeks Eriko had no idea what Shōko was thinking or feeling, but now that her emotions were so perfectly palpable, Eriko felt a sense of calm returning to her, as if she were back at the office. Oh, yeah, she remembered. It was only someone's feelings. For someone who could predict the movements of the African economy, steer Japan's eating habits and make decisions affecting hundreds of millions of yen, there was no way that the feelings of a single housewife would lie beyond her grasp.

In fact, Eriko now thought, she understood Shōko better than anyone else. She'd read her blog often enough that she virtually knew it by heart. She had perfect recall of Shōko's tastes, movement patterns and habits. What was more, she was beginning to notice the weak, sly aspects that lay concealed inside that easygoing prose. And there you were, thinking that you could hide it from us, Shōko, she thought to herself.

'Why are you smiling?' Shōko's voice shook now. 'If you do anything that crosses a line again, I'll report you to your company and your parents. You wouldn't like that, right? I'm begging you, just stop this! The endless messages, the ambushes, all of it.'

Eriko glared back at Shōko as anger flared inside her. Why did she feel the need to escalate this issue that existed between them to other people? Even if Shōko did cause a fuss, people trusted Eriko more than they did her. This order of threat was hardly enough to scare Eriko. She took a deep breath and raised her chin.

'Listen, Shōko, I'm saying this for your own sake, okay?'

'What?'

'It's not me that's acting oddly here – it's you. It's your behaviour that's the problem. No wonder other women don't like you! As soon as something doesn't go exactly your way, you run away and blame everything on the other party, without even attempting to listen to what they have to say. Blame it all on *women*. What terrifying creatures they are, eh? But think about it carefully, Shōko. Think back on all the messed-up relationships you've had with other women in your life up until now. Can you really say, hand on your heart, that none of that was your own fault?'

Realising that Shōko's eyes had glazed over, not looking anywhere, Eriko felt a rage so pure she wanted to scream. In a bid to get her focus, she leaned in and clapped her hands loudly right in front of Shōko's face. Taken aback by the coarseness of her movements, one of the servers stopped in their tracks and shot a glance their way.

'You see! It's like you just give up on thinking. But you need to THINK about stuff. With your own damn brain! What do you think you've been given a brain for? Huh? Stop turning away from yourself.'

By now, other customers were looking in their direction, but Eriko didn't feel remotely self-conscious. This was what she had to do in order to get her feelings across to Shōko. She even felt a kind of satisfaction in revealing her true feelings and confronting Shōko with them. The scenery around her was vivid in her eyes, and she could feel the blood racing energetically around her body. Something deep within her began trembling – she was truly alive. Staring fixedly at Shōko's dazed expression, the words continued gushing out of her.

'Whenever something doesn't go well for you, you try to pass it off as the fault of your surroundings, of other people's envy. But nobody's paying you that much attention, and they're certainly not envious of you. You say that friendships with men are easier, but were they actually your friends? You do realise that they don't count as friends if you're sleeping with them? I guess the question is, have you ever actually had a friend, of any gender? You told me about how difficult things were with your colleagues at work, and blamed it all on how brooding and jealous and whatever women are, but are you sure you didn't just gradually piss off everyone around you with how lazy, insensitive and soft on yourself you are? Aren't you the most needy and womanish of them all? I'm guessing that you were often late, and dropped the ball. People keep their distance from you because you're forever blaming other people, and because you run away as soon as it becomes inconvenient for you.'

Noticing that the fingers grasping Shōko's coffee cup were trembling, Eriko paused. Reflecting that she might have gone a touch too far, she switched to a gentler tone.

'And that's why the blog's as far as you'll ever go.'

'As far as I'll ever go?' Shōko's face contorted in incomprehension. Summoning all her considerateness and affection, choosing her words carefully, Eriko explained her real thoughts.

'I think you're amazing, Shōko. Someone capable of a lot more. You're not the sort of person who should be lolling around at home, satisfied with such a spectacularly mediocre husband. You should be building up a good reputation at work, creating success for yourself in the real world. But it turns out that getting a bit of attention online is enough for you. What a waste! You pretend that you're quite laid-back, but really you're just a coward.'

'That's ... so harsh.' Shōko's voice was trembling and her eyes looked bloodshot. 'What right do you have to speak to me like this?'

'Because I'm your friend.' Eriko felt somewhat surprised by the ferocity with which Shōko was looking at her. She knew that she'd been a bit tough in her assessment, but the Shōko of the blog was a master in the art of taking everything lightly, and Eriko hadn't anticipated this strong a reaction.

'That's what being friends means! That you can say the things that other people can't say. It isn't easy for me to come out with this stuff, either, but I'm telling you so that you can grow from it.'

Shōko's face was now deathly pale. A silence stretched out between them long enough to make Eriko feel very uncomfortable. Eventually she ran out of patience.

'Please just say something. Anything.'

When Shōko finally spoke, it was in a voice so quiet, it was almost impossible to hear.

'What do you mean, friends? You and I have met five times, including today. Ours is not the kind of close friendship where you can get away with saying anything to each other.' A single tear dribbled from Shōko's eye. Eriko swallowed. 'Don't ever contact me again.'

With this, Shōko got to her feet and walked out of the restaurant, her step as uncertain as when she'd come in. Eriko turned her eyes to the window to see Shōko's figure be swallowed up by the night, frail and precarious as a child. She wanted to go after her, but then thought better of it. In front of the seat across the table, Shōko's coffee sat untouched.

There would come a time when they'd see eye to eye, regardless of what Shōko had said, Eriko told herself. Shōko treated her far worse than she'd treated Shōko. Yes, she felt bad for her, but it was also true that she'd had it coming. This was only a temporary falling out. They'd get over it. She'd send Shōko a message when things had calmed down slightly. Eriko pulled the teapot towards her. The green buckwheat tea in the pot was thick and clouded. The buckwheat groats in the strainer had puffed and swollen like corpses drowned in a lake.

# CHAPTER TEN

Shōko had specified Gisele again because she couldn't think of any other cafés stylish enough to invite Satoko to, but she hadn't actually wanted to come here. For her, this place was now inextricably connected with Eriko and her family. In truth, Shōko was beginning to feel a burgeoning distaste towards this entire neighbourhood. This was the place where Eriko had been born and raised; Shōko couldn't shake the feeling that simply by being here, Eriko had her in the palm of her hand. She wanted to put all this behind her and run off somewhere completely new.

'I'm so sorry for calling you out like this all of a sudden, Satoko,' she said. 'I'm just really scared.'

Satoko's gaze dropped to the iPad on which she'd been carefully reading over Shōko's blog. Earlier that day, a number of negative comments had appeared in the comments section. This had never happened before, and Shōko was certain that it was Eriko's doing. She'd called Satoko immediately, and they'd arranged to meet and talk it through. Fighting back the tears, Shōko looked down at her knees in her faded jeans.

'I hate this. I'm going to quit the blog.'

Now lifting her eyes from the iPad, with a gentle smile on her face, Satoko spoke in a consoling tone.

'Unfortunately, criticism is part and parcel of expressing yourself in a public forum. It is crucial to learn tactics for shutting it out.'

This woman doesn't understand anything, Shōko thought, gritting her back teeth. When it came to her that Satoko was getting money for saying whatever she liked, from a position where she knew she would never be personally hurt, a wave of irritation rose up in her. Not only that – it even seemed to Shōko as though there was some part of Satoko that was entertained by Shōko's distress.

It struck Shōko now that she was a product that this woman was trying to consume. Yes, ever since their first meeting, she had been trying to exploit Shōko. She was perpetually sizing her up, wondering how best to manipulate her, busily calculating whether or not Shōko was equipped with the kind of inner workings that would later spit out vast quantities of money. You could see it in her eyes. There was no inclination there to work with her, or to help foster Shōko's talents. This was doubtless why she always came away feeling so exhausted after their meetings.

Shōko didn't have any grasp of the defence mechanisms or tactics with which one could prevent oneself from being consumed. It seemed clear enough, too, that this wasn't something that the editors were going to teach her.

Things would have been so much simpler if this was some artistic endeavour, she thought. Then she could have seen the criticism as attacking her work, rather than her, and maintained a bit of personal distance from it that way. But this wasn't any form of creative work. Maybe the very essence of blogging lay in exposing the details of your life to the general public, and thereby selling it off piece by piece. This was what Eriko's criticism had made her realise: denigrating her blog meant denigrating her entire existence. That was why she couldn't simply let it wash over her. She had to sweep away all of the opposing opinions. Unless they came begging for forgiveness, it was tantamount to an admission of defeat on her part.

Satoko's mobile rang, and she apologised before slipping out of the café. As Shōko gazed at the back of her expensive-looking jacket out of the window, her stomach cramped with stress.

Four days had now passed since their encounter, but Eriko's words from the Denny's were like thorns, still stuck in her heart. Never before had Shōko been attacked so mercilessly by someone. Her life up until now had been spent doggedly avoiding conflict. A part of her suspected that, as infuriating as Eriko's criticisms were, they were probably true, and that suspicion left her with a lingering shame and misery that she couldn't get rid of. She didn't even feel like she could talk to her husband about it. Kensuke was the port that she'd finally found, a treasured place of belonging where she felt at peace. To reveal this shameful part of herself to him would be to sully their home together, the only place where she felt secure.

'If you're at home all day, you could at least do the washing. I've got no pants or socks to wear tomorrow! It's not ideal.' So Kensuke had grumbled when he came home from work yesterday and rifled through the pile of laundry on the sofa. The laundry basket was overflowing with dirty clothes. It came back to Shōko that in the last few days, she'd been skiving off even the bare minimum of household tasks.

'Don't be mean to me, Ken-chan. I'm telling you, I didn't have time. Remember the promise we made when we got married? That we wouldn't argue over stuff like that, right? It's just pants and socks.'

'But you're here all day long! I'm not telling you to make the place spick and span, and you know I don't mind if you don't cook every evening. But you could at least stay on top of what we need to keep our lives ticking over.'

What he was saying was perfectly reasonable. Shōko understood that the person making a big deal out of the pants and socks issue was not her husband, but herself. The idea made her irate. She felt she was being confronted with the fact that what she was pouring all of her time and energy into, what was making her nerves so frayed, was nothing more than a stupid blog. Her entire life was taken up by writing this thing that neither kept her husband in good health nor helped fulfil her dreams for the future. This thing that didn't generate any money, and which she didn't even know if anybody actually wanted to read.

Saying that he couldn't run the washing machine at this time of night, given that it was located on their balcony, Kensuke slipped out to the convenience store late at night to buy fresh socks and pants for the following day.

'You don't seem yourself. Are you okay?'

Parachuted back to the present moment, Shōko looked up to see Hashimoto smiling down at her. Between his perfectly white teeth and his slender toned neck, he seemed like a shining vision of health. 'A meeting with an editor! So cool! You're a real professional now, eh?'

'Are you kidding? The book deal's not even finalised yet.'

'Do you fancy going to watch a film sometime?'

'Huh?' Shōko cocked her head in incomprehension, and Hashimoto began speaking very fast.

'I don't mean anything weird by it, I know you're married and stuff, I just thought it would be nice to hang out, like, as friends. You're fun, and really easy to be around.'

Everyone knew that there was no such thing as 'just friends' between men and women, Shōko thought, smiling inside. Still, it was nice to know that a kid like this with nothing going on in his head found her attractive. She felt her mood improving. Satoko came back into the restaurant and Hashimoto moved away from the table, as the two of them exchanged a conspiratorial glance. Something that Eriko had said flashed into her mind, but she resolved not to dwell on it now.

# CHAPTER ELEVEN

'I'm disgusted by my own ignorance sometimes,' Eriko lamented in an overly dramatic tone to Sugishita, who was sitting on the stool beside her, as she tilted her martini glass to her mouth. Spurred on by the intensity of her desire not to be on her own, she had asked him out for a drink, and now they sat in the bar of the Maru Building. 'Like, I never really bothered to find out what the situation was in Tanzania, you know? It was this upcoming trip that forced me to finally get down to some research.'

Tanzania's territory, which was about one and a half times the size of Japan, boasted vast stretches of farming land and plentiful water sources, giving it much potential as an emerging market. Yet the scarcity of materials and machinery meant that production rates and profits were low, and the reality was that most of those involved in the farming and fishing industries still lived in poverty. The social infrastructure had been insufficiently developed, and both preservation and processing facilities were lacking.

'For instance, most of the Nile perch producers still get around by canoe. Can you believe that?'

'Hmm …' Chewing on the olive in his martini, Sugishita appeared uninterested. Eriko found her tone growing sharp.

'Our company needs to be proactively engaging in trade with companies at the bottom of the pyramid. Global corporations in the West are all over this stuff already. If we're buying up Nile perch at the asking price and selling it off to the production companies for an inflated sum, then patting ourselves on the backs and calling it a day, we're only repeating the same mistake that Japan made during its rapid-growth period. We've got to identify new needs, help mature the market and develop the infrastructure ourselves.'

The so-called bottom-of-the-pyramid countries were those low-GDP countries that made up almost 70 per cent of the world. Providing products and services at a low price to these nations had the merit of enabling businesses to alleviate poverty while simultaneously making profit for themselves.

'You know *Darwin's Nightmare*, that documentary you recommended? Well, I finally got around to watching it, and it really made me think. I know that some people criticised it for making too much of a leap but ... I honestly think Japan has a lot to feel penitent about, relying on a developing nation like that for its food.'

The documentary had portrayed in unflinching detail how, in the short period of time after its introduction into Lake Victoria, the Nile perch had annihilated 200 species of fish living there, thereby gaining admission to the 100-strong list of the World's Worst Invasive Alien Species. The large numbers of Nile perch had led to the flourishing of the fish processing industry in the country, but most of this fish was exported to Europe, and didn't make its way onto the tables of the less affluent locals. The damage suffered by the lake's ecosystem led to the pollution of the water, and meant that the types of fish eaten by locals could no longer be caught there. The film had showed footage of skinny children wearing rags playing around with Nile perch corpses. An explosion in the prostitution industry, which targeted the Western pilots flying out the fish for export, meant the area had grown more dangerous. It wasn't the Nile perch's fault: it had merely been frantically defending its own territory. The tragedy had taken place because the fish had been introduced into a lake that wasn't its natural habitat. Sugishita finally looked at Eriko.

'What you're saying's not wrong, but there's no way we're going to undertake to rebuild Tanzania from scratch. Our job is sales, not politics.'

'Well, I guess, but …'

'You can't be so earnest about everything, Shimura. Take this olive, for instance. If you started thinking about who it had been picked by, in what country, was that person a minor, were they reasonably compensated, and all that, there'd be no end to it. You'd stop being able to take enjoyment in anything.'

There was a reason that Eriko was talking exclusively about work – she still couldn't chase the image of Shōko in tears from her mind, couldn't rid herself of the fear that she'd wounded Shōko in a way that she'd never recover from. The feeling made her ever more eager to perform a busy, capable version of herself.

'That's how it is for you, huh? As long as life is good in the bubble you're living in, then everything's peachy. Which is why you have no qualms whatsoever about hurting Maori. I feel sorry for her! She's a sweet girl.'

'What the hell has she been saying to you?' Sugishita let out a big sigh and lowered his well-groomed eyebrows. 'I told her so many times not to tell anyone, that if she let it slip then it would be the end of us. This entire time I've been trying to get that into her head, and what does she go and do?'

The phrase 'trying to get that into her head' stuck in Eriko's throat like a fishbone. It seemed as though Sugishita saw no problem whatsoever in treating Maori like a plaything. That was the kind of man he was, Eriko thought, staring at his jawline and the wrinkles on his neck with a scrutinising gaze.

'Don't talk about her like that. She's really into you, you know? You've got to treat her a bit better.'

'It's hard, when the other person feels a lot more than you do! I can't keep up. You know how, when you're not that serious about someone, but they get carried away and start trying to look after you, it can feel kind of stifling …? But wait, this is unexpected.'

'What is?'

'The temps confiding in you.'

Fighting off the smug look threatening to spread across her face, Eriko pressed her lips together.

'Really? Younger women approach me for advice quite regularly, as it happens. You might not see it at the office, but I'll often speak to them on the phone, or go for drinks with them after work.'

Once she'd said the words, Eriko started to feel as though they were true, and her heart grew suddenly light. If she could get close to Maori now, none of this would be a lie. And yet, despite saying that day that she would confide in her in the future, Maori hadn't spoken to her since. Maybe she was holding back, Eriko reflected. In which case, she'd have to make the first move. She should decide on a place and time for them to meet.

'Female friendships are complex. In fact, there's one that's giving me a bit of trouble at the moment …'

As trepidatious as she felt, Eriko now decided to confide in Sugishita about everything that had happened between her and Shōko to date. She told him about meeting her beloved blogger in her local café, and about how they'd instantly hit it off and become best friends, but how Shōko had mistakenly thought that the harassing comments on the blog had come from Eriko, and started avoiding her. Sugishita waited in silence for Eriko to finish speaking.

'You speak different languages, you and her. That's why you're finding it so difficult to communicate.'

'Different languages?'

'Maybe that's not a good way of putting it. Your backgrounds, the environments in which you grew up, are too different. If you try thinking of her as someone from a different country, doesn't it all make a lot more sense? You've been coddled your whole life, and totally dedicated to your work, and so you only know how to converse directly with people. For someone brought up by her dad, who did a few part-time jobs before getting married and becoming a housewife, it's too much to deal with. You don't need to think of yourself as abnormal or weird or whatever. But by the same token, it's not her fault either. It's a tragedy born of cultural differences.'

'You're so right!'

Eriko felt as if a wall that had been blocking her vision had toppled down with a single kick, and the tranquil scenery that she'd missed so much now unfolded before her eyes. She looked wide-eyed at Sugishita's face. This perspective had been awaiting her all along, she thought. She felt as though she'd woken from a bad dream. Her breathing felt less constricted, and a warmth suffused her body, right down to the tips of her toes.

'I told you, didn't I? When you were singing the praises of her blog, I told you not to get too close to her. Sometimes, when I'm travelling to this or that country with work, I wonder if globalisation is all it's cracked up to be. So much bad stuff can happen when someone who's lived in a certain place sets foot outside and encounters people from a different culture for the first time.'

'The ecosystem gets destroyed …'

It was as if Eriko herself was the Nile perch – or maybe that was Shōko? In any case, one of them had been tossed into a lake, and two creatures that were never even destined to meet ended up being thoroughly bewildered by the other. That was her and Shōko right now. Quite possibly, the situation would lead to irrevocable tragedy. A shiver ran down Eriko's spine. She still felt she wanted their friendship to go back to how it had been.

'That's why it's good being around you, because we speak the same language. It's not that I don't like Maori, but it's like she lives in a different world.'

Right now, Eriko had nigh-on zero interest in this topic of conversation. She wanted Sugishita, with all his experience, to tell her how to quash the misunderstanding that Shōko was clinging to, thereby enabling them to become friends again. The situation called for urgent measures.

'From the outside she looks like any other young girl, right? But when you actually start dating her, she's kind of full-on … She wants to cook for me all the time. It's like she's my wife or something. It weirds me out.'

Eriko began to grow irritated. She didn't have the time to listen to Sugishita carping on about his relationship. She knew full well that, although he flitted from woman to woman, he was secretly attracted to her. Surely in this situation, the best thing would be to quit his laborious game-playing and get down on his knees in front of her, shower her with the words she wanted to hear?

'Um, can we talk about something else?'

'Huh? Are you for real? You're more than happy to go on about your own worries, but you've got no time for mine?' Sugishita's face took on a look of displeasure. Panic stole over Eriko. Having grown up thoroughly spoiled, Sugishita became openly irritated when women didn't behave in the ways he wanted. And yet, Eriko didn't want to let this selfish man go home. She wanted him next to her so badly she could cry. She wanted him – needed him – to praise her.

'What do you think about going somewhere we can talk quietly?'

'Huh? But we've both got an early start tomorrow. And everywhere'll be shut already.'

His high spirits now dampened, Sugishita shot a glance at his wristwatch, his desire to go home palpable.

'We could go to Kanda and look for a family restaurant there? Have coffee or cake or something.'

'Huh?' Sugishita let out a mocking cackle. 'I'm not one of your female friends, you know. I'm not interested if there's no booze.'

What he said was true, she realised: the time she spent outside of the office with Sugishita was always mediated by alcohol. In the absence of great affection or longstanding friendship, meetings between men and women couldn't be conducted sober. It was different to dates between women, which were perfectly fun with just tea and cake as their accompaniment. That night with Shōko in the Denny's once again glinted in her memory. Feeling that if she let go of Sugishita's arm, she'd fall alone to the bottom of a freezing cold lake, Eriko's breathing grew ragged.

'I'm sorry to ask this of you, but I really need you to stay with me tonight. Please.' She caught hold of his elbow and nuzzled her cheek into his arm. After a moment's hesitation, she moved to push her chest against him. She knew from experience that when she came on strong like this, most men would freeze. Sugishita would be taken aback by the softness of the body swimming inside its cashmere covering. She could see him glancing down at her neck, her collarbone. Yet Eriko understood that even this allure wouldn't last for long. It was this knowledge that kept her throwing jabs constantly, in a frenzied bid to keep the other person interested. The two hailed a taxi outside the bar, and fell inside together. Watching the lights of the Maru building growing further and further away through the rear window, Eriko leaned against Sugishita's shoulder, allowing the fragrance emanating from her glossy hair to take its effect.

'Are you sure you want to do this?' Sugishita mumbled, seemingly unable to keep pace with what was happening. 'I didn't think that you saw me that way.' He reached for her hand and linked his fingers with hers. Eriko felt a twinge of irritation at his phrasing, implying that it was her who was into him, but in this moment she needed intense connection above anything else, so she said nothing and nodded. From the window of the taxi, she saw numerous trains interweaving as they passed over the Kandagawa River. As the taxi travelled towards Yushima, where all the love hotels were located, Eriko texted her mother to tell her that she would stay over at the office that evening, cementing her decision. At times like these, a message to her family locked Eriko into the adventure she'd set out on.

The hotel that Sugishita selected was a retro outfit, evoking 1920s Japan. Its selling point was apparently its luxurious dressing robes and open-air bathtubs, but Eriko didn't have any time to be messing around with those trappings. It seemed that Sugishita was of the same mind; the moment they set foot inside the room's dramatic crimson interior, he launched himself on top of her.

It had been a while since Eriko had last had sex with anyone, and it hurt like hell. She stung with indescribable pain. Feeling a dull ache also in her lower abdomen, Eriko realised she hadn't been for a check-up at the gynaecologist for a while. She should make an appointment, she thought. Were they open on weekends? She tried to recall. Or maybe she should take a half-day off, and go one weekday morning. She wanted to have kids someday. That 'someday' wasn't the following year, and it might not even be in five years' time. The idea that she alone might be unable to access this experience that so many other women went through without thinking twice brought on a sense of urgency in her. Eriko couldn't be sure that, as she was holding out, Shōko wouldn't get pregnant. That would only increase the distance between them. Then they'd never be able to get together just the two of them again. If both of them had children, though, maybe they would be able to restore their bond in the form of mum friends.

Moan louder, Eriko entreated herself – louder and dirtier. So long as she did it exactly as they did in the porn videos she'd watched to teach herself, then there was nothing to be embarrassed about. Gripping the sheets, digging her nails into his back, gritting her teeth and clenching her pelvic muscles so as to squeeze him tighter – none of it was remotely bad compared to being left alone on a night like this. His sweat was surprisingly viscous. He passed as slender, but a layer of softness was forming on his body. The smell of his favourite cologne had steeped itself even into his groin. When it was over, he rolled over onto his side with a satisfied expression.

'Woah. Amazing. The gap between this and everyday reality was a real turn-on. The whole time I kept thinking, like, wow, I'm actually having sex with Eriko Shimura right now ... I bet people at work would be floored if they found out.'

He chuckled, then reached a hand out for her nipple and squeezed it.

'Do you do this kind of thing a lot?'

'No ...'

'It's fine if you do. Just don't take it too far, like that woman working at TEPCO. It's okay once in a while as a stress relief, though.'

'The woman working at TEPCO ... Do you mean Yasuko Watanabe? The woman who started moonlighting as a prostitute and got murdered ...?'

Eriko was totally aghast at the idea that Sugishita would bring up a murder case in a moment like this. It seemed as though he was trying to slot her into the 'refined lady by day, dirty slut by night' cliché. Still, Eriko thought, even this was better than him believing that they were lovers now that they'd slept together once. He would most likely be enamoured with her now, but she would stay firm in her resolve. She wanted to remain friends, and only friends.

'You know what we were talking about before? About Hallie B?'

'Hey, look, I'm pretty tired. Do you mind being quiet for a bit?' His careless tone rubbed Eriko up the wrong way. She'd given him her body – surely the least he could do was to listen to her until morning? They were friends. It was as she thought this that something occurred to Eriko, and she was dangerously close to screeching. *You know people you sleep with don't count as friends* – the words she'd said to Shōko now returned to her, stabbing at her chest. Had Eriko just lost another friend?

'You're going abroad the day after tomorrow, right? You should rest. Let's sleep until the first train and then leave together. Okay?'

It was the voice of a stranger – not a lover, and no longer a friend – that now came from behind her. It seemed that she'd even destroyed the delicate ecosystem of her office relationships.

More than ever, she thought, she needed Shōko. Pulling up the sheet, she chanted the name inside her: Shōko, Shōko, Shōko.

Shōko and Eriko. One day, they would know which of them was truly the Nile perch. Eriko really wouldn't mind being savaged, she thought, if it was Shōko doing the savaging. And yet, the image that flashed clearly into her head was of her gnawing at Shōko's body, swimming naked through a lake scattered with Shōko's body parts, stained red with her blood.

Sugishita began snoring. Before she knew it, Eriko's hands were in her hair. The roots of the hairs that she pulled out glistened on the starchy sheets.

# CHAPTER TWELVE

The expensive red-brick apartment building opposite the post office stood towering in the darkness, shielded by its orange lights. Shōko had ridden Eriko home on her bike once, so the place was now imprinted on her memory. It was past nine at night, so Eriko was likely home. She'd said that her company didn't like its employees staying late, and that she tried to eat dinner at home, with her family.

Planning to cook something proper for dinner for once, Shōko's intention had been to head for the supermarket. Yet before she realised what she was doing, she found herself standing outside the apartment block where Eriko lived. A little earlier, she'd sent Satoko an email with her decision:

*I'll start updating my blog more, with a view to eventually publishing it as a book. I'll also consider showing my face in magazines.*

When Shōko thought about being exposed to the eyes of this unspecified mass of women with their harsh opinions, her stomach cramped and her legs trembled, but she was damned if she was going to let those insecurities defeat her. She'd become a model housewife – no, the model of a half-arsed housewife. She'd make her stance of not trying too hard into a new national standard. Never again would she let herself be ridiculed. She was different to her father. She'd become famous – and she'd show that bitch, who'd told her with such certainty that the blog was as far as she'd ever get. The chilly October night breeze felt glorious on her burning cheeks.

'I'm going to succeed. I won't be defeated by you. If you want to send abusive messages, then go ahead...' Shōko started composing a text, but then deleted it. A message like this needed to be delivered in person. She was aware that it was a strange decision, going out of her way to meet with her stalker. Still, however deranged this woman was, Shōko couldn't rid herself of the desire to see her. What did you call this feeling, when you knew that you should cut ties with someone, but found your thoughts returning to them again and again? Unless she did something about it, there would be no end in sight.

'You're looking for Eriko, right? She's not here.'

Shōko whirled round in shock to find a woman in a tracksuit, whom she assumed lived in the apartments, standing behind her. There was something about her delivery that transported Shōko straight back to school. Was she really a thirty-year-old married woman? In that moment, she felt she was still an unexceptional girl living in her parents' house and attending the local high school. She said nothing, and the girl went on, 'She's gone to Tanzania.'

It came back to Shōko that Eriko had been saying something about this when they'd met at the conveyor-belt sushi place. The revelation left her reeling. In theory, Eriko's disappearance should have represented an end to all her problems, but not only did she not feel pleased – she felt betrayed. At the thought that she might never again get to see Eriko, all the strength drained from her limbs. Eriko was an awful person with whom any friendship was off the cards, and yet, it seemed, Shōko still needed her.

'You don't have to pull that face ... It's only for a few days.'

As Shōko breathed a sigh of relief, she found the woman had moved surprisingly close. Unable to step back, she stood there, feeling the woman's breath on her cheek. It was warm and milky, like a baby's.

'Are you actually her friend? Surely a friend would know something like that.'

'Oh, I ... I've only just got to know her recently.'

'Right, so you don't really know about her yet. I see. My name's Keiko Ogasawara, by the way.'

Keiko smiled, revealing yellowed teeth.

'I've seen you a bunch of times. I'm always hanging around this part of town, because I don't have anything better to do. You often visit family restaurants and fast-food restaurants by yourself, right? Have you got a lot of time on your hands as well?'

Something about the directness of the question made Shōko nod, dutifully.

'Shall I tell you about her? About Eriko, I mean. She's really something else. I went to the same school as her, from primary right through to the end of high school, so I know it all. Did you not pick up a weird vibe from her?'

'Er ...'

'Did it not ever strike you that her hair and her skin are just a bit too perfect for someone that busy? How there's something a bit unsettling about the way she tries to get real close? How she seems so soft and gentle, but when you're with her for a long time you start to feel like you can't breathe properly? I'm not trying to be mean, by the way.'

The realisation that it wasn't only her that felt this way gave Shōko such an intense burst of relief that she was ready to drop to her knees. She felt a lot of guilt about her reservations towards

Eriko. The idea that a nobody like herself would find fault with someone so impeccable struck her as terribly impudent on her part.

'You've noticed all that, right? So why do you think it is?'

'I've no idea!'

'It's because there's nothing about her that's natural. She's pure artifice, through and through. She paints over everything in lies designed to represent her in the best light.'

Keiko's eyes glinted in the darkness. At first glance they seemed to be looking directly at her, but on closer inspection it was clear that they were focused on nothing. If anything, it was this Keiko who was the unnatural one, Shōko thought. Her instincts told her that she was better off having nothing to do with this person, either. Quite possibly, it would have been better for them never to have met – just like her and Eriko.

Unfortunately, Shōko wanted to hear the disparaging rumours about Eriko being dangled before her. She was practically writhing with the desire to hear them. She knew she would have sold her soul to the devil if that was what it took. She wanted to drag the woman who'd hurt her so badly down to the same level as her – or preferably, even lower. Then Shōko wouldn't need to remember the hurtful words that had been said to her. More than that, however: she was longing to speak to another woman. So urgently did she want someone to listen to her that she felt that even this loner would do. Yes, Shōko acknowledged it to herself now: sitting there at the computer, she'd been sending out a stream of words to nobody at all.

There was nothing wrong with Kensuke. It was just that the kinds of conversations that a married couple had didn't allow her to open up about everything. For Shōko, men were the pillars without which her life would collapse, the street signs without which she would be utterly lost. Her behaviour around them was always calculated to keep them interested. She might be able to reveal her laziness to them, but she couldn't let them see the murkiest, ugliest aspects of her character. Yet it was maybe those parts that represented her truest self. It was precisely because she shared the same ugliness as them that she struggled with other women, but this was, paradoxically enough, what made her need them too.

Shōko also knew instinctively that dredging up the hateful feelings festering away inside you served to bond you with the other person like nothing else. It was fair to say that the only time Shōko had felt truly connected to another person was when bitching about women with other women.

Looking at the woman standing across from her, Shōko's gaze was drawn up to the streetlight above. In the halo of its light, moths flapped their wings, the tears in them visible from below.

# CHAPTER THIRTEEN

*How do you achieve that effortless closeness with each other?*

Eriko had been internally formulating the question over and over since takeoff and now, as the plane lurched to the side, it seemed ready to slip out of her mouth.

It was as though their ears were joined together by wire.

As the plane's altitude increased, Eriko felt her daily existence growing more and more distant.

'Ami-chan, you swell up easily, like me, so you should wear compression socks.'

'God, aeroplanes are so dehydrating. I can feel the dryness on my skin already.'

'I *thought* you'd say that, and I packed some Avena spray especially. I've got face masks as well, if you want.'

'Oh my God, well prepared as ever, Fu-chan! Ah, do you want to switch seats? I feel like you need the bathroom way more than me.'

Eriko had wound up sitting in the middle of the central bank of five seats in economy class. Thanks to her presence, a group of four women travelling together had been split in two, which was a horribly uncomfortable arrangement. She'd thought about offering to switch places with them, but had been too intimidated to speak up. The eye masks, facial mists and reassuring words made their way back and forth over her knees. The women seemed to be genuinely enjoying themselves. There was no hint of any shade in their interactions, which were brimming with a palpable hunger to savour every part of the trip unfolding ahead of them. Eriko imagined that they would be holidaying in Dubai, to where this plane was headed.

Eriko's destination, the Tanzanian city of Mwanza, lay further off. She would change at Dubai and fly on to Julius Nyerere Airport in Dar es Salaam. The purpose of her trip was to visit various Nile perch processing companies based around Lake Victoria, and to decide who to contract with. She was only staying three nights, but the journey itself was a round trip lasting over thirty hours. She wanted to make sure she had as restful a flight as possible, but a mistake on the part of the person who'd booked the tickets meant that she wasn't in business class as she was supposed to be. To make matters worse, the economy seat didn't have a socket, so she couldn't plug in her laptop. She had planned to do various bits of research on the journey, so this was a setback.

And yet, being in an internet-free environment brought with it a surprisingly unhurried way of being. For the first time in what seemed like forever, Eriko felt her mind growing quiet. Of late, she had been keeping an eye out for new posts on Hallie's blog even during working hours, and was constantly on high alert for incoming emails.

'Would you like something to drink?' asked a cabin attendant, whose honey-coloured skin was traced with deep lines. Eriko requested an orange juice, and then asked for a blanket. The Western cabin attendants she'd encountered were rarely young, and often wore a thick coating of makeup on their faces. Their manner was direct and to the point, and they didn't smile that much. But surely, that only stood to reason: here they were, on their feet the whole time in this confined, arid space to which they entrusted their lives. Eriko found interacting with them in all their authenticity easier than dealing with Japanese cabin attendants, with their lustrous skin, movie-star good looks and cheery smiles that gave away no hint of their fatigue. When viewed on a global scale, the high standards that Japan demanded of its women were off the charts. How much was required from women as default! Attractiveness, chastity, youth, a calm disposition, a prestigious job, a range of hobbies, a winning smile, stylishness, a likeable aura, consideration of others ... and then, of course, popularity with other women. Eriko sometimes felt as if the perception that a woman was nothing if other women didn't love her grew stronger each year.

These days, TV series and films about female friendship outperformed those centring love stories. Everyone flaunted their female friendships on social media. Open up any women's magazine and there would be articles about the power of women supporting other women. Even at companies like hers, they were constantly doing market research oriented towards girls' get-togethers, girls' nights in and so on. Then there was the declining birth rate, the trend for people to marry ever later. The drive for women to turn their backs on the systems laid down by men and instead establish their own communities, their own rules, was becoming ever more mainstream.

The women on either side of her had the entertainment guides open on their laps, and were animatedly discussing which film to watch. In all her thirty years, Eriko had never once been on a girls' trip. It seemed to her to require some not inconsiderable self-confidence to sleep in the same room as someone who was neither a relative nor a lover – to show yourself without makeup to a person like that. Yet Eriko felt that all of these four women were her inferior when it came to appearance, possessions. They had a girlishness to them, but she guessed they were probably not far off thirty. Were they only hanging around with each other because they couldn't find a man? Were the clingy bonds that they formed their way of keeping a hold on their sense of identity? Yet when she found herself getting to this point in her thinking, Eriko experienced another stab of self-hatred.

Why did she end up feeling this malice towards girls like these, when they were clearly making no attempt to rub their friendship in her face? What was it that they had which she lacked? Consideration for other people? Interestingness as people? The ability to read the room? Or was it less that she was lacking something, and more that there was something she had to excess? Could people sense in her the tendency to search out vulnerabilities in others, for example? Was that why they steered clear of her?

Steer clear of her – she chewed this phrase over now. Yes, it was the indisputable truth: ever since early adolescence, other women had steered clear of her. Even if at first they approached her with enthusiasm, no sooner had someone spent an hour or more in her company than they'd begin to back off. She was never asked out a second time. She wouldn't have minded if these prospective friends had been explicitly critical of her, but instead they'd fade away on her, a smile still glued to their faces.

In the past, Eriko had attempted to flip the blame for this situation, asking whether the root of the problem lay with her parents. But however she thought about it, she had to conclude that she had been given the best education possible, and above all, been brought up with love. Her mother had cooked elaborate meals, kept their home clean and supported her. Her father had given her everything she asked for, so long as she could explain her reasons for wanting it. Yet neither had she been spoilt. The importance of hard work had been instilled in her, and she'd been disciplined in moderation. It was thanks to them that she'd made it this far in adult society without embarrassing herself. She felt endlessly grateful to them for that.

The one area she could think of in which her upbringing had been unique was that, owing to his position in the company, her father had rarely been at home. He would always bring her home plenty of souvenirs from his trips abroad, and she and her mother would get to visit whatever country he was in during school holidays. She was pretty sure that she was doing the job she was because she had been so enamoured by the sight of her father setting forth into the big wide world. Over time, she had come to understand that she probably had daddy issues.

Come to think of it, her father was a man of few friends too. While he'd still been working, the man who was now Eriko's boss had often come round to their house, but at some point those visits had come to an abrupt halt. Now that he was retired, he spent the entire day at home, except for the occasional stroll. These last few years she hadn't seen her father with anybody other than her mother. Still, she believed that to be a product of his taciturn nature, rather than any sign that he was disliked. Her mother was of a more sociable disposition. While Eriko was at school, her mother had gone out for meals with other parents, joined the PTA and taken an active part in school events. After the incident with Keiko, though, her mother had stopped going into school, and had given up her work at Gisele, which she'd loved so much. She'd grown estranged from Keiko's mother, with whom she used to be so close. It had taken her mother some time before she'd been able to form friendships with other women again. When, finally, her mother had grown friendly with a circle of women she'd met at a dance class, Eriko had been intensely relieved, released at last from an intransigent sense of guilt. In any case, it seemed wrong to blame her problems on her parents.

There had been a time when she'd told herself that it was her appearance and her high achievements that attracted the envy of other women. And yet, Hollywood actresses a hundred times more beautiful than Eriko would talk in interviews about their best friends, who had supported them through all those years before they finally made it. There were the female entrepreneurs that Eriko secretly aspired to be, who gave callouts in their speeches to the women in the same industry as them, whom they saw as comrades. She didn't want to admit it, but people who knew how to make friends could make them regardless of how clever or how beautiful they were. No, something inside of Eriko gave off a stench that put people off, that kept other women away.

Eriko knew full well that there was no need to let something like a bit of friend trouble affect her this much. Still, she found herself utterly incapable of getting the falling-out with Shōko out of her head. A minor misunderstanding – that had been the origin of it all. Someone as clever as Eriko should have been able to resolve a problem of that ilk. And yet, matters had escalated. Ever since Eriko, wounded by her friend's callousness, had let her words run away with her, all lines of communication had been cut. Shōko had blocked both her calls and her texts. The more Eriko struggled, the faster her fears became a reality. It seemed as if Shōko really did want to cut off all contact between them.

She had to forget about Shōko. She knew that she couldn't keep chasing her. Her life wouldn't be hindered in any way if Shōko wasn't in it. She was, above all, merely a housewife who spent her life loafing around. So long as she didn't fixate on Shōko, Eriko's life would resume its upward ascent. And yet Eriko wanted to believe that that night in the Denny's, when the two of them had been so in tune with each other, had been real. To believe that *that* was the real Eriko, the real Shōko. Through the minutest of errors, something like a wrongly fastened button, the Shōko and Eriko that had been meant to exist had been left behind that evening, and were still there, nattering away to one another with immense pleasure. Realising that her thoughts were going round and round in circles, Eriko pulled the airline blanket all the way up her body so she could bury her face in it.

It wasn't only Shōko who was being cold towards Eriko, either. Since they'd drunkenly fallen into bed with one another, even Sugishita, who had once been a valued confidant, was now being standoffish with her. Eriko had been resolute that if he asked her out she was going to turn him down, but it now appeared that he wasn't attaching as much significance to that night as she'd expected. Somehow wanting more, she'd found herself shooting him knowing glances, only to regret it immediately afterwards. Of all the versions of herself, it was the one who behaved flirtatiously towards men that she found the most unforgivable. To make matters worse, although Maori Takasugi had talked about confiding in her in the future, she'd not uttered a word to Eriko since. Sick of waiting, Eriko had said to Maori in a businesslike tone, 'I'm happy to listen to whatever you have to talk to me about. When are you free?' but Maori had just stared at her like someone encountering an alien, her mouth hanging open.

'Sorry ... what's this about again?' Maori asked, frowning, so that Eriko had been at a loss for how to reply. Why did everyone end up looking down on her like this? When her consciousness was so consumed by other people too ...

It was bewildering to her that, even at the age of thirty, the sight of a group of women getting along well with each other could be the cause of so much hurt. She found herself turning a nitpicking eye on them, praying with all her might that under the surface they were all in it for some ulterior motive or benefit. The very notion that they had developed a relationship of care, which they'd preserved for ten or twenty years, seemed capable of dragging her down to a deep, dark place. Formulating to herself that there was a harmonious world of kindness that she herself hadn't managed to access made Eriko feel ready to throw in the towel. Tears rose hotly to her eyes. The urge to smash and destroy everything around her convulsed through her body. Never before had she so fully grasped that you couldn't achieve everything through effort alone. Nobody would tell a woman in her thirties how she was supposed to make friends from scratch, and there were no manuals that she knew of. The world was so unfair.

Was it possible that she wasn't the only one feeling this way?

What about the people who met the trend for 'girls' get-togethers' and 'girls' nights out' with a scornful attitude, saying that these 'girls' needed to grow up? What about the men and women who would routinely declare that 'groups of women were way too intense' and 'women could never be real friends'? Did they not react in that way because seeing women having fun with each other made them feel as though they themselves were being criticised? When they located cracks in a friendship between women, did they not feel genuine relief?

'I'm so sorry!'

Eriko snapped back to herself to see a kind-looking, round-faced woman leaning in towards her. This was the one they'd called 'Fu-chan'. She was looking straight at Eriko with an apologetic expression. 'It must be such a pain to be seated with us lot.'

Eriko stared back at Fu-chan. Once she got off this plane, she would never see this woman again. It came into her head to ask her everything she most wanted to know:

*How do you make friends?*

*How did you meet these people?*

*Do you ever fight?*

*Do you not get sick of each other?*

*How do you get close to someone again when they're avoiding you?*

*How do you get people to call you something-chan, or give you a cute, funny nickname?*

Was Eriko's desire really that outrageous? She just wanted to have a relaxed relationship with another person, which was entirely free of sexual desire and profit and loss calculations. To have someone to go to the cinema with; someone to have tea with and talk about the things bothering you; someone whom she would invite to her wedding, and who would invite her to theirs. Someone to talk with on the phone for as long as she wanted. All she wished for was one person like that. Was that such a big ask?

'It's not a pain, but …'

But you should bear in mind that there are people out there who feel intensely hurt simply at the sight of you being so happy in one another's company, Eriko thought.

'You all seem such good friends, I'm envious,' she said emphatically, then put on a moisturising face mask, and an eye mask on top of it, to prevent any further conversation with the women on either side of her.

# CHAPTER FOURTEEN

The parfait was a picture of chaos. In addition to the swirls of fresh cream, dollops of mousse and ice cream, and the descending spiral of red berry sauce, the tall glass was dotted throughout with pieces of fresh fruit, cornflakes and chocolate chunks: altogether too high in calories and lacking in nutrition for a thirty-year-old woman to be eating after 9 p.m. at night. Seeming unbothered by its presence on the table there in front of her, Keiko languidly dipped her long-handled spoon into the dessert. Bringing the spoon to her mouth, she licked its tip before throwing it down as if having lost all interest.

'You know how Eriko constantly monitors your reactions?'

Shōko, who was sitting on the other side of the table drinking a Coke, sat up at this mention of Eriko's name. Keiko began shredding her napkin into tiny fragments.

'How she's always shooting glances at you to see if what she's saying or doing is okay, to check that she hasn't messed up in some way? When I hit puberty, I started finding that teacher's pet attitude to human relationships a bit embarrassing, you know? This need to get full marks not in academic subjects or sport, but friendships too.'

Shōko felt as though the faintly dingy corner of the family restaurant where they were sitting had been lit up by a spotlight.

Yes, she thought, those constant appraising glances! That was it: it was Eriko's eternal approval-seeking that made her so tiring to be around. The mystery had finally been solved. Her difficulties with Eriko weren't born out of envy, and didn't mean that she was heartless, either. The reason that Shōko would feel conflict in her chest whenever Eriko came out with something that seemed calculated to butter her up was that such behaviour was intrusive. Relief flooded through Shōko's body. There was suddenly a purpose for being alone with Eriko's weird neighbour. As Keiko began twisting the shredded napkin into a tight cord, she said, 'I guess it was around the time that I moved from middle to high school that I realised how draining it was to be around her. It's not that she's inept at social relationships. It's that she always wants to be the best.'

Shōko was twitching in her eagerness to break into the conversation. She took a sip of her over-chilled Coke before speaking.

'Right! She's got this image of what the perfect female friend looks like, which she tries to foist on you. If you're so much as a millimetre out, she loses her rag. As if everything's your fault.'

Shōko was beginning to feel a form of respect for this woman in front of her, who'd voiced so plainly the discomfort she had with Eriko. She looked at her again, taking in her tracksuited figure, her small, bare face, her messy hair. The nail varnish on the fingertips poking out of her sleeves was chipped. Her powdery skin with its red patches was covered in a fine down. All in all, she looked far more unkempt even than makeup-free Shōko, in her loungewear. And yet this also seemed to cement her status as a special entity, gloriously detached from the world. Shōko asked herself if she was overestimating the woman. They had, after all, only just met. Keiko went on, oblivious.

'Relationships between people are a mixed bag, right? I'm not only talking female friendship, but all relationships. You've got to take the rough with the smooth. In a way, Eriko's perfectionism is one of her good qualities. She believes that if she only puts in the effort, then everything she wants will come to her. But she needs to realise that it can be stifling for the person she's with.'

Shōko had been expecting Keiko to be hysterical and dirty-mouthed, and she now felt stunned to find her perspective actually quite balanced. She'd been hoping, she realised, for someone with a more similar take to herself.

'Ever since she was very young, Eriko has been the pampered princess. Clever and gentle, kind and serious. In primary and middle school, everyone admired her and aspired to be like her. The parents and the teachers all trusted her. My mum often compared me to her. Thinking about it, I think my mum might have really idolised Eriko's mum. I was constantly being told to do as Eriko did. Weirdly, it didn't bother me. It seemed natural that any mother would want her daughter to be like someone that exceptional. I felt proud that I'd known her since I was small. When I heard that Eriko was applying for a private middle school, I started studying like crazy so that I could get into the same one. I got put on the waiting list, and I was over the moon when I found out that I'd got in, and we'd be going to the same school. I remember how proud I felt wearing the same uniform as her, getting on the same train. We weren't allowed to cycle to school, so took the train in, even though it was in Setagaya.'

Shōko remembered Eriko's words when they'd first met in this very restaurant, about what a pain it had been to take the convoluted route by train to a school that was geographically so close, and about how she'd envied people who'd cycled in. Maybe Keiko hadn't changed a jot since adolescence, Shōko thought, just as neither she nor Eriko had.

'Do you remember how it was in the first year of high school? How the class was suddenly divided clean in two, into the girls who were now women and the girls who were still children?'

Shōko nodded deeply. A vision of her high school in that riverside town came rushing back to her. She had been on the women's side. That year, the same one that she lost her virginity, a lot of the girls in her year suddenly looked like kids to her. Her home life might have been falling apart, her grades might not have been good, but just riding on the same bike as her boyfriend made her heart feel round and full. Quite possibly, that was the first time in her life that Shōko felt as though she could breathe properly.

'I got friendly with a bunch of girls who'd joined for high school. They were totally unlike Eriko and the other girls who'd been in my class. They were glamorous, and they knew all this stuff about makeup and boys. They were fun to be around. After school we'd go to karaoke together or go into Shibuya to hang out. All pretty tame – but as dramatic as it sounds, that was my first taste of freedom. Eriko ceased to be the person that I wanted to turn out like.'

Keiko went on rolling the napkin into tiny paper straws as if to demonstrate how little her emotions were stirred by the topic.

'I had this realisation that I'd moved into that apartment building at the age of seven, and for the years since, half of my life up until that point, I'd been inseparable from Eriko. At the age of fifteen, I finally worked out that the world was full of incredibly fun people, full of stuff that I'd never encountered. But it seemed like Eriko couldn't forgive me for moving on. Her behaviour was something else. At that time people didn't use the word "stalking" as much as they do now, but that was totally what it was.'

When Keiko began avoiding Eriko, the story went, Eriko began doggedly pursuing her. The onslaught began with her lying in wait for Keiko to leave school. On occasions, she'd drawn on her favour with Keiko's mum to sneak into Keiko's room and rifle through her desk. Not knowing what else to do, Keiko had lied and said that she had a boyfriend, that she didn't have time to spend with Eriko any more. That had only made things worse.

'What do you mean, a boyfriend? Where? Where is he, huh? I think you're lying! You're lying to me, to keep me away! Show him to me. If he really exists, then bring him to me!'

Seeing Eriko with her eyes huge and glinting, tearing at her hair and wailing as if something inside her had broken open, Keiko said she had felt genuine fear.

'I didn't feel like I had a choice. I had to do or say something, even if it was a lie. So I told her that he was married, that he was much older. He was someone with social standing, so I couldn't tell anybody about him, couldn't reveal his name.'

Shōko could barely stand to listen. By this point, she knew all too well: Eriko would never forgive anybody lying to her, even if it was about the smallest, most insignificant thing.

'She kept on showering me with questions, so I told her that I'd met him through a telephone-dating service. I thought that would stop her poking around to find out who he was. You know how compensated dating was popular back then? All those older men paying to go out with schoolgirls. And after that, she really did stop hanging around me. I felt relieved, thought I'd freed myself. But I didn't have to wait long for the chaos to begin. What do you think she did?'

Shōko felt that she knew the answer, without being told. Amid all the ups and downs of this past month, she had come to grasp Eriko's behavioural patterns. Shōko found both her hands were clenched tightly into fists. Eriko made no distinction between normal and abnormal behaviour. She spouted off righteous arguments until she had you cornered, working efficiently to strip you of your escape routes, one by one.

'She spread rumours all around the school that I was doing compensated dating. She wrote letters not only to my form tutor, but to the chair of the board of school governors. The teachers came round to my house, and there was a huge hoo-ha. Eriko was an A-grade student, trusted by everyone around her, so even my parents believed the rumours. My father hit me, like, properly. I've still got a scar from it.'

Keiko raised her jaw and showed Shōko a mark beneath her neck.

'Eventually the misunderstanding was resolved. But it was impossible for things to go back to how they'd been, for either me or Eriko. Eriko had come to be branded as a stalker, and nobody in school would talk to her. The school required she have counselling. We stopped speaking. That whole incident really opened my eyes. Your parents won't necessarily be there for you when you need them, and the person that you thought of as a close friend can become an enemy in an instant. Poof!'

For a while, Keiko stared into the darkness outside the window. The thin paper strings she'd created were strewn across the tabletop. Her parfait had melted into gloopy liquid. The whole table looked a horrible mess. A passing server winced in distaste.

'I think I stopped giving a shit, after that. About my studies and my friendships, and also about what other people thought of me. I only managed to graduate because the teachers took pity on me. I took a couple of years out before finally going to uni, and even then, I didn't go in a lot. I got a full-time job that didn't last, and then shifted to casual work, but it was the same story. I figured that, given all that, I was probably best off getting married, so I got hitched to the guy I was seeing, but it quickly fell apart. There was a time when I worried about why it was that my life seemed to be going so badly, but recently I've finally understood. It's not that there's a problem with the people around me, and it's not Eriko's fault either.'

'Do you really think that you need to give up on everything just because you had one slip-up?' Shōko said hesitantly, and Keiko opened her eyes very wide. In the bright fluorescent lights, the whites of her eyes were tinged blue.

'Why does everyone think that you have to be doing something all the time? Why is doing nothing such a bad thing? It's the same for you. You could live off your husband's money if you wanted, right? Are you that scared of admitting your own insignificance? Or is there something that you truly want to do? I think it's fine to do nothing.'

Keiko spoke languorously, in a tone that seemed to push the clamour of the family restaurant far away. Shōko began, suddenly, to understand why it was that the fifteen-year-old Eriko had been so attached to this strange woman who wasn't particularly attractive, and didn't have anything else going for her.

'Doing nothing ...' Shōko repeated dumbly. She felt as though a host of invisible hands had reached down to pull her up from a deep hole towards a quiet, comfortable world of harmony.

'Yep. Just floating along like a fish in a tank. It's amazing how placid your soul becomes. I like doing nothing. You're the same, right?'

Keiko seized hold of her spoon again and looked up at Shōko. She began stirring the melted parfait with a squelching sound.

'You're like me. Since the moment you were born, you've found the whole business of living profoundly exhausting – working for other people's sakes, having big visions for the future, expending effort to get what you want. So you know that having a lazy disposition is not an easy fate. I'm exactly the same.'

'No, I ...' Shōko's lips were dry. Why had she ordered a Coke? The tips of her fingers felt frozen.

'It's okay, I get it. I see you out all the time. Sitting there in the fast-food joints and chain restaurants that exist everywhere, staring hollow-eyed into space.'

Shōko's father was the same. All this time she had wanted to believe that he was lonely – and then another part of her wondered if he was just inept. But maybe the truth was that the way he was living right now was what contentment looked like for her father. And Shōko too – wasn't her greatest wish to simply drift along? She didn't want to have to deal with other people. She didn't want to work. She wanted to be on her own, as much as possible. That was how she truly felt.

She didn't really *do* anything, and yet this unshakeable sense of fatigue wouldn't leave her. It had grown more and more pronounced of late. Was she just exhausted from the very depths of her soul? Was that why she found everything such a pain – and had done, from long before she ever came to Tokyo? What Keiko said was true: from the moment she'd been born, she'd found the whole business of living tiring. Celebrations and special occasions were too much hassle. When she'd first found a job, she'd been upbraided by her superiors at work for forgetting to pass on trivial messages and making mistakes on the orders, only to find herself repeating the same mistakes almost immediately. It was less that she was incompetent, and more that constantly seeking to improve oneself seemed to her like a right pain. She would try hard to get a grip, reprimanding herself that she couldn't go on this way, but at the very point that she had forced herself to more or less keep up, her health crumbled. Shōko knew it all too well: her greatest wish was to do nothing. Staring at this odd woman across the table, she reflected that Keiko truly did have eyes like a dead fish, and felt a chill grip the pit of her stomach.

'I'm going to go. I've remembered there's something I've got to do.' Shōko got to her feet hurriedly, but Keiko didn't reproach her in any way.

She merely said, 'Okay,' and began once again to stir the remains of her parfait. Shōko set the bill down on the table and then practically ran out of the restaurant. She felt grateful for the chilly October air around her. As a train passed overhead, Shōko came back to herself. She picked up her pace and dashed out from under the overpass. It was only when she got to the shopping arcade that she finally breathed a heavy sigh.

Eriko was nothing but bad luck, she thought again. It was best to keep as much distance from her as possible or she would end up like Keiko, unable to function in society. Eriko clearly had an aptitude for ruining people's lives. Hearing a message alert, she took out her phone. The text was from Hashimoto, the waiter at Gisele. She still hadn't replied to his invitation to go watch a film in Shinagawa, but she should, soon. She didn't feel guilty about the prospect of going out with him, and thought it might cheer her up to do something different.

It was okay, Shōko said to herself, she was different to Keiko. It wasn't only her husband who wanted her, but young men like this too. Above all, she still had her blog. She had the support of all those people who followed it. So long as she took care of her readers, she wouldn't stray from the path. With their eyes on her, she would be protected from the fate of frittering her time away to no purpose. Her readers were her emergency brakes, keeping her on the right track.

Her breathing now coming more easily, Shōko's stride grew wider. She would stop in at the supermarket, buy some colourful vegetables and seasonal fruits, and cook something that she could photograph and post for her followers.

# CHAPTER FIFTEEN

A stifling hot wind whipped her cheeks. Before her stretched an endless sky of a blue so intense that it stung her eyes, merging seamlessly with the Indian Ocean. This was the tropical coast of Africa. The leaves of the windmill palms that served as a canopy to the café terrace rustled coolly in the breeze. The modern white buildings drew Eriko's gaze over and over. The immaculately paved road that traced a straight line into the distance had been clogged with cars all the time she'd been sitting here, but for some reason, she didn't sense any great impatience there. As implied by its name, which meant 'home of peace' in Arabic, Dar es Salaam was a cheery, tranquil place.

'This is the rainy season now, although there's never much rain. It'd be better termed the drizzle season. You're lucky, having this good weather on your last day.' Naomi Akagi, sitting opposite Eriko on the terrace, was her local coordinator, and had been living in Tanzania for five years. She'd started out working as a tour guide for a big Japanese travel company, but had then married someone working at the Dar es Salaam branch, and now lived in an apartment in the city. She told Eriko that she'd written a book about Tanzania. She was in her mid-thirties, but despite the freckles and dark patches dotting her tanned skin, the bare arms protruding from her tank top and her hair casually tied back gave her a youthful appearance. In contrast to her laid-back presentation, her Japanese was erudite and pleasant to listen to. Eriko discovered that she'd done a master's in South American literature at a women's university.

'I feel bad! Your company specifically requested my help, and yet all I've done is show you around the city on your final day.'

'No, no! These days most of the people working in the processing companies are of Indian heritage, so I can get away with using English.'

Yesterday, Eriko had been to visit over ten processing factories in Mwanza, close to Lake Victoria. She'd spoken with the workers, asking them questions about their working conditions and the quality control. It had been her first time seeing a freshly caught Nile perch. Silver scales glittered across its large body, and its flesh was snow white. Eriko had never imagined that a dead fish could have such beautiful eyes.

'I didn't expect the factories to be that modern. They had Western-style conveyor belts and metal detectors, and some of them were fully automated. Excellent hygiene standards as well.'

'Right? You get a different impression when you actually come to visit. The image that Japanese people have of Tanzania sorely needs updating. I'm not blaming you, of course – it's that there isn't a sufficient flow of information. As you see, the capital is pretty affluent, and it's been built in a way that makes it easy for people from overseas to live here.'

If she'd had the time, Eriko would have liked to visit not only the factories, but the villages positioned around Lake Victoria. She was fully aware that it was only the most sophisticated parts of the country that she'd seen on this trip.

'That said, the lives of the low-salaried workers living by the coast are really tough. Tanzania's economy is growing, but there's been little improvement to the infrastructure. Venture businesses are popping up here, there and everywhere, but there are still no adequate financing systems in place. Still, I'd like people to know that it's a country with abundant natural and human resources, with plenty of investment potential. Ah, let's order.'

Naomi Akagi hurriedly opened the leather-covered menu. It was lunchtime and the café was crowded. The sole waiter was rushing around busily. Naomi took in the menu with the evident delight of a true foodie.

'Ah, they've got tilapia! Nile perch is popular overseas, but it's not that well loved by Tanzanians. People find it a bit lacking in flavour and smell. There's much more of a taste for tilapia, although its numbers have fallen off dramatically after being gobbled up by the Nile perch. It's got a really rich flavour that can hold its own against spices. Perhaps a bit of an acquired taste. My top recommendation would be this green banana stew. They call it banana but it's less like a fruit and more like a chewy potato. It's a pretty common Tanzanian dish, cooked with tomatoes and beans. There's also all kinds of rice dishes, if you prefer.'

'Oohh, I'll order the stew. It sounds good. I'd like to try tilapia too.'

'Wow,' Naomi said, raising her eyebrows and looking directly at Eriko. 'You're different to other business types. There's a flexibility about you ... I must say, I was quite taken aback when you said that you'd prefer to eat somewhere popular with the locals than in an expensive restaurant.'

It was clear that Naomi was impressed. Eriko's conversation with Shōko at Smile Sushi came flooding back to her. Shōko had declared that she didn't want to know the provenance of each and every bit of fish that she was eating, that she was happy so long as it tasted nice. Eriko still couldn't get her head around that attitude.

'In Japan, fish like Nile perch and tilapia used to be sold a lot under false labels: Nile perch was passed off as Japanese sea bass and tilapia as red snapper. Even though they'd clearly taste better when cooked in recipes designed specifically to bring out their unique qualities, rather than those modelled on the qualities of a different fish! The Japanese have a resistance to freshwater fish, in general. Maybe it's because people automatically associate them with koi carp and goldfish? But it just goes to show that in Japan, the name is more important than the taste. In the current situation, where we have to rely on overseas producers for food, I think consumers should be shedding their preconceptions and taking an active interest in experiencing tastes from other cultures.'

'Absolutely. I don't really like cooking Japanese food with the ingredients available here. We're of the same mind.'

Naomi shot Eriko a grin indicating her agreement, and then briskly placed their order with the waiter. Eriko breathed a contented sigh. So long as work was involved, it was possible for Eriko to get on with other women. She could approach them temperately, without exaggerated expectations or excessive nerves. She wanted to believe that this was her true self – that it was the other self of hers, who had been so mean to Shōko and scoped out her movements like a private detective, who was the impostor.

'This is embarrassing to admit, but I work for the same company that my father did. I've followed directly in his footsteps. Underneath it all, I think I'm pretty strong-headed and conservative in my attitudes.'

'Does that mean you moved around a lot as a youngster?'

'No, my father moved around a lot, but my mother and I stayed behind in Tokyo. They thought that would be best for my education. I always envied my father so much. I thought of him like the travellers I read about in fairytales.'

Why did Eriko find herself capable of telling Naomi, who she had only met three days ago, all this personal information? Was it the smell of the sea, the blue of the sky, that liberated her in this way? She noted that the warm, laid-back atmosphere here was similar to Taiwan. A memory came flooding back to her, from long ago. Her father's apartment had been in the very centre of Taipei. While her mother was having a massage, her father had taken her along to the night market. Seeing the deluge of lights spreading as far as the eye could see, her eyes grew wide, and she declared that it was 'like a temple festival!' At this, her father gave a knowing smile.

'I know it looks that way, but this is no festival. This market is here every single evening. We can buy our dinner at one of these stalls.'

Though it was nearly nine at night, Eriko went galloping excitedly around that market with another girl close to her age. The rows of stalls sold a whole assortment of delicacies: rice bowls topped with chopped meat; fresh spring rolls; various chicken parts simmered in sweet and spicy sauce.

'You don't even need to own a knife when you live here. People aren't in the habit of cooking at home because there are so many places to buy takeaway food.'

How easy, how free it all sounded, Eriko thought. The sight of her mother slaving over the meal preparations, the hassle of dishwashing: these seemed to her in that moment to belong to a different world. The notion that what was considered 'common sense' shifted according to one's environment brought with it a rush of excitement. She asked her father to buy her strawberry tanghulu. The hot candied strawberries were sweet, sour and soft, and though she burned her tongue eating them, they were so delicious that she could recall their taste even now.

'I started wanting to go to lots of different countries and experience different cultures. Encountering new ways of perceiving things made me feel a lot more at ease. Back then, at least.'

For the first time in forever, words that felt authentic came slipping right out from Eriko's lips. In this moment, she remembered anew how important her work was to her. It wasn't just something she did for status or income. It was what made these moments of relaxed connection with others possible. Naomi Akagi would never hurt her or betray her – because she was someone Eriko was doing business with. That immovable safety blanket brought Eriko great comfort. She resolved to make sure that this Tanzania deal was a resounding success.

'After this, I'll take you to Coco Beach. The waves will be relatively tame today. It's beautiful – white sands, palm trees, the whole package.'

It was like they were friends …

Thinking this, Eriko turned to Naomi and smiled. The very idea that conversing with another woman could be this enjoyable was extraordinary to her. Still, she remembered what someone working at the processing factories had said today: 'You have to make sure the Nile perch are fed well enough. They're carnivorous, so when they run out of food, they will start to eat one another.'

When the environment became saturated, then even those who had previously got along fine would set off down the road of attacking and killing each other. If Eriko began meeting Naomi Akagi privately, relations between them would falter. Naomi would start pushing Eriko away, and Eriko would chase her down to stop that from happening. That was the kind of person that she was. It was dejecting, but she knew it to be true.

She decided therefore to treasure this fleeting moment, to etch it inside herself along with the blue of the sky.

# CHAPTER SIXTEEN

Shōko heard the door opening. Her eyes still fixed on the plate she'd just arranged, she let out a proud, 'Ta-da!'

When Kensuke walked into the living room and spotted the plates on the table, he started and his eyes grew round. The menu this evening was the *Easier Than it Looks! Acqua Pazza* that Nori had told her about, along with *Spaghetti alle Vongole in Bianco* (*In the Microwave!*). Both recipes had been simple enough for even Shōko to manage, and they looked impressive. The only issue was the cost. Shōko had to set foot into the high-end supermarkets she didn't usually go to in search of all the herbs and spices that the recipes required.

'Well, this is a surprise. What's going on?'

'Don't just stand there! Tuck in, quickly! Give me your feedback.'

'It's like a product-tasting session at work,' Kensuke said with a wry grin.

Exactly, Shōko thought. This was work.

'You know I've no objection to the usual dinners you make, right? Umeboshi ochazuke and whatever.'

But that wouldn't do. Not for the new Shōko.

Yesterday, at the *Melanie* product-tasting session, Shōko had met a whole group of stay-at-home wives. She didn't even know how many years it had been since she'd last been around that many other women. The day before she'd been so nervous that she'd barely slept, agonising over what to wear and what she could possibly talk about. But the women who assembled in that large meeting room of the major publisher were casually attired, and treated her with friendliness. Maybe owing to their plentiful media experience, they were masterful at negotiating distances with others. Seeing that Shōko was a new face, they didn't rush her, but nor were they standoffish, approaching her very naturally. 'I'm a huge Hallie B fan! I know I might not seem like it, but I'm actually *very* slack around the house. Genuinely!' they would say, expertly combining flattery and self-deprecation. Shōko knew that these were no more than pleasantries, not to be trusted, but she felt grateful for their brand of consideration for others, which didn't tire the other person out or intrude too far on their business. Of all the women, it was the superstar blogger Nori whom she had connected with the most. Truth be told, until meeting her in person, Shōko had found Nori's persona quite grating. Reading her cheery prose, she couldn't help but come away with the feeling that she was being reproached. It wasn't only her housekeeping and child-rearing that she wrote about, but her modelling jobs, her work in developing new products, and so on. Shōko also objected to the way Nori insisted on making out like she had the common touch, when she could only assume that someone of her level of fame must be really quite affluent, and the sight of her navigating her murderous schedule with total apparent ease irked her. And yet, meeting her in the flesh, she found her to be straightforward and kind. Her boyish haircut and baggy dungarees gave her a fresh look. From a comfortable-looking tote bag, which she had apparently designed herself, she produced a magical array of items: a notebook, a digital camera, a sketch pad. Sitting next to her during the tasting session, Shōko felt increasingly charmed by her, and before she knew it, she found herself opening up to her a little. Nori nodded as Shōko confided in her that she was reluctant to reveal her identity, and that she was having problems with a stalker fan.

'I so get that. There's a pretty high chance when you get to know people who identify as fans that something like that will happen. I've experienced tricky situations myself,' Nori said with a smile. 'Of course, it's important to try not to let it affect you. But I also wonder whether, if that person understands that you're not the same Hallie B that you used to be, they might stop feeling so attached. You could start really pouring your energy into your blog. I'm sure that you'd see a good outcome.'

Nori was amazing, Shōko found herself thinking. Whatever negative turn of events she encountered, she found a way to convert it into a business idea – into material to make herself shine.

Above anything else, Shōko enjoyed Satoko's look of faint irritation at the sight of her and Nori getting on so well. She must love to see the bloggers competing and wounding one another while she watched on from her safe position on the sidelines, Shōko thought. It was undoubtedly unexpected and even objectionable to Satoko that someone like Shōko, who usually struggled with other women, would, once taken under Nori's wing, meld so well with the gathered company. That much was clear from the text she'd received afterwards, which read:

*You seemed to be getting on so well with everyone, I'm guessing you don't need me any more! Haha.*

Shōko began composing today's blog entry in her head:

*Today's recipes were suggested to me by fellow blogger Nori, who I've got to know recently. I know it's hard to believe, but they honestly took less than twenty minutes! Could my slacker-wife era be drawing to a close?!*

In truth, if you took into account the chopping of the vegetables and the assembling of the ingredients, the dishes had taken over forty minutes to prepare, but Shōko felt this degree of exaggeration was permissible. She'd just brought out the gingham placemats that she'd not yet used once and arranged them on the table with the plates when the home phone rang.

'Will you get it? I can't now.' She spoke loudly, but her voice was drowned out by the fan, and Kensuke, who was in the other room changing into his home clothes, didn't hear. She wiped her hands off with kitchen roll before reaching for the receiver. It was her brother. His voice sounded harrowed, and he started in without any small talk.

'Things are bad, Shōko. Urumi's gone for good this time. She left behind divorce papers, and a note that said he was only to contact her through the lawyers from now on. Dad is in a total daze.'

Not this again! Shōko felt irritation surge through her. Among the homemaker bloggers, there had been those who had made no secret of the fact that their family homes were in Tokyo and that their parents supported them. Shōko's family, by contrast, was of no use whatsoever. They had never once considered her needs. Hers was a family by name only.

'I can't come right now. You sort it.'

'What!? Why?' There was palpable surprise in Yōhei's voice.

'If Dad was really in trouble, he'd be in touch. Let's leave him.'

'Well, I guess, but ...' After a pause, Yōhei went on hesitantly. 'You know how he can't ask for help. So I dunno, I think it's times like these that the women need to step in and show a man some kindness.'

How incredibly dated her brother's values were, Shōko remarked to herself. When she was growing up, she'd adored him: his reams of bravado, and the soft heart that lay beneath it. But maybe, as a result of this adoration, she'd let him get away with too much. Shōko felt an anger, which had been shut away firmly inside her for so long, finally exploding.

'Why is it the women's role to be kind? You do it! You step in and show him some kindness! You're the one who lives there! Doesn't it occur to you that the reason Mum and Urumi lost it was precisely because they had all of this thrust upon them? And now, what – I'm the next victim? Give me a fucking break.'

'But I ... I'm not good at handling Dad,' Yōhei said in a wavering voice.

'Me neither! There's nobody on this earth who knows how to handle him. He likes being alone. He likes making out like he's turned his back on the world. This time, it's you that's got to sort it out. I'm busy with my blog.'

Shōko slammed down the phone. Kensuke, who had appeared by now, spoke hesitantly.

'Don't you feel a bit bad for him, Shō-chan ...? He's still practically a student. Maybe you should go back home. You can connect to the internet wherever.'

'No. My blog is *The Diary of Hallie B, The World's Worst Wife*, which means I've got to write it from home, in Tokyo, by your side. There are readers and editors counting on me.'

Kensuke's lips, which usually traced only the gentlest of arcs, now distorted into a sarcastic sneer.

'Wow, you're talking as if you're some renowned author or something.'

'What's with that tone? You think it's only a silly blog, don't you? Do you have any idea how much effort I've put into this?'

The shrill voice that leapt from her mouth was one that Shōko barely recognised as her own. Kensuke's face tensed. Shōko's eyes grew hot. She didn't know why she was this worked up. When had this enterprise, which had started out as something she did for pleasure, become a binding obligation? When had their lives, which were supposed to be theirs alone, become something that belonged to everyone? She knew instinctively that Kensuke had shut an invisible door between them. He turned his back on her and made for the entranceway.

'Where are you going? It's late.'

'I'm going to eat out.'

When she glanced over, Kensuke already had his trainers on. She flew over to him and caught hold of his arm. The voice that emerged from her mouth sounded humiliatingly desperate.

'But I've made dinner especially!'

She had been about to take a photo and upload it to the blog. She wanted a witty comment from the Demon King to add in, something along the lines of: *What's all this? I never thought the day would come when I got to eat this type of food at home.* He was ruining all her plans.

'It's better if I'm not here, surely. You can write your post in peace.'

Kensuke gently shook his arm free of her grasp and grabbed the doorknob without turning to look at her. The door shut behind him, and Shōko was left alone. What had just happened? She'd gone out of her way to cook properly for once, welcomed him home with a lavish meal – why, then, had it resulted in such a grim exchange?

That Girls' Festival day when her father had spat 'I can't eat this' at her mother now came back to her. The sight of her mother's face when her father had refused to touch the meal she'd gone to all that trouble to make. Giving in to her annoyance, Shōko stomped back to the kitchen. She picked up the plates and was about to toss their contents into the sink, but she then realised: without photos, none of this would have any meaning at all.

# CHAPTER SEVENTEEN

Her boss had said that she could take the morning after her return off, but Eriko went into work at the usual time regardless. She'd been away only a few days, but the office circulars and pieces of post had formed mountainous piles on her desk, and even after spending the whole morning sorting them, she'd only made her way through half.

When she got back from an external appointment it was already 7 p.m., and her desk was still strewn with papers. Defeated, she called up a temp named Emiko Yamamura on the internal line and got her to bring over a small cardboard box to put the documents in. As Emiko was kneeling on the carpet, constructing the box, she looked up at Eriko, apparently remembering something.

'Did you know, there was an announcement in the morning meeting while you were away? Sugishita and Maori Takasugi are getting married before the end of the year. It's great news for Maori.'

'Really! I had no idea they were a couple. That is great news.'

'She'll be leaving the company, so we're going to throw a joint farewell and celebration party next month.'

Once Emiko had walked away, Eriko sat down at her finally clear desk and started up her computer. Her heart was thumping.

It was nearly November, and yet a coating of sweat made her tights cling suffocatingly to her legs. In one corner of the office she saw Maori, working late for once, encircled by other temps, all of them joking around. The girl was always surrounded by other women.

Suddenly, Eriko felt like some kind of clown. Were Sugishita and Maori laughing at her behind her back? It was all so stupid. She hadn't felt anything for Sugishita, and had no desire to get married herself – why, then, did this news make her feel so miserable?

The trajectory of Maori and Sugishita's courtship, from their meeting through to their marriage, was more or less identical to that of Eriko's parents. Her father and mother had met when he was a trader and she a clerical worker. They had got married after her mother had fallen pregnant, and she had given up work. Hearing this news about Sugishita and Maori, she felt confronted by the awareness that there'd likely been this same faint note of squalidness about their relationship, which brought on an unpleasant feeling.

This was just like the first term of high school, Eriko thought: the sense that everyone was leaving her behind. She hadn't been envious of the other girls and she'd had no interest in makeup, or going out, but when even Keiko, whom she thought of as a sister, had turned her back on her, Eriko had been so lonely, she'd wanted to die.

Was it just her imagination that the whole world was criticising her? The sense of peace she'd achieved in Tanzania had vanished without trace.

When her computer was up and running, it wasn't her emails that she glanced at first. Instead her mouse moved immediately to her bookmarks to open up Hallie B's blog. By now, any qualms she'd once had about reading the blog during working hours had evaporated.

Ah, not that stupid woman again, Eriko mumbled. It seemed as though while Eriko had been away, Hallie had taken part in some bloggers' meetup and fallen in with a crew of tedious housewives.

'What I love about Nori is the way that, even though she's a super-mum with a successful career, she never seems like she's trying too hard. Women with busy jobs can be quite highly strung and demanding, but Nori isn't like that at all. I feel so relaxed when I'm with her, it's as if we've been best friends forever …'

What the hell …? Eriko could only read this as a personal attack. Shōko had never been like this before; she'd never been the type to use words that functioned like a secret code comprehensible only to certain people, lifting favoured people up and dragging others down into the mud. Above anything, the words 'best friend' stabbed her right in the heart. This wasn't Hallie B who was writing this. It wasn't Shōko, either.

Eriko's neck flushed in rage. She immediately typed the words into the search bar: *Hallie B's World's Worst Wife boring.*

Within moments, Eriko was looking at a handful of negative comments left on a well-known forum. All of them seemed to be saying something similar:

*I always liked how gentle and not try-hard it was, but recently it's just like all the other wife blogs :(*

*I preferred it when it was rougher around the edges! Is she doing this because she wants a book deal?*

Shōko's blog wasn't that widely read, so the comments weren't numerous, but even this sprinkling of them assuaged the heavy feeling in the pit of Eriko's stomach. Then her eyes landed on a particular comment, and she instantly felt her breathing grow easier.

*I can't relate to this new Hallie at all!*

So it wasn't only her! There were other people out there who felt the same way as she did. If comments like this existed, she had to be in the right. She would print it out, and stick it in her notebook.

*Relating to other people* – now Eriko thought about it, it seemed to her that this was the most valuable thing in all the world.

She was fairly sure that she wasn't the only one who felt this way about this connection, either. Other people, too, wanted it so badly that it had them in knots, in tears. They would pay any amount of money to find people who felt the same as them. It was this desire that made it so hard for people to give up the internet. In allowing people to leap across time and space in an instant, the internet had an intoxicating power to make people feel that they weren't alone. If someone was given a platform to speak from, they still had to draw people in and make them feel understood. Women who weren't relatable made people feel lonely. They made the already cold world even bleaker. The divine mission that Hallie had been appointed with was to light a candle on a chilly, lonely evening, and make her readers feel that they were okay just as they were. Her duty was to shower people in light. She needed to rectify her mistake.

Eriko suspected that the fact that Shōko was hanging around with this cheap mummy blogger Nori was an act of betrayal that her readers would find as hard to accept as she did. Just the thought of Nori and Shōko eating out together and acting all chummy made Eriko want to scream. If Shōko only used a bit of imagination, she would be able to figure out how this was likely to make women like Eriko and her other friendless readers feel. All Shōko was saying was: look at me, I'm close to a celebrity like Nori, so I must be doing fine. I'm great, just the way I am ... As she thought this, it crossed Eriko's mind how over the moon she'd been when she'd met Hallie B, whom she'd admired for so long, and her feelings grew even more bitter. It was because Hallie B didn't have any female friends, but still enjoyed her own company, that Eriko had been able to relate to her. Nowadays, her blog was all time-saving this, paraffin paper and salted kōji that, and other words that held no interest for Eriko whatsoever.

Why had she stopped writing the witty prose she used to, full of junk food and the titles of TV programmes, books and films?

What about criticism of Nori? Eriko wondered. Was there any of that out there? Her fingers struck the keys again – and just as predicted, there it all was. Eriko couldn't stop herself from smirking. The internet was littered with attacks on Nori and her myriad commercial collaborations.

But no, this was bad. Eriko glanced behind her to check that there was nobody behind her. At this rate, she'd find herself falling down a rabbit hole. Tomorrow there was a big meeting in which she had to give a presentation about her Tanzania trip. She had to sort through her notes, compile the data, and present it along with slides showing the photos she'd taken on her trip. Yet right now, she felt incapable of thinking about anything except for Hallie B.

Could she not stay over at the office? With that thought, Eriko felt a weight lift from her shoulders. Suddenly, the evening seemed to swim, dizzyingly capacious, around her; the office appeared like her own bedroom.

Here, she had her work and she had the internet. This way, she could cut out on commuting, would never be late for work, and wouldn't have to spend weekends all by herself either. Here, in the office, it didn't bother her that she didn't have friends. If she could only live in the environment that was right for her, as the Nile perch had been doing before it had been transplanted, she didn't need to get hurt or get lost. What Eriko was searching for was a harmonious, sympathetic world, where she could relate to everyone. Such a place had to be out there somewhere. How many more evenings like this would she have to spend before she could find it? It was difficult for people like Eriko to establish relationships in this society, replete as it was with mind-bogglingly complex rules. In opening up to people, you had to accept their differences and be considerate of where they were coming from, while also holding onto your own sense of identity. To Eriko, it seemed like an impossible juggling act.

In a short while, everyone else would have left the office. Until then, she simply had to stay here tapping at the keys with a butter-wouldn't-melt expression.

A single tear ran down Eriko's cheek and landed on the keyboard, taking her by surprise. She looked around furtively to check whether anybody had seen. She didn't feel the slightest bit melancholy. Maybe her eyes were just dry. She took out her strong eyedrops from the desk drawer and arched her neck back to put one in each eye. The room distorted wildly. She felt as though she could feel eyes on her chest, exposed in this posture, but she didn't care any more.

Since coming back from Tanzania, she had begun to experience this soft female body of hers, the vessel she had been given to navigate the world in, as a real nuisance.

As she was here doing this, the Nile perches were busy evolving. They would devour their friends, if that was what it took to keep themselves alive. Nobody knew how big they would go on to become. A clear mental image now took hold of Eriko and wouldn't let go: a huge Nile perch, dozens of metres in length, swimming leisurely around a Lake Victoria that now contained no other creatures, its silver scales glistening. Just one mammoth fish. And yet, the Nile perch wasn't lonely. It wasn't lonely because it contained inside that enormous body the souls of the hundreds of thousands of creatures it had eaten.

Eriko had to bring the old Hallie back. It was a reasonable demand, coming from a friend – no, coming from a treasured reader who had helped Hallie's blog grow. She was not Hallie's enemy. She was a devoted fan, with Hallie's best interests at heart. It was her words that Hallie should be listening to, not this Nori who'd cropped up out of nowhere. Shōko had taken a wrong turn, and the only one who could help her was Eriko, who not only knew her back to front, but was also equipped with plenty of common sense and business know-how. Shōko didn't have any other real friends.

Before Eriko knew it, the now-deserted office was pitch black, with only her computer and its surroundings bathed in white light. Throughout the night Eriko typed, pouring all her strength of feeling into text. Little by little, Hallie B's comments section filled up, subsumed by harsh critiques, comforting words of kindness and nuggets of helpful advice.

# CHAPTER EIGHTEEN

When was the last time that Shōko had read a book? The November light filtering through the leaves of the trees and in through the windowpane lit up the paper, bringing its texture into focus. Shōko had always had a horror of spaces this quiet. The sense that it was only her and the printed word left her uneasy, and as she turned the pages, the paper responded pliantly to the touch of her fingers, so she felt as if they were sucking something from her. Time dripped by, slow and smooth, like soup filtering through a strainer.

How long had she been here now, sitting in the window seat of Gisele with a highlighter in hand? Shōko darted her eyes to the clock on the wall to see that it had only been twenty minutes since she came in. She was taken aback to note that the clock hands seemed to be moving far more slowly than usual. Maybe this had been her state of mind before she'd thrown herself into the world of the blog. Yet somehow she'd stopped feeling as though she wanted to return to that way of being.

Her eyes followed the lines of text from the top of the page to the bottom. She had never disliked reading. That said, she wasn't a fan of anything too complicated, favouring light essays about everyday life or cheerful escapist fiction. Recently, though, she hadn't been going to the library as she used to. While she pored over the words filling the bright liquid crystal screen of her laptop, whole days seemed to evaporate. Kensuke said nothing about how her eyes remained glued to her phone during mealtimes, or how she was publicising various scenes of their lives at a far greater frequency than before. It wasn't as if their relationship had soured entirely since their argument last month, but there was more distance between them than there previously had been.

Still, Kensuke was a generous-spirited man who rejoiced in the achievements of others as if they were his own. Shōko took the optimistic view that he would get used to the situation in time. He didn't have any reason to complain, either: of late Shōko was being far more proactive about the housework. She made simple but colourful meals to upload to the blog, and was trying to keep the flat as clean as possible. Little of her time was spent lazing around. She was getting more income from affiliate ads, and if her blog did end up getting made into a book, then she'd receive royalties too. The situation was full of benefits for Kensuke.

Shōko continued to correspond with Satoko. She still hadn't given her a definite yes about the book, but her feelings about it were rapidly solidifying.

The book she was currently reading, *The Food Bloggers Who Turned Dreams Into Reality*, she'd bought online after it had been recommended to her by Nori. Each sentence seemed to sink into her like nourishment that she sorely needed. The checklists at the end of each chapter were as helpful as Nori had said:

❑ *Have you tried making your writing easier to read by emphasising key points and inserting frequent paragraph breaks?*

❑ *Do you have a good grasp of what it is that attracts readers to your blog?*

❑ *Have you tried techniques to ensure your food looks good in photos, such as shooting in natural light?*

Quite possibly, Shōko thought, she had been too negligent of how she was perceived. She should maybe invest in a proper camera. But then, that kind of try-hard attitude wasn't very Hallie at all, and it might put off her existing readership. It was fine to keep taking photos with her phone as she'd done until now – she'd just make some slight technical upgrades. She had the sense that she'd finally reached a turning point, and was on the verge of an evolution from an amateur homemaker blogger to a professional one. She couldn't afford to be rejecting publicity requests at a moment like this. Finishing the book, she closed it, sat up straight and drained the cup of now-cold herbal tea in front of her in a single gulp.

Yesterday, Shōko had done her first photo interview for *Melanie*. Part of a special issue about bloggers, hers was to be a two-page spread entitled *The Rising Stars of the Blogging World: Introducing Hallie B! Representing the Child-Free Homemakers*. It was unprecedented for a relative unknown like herself to be featured in this way, Satoko had told her excitedly. Shōko could only guess that Nori had had a part to play. The issue would go on sale next month. Once it was on the shelves in the bookshop, Shōko suspected, she would no longer be able to continue living under the radar as she did now. She felt, too, that she was ready for the change.

'I'm committed to a slow, relaxed approach to life! When it comes to things like housekeeping and having kids, I've made a pact with myself not to compare myself to others. I'd always rather step out to a cheap restaurant with my husband, or call in pizza and watch a DVD, than snap at each other about who's going to wash the dishes. That's the rule the two of us have.'

The night before the interview Shōko had been too nervous to sleep, but there in the office of the publishing company, drowning in countless camera flashes, a dam had broken, and she'd become incredibly talkative. It was as if everything she'd been working on since meeting Nori had suddenly burst into flower.

She'd only met Nori in person that once, but through reading her blog and exchanging messages with her, Shōko had been able to glean a lot about her approach to life. In contrast to her soft, friendly appearance, Nori had an almost merciless objectivity and was a gifted marketer.

'One of your most appealing qualities as Hallie B is that you don't take yourself too seriously and people find you very real, but I think the time's coming when it's important to draw a line, to let people know that you're different from a regular person,' Nori had told her. 'You have a platform. That doesn't mean you have to become a superstar in any way. If you have the awareness in yourself that you're imparting experience, people will naturally come to listen to what you have to say.'

Shōko felt as though with this advice she'd been handed a magic wand. The way that somebody presented themselves, the words they used – these things could make a person. It didn't matter what your past held: the key point was not to feel any shame. As she spoke into the voice recorder that Satoko had given her, Shōko found her heart opening. She'd always been embarrassed about how empty she considered her life to be, but the truth was that most people felt the same. Her role was to represent all those nameless people, to open up a breathing space in the lives of all the stifled housewives. She had to correct this mistaken belief that a person without achievements had no value. She needed to tell them to have confidence, that they were fine as they were. In the end, it was people who stayed real who captured people's hearts. Affirming the unremarkable quality of everyday life was in itself a distinctive take.

In the interview, Shōko spoke proudly of how, though it wasn't easy financially, she had no intention of getting a part-time job or having kids right now, and how her attitude as a blogger was built on her being a nobody. She understood that there would be people out there who'd find fault with these statements. Still, she no longer felt in the mood for heeding their criticism. She'd taken Nori's advice and stopped googling her own name, and had decided to turn off comments on her blog.

The astounding number of messages that had been posted to the blog in the early hours last Tuesday were clearly all written by the same person.

> *Where has the fun, cheerful Hallie B gone? It's like you've become a regular try-hard wife blogger. I miss the old Hallie!*

> *It's incredibly alienating to see you off having fun in this circle that we're not invited into. You could be so much better if you only had a bit more empathy for others. As a woman, it's a real pity to observe.*

> *You're someone that could do anything if they set their mind to it. This isn't what you're destined for, surely!? You can scale greater heights than this. Please shed this fake skin of yours. This is a sincere plea from a committed fan.*

As the timestamps on the comments neared dawn, these plaintive, earnest pleas grew more intense, encompassing more and more contradictions:

*Don't put on airs with us! The world doesn't revolve around you, you know!*

*This is a terrible act of betrayal for your readers. We demand an apology.*

*You're being led around by the nose by the media. You're a sad, ignorant, uneducated woman. I bet you didn't even go to a decent university.*

*When your book comes out I'm going to dedicate myself to writing bad reviews of it. You're talentless! You've never had an interesting thought in your life. I'm going to follow you around for the rest of your life and troll the hell out of you!*

Then, after resorting to unbridled attacks, the comments suddenly grew whiny and weak, as though the tide had suddenly receded.

*Please, just reply ... Why do you neglect your fans like this? Come back! Remember that it's us who've supported you this entire time!*

Both the line of argument and the choice of words made it impossible to think that this was anybody other than Eriko. Shōko no longer felt afraid or hurt. In part this was because most of her fans had been sympathetic, leaving comments like, 'Don't let the weird troll get you down!' and 'It seems like you're getting some flak from a crazy lady, but trust me, she's just envious.' Shōko had long since ceased to feel any strong feelings toward Eriko. She had passed through the annoyance, and now she was enveloped in an icy tranquillity.

The reason she'd come out today to Gisele, with its connections to Eriko's mother, was to prove to herself that Eriko was nothing to be scared of.

The Shōko who, not so long ago, had looked up to Eriko like a goddess and found her dazzling in her brilliance had been lacking in worldly wisdom. She had only been seeing the superficial aspects. One's academic record, appearance and profession – these things didn't actually mean anything. Watching Eriko staging her pathetic one-woman show in the comments column, Shōko had finally had an epiphany. The reason that Eriko was so unfulfilled, so thirsty for connection with others, was because she was so tied up by status and appearances. It wasn't that Shōko had no sympathy for her plight. She felt bad for Eriko, but she knew that she couldn't do anything to help her, and that she had no obligation to, either. What Eriko had done constituted a huge attack on Shōko's business.

'Would you like a top-up?' Looking up, Shōko saw Hashimoto, his eyes narrowed into a friendly smile, holding up a glass teapot. The herbs inside the water had swollen. It was already getting cold outside, and yet he wore only a thin T-shirt. The sight of his bare arms emerging from his sleeves tugged gently at something inside her.

In all honesty, that was her other reason for coming here today – to see him. Taking advantage of the lack of other customers, he now crouched down, placed a hand on her table and looked straight at her. The pose was like that of a prince, kneeling for her. She remembered talking in the classroom with her boyfriend like this, back in school. Shōko had felt glad to be on the receiving end of the jealous glances darted her way.

'It was fun, the other day.'

The two of them had been to the cinema the previous week. Shōko hadn't told Kensuke about the outing, but she didn't feel guilty about it; before getting married, she'd often done similar things with male friends. They'd been to watch an American slapstick comedy at a Shibuya movie theatre, had had a coffee in Starbucks, had taken the train home together and parted outside the station. Messing around innocently with a young man like that, whose muscular physique exuded a fresh musk, had given Shōko an unexpected burst of elated energy. Of course the time she spent curled up cosily in bed with Kensuke was indispensable to her and she had no intention of throwing that away. But, experiencing the rush of excitement caused by flirting with Hashimoto, she realised that for many years now she'd more or less forgotten that she was a woman. She wanted to continue seeing him, never actually crossing the decisive line, but savouring the most delicious dance that lay before it. She had no intentions of hurting or betraying anybody.

In fact, Shōko thought to herself, since she'd started taking her blog seriously, her life had become incredibly enjoyable. Her body coursed with satisfaction, right down to her fingertips. She now had the confidence to navigate all kinds of situations.

'You're not all excitable like girls my age, and you don't tell me to start looking for a proper job, either. I loved talking with you. I find being with you very comforting.'

Hashimoto pouted his thin lips like a baby angling to be fed. She'd found out on their outing that despite being twenty-five, he was still a student, living with his parents and attending the local university. Maybe because he'd taken a year out, and repeated two others, he seemed to be terrified of graduating and getting a proper job, and was doing all he could to prolong this carefree way of life. Shōko understood very well how he felt, so she didn't lecture him – if anything, she was tempted to join him in thinking through whether there wasn't an easier path open to him.

'Do you want to go on more of a *date* date, next time?'

'Hey, I told you! These aren't dates. But yeah, sure. How about … the aquarium?'

When Shōko was a teenager, date destinations had been limited to the aquarium and the shopping mall. Thinking this, Shōko wondered how her father was getting on since Urumi had left. The thought took hold of her for a split-second and then vanished without trace. Hashimoto's skin was perfectly smooth, except for the section from his jaw to the bottom of his neck, which was pocked with acne scars. That roughness was somehow heavenly to her. It seemed to her that if she were to trace her finger over it, poignant memories would come flooding back to her.

'The aquarium, eh? Got it. I'll text you.' Catching sight of the outline of a customer about to push open the door at any second, Hashimoto straightened himself up in a smooth motion and glided towards the entrance. Two middle-aged women made their way in, chatting amicably to one another. Feeling a twinge of melancholy, Shōko put her book in her bag and took out her mobile. If she didn't write her impressions of the book while she still remembered, she'd miss the precious opportunity for a blog post. The frozen time inside the café began to move again, the ticking of the clock suddenly much louder.

# CHAPTER NINETEEN

She had no idea Maori was standing right behind her until she felt the tap on her shoulder.

'Morning, Eriko! Have you been working through the night? Ah, your teeth are all green! You'd better look in the mirror before the others get in. Oh, and there's some on your cheek as well. Like a little baby!'

At Maori's burst of shrill laughter, Eriko felt her face grow hot. She reached for the tissue box placed on one side of her desk. Maori had caught her in the middle of the Kyoto Uji Matcha and Chocolate Croissant with Warabimochi that was her breakfast. It was a new product at the convenience store that Hallie B had featured on her blog yesterday, with the review: *Crazy chaotic deliciousness. Why has nobody thought of this before!? Crispy croissant dough, softly melting chocolate, and the jelly-like squidge of warabimochi, all in a single bite.*

Of late, Hallie B had thrown herself headfirst into home cooking, and it was now something of a rarity for her to review this kind of junk food. In her excitement, Eriko had ended up buying three.

This was the fifth time this November that Eriko had spent the night at the office. Next to her dishevelled hair, bare face and bloodshot eyes open wide behind her glasses, Maori's curled hair and natural makeup seemed to belong to a different world. She definitely wasn't what you'd term a beauty, and yet, bathed in the morning light, her white cheeks and dyed brown hair seemed to glisten, and there was an upright freshness about her that could have won anybody over to her side. Since the announcement of her marriage to Sugishita, Maori seemed to exist as if in the very centre of a spring, emanating rippling circles of water. Had things turned out just somewhat differently, the life that Maori carried inside her might have been growing inside Eriko's body instead. She wasn't envious, but it did occur to her that such a turn of events might have freed her from her obsession with Hallie B, and enabled her to live a more respectable existence. As Eriko was gazing absent-mindedly at her, Maori's gaze slipped past Eriko to the computer screen behind her, and a dark look flashed into her eyes.

Eriko started. Turning quickly, she grabbed her mouse and closed the window open on her desktop. Had Maori seen it? Her heart was thumping, and a tendon in her neck began twitching. Her throat felt itchy and dry. Maori had caught her in the act of typing a negative comment about Hallie B on a certain forum. The thread that was specifically about Hallie B had been started by Eriko herself. She didn't feel great about using the internet in this way, by any means. But now that Shōko had blocked her calls and texts, and closed the comments section on her blog, this was the only place she had to vent her criticism and affection. Knowing that, beneath her carefree front, Shōko was very concerned with how she was perceived by others, Eriko could only imagine that she'd find her way here soon enough.

The thread still wasn't that extensive, and was mostly sustained by three or four people who seemed aggravated by the recent change in Hallie B. In all honesty, Eriko not only found their opinions off the mark, but also construed their particular brand of jealousy as a kind unique to women lacking in intelligence who hadn't been gifted with much fortune in their lives. She scrimped on sleep, scouring Hallie B's blog and then converting her thoughts into sparkling, constructive prose, partly in a bid to draw more like minds to the thread. This was the only means of contact with Shōko that was permitted to her. She had no intention of giving up until she got through to her.

'Didn't you pull an all-nighter the other day as well? Have you got a busy project on at the moment?'

'No, it's just become a habit.' In the attempt to escape Maori's searching gaze, Eriko's eyes landed on her boss's seat directly behind her. The morning sun was streaming in at an angle, illuminating the pictures of his wife and two children on his well-organised desk. The boss had once been her father's direct subordinate, and had often come over to their house before his promotion. She remembered him, slightly embarrassedly, calling her 'Eri-chan'. It wasn't simply the fault of the morning light – the perception that everyone other than herself was perpetually advancing in their lives made her wince.

Eriko's motivation for spending the night here wasn't purely to keep tabs on Hallie B. It was also because she'd been feeling tired of late, and her efficiency was dipping. She knew that she was falling behind.

The series of actions that she had once accomplished daily – finish up work for the day, get on the train and go home, have dinner with her family, take a bath, get a good night's sleep, wake up, do her makeup and hair, then get on the train to work again – had recently come to seem like far too much hassle. By skipping this entire sequence, Eriko found she was suddenly gifted with a huge chunk of free time. The office at night was a vast, comfortable box. She would wait until everyone had left, then remove her makeup with a cleansing sheet, take out her contact lenses and clip up her fringe with a barrette. Going to the convenience store in front of the company to buy both dinner and breakfast, she felt the thrill of preparing for an excursion. In addition to conducting the research that she needed to for work, she'd spend the time monitoring Hallie's movements on the internet and keeping the thread on the forum ticking over. She took care not to be discovered by the security guard on his patrols. When she felt sleepy, she would set an alarm on her phone and lie down on the sofa in the office kitchen. In the morning, before the others came in, she would apply thick foundation and eyeshadow, cover the sweaty tang of her body with perfume, and tie her hair into a chignon, so that nobody raised their eyebrows at her appearance. It made her feel faintly powerful, pretending that nothing out of the ordinary had happened, while secretly having this understanding of the office that nobody else had – this knowledge of how it felt to be at her desk, floating there like a solitary island of electric light in the velvet darkness.

'The temps are worried about you as well. If there's something we can do to help, please do let us know. We all know what a hard worker you are.'

Maori's tone was calculated to sound caring, but it was laced with ridicule, in a way that riled Eriko. This way of subtly showing off her closeness to her friends was the worst. It reminded her of Hallie's blog of late, with all its Nori this, Nori that nonsense. Maori was just an incompetent young woman. Why did she think she had the right to throw her weight around like this? Eriko's lack of sleep wasn't helping. Antagonism rose inside her throat like vomit. She narrowed her eyes and looked up at Maori.

'You're looking very beautiful recently. I'm envious.'

'Ah, no, that's not true! I'm no match for you!'

'Maybe it's your happiness about getting married shining through? Congratulations, by the way!'

Eriko did her best to pick her words so as to avoid being seen as the villain in this scenario. She needed to coat her poison in sickly-sweet phrases and force it inside the lips of this woman getting ahead of herself, like other women did. Just a microdose of poison, which would spread through her body over time, not making her unwell but somehow affecting her mood, leaving her plagued by an anxiety she couldn't articulate. She dropped her voice into a whisper and let the corners of her eyes droop, in a look of sympathy.

'I'm worried about you, though. Are you sure that getting married is the right choice? That you'll be happy with Sugishita? There's no turning back with kids, you know? You don't know what's going to happen with your contract either. And to be going into that as a temp, which is the least stable of all the positions. The risk with marriage and having children is that they put your career right back to the starting point …'

'Sorry?' Maori's fleshy face slowly distorted. She had something approaching a double chin to begin with, and when she pulled back her jaw and drew her eyebrows apart, she exuded a quiet intensity. Eriko had been planning to continue in on the offensive, but she quickly thought better of it.

'What the hell? This sounds a lot like serious gender discrimination to me. Whatever it is, I don't like it. I'll happily take you to court. It won't look very good for you if you're sued for sexually harassing another woman, will it?'

Faced with this totally unpredicted line of response, Eriko found herself unable to draw breath.

'Take me to court?'

'I could probably only manage a small lawsuit of about 200,000 yen, but so long as there was a lawyer involved, it would be clear to people that the fault didn't lie with me. Word would get out that you had problems.'

The woman standing in front of Eriko was younger than her and lower in status. She was bad at her job, and had most likely only graduated junior college. Yet in this moment, she seemed indomitable. Gathering herself, Eriko tried to put together a strategy that would ensure her a stable footing. She needed to maintain her status at work, at the very least. It seemed to her that if she didn't urgently try to remember that her career and her talents far exceeded those of Maori's, her heart might actually break apart.

'Oh, I don't think I explained myself properly. I'm sorry. Let me try again. I don't like having to say this, but I think you're so great, and I'd hate to see you getting hurt. Just know that I'm doing this for your benefit, though?'

Eriko took a deep breath and looked Maori in the eye. Sugishita's hot breath, the sticky touch of his fingers on her body, returned to her with alarming vividness, and though she knew it was hardly the time, she felt a twinge in her crotch.

'Sugishita isn't the man you believe he is. I think he's cheating on you.'

'Oh, yeah? And what if he is? Can I go now, please? I've got things to do.' Maori made to go back to her desk, her expression utterly unaltered. Eriko found herself not only flabbergasted but hurt. It was always this way. When she'd finally found an excuse to speak to someone, when she felt like her preparations to engage with someone were watertight, she would be coldly pushed away.

'Wait. Please! Don't deceive yourself!'

Maori let out an exasperated sigh and began to turn away. Eriko felt herself flushing to her ears. She had to do something to maintain her position of superiority. 'I'm doing this for your own benefit!' Flying at Maori, Eriko seized her wrist. As she opened her mouth to yell, her hair flying everywhere, there was some part of her observing the situation coolly from a position outside herself. *What is this farce you've got yourself swept up in?* the observer asked. *And with this girl, who's all of twenty-three years old?* Eriko had gone after her, though she'd done nothing wrong, and when Maori wouldn't give her the time of day, she'd lost control of herself. What, exactly, was she aiming to do here, when she didn't feel anything towards either Maori or Sugishita? Maori screwed up her face into a look of pure animosity. Her mouth contorted into a leer, she fixed Eriko with a look that said she was utterly sick of the sight of her.

'What the fuck do you want, you dumb bitch?'

At this sudden burst of language of the kind she'd never heard outside the TV, Eriko felt as though her heart might stop. Maori's face had assumed the expression of an adult struggling to deal with a grizzling baby.

'Coming up to me with that stupid wheedling grin on your face. What the fuck do you want? Huh?'

Unable to answer, Eriko bit her lip.

'You don't even know yourself, do you?'

She was probably right, Eriko thought. She only knew that she was craving to be part of an intense connection, to ascertain her own contours through another. That said, her choice of person had been misguided. Her usual friendly smile now nowhere to be seen, Maori stood there, imperious. Her chunky shadow spread out across the floor. From the look in Maori's eyes, her worldly-wise tone, Eriko understood that she had opened a box she never should have touched.

'I really couldn't give a flying fuck whether Yasuyuki is playing around or being unfaithful. My parents got divorced when I was young, and I watched my mother struggling throughout my childhood, so I never had any grand romantic vision of marriage. The important thing for me is to marry a man from a good background with decent savings, so my mum doesn't have to worry any more. If my younger brother can just graduate from high school, I'll be happy. I'm sick of making barely enough to send them money and cover my rent, and panicking each time about whether I'm going to have my contract renewed. Of not spending more than 300 yen a day on lunch. What I want is to be able to bring up my kids without having to worry about money all the time. So long as I've got my girlfriends, I don't need anything else. I've never held out high hopes for men. If I've got a man who's healthy and who doesn't get in my way, that's good for me.'

As Eriko looked at Maori, the area behind her seemed to expand before her very eyes. Did she have eye strain or something? The lines traced by the same-shaped desks led off endlessly into the distance. What a cavernous space she'd been working in all this time! Was it really her who'd been sitting in this desert-like place by herself the whole night through?

Sugishita had once said to her with a smug expression that she and Maori inhabited different worlds, his implication being that she and he were on the same level. Now she understood that this was wrong; just because Sugishita and Maori were different, it didn't make her and him the same. Everyone was inescapably different. A company was like an enormous tank into which innumerable different species of fish had been set free. Which was why she should have been more cautious. From the force with which Maori grabbed her hand then, Eriko understood that she had been foolish enough to throw an unsolicited punch at someone who was better given a wide berth. She couldn't predict either Maori's method of attack or her level of force. She was a totally unknown opponent. What could she do? Eriko's legs began trembling.

'You say that Yasuyuki's cheating, but with who? Hm?'

'I'm sorry! Please ... forgive me ...'

Eriko contorted her body, attempting to squirm free of Maori's grasp. What extraordinary strength, she thought. Maori's long, pale blue nails studded with stones and beads dug into the flesh of her arm, ready to draw blood at any moment. Maori's appearance was otherwise subdued, but in seeing the aggressive colour scheme of her manicure, Eriko felt like she'd glimpsed her true nature. *Mum! Dad!* she found herself internally calling for help, like a child. Maori's hot breath scented with artificial sweetener struck her ear.

'You're not trying to tell me it was you, surely? Hm? Is that why you're so fucking bullish about it?'

The nails finally released their grip. For a second, the heat in the air dropped away. Maori sat herself down roughly on a chair next to Eriko and grinned slyly. Eriko's relief at being released lasted only a moment. Now Maori's exacting gaze ran itself up and down her body, sizing up her worth. Eriko found herself speechless. There was nothing that she could do other than hug her body with her hands and look at the floor.

'Well, well! You and Yasuyuki! Huh. I guess that figures, I know that guys your age think you're kind of hot. Do you know what the temps say about you, though?'

Eriko didn't want to know. She covered her ears in a bid to shut out the taunting voice.

'That the goody-two-shoes act is tedious as hell. That you're way too old to be acting like you're still the class prefect. That nobody's envious of you, and it's sickening to watch you simper and play nice as if they were. You don't have any friends, do you? "The only thing missing from my flawless life is female friends! Aahhh, I'm just dying for some! It's the last piece of the perfection jigsaw for me! Pretty please will somebody talk to me?"'

Maori's impression of Eriko's voice wasn't at all bad. As she spoke she twisted her torso, clasping her hands at her waist. Given how popular Maori was, Eriko thought, she'd doubtless performed this countless times in front of people. A lump formed in her throat and her body was suddenly feverish with heat. She would have given any amount of money to be able to run away. Finally, Maori let her hands fall heavily by her side and looked at Eriko again.

'Yasuyuki loves being fussed over, that's his problem. I don't particularly care who he's been with, but the thought of him sleeping with you makes me want to puke. Wow, though. All that "I'm only doing this for your benefit" bullshit, when this whole time it's you who's acted out of line – you really don't disappoint, do you? It's clear as day that you look down on my background and my academic record and whatever, but from where I'm coming from, it's you that's the lowest of the low. Ah, man! I was so over the moon that I finally managed to get him to agree to this wedding, and now all the good feeling's gone out the window. Do you have any idea how tough it's been for me, to get to this point? So what are you going to do, hm? Perfect little Eriko, who has no idea what real suffering is, who has not the remotest idea of how other people feel – how are you going to make it up to me? I bet right now you're thinking about nothing except how to escape this situation.'

With this, Maori stood decisively to her feet, and shoved Eriko's shoulder, hard. Reflexively Eriko's hand slammed down on her desk, striking the keyboard, which let out a high-pitched noise of the kind she'd never heard it make before. Maori didn't look away for even a second, but kept her eyes pinned on Eriko. Her face had turned an unsettling mauve colour, and her veins were popping out. She looked not unlike a cartoon demon.

'I'm really, really sorry.' Holding back her tears, Eriko gave a low bow. It was just as Maori had said: what she was feeling was fear, rather than any particular remorse. She wanted to clear up this situation as quickly as humanly possible, and return to how things were before. She wanted to go back to observing Hallie from a safe distance, as if nothing had happened. Yet still she couldn't restrain herself from asking Maori: 'Why is the wedding so important to you, if you don't trust your fiancé?'

'Because I'm inviting all my friends, and I want to make sure they have a good time. Yasuyuki's colleagues and school friends all come from these mega-elite backgrounds, so I'm planning to introduce them to all my friends who are looking for husbands. I can't tell you how long I've dreamed of the day when I get to throw a beautiful bouquet to my single friends.' Maori's tone seemed genuine. There's no way I'm going to win, Eriko thought. Not against this girl. Not in a million years. She slumped her shoulders and bowed her head again.

'I'm so sorry for putting you in an uncomfortable position. I'll do anything to make it up to you. Anything to repair the damage I've done.'

'Anything?'

'Anything.'

'Okay. There are twenty-three men in the sales division, aside from Yasuyuki. I want you to sleep with all of them.' Maori's tone was breezy, as though what she was saying were perfectly sane. Just before her dried throat closed up entirely, Eriko let out a cry that didn't seem to have come from her.

'The fact that you'd done it with Yasuyuki wouldn't bother me half as much if you'd also slept with the head of division, and the team leaders, and the section heads. If you really care about my feelings, then you've got to sleep with them all. I want you to take photos on your phone, and send them to me as evidence that you're doing what I say.'

As Eriko was sitting there at a loss for how to reply, Maori shoved her shoulder again. She didn't appear to be angry any more. She was simply doling out instructions, like an efficient boss, and her real feelings were inscrutable.

'If you could sleep with Yasuyuki on the spur of the moment when you're not that into him then you're capable of doing it with anyone. What's that face for? Are you going to tell me you can't? You said you'd do anything, didn't you? Was that a lie? A half-baked apology? You've hurt me, and now you're not going to make amends, is that how it is? Hm?'

'It's not a lie. But I just …'

Feeling herself tearing up, Eriko glanced in the direction of the door. If only someone were to come in now – come in and extend her a helping hand. Maori stepped to the side, obscuring Eriko's view. She looked down at Eriko with an all-piercing gaze. Her low, resonant voice seemed to reach straight to Eriko's core.

'Do you realise that practically all the women who become permanent employees here come from families like yours? Everything is determined, from the moment you're born. Every day, I have to live with the knowledge that hard work gets you nowhere. You make out you're this gloriously independent adult, but you know better than anybody that when push comes to shove, someone will step in to help you. Stupid women like you make me sick, going around with their noses in the air when they've been spoiled and given everything they want throughout their lives, are still being supported by their parents at this grand old age, and yet, for some reason, believe that they've done everything themselves. While we're here panicking about whether we'll get our contracts renewed, you permanent employees sit there surfing the web, believing that you're working your balls off. It's a fucking joke. Your dad was a big shot in this company too, wasn't he? Did you try weely weely hard with your job application so that he'd sing your praises and tell you what a good girl you are? Then you come in to work dolled up every day in the hopes of meeting a man like your dad. Pah! It's fucking laughable. You're just a big joke. Shall I tell you why no one likes you? It's because you never think about anybody but yourself!'

Eriko had reached her limit. The tears came spurting out. Barely thinking about the snot running down her face, she grabbed at Maori's thick waist.

'I'll do it! I'm sorry! I'll try and do it! I'll sleep with them. I'll have sex with all the men on this floor. I'll try. Please, please forgive me.'

Eriko got down on her knees on the floor, and once again bowed her head down low. Her greasy, unwashed hair made contact with the floor. Maori took hold of her hair with full force and pulled Eriko's head up so she was looking directly at her.

'You mean it, right? You know what's going to happen to you if you're lying to me now, don't you?'

As her parting blow, Maori struck Eriko's head. A burning pain ran across Eriko's skull and her vision flickered. She stumbled to her feet, picked up her stuff and walked past Maori, before running out of the office. In the corridor, in the elevator, in the bright glass-fronted lobby, her colleagues who were only now arriving for the day called out to her, but she didn't stop. With each male glance thrown her way, she felt more sordid. She hailed a taxi outside the office and told the driver her home address. In the back seat she clenched her eyes tightly shut. Several times her mobile rang in her bag, but she ignored it. This was the first time she'd ever missed work without permission.

*You're like that TEPCO employee who turned into a prostitute ...* Sugishita's words when they'd slept together came back to her. She'd learned about the case of Yasuko Watanabe in sociology class at university, but hadn't been that interested. You occasionally found professional women who seemed mesmerised by the case, but to Eriko this seemed no more than a perverse way of drawing attention to themselves. A high-achieving girl entered the same company as her respected father, had her dreams ripped apart, lost herself, started working on the street, and wound up being killed ... It sounded like the storyline for a clichéd TV drama, and it now surprised her to note how much it resembled her own situation.

She was sure that Yasuko Watanabe hadn't had any female friends. Looking down from the expressway on the surface of the Imperial Palace Moat, Eriko tried to picture her life: an existence that consisted entirely in coming and going between her home and the office, with no female friends to share her concerns, her misfortunes with. Like living her life as an invisible person, where she herself didn't really know what her own tastes or preferences were. That was why she had gone to seek out her own contours among all those unknown men. To a woman with no female friends, the only way of ascertaining her own existence was to sleep with people of the opposite sex. Was it then possible that sleeping with all the men in the sales division would make Eriko feel more alive? Would enable her to discover what type of person she was, help her to better grasp her distance from her surroundings? She was aware how idiotic it sounded as an idea, but she also felt that it was the only path now open to her. Maori believed in neither love nor work; she saw value only in her friendships. Having observed the transformation in Maori's demeanour, the imperiousness she had assumed, Eriko now found her words persuasive. Viewed from a certain angle, Maori was an unwavering sort of person. She trusted other women, and other women trusted her. Eriko was mesmerised by the glow that this way of being generated. Maybe if she followed in Maori's footsteps, went wherever Maori led her, she'd be able to get Shōko back. She wanted to succumb to a greater force, to obediently carry out the mission she'd been entrusted with. That she was feeling this way must mean she was really quite exhausted.

The priority for the moment was to go home and rest. Eriko was confident she'd have no problem fooling her parents. The taxi now pulled up in front of her apartment building. Outside, the bright sun left her feeling dizzy, and she hurried in through the door to the lobby. Making her way over to the elevator, she bumped into Keiko. Dressed in a tracksuit, Keiko was slumped against the railings of the outside corridor, just as she had been the previous time, smoking a cigarette and holding a plastic bottle in one hand. She slung her glance in Eriko's direction.

'What's up? It's still the morning! Did you forget something?'

'I left work early. I'm not feeling well,' Eriko said curtly, avoiding eye contact. It suddenly came to her that today was the day of the monthly sales strategy meeting. Not just that: she had an arrangement to meet with a new client for sales talks. But there was no way that she could sit side by side with the men from the sales division in her current state. Was tossing aside her important duties and running home like this proof that she was as soft as Maori said?

As she went to move off, Keiko murmured, 'You should give it a rest, you know. All this following Hallie around. The stuff online too.'

When Eriko turned back to look at her, she was leaning against the railing with a perfectly impassive expression. She exhaled a puff of smoke in a manner that seemed to confirm she'd read Eriko's mind perfectly.

'I know what's going on. Anybody who knows you would. You think you're doing a good job of hiding it, but my guess is that the people at work and your parents have all noticed that something is up. I know that the person who dropped you here on her bike is a blogger called Hallie B. I've spoken with her a bit. She's terrified of you. She ...'

Eriko didn't want to hear any more. Desperate to cut Keiko off, she squeezed out the words, 'You've got it wrong. It's all a big misunderstanding!'

Suddenly incapable of standing up straight any longer, Eriko slumped against the railings. She and Keiko were now adopting a similar posture. She remembered how, a very long time in the past, the two of them had talked for hours in this very position: by the high bar in the playground, on the roof, at the ice-cream shop counter. The time she'd spent with Keiko had been the most precious thing in the world to her back then. Once again, Eriko felt tears spilling from her eyes.

'I met with Hallie B in a Denny's, late one night. We had such a fun time. She said all this stuff to me, like, let's meet regularly, and, we live so close by, so we can hang out and talk all the time. She even gave me a lift home on her bike ... I'm not lying. You saw, right?'

Keiko kept silent, smoking, until Eriko had finished talking. Finishing her cigarette, she dropped the butt into her half-drunk bottle. The flakes of ash swirled round slowly in the water, before floating down to the bottom, catching the light. It seemed to Eriko as if the bottle contained the sea bed in miniature.

'Listen, there's nothing unusual about what you just told me.'

Eriko looked at Keiko in shock. Keiko launched into a slow explanation, as if to a small child.

'You don't know how to connect with people, so you mistook a regular connection for something special. You blew it up and gave it more meaning than it actually had. That's all it is.'

'But that's not true! Hallie …'

'Hallie nodded and told you that she understood. She was attentive. But that's not a special occurrence. It's part of the conversational rules shared by women across the world. It's a form of courtesy.'

'No, you're wrong.'

'It pains me to say this, Eriko, but however hard you fight, you're not going to win that evening back. Hallie's looking out on a different scene.'

Eriko let her body slide down from the railings to crouch down on the floor. Still Keiko didn't stop talking.

'You can still keep that as a precious memory. It's good that you got to have a bit of fun like that, even if it was an illusion. If you really were connecting with one another, as you say, then that night's a precious gem. Precious precisely because you can't get it back. You need to stop making demands on the other person to give you more of whatever you want.'

Keiko's lecturing tone was permeated with a species of affection. At the speed of light, she had crossed that decade-long blank space that existed between them. Eriko was left reeling. Oh, yes, this, she found herself thinking – this was how Keiko had been. She was bad both academically and at sport, and hadn't stood out in the classroom. Yet when the two of them were alone, she was like a big sister to Eriko. She seemed to understand everything, to always be a few steps ahead. She had the power to soothe Eriko, in all her inflexibility. Unlike her classmates who were always pining after this or that thing, Keiko seemed to understand her place in life from early on, and took a philosophical outlook. Feeling herself on the verge of recalling her utter dependence on Keiko, Eriko pulled a severe expression and stood upright.

'What would someone like you know about it? Someone who doesn't have a single friend herself? I know what you're playing at. I know that you're living like this, this pointless existence where you sit around doing nothing, as a way of accusing me. Well, pull yourself together. Find yourself a proper life! How am I supposed to move on from high school if you're lurking outside my house the entire time looking pathetic?'

'That's not a line for a perpetrator to say to their victim, you know,' said Keiko. She didn't seem remotely hurt. On the contrary, she snickered as she spoke. It was as Eriko made to walk towards the elevator that Keiko said in a friendly tone, 'It's kind of weird that someone so high-achieving finds it so impossible to get on with people, isn't it?' Eriko glanced back at her. 'I guess the conclusion is: there really are things in the world that you can't achieve through will alone. Like friendship.'

# CHAPTER TWENTY

Ripping open the seal of the large envelope with the name of the publishing company printed on it, Shōko tried to keep a handle on her excitement. The stars of the bumper New Year's issue of *Melanie* were Nori and renowned bloggers like her, all dressed up in glamorous outfits. Shōko's section was a long way towards the back. When she finally reached the two-page spread in question, she let out a sigh of disappointment. Under the fluorescent lights of her living room, the glossy photograph of her was that of a hopelessly unrefined, flat-faced woman.

'You look pretty. It's a nice shot. You really are beautiful, you know.'

Kensuke, who was sitting opposite her at the table sipping a can of beer, was generous with his compliments, but they weren't enough to satisfy Shōko. The her that existed in her imagination was leaner, maybe not exactly glamorous per se, but certainly someone who exuded an appealing, stylish aura. The day before the shoot she'd been to the hairdresser's for the first time in a while. The day itself, she'd woken early and massaged her face, taking her time to apply her makeup. She wore a shirt with trousers in a fashionable print that she'd carefully picked out in Isetan in Shinjuku, and yet on the page, the outfit looked cheap. Where had she gone wrong? Deciding not to give herself the chance to get down about it, Shōko resolved to come up with a list of improvements to make next time. That was undoubtedly the tack that Nori would take.

It didn't take her long to understand. Of course she looked plain. The carefully selected clothes, the haircut, the face massage, the makeup – all of these were things that women in their thirties did regularly. For someone like her who usually went around makeup-free in worn-out clothes, going to the hairdresser was a big deal, but it wasn't going to make her shine in a setting like this. She had to take more care with her appearance. Shōko endeavoured to think optimistically. Having formerly worked at a popular apparel brand, she would soon be able to find her way into that world again. She was on the path to becoming someone with a media presence, which meant she never knew who would be watching her, and when.

Her mobile on the table vibrated. A text from Hashimoto: he'd remembered her request for him to take her to the aquarium. Shōko's expression softened. When she got to the words, *I bought two copies of the magazine you're in. You look hot!* her former feeling of despair evaporated entirely.

'Is it okay to go out with a friend next Saturday?' she asked Kensuke, without lifting her eyes from her phone screen.

'A friend?' came the doubtful reply. 'I didn't know you had any friends?'

Dammit, she thought. It was true. She didn't have any friends. She racked her brain, and then looked up and shot her husband a smile.

'You know that girl we saw downstairs? Eriko Shimura.'

'Her? Are you sure? She was getting a bit stalkery, wasn't she? Are you sure it's not her who wrote all those weird messages on the blog?'

Seeing Kensuke's face screwed up in distaste, Shōko almost burst out laughing. How childish, how unsubtle Eriko was! The idea that even her slow-witted husband could see straight through her trolling made Shōko feel a touch sorry for her again.

'No, she's okay. She's sweet, in her way. That time when she came to our apartment there was lots going on with her at work and in her love life, and I think she went a bit funny in the head.'

'Well, be careful, okay. Women's jealousy is a scary thing.'

'Women's jealousy, eh ...'

'Honestly, I can't stand all that cat-fighting. It freaks me out. You're too pure for any of that. That's one of the things I like about you.'

He understood nothing, Shōko thought. There was nobody on this planet who didn't experience jealousy – not only women, but everyone. The reason that Shōko had distanced herself from relationships with other women was because she understood that she was the worst for comparing herself to others and feeling down about it. She was the least 'pure' of them all.

'You're so *active* recently, Shō-chan. It's like you've become a different person. I've been meaning to ask, though, is everything okay with your dad? Is it okay to leave it all to your brother like that?'

Silently, Shōko pulled the cookie tin towards her. Inside were biscuits from a famous shop in Tokyo, known for their refined taste. They had been a present from Satoko. In truth, Shōko preferred the cheaper kind of biscuit – lighter tasting, crunchier ones that smelled of emulsifier – but these weren't bad, either. She hadn't heard anything from home since that phone call from Yōhei. Maybe Urumi was back already. Both her brother and her dad were physically healthy and had plenty of time on their hands.

They weren't worried about her, she thought, so she had no cause to worry about them.

'Let's not talk about that. I'm thinking about joining Twitter. What do you think? Nori says my style of writing would be well suited to tweets.'

'You really have changed, haven't you?' Kensuke's face took on a bitter look.

Is it not you that's the jealous one? she wanted to ask him in reproach. She crunched on the biscuit, and began composing a reply to Hashimoto.

# CHAPTER TWENTY-ONE

A hand resting on the utility pole, Eriko groaned loudly enough for the passersby to turn to look at her, then crouched down on the street. This part of town, Shinsen, was concave, dipping in its centre. Crouching down even slightly made the buildings and love hotels hemming in the circle of night sky appear even taller, so high that they seemed ready to snap and come falling on her at any moment. Was it her drunkenness that made the scenery look a lot like a face, baring its teeth and laughing at her? Overwhelmed by the sight above her, Eriko stared down to see a collection of cigarette butts and old dog excrement on the pavement.

'Eriko! Are you okay?'

The feel of a large palm at the base of her back. Lacking any sensual quality, its touch took her right back to being a little girl. How was she supposed to break through this barrier of sterile warmth that existed between him and her? Her boss was in his fifties, and belonged to the list of people who had shielded and supported her throughout her life, along with her parents and her teachers. Maybe that was why she couldn't cross over to the place where Maori and the others all stood. Looking up, she saw his balding head glistening in the streetlight.

'I think I'm going to be sick.'

At the smell of her own breath, Eriko's stomach twisted.

'What? Hold on a minute!'

Eriko arched her back so her face would be out of sight of her now-flustered boss, then jammed her right index finger deep into her throat. As her fingers struck against hard bone cloaked in wet flesh, she tried her hardest to bring up the contents of her stomach the way she used to. As she'd run her eyes down the izakaya menu earlier that evening, the trick of eating and drinking with the express purpose of vomiting came back to her immediately. When the magic ingredient that was alcohol was involved, the objective was simple enough to achieve. By the time she'd left the restaurant she was feeling light-headed, and the need to crouch now wasn't play-acting.

Eriko squeezed her eyes shut. She imagined herself five centimetres tall, standing inside her own mouth. Digging in her heels so as not to trip on the bumps dotting her tongue, she peered down into the hollow of her throat. That profound darkness was like the Inokashira Line tunnel next to the level crossing, which she'd glimpsed before entering the izakaya. If she were to make one misstep, she'd go plummeting down, headfirst; she'd fall into that pool of bubbling liquid that dissolved everything, and never return.

In the next moment, Eriko felt the burning-hot bitter liquid bursting up. Proud that she'd finally managed it, Eriko emptied the contents of her stomach across the pavement. With her most flirtatious eyes, she looked up at her boss. Now that the pressure in her chest was alleviated, she felt positively fresh as she wiped away the warm liquid from around her mouth with the back of her hand.

'It's gone on my clothes ... A taxi driver won't pick me up like this. I'm going to have to go to a hotel nearby and wash them, and wait for them to dry. There's no way they'll let me in by myself, though. Will you come with me?'

Backlit by all the neon lights, her boss appeared to Eriko like a giant tree. His feelings were hidden by his branches and leaves, and she couldn't make them out.

'Don't be stupid, that's a terrible idea. I'll call your parents and we can get them to come and collect you.'

Aghast at this proposal, Eriko groaned once more loudly, shaking her hair and hiding her face. She knew that her boss was standing there flummoxed, unable to walk away but unable to reach out and help her either. After hesitating for a moment, she grabbed his suit with a vomit-slick hand and hauled herself up. With this same momentum, she dragged him in the direction of the love hotel in front of them, modelled on a tropical resort. She could sense that the sole of his foot had left the asphalt, but he didn't move. He might only have been of average height and weight, but his body, which had withstood thirty years in the sales division, was pure tenacity. Eriko quickly brought her wet lips to his ear.

'People are watching. You know that people from team three often go to a wine bar around here? We'll be in trouble if they see us. You wouldn't want there to be rumours, would you? Your wife and the girls would be sad. Emiko would be sad. It'd affect your position at the company. If we go into the hotel, I promise we'll leave separately.'

Eriko could tell that her use of the name of his daughter, who was just entering high school, had had an effect. Seeing him waver, she summoned up the last of her physical energy, and finally dragged him inside the entranceway adorned with fairy lights and plastic coconuts. In front of the automatic doors stood a fountain, the noise of the water spilling from a tray held aloft by a naked cherub resonating at a volume that seemed faintly obscene.

Apparently resigning himself to his fate, the division manager followed after her. This well-respected man, whose usual manner was light and comical but who commanded great authority when steering others, appeared suddenly small, and Eriko felt that she had got what she wanted. At the reception desk, designed so that the customers' faces were hidden, she picked a room number at random and was handed a key. She got in the elevator, and smiled at her boss, doing her best to look as appealing as she could. They got out at the third floor, and Eriko opened the door with their room number on it. The eruption of the smell of old cigarette smoke made her wince. The room was small, its space almost entirely taken by the large bed lit up in blue.

It hadn't occurred to Eriko until very recently that she contained this kind of destructive impulse. She was glad that she hadn't been entrusted with a button that could bring the world to an end at a single touch. Or maybe everyone had a button like that – they simply didn't realise it. Once you realised, you could never get its presence out of your head. You felt the weight of the world growing less and less significant by the day.

Eriko flung off her bag, sat down heavily on the bed, and gazed at the manager in the most seductive way she knew how. She had to make a start on the mission she'd been set by Maori. There were twenty-three men in the food product sales division. Sugishita's and Maori's wedding was fast approaching; there was no room to hang around. Every time her eyes met Maori's in the office, Maori would shoot her a terrifying glare. Rousing her courage, Eriko had invited the division manager for drinks.

Until she'd entered middle school, this man had been like family to her. When she was a little girl, she'd seek attention from him, and he'd pat her head. One time he'd played dolls with her for hours. His wife had visited their house several times too, and when his daughter Emiko had started middle school, Eriko and her mother had spent hours in the department store picking out a pair of trainers as a celebratory gift for her. But none of that mattered now. She had to put all of that out of her mind, so that her feelings didn't get the better of her and foil her plan.

She'd asked him out to dinner on the pretext that she had something to talk to him about, and as soon as they'd been shown through into the private room in the izakaya in Shinsen, Eriko had pressed herself against him. Shinsen was the perfect part of the city for a plan of this kind, containing as it did both love hotels and upmarket bars and restaurants favoured by people in the know. The high-low contrast was extreme, and it was peppered with spots of darkness that threatened to engulf the unwary. With the night sky so far off in the distance, everything lost its sense of reality.

The manager's body didn't exude the greasy smells common to middle-aged men. Instead, he smelled faintly citrussy, not unlike the lemon peel in the pound cake that he would bring into the kitchen at work, saying his wife had made too much. She imagined that his wife had a significant role to play in his physical upkeep. His clean, inoffensive presentation enabled Eriko to act more boldly. And yet, despite her casual solicitations, he didn't seem to be taking the bait.

'I think you're tired. You should think about taking some time off.'

The man who was usually cracking dad jokes now directed on her a caring look of the kind she'd not seen from him before. When she'd joined the company he'd said to her, 'I want you to forget all about my connection to your dad. You're part of this division now, and I'll be just as hard on you as I am on the others.'

Since then, he'd never been like this with her. Now, Eriko was attempting to destroy everything that they'd built up over time with her own two hands.

'Look how dirty my clothes are! Do you want to get in the bath with me?'

Taking care not to let her voice waver, Eriko gave a flamboyant laugh, then threw off her cardigan and blouse, balled them up and tossed them at her feet. She could feel the skin across her upper body tensing. Of late she'd had no time to spare on lavishing over her appearance. She had no perfume on, and her nail varnish was peeling off. She couldn't remember what underwear she had on, either. Still, she was at least far younger than him. This, surely, would put her at an advantage. She was about to explode their trusting relationship. Her parents would faint with shock if they knew. If she could only get rid of her life up until now, all the time she'd spent at the office, then she could rebuild it from its foundations – this hopeful thought flooded her head like a bright white light, washing it clean.

'You truly believe that if you can create the right conditions, manipulate the circumstances in a certain way, then people's feelings will behave exactly as you want them to, don't you?' the division manager now spoke. 'You've been the same since you were young.' His tone was cool and detached, completely at odds with the situation they were in. If anything, he sounded pitying of her. She looked into his eyes, and found none of lust's cloudiness there. For a passing second, she felt like a flasher, exposing herself and getting off on it without the other party's consent. She hadn't imagined things panning out this way; she'd been convinced that he'd respond just as she wanted him to.

'Your mum and your dad were the same, so I know. They're not bad people. Of course I don't dislike them. They were good to me, and I'm grateful for that. Your house was always immaculate, your mum was young and pretty, and she cooked the most exquisite meals. I bet they're the type of couple who've never argued. But I don't think I ever spoke with your dad about our real feelings. I don't think that was only with me, either – I suspect the same went for everyone. Whenever he praised, comforted or encouraged me, it was always in a very formulaic way, which sounded like lines he'd picked up from somewhere. As if he were reading from a script. That was why I stopped going round there. I think you're a similar personality type. You're totally oblivious to your myriad privileges, which makes you hard on others and blind to your surroundings.'

Eriko wanted to cover her ears and scream until she couldn't breathe any more. It was unbearable to her, to hear someone's verdict on her family, delivered with such chilly objectivity. Criticism of her family was the one thing that Eriko couldn't tolerate. Her insides burned. Being stripped naked in front of her entire division, having them assess her body, would be nothing compared to the humiliation she now felt.

It wasn't sexual desire that went ripping through Eriko now. No, the violent desire that erupted through her body was to pin this insolent man to the floor. She had to get him to want the same thing.

Eriko had to be compensated for what he'd just said. She stood up and, pushing her breasts into his body, wound an arm around his waist. Yet despite the honeyed voice with which she entreated him to kiss her, he only averted her eyes. Finally, he shot her a dirty look and shoved at her knee with his hand. Eriko stumbled, grabbing onto the corner of the bed. She would not let herself be humiliated in this way, she thought, staring menacingly up at him. She now felt that she had to make him submit.

His voice had taken on a tinge of exasperation.

'Deep down, you don't trust anyone. That's why nobody wants anything to do with you. Who on earth would feel like they could be themselves around you, when everything you do and say is so meticulously calculated? The same could be said about the way you work.'

Saying this, the manager seemed to cast off the hesitation he'd previously been feeling, and struck Eriko's bare shoulder with his elbow. A stinging pain that penetrated to her bones ran through her, and she toppled back onto the bed. She felt the springs bounce beneath her bare back. Even her boss, who she'd always believed had a soft spot for her, had seen through her. She felt so mortified, she wanted to scratch her throat to ribbons.

'Why is it just me?' she said, and smelled a whiff of vomit.

'Why do you still bother trying to involve yourself with people, when all there is to you is the front that you put on? Stay on your own until you can trust others. Being alone isn't anything to be embarrassed about. It's time for you to grow up.'

The manager's words seemed to fall upon her from a great height, so high up that she couldn't even make out his face. He seemed to her loftier than even the Shinsen night sky. Her father had never spoken to her like this. He'd always affirmed her.

The idea that someone like her, who'd been raised with such loving care, would be rejected in this way – something must have gone wrong. Whatever happened, Eriko didn't want to be on her own. In her heart of hearts, she wanted someone by her side at all times, holding her hand.

How heartless he was! The only person Eriko could think of who was genuinely alone in the way he spoke of was Keiko. There was no way that Eriko was going to end up the same as the woman who had once cut her out so brutally. Who was Eriko that some trifling comment could make her want to die? She felt that she'd never be able to take a step of her own volition, without carefully checking her reflection in the eyes of another.

In one corner of the room was a flare of colour that she'd missed before. Looking closer, she saw a poster reading:

*Enjoy Our Girls' Night Out Discount Plan!*

*Missed the last train? Stay together until morning! An excellent range of toiletries and all-you-can-eat sweets. See rates below.*

The images on the poster showed girls laughing together alongside a selection of red and green fruits, and a pile of pancakes drizzled with honey and butter. Were there really women who'd come to a love hotel to spend time together? She imagined this desolate space filled with the sound of women's laughter, brimming with all sorts of delicious fruit and cake. Just because you were in a love hotel didn't mean you had to have sex. True friends would be able to alter the significance of that space.

'And you can say with certainty that you don't have any front, can you? You must have had dirty thoughts about me at some point. Has it never struck you that that little girl you used to know has grown into a fine woman?'

Summoning her strength, Eriko threw off her skirt and then reached for the manager's groin. It was warm and squishy. Still, she arched her body as though she'd burned her fingers, and held up her head in a look of exaggerated triumph.

'Look, see, you're hard! How pathetic! You go around spouting all this high-blown nonsense, but you're pretending like everyone else. With your nice suit and your friendly smile, you're masking the fact that you're just a filthy old man.'

Eriko wanted to clap her hands and scream with laughter. She remembered when the two of them had played the board game Othello in her childhood. She had always persuaded him to continue playing until she managed to beat him. Now finally, with this tactic, she had got him. His cheeks flushed and his eyes moved furiously from side to side in shock. She couldn't let him get away with this humiliation. Digging her fingers in harder, she thought she sensed a faint stirring in his unresponsive body.

'What's so terrible about making an effort, with trying to get other people to like you? You're arrogant, that's your problem …'

At that moment, there was a ringing in her head, and she was pushed back onto the bed. The manager was gripping the stem of the bedside lamp. She understood instantly that it had struck her forehead. When she lifted a hand to it, she found it burning hot, and could already feel a lump forming. She opened her mouth to scream, but nothing came out. Was she going to be murdered here? Then she really would be like Yasuko Watanabe …

'Effort? If you're that keen on effort, then why not try making some real effort.'

How dare he, thought Eriko. There was nobody on earth making as much effort as she was. What was she supposed to make more of an effort with? The pain blurred her vision. Regaining his breath, the manager answered her unvoiced question.

'I'm not talking about the hollow act of pretending to be someone you're not. Look, everyone's noticed that you've been acting strangely recently. We're all worried about you. Coming in looking like a dog's dinner, skipping meetings and sales talks unannounced. You're violating company rules by staying over at the office and looking at disreputable websites. Your work is riddled with basic mistakes. I was planning to say something at some point, but I think maybe you need to rest for a while. Take a good hard look at yourself. I'll take you home. I want to speak to your father.'

With a strong arm hoisting her up from the shoulders, the manager pressed her clothes on her, then dragged her up from the bed. He flung open the door to the room with all the impetuosity of an oxygen-starved man searching for air. A cold breeze blew in, and Eriko hastily put on her vomit-stained clothes. She noticed for the first time that the corridors were lit up in red, forming a contrast with the blue rooms.

The borderline between the two was stained purple, and there the shoes Eriko had kicked off before lay, facing in different directions.

Eriko didn't know what her boss had said to her parents late that night when he saw her home in a taxi, but from the following morning on, her mother stolidly refused to let her out of the apartment.

Eriko lay curled up in the blanket steeped in her own smell like a bug in a chrysalis, and spent all her time scrolling on her phone. Waking after lunch, she would spend over two hours in bed, reading through Hallie B's tweets. From the people who she replied to and the products that she mentioned, Eriko could make guesses about who she was seeing and what she was doing:

> *Today's breakfast is udon with shiso mayonnaise, topped with poached eggs! I had something similar in a local izakaya, and decided to try making my own version. I know it's designed as something to soak up the alcohol when you've been drinking, but the way it slips so easily down the throat makes it great first thing too. And it's super easy!*

*Here's our home collection of the capsule toys on sale by the register in family restaurants, which the Demon Lord just loves to buy …*

*My absolute favourite overseas drama is* The Wonder Years *on NHK. Why haven't they released it on DVD, though? Is it a problem with the music rights?*

The Twitter account that Hallie had set up a week previously was now a key form of emotional support for Eriko. She had 230 followers – not too shoddy, Eriko thought, given how new it was. The goody-two-shoes vibe of Hallie B's blog of late had been an irritant to Eriko, but it seemed as though the short-snippet format was well suited to Shōko's disposition. Her relaxed, peaceable prose was a breath of fresh air.

Eriko had been at home for four days now. Right away, she'd had a call from Maori.

'So you're trying to get out of it by playing the mental health card? I knew this was how it would go.'

'I'm really sorry. I … um …'

Maori mercilessly cut through Eriko's apology. 'Why the hell did you go for the manager first?'

Eriko guessed that she'd probably had a misguided confidence that he'd envelop her in his kindness.

'Because he's like your daddy? Did you think he'd protect you?'

Eriko found herself unable to answer this simple question.

'You always get someone to save your arse, in the end. You only know how to live in a way that's utterly reliant on others. That sounds like privilege, but in a way I feel sorry for you. You're like a pet that'll never leave its cage, an ornamental fish that has to spend its entire life in its tank. Yasuyuki will send you a wedding invitation, but you're not to come, you hear? If possible, take the whole month off and stay at home. Don't leave your house.'

Maori put down the phone. For Eriko, Maori's instructions were now inviolable commands. She didn't know if she could drag out her time off work for a whole month, but for the moment she was determined not to leave the house. She wanted Maori, at least, to acknowledge her efforts.

She knew that the demand that she slept with twenty-three men to make her amends had been insanity – and yet, she had wanted to do it. She wanted to force Maori to see her bravery and her resolve, and to start treating her humanely as a result. Why, oh why, could nobody really see her?

There had been no contact from Maori since. Just once, she'd plucked up the courage to try to call her, but it seemed as though Maori had blocked her. Her texts didn't go through either.

Succumbing to tedium, Eriko made her way idly through Hallie's tweets. Seeing a new one, she sat up.

*At the aquarium with a friend. I'm remembering how much I love the smiley faces on the rays' stomachs. Photo dump incoming …!*

An array of aquarium snaps followed immediately. There was a sea turtle, jellyfish, starfish, and then … Seeing the large grey fish with a horse-like profile, Eriko yelped. A Nile perch! There were very few aquariums in Japan with Nile perches. Which meant – she knew where Shōko was. This was the new aquarium in Shinjuku, where Sugishita had previously invited her to go and see Nile perch in the flesh. If Eriko left the house now, she might be able to bump into Shōko. She got up with her phone and wallet in hand, and left her room for the first time in half a day. Her parents sitting in the living room looked at her wide-eyed.

'Where are you going? Wait!' Her mother's shrill voice chased after her. Her father, who'd been reading his newspaper on the sofa, also got to his feet. The dark blue sweater that her mother had chosen for him suited his white hair well. She didn't know any other men in their sixties who were as well presented as her father, but she also knew that was all down to her mother's efforts. Taking in the dark bags beneath her father's eyes, it struck her that without her mother around, her father may well become a far less palatable proposition.

'I'm going to meet a friend.'

'But you don't have any friends!' To Eriko's surprise, her mother's eyes were rimmed in red. It was rare for her mother to come out with statements like this. 'You've never had any friends!'

So, Eriko thought, it was just as she suspected. Even her mother didn't trust her. Her boss's words began to make faint sense to her. Her father said nothing, simply stood there stock still behind her mother.

'Why, Eriko? We did our best to give you a normal upbringing. Why do you struggle so much with people?'

That was the question Eriko most wanted the answer to herself. Why, when she wanted so badly to get close to others, was she so comprehensively rejected by them?

Not wanting to worry her parents any further, Eriko said calmly, 'It's Shōko Maruo.'

'Who's that? Listen, please … If you're looking for something to do, how about you go and see Doctor Nishi?'

This was the name of the therapist at the psychiatric department whom Eriko had visited periodically since the incident. Eriko loathed the tone he had, shot through with the conviction that there was some kind of issue with Eriko's family. He spoke as if there was some grave defect with her. Eriko wasn't abnormal.

She could take an objective view, and she believed herself to be kind too. She just hadn't been blessed with the opportunity to show these qualities to other women.

'She's a married woman, who's a regular at Gisele. She lives in the shopping arcade over there. She knows Keiko too. I'll be back soon. Ask people about her, if you don't believe me.'

While her parents were frozen still, processing this information, Eriko shoved her feet into her dad's sandals lying by the entranceway and launched herself through the door. She was wearing the fleece jumper and joggers she used as pyjamas, but right now her appearance was the last thing on her mind. She hurled herself down the stairs and, when she got out to the street, hailed a taxi and jumped in.

The roads were clear, and in less than half an hour, the taxi was pulling up outside the aquarium. She paid her fee at the ticket desk and stepped into the darkened entranceway. For a Saturday, there were surprisingly few children around. She had an inkling that she'd read a review saying that this particular aquarium wasn't popular with kids because there weren't so many different kinds of fish on display, and they had a poor selection of merchandise. Guided by the blue lights of the tanks, Eriko moved through the dark corridors as quickly as she could. She had no time for looking at fish. When she finally spied Shōko standing on the other side of the tank containing rays, she almost cried out.

Shōko …! But who was the man next to her? Tall and skinny, he was definitely not her husband. Eriko had a hunch that she'd seen him once at Gisele. Did he work there? Eriko gasped to see that the pair were holding hands. She snuck round to the other side of the cylindrical tank and followed in their wake, maintaining a decent distance. They seemed to be making for the freshwater fish section, where there weren't so many people around.

Shōko came to a halt right in front of the Nile perch tank. The pair of fish there, each two metres in length, were drifting through the water. Covered in scales of a deep silver, their bodies assumed different colours with each movement, turning purple, grey and then iridescent white. Their big eyes glinting red betrayed no feelings at all, but had a stately quality that suggested they could see through everything. The line running from their dorsal fins to their mouths traced a steep arc, which ended in their thick lips. Their tail fins, shaped like flat round fans, undulated elegantly. For a while, Shōko looked on, entranced.

Eriko gazed expectantly at Shōko's blue profile, which looked as though it were drifting on the bottom of the tank. Is she thinking about me right now, Eriko wondered. Is she remembering her friend who, in her job at the major trading company, is responsible for Nile perch sales? But right at that moment, Shōko giggled and brought her face up to the man's ear. He laughed, and suddenly moved his lips to hers. This seemed to take Shōko by surprise, and for a second her shoulders tensed, but it wasn't long before she encircled her slender arms around his neck. In no time, the two were kissing hungrily.

'Excuse me, flash photography is forbidden in here.'

It was only as the small fish that were presumably food for the Nile perch sped away, and the woman who'd come running over said these words, that Eriko realised her phone was flashing. It seemed as though, without ever consciously deciding to, she'd taken a number of photos of Shōko and the man kissing. Why had she wanted to record an event like that? Eventually, perhaps finding the sight of Eriko gazing down at the images she'd captured somewhat unsettling, the member of staff gave up and went away.

When Eriko looked up again, Shōko was staring at her, mouth agape. Finally, she's looking at me, thought Eriko. She could have jumped for joy. It had been such a long time since they'd looked at each other like this. For so long she'd had to imagine Shōko's life, her feelings, through the information she was provided on the internet, and she had been on the verge of suspecting that Shōko was a kind of illusion, that she didn't actually exist in this world. Shōko's long, narrow eyes like brushstrokes; the clean, fresh look she had about her, with her bones swimming around under her loose top. How Eriko had been longing to see her. Had she ever needed someone this much before?

'Oh, is this a friend of yours? I'll go ahead. I'll meet you outside.'

The young man promptly moved away from Shōko's side, apparently running away in a panic. What a pathetic specimen, she thought. He was no match for Shōko. Eriko moved quickly over and shot Shōko an affectionate smile.

'I had a hunch you might be here! I saw your tweet and came dashing over. You're indiscreet as ever, eh? It's much easier to figure this stuff out than you think, you know! You might think I'm snooping around, but you're the one who puts your private life online in its entirety. You're the one at fault!'

Determined not to give Shōko any window for blaming her, Eriko mobilised all of her energy and spoke with animation. Shōko said nothing, simply stared wide-eyed at her. As Eriko returned her gaze, something occurred to her. Opening up her photos folder on her phone, she brandished the shots she'd taken in front of Shōko.

'It wouldn't be good if these photos got out, would it? You're famous now, and your face is in magazines. You'll lose your fans, and I imagine your husband would have something to say about it too …'

'Why do you feel the need to do this?' Shōko said, when finally she spoke. 'Are you aware this is blackmail?'

Delighted at having elicited speech from Shōko, Eriko felt a rush of elation. It was as if she'd suddenly been handed a trump card.

'I won't tell a soul about it. But there's a condition.'

Eriko reached out and grasped Shōko's arm with both hands. In the short amount of time they'd not met, she seemed to have lost a lot of weight. Was that why, even in her profoundly everyday attire of a cheap-looking wool overcoat, a jersey top and skinny jeans, she looked somehow more sophisticated? This wasn't the real Hallie B. Eriko had to get her back.

Should she do as her manager had said? she wondered now. Should she learn to trust people by practising little by little? By telling people how she really felt, for example. By putting in the time it took to understand another person, if she couldn't immediately relate to them. By learning to coexist with others. But no, it was useless. Eriko couldn't be bothered with all that hollow, purposeless effort. What was the point of scrabbling around in the gravel for the odd shining fragment? Instead, Eriko would secure for herself an absolute, unbreachable trust in one fell swoop. With her own hands she would secure for herself a guarantee that she couldn't be betrayed, which would finally enable her to enter the ranks of normal people.

'The condition is, you have to be my best friend. I want us to start over again. You have to promise right here that you won't dislike me, or ignore me, or move away from me. Then I won't threaten you in any way. I won't do anything like this again. If I know that I can relax and enjoy your company, I really can be the best friend in the world. I swear.'

Don't look so terrified, Eriko entreated Shōko internally, feeling close to tears. Don't stand there with those dead-fish eyes and your mouth gaping open. We're both victims here. We're strays who've fallen from the intricate net of rules ensnaring Japanese women. Look up. See all those tiny threads crisscrossing the surface up there? You and I, we can't traverse those threads on tiptoes like ballerinas, as the other women can. That's why we've got to take each other's hands, here in this dark, quiet haven at the bottom of the lake, and help each other. I've only got you, and you've only got me. It's just the two of us.

'I wish you could see that the real me isn't like this.'

Whatever you do, though, stop pulling that frightened face! It had been exactly the same with Keiko, back when Eriko was fifteen. She liked Shōko, as she'd liked Keiko before her, and she simply wanted to be friends with her, but the harder she tried, the more she was shunned and feared. Frustration simmered in her, but she resolved not to give up. Now that Eriko had grasped Shōko's secret, she intended to get what she wanted. As two people who'd fallen through the net of the usual rules, it made sense that they'd need new guidelines to create a relationship between them. Eriko had to take responsibility for steering their boat, to make sure that it didn't stray off course. The tiny boat might falter and sink, or it might arrive safely at shore – it all depended on Eriko. What a fragile, brave, lovely ship it was! Eriko wanted to reach a hand out to it and eat it up. She felt that she'd probably enjoy the taste, even though she herself was contained by it, in miniature. She wanted to take this friendship into her body and become one with it. That way, she'd never need to worry or lash out in panic, feeling herself on the verge of suffocation.

Lit by the blue-white lights and the flickering reflections of the water, Eriko's beloved best friend's lips trembled. Here Eriko was, alone with her friend at the bottom of all this wavering blue. She wanted to take off all her clothes, to have Shōko take off hers too, so that the two of them could swim together. Their bodies free, she and this person who would never betray her would swim alongside one another, their bodies interlocking as though they were dancing, sensing the cool water on their skins as they embarked on a journey without any destination. It had been so long that Eriko had been starved of this kind of tranquil, fulfilled time with her friends, undisturbed by work, family or men.

Her breathing was steady. For once, her feelings felt smooth, free of any sharp points. She'd been hurt, plentifully, but she felt right now that she could forgive everything. Shōko was a woman with flaws. Eriko had to be tolerant.

In the tank, the two Nile perch crossed paths. Without looking at the other, they slid past each other with awe-inspiring grace, at a distance of just a few millimetres. They, too, had their unspoken rules of engagement.

It seemed to her that the Nile perch were far more gifted at maintaining a comfortable relationship with each other than she and Shōko were.

# CHAPTER TWENTY-TWO

Under the merciless glare of the fluorescent lights picking out every last detail, a parade of plates moved past Eriko on the conveyor belt: faded sea urchin atop its bed of gunkan-maki, drying ham perched on stiffening slices of melon, maguro gradually turning purple. The last time Eriko had come here with Shōko was in September. Back then the plates had seemed to whizz by so fast that she'd been nervous to reach for them in case she missed, but now their pace seemed positively leisurely. It was like someone had adjusted them especially for her. She envisaged some entity watching over her every move from some invisible control tower. She extended a hand and picked up a plate of engawa with ease. Just this was enough to make her feel like a person living frictionlessly with the world around her. She felt like humming a pop song she vaguely knew, dancing her shoulders along. She dipped the engawa nigiri in soy sauce and moved it to her mouth. It tasted nothing like the engawa she'd had before, made from olive or righteye flounder. Each time her teeth bit into it, cold oil spread through her mouth. The ridged flesh resisted her bite, as if saying that there was no way it was going to be chewed so easily. So this was the strength of the mighty halibut, Eriko thought, that you had to pacify with a shotgun. It might not have been the engawa that Eriko was accustomed to, but whatever it was, it had a different kind of charm, an appeal not dissimilar to salmon jerky or some similar snack. Since her childhood, Eriko had been forbidden by her mother from consuming anything artificial – the sweets teeming with colourings and the hamburgers made of goodness knows what kind of meat that her classmates shoved into their mouths with great satisfaction.

*Those sorts of things aren't good for your body, you should be eating food made out of ingredients that haven't been tampered with* – these were the principles Eriko had been raised with. Yet the demonic colours that food was able to assume precisely because it was artificial seemed dazzlingly attractive to Eriko. She was an adult now, who could make her own decisions; she resolved on the spot to start eating more fast food, more convenience store snacks. Maybe her inability to make friends could be put down to her mother's rules meaning she'd only eaten healthy food, she started thinking, in an attempt to shift the blame. Finally, she had come to share Shōko's tastes! Feeling her perspective on the world seem to open out, she felt like shouting for joy. She would try making casual conversation with the staff, Eriko thought. She prepared what she was going to say, and then, while wiping her hands with the wet cloth, said in a cheerful yet worldly manner,

'Wow, this is delicious! This taste for just ninety-eight yen is quite something! Your company must be doing something right.'

'Oh, er, thank you …'

The middle-aged chef on the other side of the conveyor belt blinked in apparent awkwardness. The couple to their right said something inaudible, and the chef smiled faintly. Just as the anxiety began creeping over Eriko, she heard the automatic doors behind her opening, and that scent of fabric softener like cotton candy carried over to her on the night breeze. A smile surfaced on Eriko's face quite naturally, and she wrapped an arm around the shoulders of her best friend, who had sat down next to her. She was dressed boyishly in a long cardigan and harem pants.

'You're LATE! A whole TWO MINUTES!' Eriko grinned.

'I'm sorry.' Shōko bowed her head in apology, not a trace of a smile on her face. There was a palpable twitchiness about her that was dampening the excitement of the occasion, Eriko thought, a touch irritated. And this was their first dinner out together since swearing their oath of friendship at the aquarium too! She scooped a little matcha powder into a teacup, in the way that she'd learned on her previous visit, and pressed the hot water dispenser button above the counter. When she set the full cup of tea before Shōko attentively, Shōko hunched her shoulders and looked down at the floor again.

'What were you up to today? You haven't updated your blog since yesterday. I was worried about you.'

'Nothing much ... Just cleaning and airing the futons, that kind of stuff.'

'Whaaaaaat?! That doesn't sound like the Hallie B I know and love. You sound like a regular housewife! I'm way outdoing you in the slacker stakes these days!' Eriko let out a peal of laughter. Today she had woken up after noon, read some stuff on the internet, eaten the lunch her mother had made, and then felt at a loss for what to do next. She'd almost been tempted to try going back to sleep, to reduce the number of hours until her evening arrangement she was so looking forward to. It struck her once again that she didn't really have any hobbies or interests. Occasionally she'd open up a book, but after passing her eyes over those inert lines of letters for a while, she'd grow so irritated she wanted to hurl it at the wall. To give her the nourishment she needed, she wanted things to speak to her more directly, to drag her right in.

'Are you not going to update it? Is it okay to leave it for two whole days? Won't it put your book contract in jeopardy?'

An announcement rang out across the tannoy, reporting a large number of tuna scrape gunkan-maki making their way onto the belt. Shōko waited for the vociferous voice to finish and then mumbled, 'I'm thinking I might take a break from the blog for a bit. I'm just not feeling it at the moment.'

That much Eriko had already noticed. Hallie's prose was stilted of late, and contained none of the unaffected outpouring of feeling that had characterised it in the past. It was no longer any different from all those mummy blogs, with their trademark blend of self-consciousness and desire for enlightenment. Eriko could easily imagine that increased attention brought with it a sense of pressure. She wanted to do all she could to ensure that Shōko's blog reclaimed the unaffected, pleasantly unstreetwise quality of before, which effortlessly won over her readers' hearts.

'Shall I write it for you?'

As she reached out a hand for her second plate of engawa, Eriko articulated the plan that she had been formulating this whole time. She thought it was a pretty genius idea, though she said so herself, and she smiled as her mouth formed the words. Shōko's mouth hung open, creating a perfect little circle.

'I'm pretty sure I have a better handle on your vibe, your pacing and your word choice than anybody. It'd be super-easy for me to replicate. I bet I could write something that sounded exactly like you. How about I do one entry to begin with, and you can check it and tell me what you think? If you don't like it then I'll quit right away.'

'Oh ... um ...'

'It's obvious to the readers that Hallie B's out of sorts at the moment. I think it's best if you take a rest. You know you can always count on me when you're in trouble! That's what best friends are for.'

Even just saying these words, Eriko felt her whole body melting with joy. She'd always envisaged this version of herself: extending a helping hand to other women, guiding them like a kindly big sister. This was the version of herself that she'd imagined becoming since she was a little girl. Leaving aside the caveat that Shōko still hadn't agreed to the plan, was staring down into her cup of powdery tea with an agonised expression, everything was precisely as she'd pictured it. She suddenly thought back to the days when she had worked in the office as though they were a memory from the distant past. Even when she'd secured a big deal, had won the praise of her boss and her colleagues, Eriko had never been able to give herself a passing grade. When she remembered that she didn't have a single female friend, she felt an emptiness that nothing could assuage. It seemed to her that she was the only one who didn't understand the tastiest part of life, with its complex, delicious flavour.

Eriko reached out for a plate of fresh, thick rolled omelette, which she knew from the blog was a favourite of Shōko's, and set it down in front of her. Shōko didn't so much as thank her, instead continuing to stare vacantly at the conveyor belt. The yellow egg rapidly shed its sunniness. To her satisfaction, Eriko managed to extract the password to her blog from Shōko.

'You can totally depend on me on this one! I'm off work at the moment anyway. I'm imagining I'll be off for another month or so. I've been working so non-stop these past eight years, and I know nothing about the world outside, so it's about time! My dad's on good terms with people at the company, so I imagine he'll have some leverage. I'm intending to study for a qualification, pick up some new hobbies and properly take it easy. Hey, what do you think about us going along to the same class? Or else taking off on holiday somewhere, just the two of us? I've always wanted to go on a girly holiday. We could go to Hong Kong! Or Hawaii? Or stay in Japan, and go to Hakone, or Atami?'

'A holiday ...? I've never been on holiday with another woman,' Shōko mumbled in a voice so quiet Eriko struggled to hear it. If she was going to press the matter, she thought, then now was the time. She leaned in towards Shōko. Her stomach, into which the cold fish had just dropped, let out a gurgle. It was as though that small slice of fish had taken on life, and was swimming around and splashing inside her, creating a lapping sea. Big waves drove across its surface.

'Me neither! Which is all the more reason why we have to do it! It'd be so much fun, going away together. Have you ever ridden the Romancecar?'

'No.'

'I thought not! You and your husband are real indoor types, aren't you? Why don't we say Hakone? The autumn leaves will be so beautiful there at this time of the year. We could go next Wednesday and Thursday, stay overnight.'

Shōko looked uncomfortable. Eriko had in part expected this, and it wasn't unreasonable. In a single leap, Eriko had strode through a boundary line that most women would doubtless spend months timidly padding around. It stood to reason, then, that Shōko wouldn't be instantly brimming with enthusiasm, Eriko told her heart, which was even now on the verge of withering up in defeat. She had to catch the wave. She was damned if she was going to think about what her manager had said to her right now. After mulling it over endlessly, the conclusion she'd come to was as follows. What she and Shōko needed was neither time nor words but a kind of structure, a mould to contain them. If their feelings were turned in different directions, they had no option but to pour them into the mould that was commonly understood as closeness – which consisted in conditions such as meeting three times a week, going on holiday together, texting five times a day – and then watch them set, like terrine. Eriko knew from experience that if one only had the confidence to give them a structure, most things would turn out all right. She felt convinced that if she and Shōko could only surpass this awkward phase, what awaited them on the other side was a world brimming with ease and comfort, of the kind that neither had yet experienced.

Shōko said nothing. She was dying to run away. Determined not to displease Eriko, though, she remained sitting there.

Unfortunately, it was mediocre types like Shōko who feared these moulds the most. Eriko had witnessed this phenomenon not only as a student, but as a working person too. When she'd first joined the company, she'd observed how, the more people resisted the rules and made clumsy attempts to wield their own individuality, the less able they were to succeed. These were the types who soon quit. Those who got ahead were those like her and Sugishita, who had endeavoured to do things in the manner they were shown by their predecessors, before they learned, slowly and patiently, how to apply their own original touches. The same principle applied to the mould that was marriage. Eriko's parents didn't appear to her to be passionately in love or tied together by mutual trust, but in living their lives together, protected by the title of man and wife, they had developed bonds and feelings for one another. Why, then, could one not apply this kind of template to female friendship? Still Shōko said nothing. Her body was stiff and her eyelashes quivered, as if she were absorbing Eriko's idea with her entire body. Eriko's recent experiences had made her wiser. She now adopted a warm, permissive tone.

'Okay, so an overnight trip it is! You don't have a job, so you can go any time, right? I'll book the Romancecar and the hotel. We'll go and bathe in a Hakone onsen. It's a plan!'

'I've got to check with my husband first. It's all a bit quick …'

'Let me know if there are places you'd like to visit while we're there. I really want to go to the Pola Museum of Art. I've always adored the Impressionists.'

Thinking that voicing her own desires might make it easier for Shōko to do the same, Eriko tried this tack out for the first time. She remembered how when Maori invited her colleagues to lunch, she never said 'I don't mind where we go', but nonchalantly voiced her own preferences. Eriko felt quite proud of her own progress.

In all honesty, she wished that she could ask Maori for guidance. She had no confidence that she was doing the right thing, and the tension that came with feeling one's way through the darkness lingered persistently. What would Maori do in a situation like this one?

Hakone had occurred to Eriko as a holiday destination that they could get to in just an hour and a half on the train known as the Romancecar, which stopped at a station not far from where the two of them lived. She understood that, as a stay-at-home wife, Shōko had a limited amount of time and money at her disposal, and it was best to stick to somewhere relatively close at first. She wouldn't have minded covering Shōko's share of the holiday, but as friends, it was best to go halves. Eriko resolved to look for an onsen resort hotel with a Ladies' Discount Plan for something in the region of 10,000 yen a night, with breakfast included.

Eriko was going on an onsen trip with her friend! This was bound to bring them closer. The cloudy water and the vapour rising up from the volcanic valley would dissolve all the awkwardness between them. They would see each other naked, without makeup, and have honest conversations in their post-bath face packs. She wanted Shōko to understand the less cool, more perfectionist aspects to her personality. She wanted to find out more about Shōko too. They would share the kind of contented time, undisturbed by power dynamics or sex, that everyone else took for granted. It lay so close that Eriko could practically reach out and touch it. They had come this far. There could be no mistakes now. Shōko was staring down silently at the floor. Reflected in the soy sauce in the dish, her narrow jaw quivered, along with the ceiling lights. Eriko had no intention of rushing her friend into anything. Knowing that she herself had no occasion to panic, she moved her eyes to the leisurely revolving sushi. Shōko wouldn't betray her. She could only say yes. Her exit route was blocked. To think that knowing this could bring Eriko such calm!

Seeing a new nigiri go floating past, Eriko suddenly straightened her posture. Her mind filled with thoughts of the product for which, until a few weeks previously, she had been working diligently to secure a sales route with Japan – for whose sake she had travelled overseas and inspected processing facilities, and had been thinking up sales promotion activities on a daily basis.

'They used to sell Nile perch as Japanese sea bass, you know. Smile Sushi was one of the buyers. Nile perch, like we saw in the aquarium. That was why you chose that particular aquarium, wasn't it? Because you knew that that's the fish I was in charge of at work, and there's only a handful of aquariums in Japan that have them.'

'Nile perch …? Sorry, what …? I don't think I saw them.'

The word aquarium had elicited a reaction from Shōko, but she seemed flummoxed by what Eriko was saying. This expression sent ripples drifting across Eriko's formerly placid heart. The root of her tongue grew dry. Why did this woman so stubbornly refuse to show enthusiasm in her in the way that Eriko wanted her to? She could have at least perceived her as a woman who did a big, important job handling weird and wonderful food items. Maybe this was something that a contractual arrangement couldn't fix. Maybe it was Eriko's loss, for being drawn to someone like this in the first place. Seized by a reckless impulse, she grasped a dish of Japanese sea bass and set it down roughly in front of Shōko. Sheepishly, Shōko pushed the plate back in her direction.

'I think I'm better off steering clear of raw fish for the moment. I've got a bit of a bad stomach. Sorry.'

It was true that since arriving, the only thing to pass Shōko's lips had been tea. Now Eriko looked, she could see that she was off colour. As her best friend, she should have noticed immediately, Eriko reproached herself, and patted Shōko's back in a bid to comfort her. She didn't feel her gesture to be particularly forceful, but Shōko's fragile body jolted forward.

'Are you okay? If you're feeling bad I can come round to your place and take care of you at home, if you like?'

'No, that's okay. But thank you. I appreciate the offer. I'm sorry.'

Seeing the look of fear in Shōko's eyes as she batted off her suggestion, Eriko felt faintly hurt.

'You're not allowed to apologise. Point deducted! Promise me you won't say sorry any more. You apologise way too much. You've got to go back to your old happy-go-lucky self! It's boring if you're apologising the whole time.'

Shōko was on the verge of saying sorry again, but catching herself just in time, she pursed her lips and then smiled awkwardly.

'Well, anyway, a good rest at the onsen should sort you out in no time! You've been over-exerting yourself. Leave next week open, okay?'

Even as she said it, Eriko knew that there was no way Shōko had been overdoing it. Eriko perceived that inside, she was sneering. Try as she might, she couldn't rid herself of vexation towards this best friend of hers, who simply refused to act as she wanted her to.

Eriko was only on temporary leave from the first-rate company where she worked. Once she'd made her way back to herself, and stabilised her relationship with Shōko, she intended to go back to her former life. She would meet up with Shōko after work; at weekends they'd go and eat buffets at hotels, go away on mini-breaks. With a friend like that, she'd be even better able to focus on her work than she had been before. No longer would she have to pretend to have chosen to be alone at lunchtime; no longer would she have to try to get along with the temps, either. Not when she had the best friend of all time for her very own ...

The conversation was hardly flowing, and with Shōko looking peaky, their dinner finished far earlier than expected. Eriko had accumulated a stack of almost twenty plates while Shōko had just two. As Eriko and Shōko crossed under the overpass, a bike went sliding past them with two schoolgirls on it. Their bright, soaring laughter, their flapping skirts, their sweet watermelon scent all blended with the night breeze.

'Oh, look, she's giving her a backie!'

Eriko's eyes were caught by the white legs extending from the pleated skirt of the young girl perched on the luggage rack of the bike. As she watched the girls cycling off, she linked an arm through the slender one alongside hers. It was in that moment that she was struck by the sudden premonition that she would be alone for the rest of her life. How strange to feel something like that, she thought, when her friend was right next to her. Seeking salvation, she turned to Shōko and cooed, 'You gave me a backie on the way home from Denny's, remember?'

'Did I?'

'I'd love to do that again. Promise me you will? The next time we meet locally, come by bike. You promise?'

The two parted in front of Eriko's apartment building. Watching Shōko's figure receding into the distance, Eriko prayed that she would turn back to look at her, but that fragile back with its protruding bones moved steadily away. When Eriko finally passed through into the entrance lobby, Keiko was leaning against the railing, smoking. Not again, thought Eriko, averting her eyes.

'Are you still not back at work?'

'You've no need to worry about me. I'll be spending my time with Shōko now. We've resolved the misunderstanding between us, so it'll be girls' time every day! Going on mini-breaks, taking lessons together and so on. We're going to Hakone next week. I'm reclaiming the adolescence that I lost out on, thanks to you!'

This was revenge, Eriko thought triumphantly. Through her own perseverance, she'd finally managed to find a friend who would never let her down. Now Keiko would finally understand the loneliness, the grief that she'd experienced as a fifteen-year-old.

'Wow, that's a quick turnaround. Have you got dirt on her or something?'

Eriko was so taken aback she didn't know how to reply. To prevent Keiko from perceiving that she was flustered, she stared into the light that was blending with the darkness over Keiko's shoulder.

'Well, whatever, I'm not bothered. But I think you'd be better off taking a bit of care with your appearance. You're getting worse than me. You're always talking about girls this and girly that, but you're not a girl any more, Eriko. You're a middle-aged woman.'

What right did an unemployed woman, wearing fleece from head to toe, have to say such a thing, Eriko thought indignantly. Her shoulders held erect, she strode straight ahead.

Now that she came to think of it, though, Eriko couldn't remember the last time she'd been to the hairdresser – but this thought was dissolved by the sudden Christmassy smell. An ivy-scented night breeze grazed her cheek, reminding Eriko of the carol service they'd had at school. If she could still recall her memories from her teens this vividly, she thought, then she *was* still a girl.

All of a sudden, December was fast approaching.

# CHAPTER TWENTY-THREE

Even when Shōko closed her eyes, she couldn't get rid of the sight of her. She wished more than anything that she could leave the neighbourhood. If only she had a fixed income, or sufficient savings that she could move without having to rely on her husband to fund it. Then she wouldn't have to feel like she did, as if she were trapped inside a rusty birdcage. Why, oh why, had she quit her job? Or, more to the point: why, oh why, had she ever got involved with Eriko in the first place?

Wanting to rip out her hair in frustration, Shōko turned over heavily. Since yesterday, she'd felt so awful that she'd stayed curled up in bed without eating a thing, and her husband was worried about her. The tension between them that had defined their relationship of late had been suddenly swept away, and he was rushing around tending to her like a caring older brother.

'Are you okay?' he said now, as he appeared with a bowl of rice porridge with sliced umeboshi and beaten egg. 'You've been spending too much time on the blog recently. You've barely been going out. You need a proper rest.'

It seemed he'd shunned the ready-made stuff and had prepared the rice porridge from scratch, and there was a clear sweetness to its flavour. With the initial mouthful, the delicate taste suffused her body, and she felt herself reviving. For the first time, she felt ashamed of herself for relying so exclusively on time-saving recipes and fast food, on the basis that they were cheap and delicious, that cooking properly was too much trouble, and that it saved on the washing-up. The time that home-cooked food took to prepare was what gave it the power to touch people's hearts, she reflected.

'You know how I've been kind of tetchy recently? Well, work's been really tough. A big supermarket that's opened up close by is stealing away a lot of our customers, which means we're struggling to reach our sales targets, and all my trusted part-timers are quitting one after another. I think seeing you doing so well has made me panic a bit. But ultimately, I've come to the conclusion that if people other than me come to realise how great you are, then that's a good thing, and I have to do my best on my own terms. I've got an interview next week, and depending on the outcome, I might move to the sales team in the head office.'

Kensuke smiled, and his face, which had grown a little rounder recently, creased happily. Although Shōko told him he didn't need to, he wiped down her body with a hot, wet towel and changed her pyjamas. She felt the damp and steam passing across the tops of her thighs, the undersides of her knees. She'd slacked off shaving recently, and when he reached her armpits her shoulders tensed slightly in apprehension, but he didn't seem bothered by the hair there.

Staring up at the ceiling, Shōko thought to herself that if she let Kensuke get away, she would never again get this close to a perfect stranger. There was no way she could be like this with Hashimoto, who was currently at the peak of his attractiveness. Even if it were possible, it would take an extraordinary amount of time to get there.

Shōko had still not been able to come out and tell her husband about the onsen trip with Eriko. She was sure that his reaction would be one of bewilderment; that he'd tell her not to go. How could she tell him that it had all turned out to be a misunderstanding on her part, that Eriko's behaviour was perfectly above board, and the two of them were now best friends, in a way that didn't sound like she was lying outright? She had no idea.

Why had she been so oblivious to what her husband was going through recently, she now asked herself. What had she been thinking, cheating on a kind and considerate man like this? Feeling ashamed and disgusted at herself, and utterly miserable, Shōko folded herself over and gritted her teeth. She was no different from her dad, who'd made her mother suffer for such a long time without ever having had any intention of doing so. It wasn't only that, either. She'd created a blot on their life together that would never go away. Thinking of the text she'd received from Hashimoto yesterday, sour bile rose up from her stomach:

*The strange woman we bumped into at the aquarium – isn't that the daughter of the owner's friend? It'd be really bad if she told people about us. I wouldn't know how to explain, and I'm guessing you don't want your husband to find out either. Maybe we should stop seeing each other for the moment.*

The cowardly bastard, she thought. She felt no relief at the idea that they'd be ending things definitively as opposed to letting them drag on; instead, she was filled with a seething rage. She read his text once more now, then hurled the phone at the wall. It fell down onto the bed and rebounded to the side.

Why was he permitted to get off scot-free, when he'd worked so hard to chase her down? It was true that she had probably been starved of male attention other than from her husband. She knew that it couldn't have lasted long anyway. It was destined to fade, regardless of whether or not she responded to it. The idea that she would be paying such a high price for a spot of messing around, not even a proper fling, was wild to her. Thanks to a kiss that had come out of a momentary lapse in caution, Eriko Shimura now had her by the throat, and she had lost her freedom of movement and choice as a result. Shōko could now do nothing without Eriko's permission. She had less liberty than a collared pet. Eriko was a veritable volcano of a woman, the kind of person who might lose her temper and erupt at any tiny thing, and so all her orders had to be obeyed. Even as Shōko lay there in bed, she had the feeling that Eriko was somehow watching over her, and she felt unable to relax at all. Since the day at the aquarium she hadn't slept, and hadn't been able to eat much either.

Now she was being forced to go to Hakone. The two of them had never spent longer than two hours in each other's company, and now they'd have to be together in the baths, and while sleeping. Bad enough that Shōko had never done this with any other woman – now she had to do it with Eriko. With the thought that she had no choice but to go, Shōko's nose grew stuffed and she heard a ringing at the back of her head.

Kensuke had been wary of Eriko ever since she'd shown up in the lobby of their apartment building. Shōko could potentially lie and say she was going to her dad's, but knowing Eriko, she would doubtless write all about the trip on the blog in Shōko's name. She had to think up something to tell him that would convince him, and quickly.

How on earth had things got to this point? She felt as though, if she were to tell her husband the truth about what had happened, she would be confessing not only her infidelity but also her own shallowness and self-obsession. The idea was petrifying. To him, at least, she wanted to remain a cheerful person, a woman who didn't give off any sense of clinginess.

Craving a cigarette, which she'd been cutting back on of late, Shōko finally stood up from the bed. She headed to the living room, dragging her heavy lower body, and pulled the pack of Camels and a lighter from the back of the bookshelf. She lit the cigarette and, savouring its sweet aroma, lay back on the sofa. Breathing the smoke in, her tattered feelings settled slightly.

Shōko looked out at the clothes flapping about on the balcony of the apartment block opposite. She could hear the loudspeaker announcement from what she thought was a roasted sweet potato van. Beyond the curtain stretched the bright pale sky, the sunlight falling on her midriff. She hadn't been cleaning of late, and piles of dust and hair had built up in the corners of the room. The air felt dry – it was probably time to think about buying a humidifier. The morning passed in the way that it used to until not long before. Ironically enough, now that Eriko had seized her account and she no longer needed to update her blog, Shōko's days had regained some of their former quietude and ease.

It wasn't like she was paid for the blog, and there was no obligation for her to write it. The agreement with Satoko hadn't been formalised. In fact, perhaps fed up with Shōko's hesitancy to take the plunge, Satoko hadn't been in touch much lately. What on earth had Shōko been getting herself so worked up over, when ultimately that was the extent of the enthusiasm that people had had about it? The blog had started out as a bit of fun, but then she'd fallen headlong into it, and had started experiencing all the cravings of a drug addict, leaving her incapable of being present in the rest of her life. Whatever she laid eyes on, she could only think about in terms of a potential blog post.

A little while ago, she'd taken a look at the entry that Eriko had written in her stead. Eriko's word choice and the angles at which she took her photos were perfect:

*Today I went to the conveyor-belt sushi place with my best friend, who lives locally. I'm obsessed by the engawa they have there – a steal at ninety-eight yen! The amazing thing about conveyor-belt sushi is that you can have tea, and dessert, all in the same place without having to move, which is ideal for neverending catchups with friends. Every time I visit, there's some wacky new sushi topping to marvel at (this time it was tuna mayo with aubergine, lol)! I so much prefer it to stuffy, expensive sushi restaurants.*

How very Eriko, Shōko thought, to refer to herself so brazenly as her 'best friend'. Still, the entry was convincing enough that, if Shōko had been asked if she herself had written it, she might have to think for a moment. The thought that her individuality, her writing skills, were limited enough to be so easily feigned gave her a pang for a moment, but ultimately, she'd already resigned herself to this reality. The awareness had been dawning on her since she'd begun appearing in women's magazines. In fact, Shōko was coming to reflect, quite detachedly, that maybe it would be possible to entrust the blog to Eriko completely, to wash her hands of it. She felt miraculously undisturbed by the prospect. The intensity of her prior involvement, how thoroughly she'd staked out her territory online, now seemed to her like a dream. What mattered far more to her was regaining her sense of peace.

From where she lay facing up on the sofa, Shōko lit her second cigarette. Watching the ribbons of smoke drifting up towards the ceiling, it struck her what a contented, secure and complete existence she'd had before, and tears pricked her eyes. She'd been without worries, she'd had her husband to protect her, and she'd valued the elements composing her daily life. She had perceived herself as someone who, unable to feel like she belonged either in her hometown or at the workplace, had simply drifted from one thing to another, but she now saw that she'd been in possession of everything that she wanted without realising it.

While it wasn't especially well kept or tidy, the living room surrounding her didn't look remotely out of order. The manga and magazines she and Kensuke liked were arranged in stacks. Opened bags of snacks were sealed with laundry pegs. There was nothing here that felt out of control. Sure, there was nothing thrill-inducing about this way of living, but by the same token, it lacked unpleasant tension and disappointment.

Perhaps this was what she had been craving so badly as a young girl. It wasn't that she was lazy, as Eriko had once reproached her for being. Rather, she had simply been moving towards what she wanted, slowly and carefully – and then, she had secured it for herself. There had been no need for Shōko to carry the judgements of a deranged woman like that around inside her. Why was Eriko so disdainful of her way of living?

Before she knew it, Shōko had come to value other people's opinions of her over her own assessment of herself. In her eagerness to transmit to the world the feelings and opinions that she should by rights have kept to herself, her eagerness for their evaluation of them, she'd been neglecting her life with her husband and the changing seasons right in front of her. Being accepted by other women, releasing a book, shifting the way that other homemakers felt about themselves, becoming a person of importance – all these goals now seemed irrelevant to her. None of that had any meaning anyway. It was the everyday moments with Kensuke that held the most significance for her. That was what the aquarium incident had shown her.

Turning over on the sofa, she felt the rice porridge slopping about inside her stomach, forming waves.

She had to get Eriko to delete the photos of her kissing Hashimoto. Then she would cut her connection with her, and return to her regular existence. The question was, how? Shōko let out a great sigh. She felt one of the springs in the sofa pinging beneath her.

The whole affair felt like navigating a labyrinth – even if she were to come up with a plan for moving steadily through, she had no conviction she'd ever reach her goal. It all seemed so arduous. Even the thought of getting up again was too much now she was lying down. Besides, if effort alone was enough to get you places, then she wouldn't be living this kind of existence. She knew for certain that she didn't have either the wisdom or the energy to get herself out of this situation with Eriko. Maybe if she did exactly as Eriko said for a while, things at least wouldn't get any worse.

Which meant she didn't have to do anything. Smiling, Shōko stared out again at the apartments beyond the curtain.

She would obey Eriko, mindlessly. She'd await her instructions. This way, her life with Kensuke would be protected. In one way, it was maybe quite a cushy deal. She'd do what Eriko said while internally poking her tongue out at her, just like she'd done with the teachers at school.

Keiko's words filtered back to her now: *you don't have to do anything*. In that moment, Shōko had felt a momentary surge of admiration for the woman in front of her, who drifted through the void totally alone. Her way of neither expecting things of others nor having others' expectations placed on her represented a kind of ideal state, Shōko felt. And yet, Shōko knew that right now she was a far more ethereal presence even than Keiko. She couldn't even bring herself to say the words she needed to say. If she ended up disappearing, becoming invisible, that was okay with her.

The windows, which she never cleaned, stippled with dusty raindrops, were firmly shut, and yet it seemed to Shōko that she'd been enveloped by the air outside. The late-autumn breeze that carried her was chilly and sweet, with an innocent quality that instilled in her the desire to join in its play. She wanted to become a leaf and be swept up in its momentum. The desire wasn't far from wanting to become the air itself. Becoming one with the air and wafting about was more or less the same as being here and doing nothing. All she had to do was entrust herself to the wind, the waves.

The roasted sweet potato van seemed to have pulled up outside her apartment. The drawn-out voice of the tannoy announcement grew louder, and was then cut off suddenly, as if by a guillotine.

## CHAPTER TWENTY-FOUR

Every day, the Odakyu Romancecar would slice effortlessly through the part of town in which Eriko and Shōko lived, scattering wind and sunlight as it went. Locals would see the carriages of white and Vermeer blue go streaking across the edge of their vision, like straight lines across a canvas. Eriko, who had grown up with this scenery, was so accustomed to glimpsing the Romancecar that it barely ever occurred to her to board one as a passenger. The same was true of her parents. She'd ridden one just once, on a family holiday when she was very young, but her memories of its interior, or what she'd seen when she got there, were very hazy. She wasn't even sure whether the destination had been Hakone.

Now, sitting alongside Shōko in the very front seats of this train that was so much a part of her everyday made Eriko feel a bit like she'd leapt inside the reproduction of the Matisse painting that hung on her wall at home, and was going further and further in. Even more than when she'd set foot inside the love hotel with her manager, or decided to take a break from work, she had the sense of having stepped outside her daily life, in a way from which it would be impossible to return. She was crossing that line of her own volition. Maybe she was finally on the verge of becoming something other than herself.

At the very front of the carriage was a semi-circular window of convex glass, through which the tracks appeared remarkably close by, appearing only to disappear again immediately. It felt as though they were being covered up by the lower half of her body, Eriko thought, resting a hand on her abdomen.

The seats were as comfortable as any business-class chairs on a plane. She saw a bowling alley pass by, and a supermarket chain that you found only in this area of the city. Soon they'd pass the neighbourhood that they both lived in.

For a moment, Eriko was filled with a powerful urge to turn back – to return home to the time that felt like an extension of her own childhood, where she could curl up in the blanket suffused with her own smell, knowing that her parents were looking over her, and simply await the meals her mother would make. The desire confused her. Why would she feel something like that?

It was bizarre to be afraid of what lay ahead, when that was a parade of things that she had wanted so badly. Perturbed, she attempted to put herself in a positive frame of mind. If she let herself get anxious, she might be dragged down to a place from which there was no return. That, at the very least, she wanted to avoid. She'd travelled long distances for work numerous times – this trip was only taking her to the next prefecture! The nerves, the vulnerability she felt must be about the presence of another person. Eriko now glanced at Shōko, whose body was pressed up against the windowpane, smelling of fabric conditioner and sunlight. The old jersey top that was the source of these aromas was crumpled and bobbled, gesturing towards a more intimate, domestic side of Shōko that Eriko didn't yet know. She imagined that Shōko's husband had the exact same smell. This relaxed family environment enveloping Shōko like an aura created a strong flare of rejection and envy in Eriko. She wanted to sleep with Shōko's husband, to make him a shared possession of theirs.

'I'm taking a trip to Hakone with a friend, for a bit of a change of scenery. Don't worry about me!'

How momentous it had felt to utter those words to her parents. Indeed, it had made Eriko think that the worst part about having no friends was being incapable of saying things like this to her mother and father. Quite possibly, her parents' belief that nobody liked their daughter was harder for Eriko to bear than the reality of being all on her own. At this announcement her mother's thin eyelids twitched, and a stern expression fell over her father's face. Summoning all of her enthusiasm, Eriko started up her computer and talked them through Hallie B's blog, explaining what kind of a person she was and conveying how perfectly well they got on. After listening to their daughter's explanations for close to an hour, her father asked slowly, stressing every syllable, 'You're sure about her, right? You're sure she's someone you can trust? Just remember that you're currently taking time off work. There are many people bearing the brunt of your absence. If you do anything irresponsible, you'll be betraying the people who have your back.'

*You don't have anyone that you can trust like that, do you, Dad?* The words rose up to the back of Eriko's throat. All this time, she'd been mulling over why it was that her father had no friends, but she couldn't alight upon an answer.

There was no way that her quiet, kind, forbearing father contained the miserable, ridiculous, inexplicable parts that existed within her. Just the thought that he might brought a terrible shame and fury rising up in Eriko, so that she felt as though her whole body was crumbling. Was it possible that the trait of making life hard for oneself was genetically transmitted? The very thought made her look away from her father, gave her the urge to dash out of the house – the last place of sanctuary available to her.

Both her parents seemed suspicious of Eriko's attempts at persuasion, but when she'd stressed to them Hallie B's renown as a blogger and mentioned the book deal, handed over the details of their hotel, and walked them through a detailed itinerary, they reluctantly let her go. She'd spent the entirety of the last few days preparing for the trip.

So why did she feel so on edge? Why was her throat dry as a pebbledash wall?

Eriko took a sip of the sake-in-a-cup that she'd bought in Shinjuku where they'd boarded the train, and gazed at Shōko's profile, attempting to etch it into her memory. Static electricity had stuck the ends of her short hair to the windowpane, creating a sculptural object like a small birdcage. She took in the flecks of dust hovering at the tips of Shōko's eyelashes. Even the grain of her butter-coloured skin and its soft, downy coating stood out clearly in this light. Shōko was far from a great beauty, and yet Eriko couldn't take her eyes off her. She knew that Shōko's life, her perspective, were quite narrow, but it was as if her heart was always yearning for somewhere other than where she was. Eriko was ineluctably drawn to that precarious quality about her, which suggested she could spread her wings and take off at any moment. She wondered if the men who'd been with Shōko had thought something similar as they gazed at her.

Now, though, there would be no more escaping. Eriko had emerged victorious – over that young man, over Shōko's husband, and indeed, over any other of Shōko's men. Finally, she was creating with Shōko a world that men couldn't enter.

As Eriko listened to the sound of the train, she totted up the gains that she had brought about through her own efforts. She was currently heading to a Hakone onsen with her best friend – in other words, she was finally doing the kinds of things that adult women did. All the frustration and anguish that she'd experienced up until now had been wiped clean. Or rather, she had to wipe it clean, now. After repeating this to herself internally, Eriko leaned forward to stare right into Shōko's face.

'Look! We're about to pass our neighbourhood.'

'Oh, yeah,' Shōko responded without enthusiasm, glancing at Eriko as if registering her presence for the first time. In the sunlight, her eyes looked pale and somehow glazed over. This was supposed to be a girls' getaway, where they felt totally comfortable in one another's presence, and Eriko would have liked to have a little more to work with. The first night they'd met, Shōko had struck her as someone with plentiful wisdom and quick intuition. Perhaps sensing her frustration, Shōko now asked, 'You've lived in this part of town your whole life, right? Have you never thought about leaving?'

It was rare for Shōko to ask questions. What a truly perfect moment, Eriko thought. Here they were in a Romancecar, heading for an onsen mini-break together, talking intimately with one another. She felt suddenly so euphoric, she didn't know what to do with herself. Entreating herself to calm down, she smiled a pensive smile.

'I probably will end up moving away if I get married, but when push comes to shove, I do really like this part of town.'

This was neither a lie nor an exaggeration, but a faithful expression of her true feelings. Of course she was sometimes taken by the impulse to leave everything behind and experience a wholly new environment, but she couldn't identify any real reason to leave, and even if she were to, she was fairly sure she'd end up ultimately searching for some place that closely emulated this one anyway.

'Oh, really? I was so desperate to get away from home. I hated my hometown and my family. Particularly my dad.'

Right at this moment, the very neighbourhood where Eriko had grown up was visible on the other side of the tracks, in the direction in which Shōko's gaze was pinned. Sighting her local supermarket, elementary school and shopping arcade from a different angle to usual if anything inflated the sense of familiarity she felt towards them. In her joy, a strange noise emerged from Eriko's throat. Driven by some particular feeling, Shōko had spoken to her, spontaneously, about her upbringing. This moment surely marked a turning point for their relationship. Everything would be plain sailing from here. She felt as though they'd surely just experienced the high point of their trip – and so early on. Her heart was thumping.

'Oh – really. Really! I'd love to hear more. What's he like, then, your father?'

'He's a typical country landlord. He owns an apartment building in front of the station, a parking lot and a mountain. A mountain that looms over the whole town.'

'Wow, so you're quite the little princess!'

That the discovery that Shōko had been born into an affluent family delighted Eriko this much was surprising to her. She felt like she had understood why it was that, even when Shōko's lifestyle was slapdash, she managed to keep an air of class about her.

'But God knows how much that's all worth now. It's such an out-of-the way location, anyway. My dad doesn't seem to feel worried, but I don't think he has any assets at all. He's not a bad person but ... he's so reckless about everything. His behaviour is very odd. Most of the time he's joking around and grinning and won't say anything of substance, but then he'll suddenly lose it, and get *really* mad, like a yakuza or something. He doesn't know how to communicate with people. His great loves are drinking and pachinko, and he slobs around, filling his time with those. You can never tell whether he's in a good mood or not, either. Ach, I can't really explain it. It's just I … I find him difficult. He's not a bad person, but I get so tense whenever I'm around him. Everyone in my family's the same. Ever since my mum left, both my brothers have kept their distance from him. Now it sounds as though my stepmum has upped and left too, so God knows what will become of him.'

This was the longest that Shōko had ever spoken about anything. Eriko shifted in her seat in discomfort. She'd never heard of such a messed-up father as this one. If he was violent, or made no money, that would be easier to comprehend. What was hard was men like this, about whom it was impossible to say whether they were good or bad. Yet Eriko felt that she didn't want Shōko to know that this was her experience: she might take it as Eriko looking down on her upbringing, and she was also scared of revealing her lack of experience with matters of this kind. She even felt a faint sense of anger – both towards Shōko, for having a hard-to-read background, and towards her father, who had made that the case. She tried to formulate a response that wouldn't rub Shōko up the wrong way.

'You should be meeting him where he is. He's an important member of your family, who gave you your life, after all. You have to be brave and face him. There are plenty of people with far worse situations than yours. Why not stop blaming other people and try putting in the work?'

None of this was untrue, as it happened. It was thanks to Eriko summoning up her courage that she'd managed to resolve her and Shōko's misunderstanding, and smooth over relations between them. Feeling this to be a far more authentic response than making a half-hearted show of understanding, Eriko felt a burst of self-satisfaction. 'You've got to tell people how you really feel. Truthfully.'

For a moment, Shōko gazed wide-eyed right into Eriko's eyes, and then she looked away.

'You're right. I'm not making enough of an effort. I've always known that. It's just that when I'm around him, I don't know how to make an effort. I don't know what the solution is. There's nothing I want to say to him.'

'Ah, that's kind of tragic …'

Sensing that she'd been pushed away, Eriko panicked. Not knowing what expression to adopt, she let out a sigh, pulling something like a wry smile. She felt the same as Shōko, that she didn't know what the solution was, and yet somehow Shōko's honest confession had led her further away from Eriko. Shōko smiled a faint, pained-looking smile, and turned her eyes back outside the window. Their neighbourhood was now far behind them. Small patches of trees she assumed were parks and the platforms for stations that she knew by name only rushed past.

'Say more, if you'd like. I'd like to know more about your family.'

'Sorry, that's it, I'm afraid. You've heard everything there is to say about my dad. Really, there's nothing more. Finito.'

With that, Shōko closed her eyes, apparently signalling a reluctance to be spoken to any further. Her eyelashes cast a shadow on her cheeks. Replete with the anger and frustration of being rejected once again, Eriko wanted to smash the windowpane open and jump right through. Where, and how, had she gone wrong? She checked back over her words from dozens of seconds previously, but couldn't identify any definitive blunders. If anything, her utterances seemed to her utterly ordinary – perhaps too ordinary.

She'd shown her understanding, and hadn't said anything off. She simply wanted to create a nice, gentle atmosphere between them – otherwise this holiday of theirs, and all the time she'd spent planning it, would be wasted. Even this prickly feeling she was battling seemed unforgivable to her. Desperately she clawed around for a diverting conversation topic.

'At the Pola Museum of Art, they sell cookies with pictures of Monet's *Water Lilies* on the box. I was thinking they'd make great souvenirs! Is there anywhere you want to go? Did you think about it?'

'No, not especially. My priority is to space out in the onsen. Otherwise I'm happy going where you want to go. Will you wake me when we get there?'

With that, Shōko closed her eyes and kept them shut. Eriko knew that she was only pretending to be asleep, but for some reason she felt she couldn't shake her and say as much. At the same time, she felt something akin to envy towards Shōko, who was doing things very much at her own pace.

Maybe there was some part of her that felt relieved, though. She faced forward, reclined her seat and let out a small sigh. If Shōko had gone on speaking about her family, Eriko wouldn't have known what to do. Eriko had never known anybody who'd grown up in such a complicated home environment before, and so she didn't know what the appropriate response would have been. Or maybe she had known people from similar situations, but they hadn't opened up to her about them. Come to think about it, she had never shared her feelings with anybody who was in a very different position to her own.

When dealing with something like poverty in Tanzania, Eriko could process it as data and deliver a verdict. Confronted by the experiences of an individual other than herself, though, she would find her head shrouded in a haze. The haze encouraged her to resign herself to the fact that it was impossible for someone like her to truly understand other people. When she tried to bat it away and move forward, she would always find Keiko standing in her path. There would be the face of the young girl who'd pushed her away as if her life depended on doing so, wide-eyed and trembling as though she'd encountered an unknown animal. Eriko couldn't go any further. What if her imagination was very different to the reality? What if she ended up terrifying and hurting the other person? The thought made her body shut down.

That was why she needed the writing of Hallie B so badly, allowing her as it did to feel connected to someone. It wasn't this incomprehensible Shōko that she wanted, but that old Hallie B, who was so easy to feel close with.

Eriko wanted to be reconciled with the world. The train passed through a neighbourhood that looked identical to her own, but which she'd never visited. There was the sign for the same supermarket as her local, rows of the same build of houses. How great it would be if she were possessed with a kind of telepathic power that enabled her to understand the feelings of another person in one fell swoop, she thought. With a power like that, maybe she wouldn't need to book the very front seat of the Romancecar. Maybe she wouldn't need to go on holiday with a perfect stranger at all.

# CHAPTER TWENTY-FIVE

Stepping off the train onto the platform of Hakone Yumoto Station, Shōko wrinkled up her nose. This was the same smell as the mountain air back home. The temperature here was cooler, and though the sky that she glimpsed through the roof of the platform was clouded, it seemed high and somehow invigorating.

This was the sweet, moist scent that filled the garden of the house in which she'd grown up, where wet leaves gathered on the ground and silently rotted. She imagined that, if she were to share that impression, the city girl beside her would have no idea what she meant.

The mountain that Shōko's father owned was the biggest in the region. At its foot was a bamboo grove of the kind that often appeared in fairytales; come spring, their uncle, who lived locally, would come to dig up the bamboo shoots. Shōko and her brothers all preferred her mother's rice with bamboo shoots when it had been left to cool, its flavour deepening. Her father had loved umeboshi paste wrapped in bamboo leaves, while Shōko found it unbearably sour – and she didn't like the sharp taste of raw bamboo shoots either. On the whole, her father left all the housework and childcare to her mother, but when it came to the cooking projects he embarked on when the mood struck him, he was terrifyingly strict about every aspect of their consumption, from how it should be eaten to when it must be finished. Most of the meals he put his hand to were carb-rich, often so strongly flavoured they made her tongue tingle.

'Do you want to go and get something to tide us over at the soba restaurant in front of the station? I found it in the guidebook, it's homemade and apparently very well known.' Eriko darted a cautious glance in Shōko's direction. By now Shōko had stopped feeling irritated or offended by these appraising looks.

Eriko's overbearing advice in response to Shōko's confession about her family had liberated Shōko in some way. Until that point, there had been some part of her that hadn't been able to entirely throw away the hope that they might some day come to understand one another. Quite unexpectedly, Shōko had found herself wounded by Eriko's comments – and this hurt allowed her finally to cede her hope. Eriko wasn't ever going to understand her, whatever she said. It was best not to think of herself as dealing with a person – to imagine the figure beside her as some kind of human-shaped bolster. Come to think of it, with her immaculate looks and extreme behaviour, Eriko wasn't dissimilar to a puppet. When Shōko took the decision to think of this as a holiday she'd come on alone, and make the most of it in that way, she felt the colours around her suddenly growing brighter.

She found it amusing that the only type of person who could stand to spend long periods of time together with this woman were people like herself: undiscerning, with a huge amount of time on their hands. Past the age of thirty, those people were truly few and far between. Considering Keiko and herself, it seemed as though Eriko had a tendency to fixate on lazy women, who drifted half-heartedly through their lives. It seemed as though she enjoyed getting close to people like that, and then coercing them into becoming more like her. In which case, would it not be better to search out neurotic, overbearing elite types like herself from the beginning?

Shōko held up her mobile phone to the Romancecar that was stopped at the platform and took a few photos. Exiting through the ticket gates, they browsed the souvenir shops inside the station. Shōko didn't dislike visiting new places and trying regional specialities she'd not tasted before, but was always put off going on holiday by the laboriousness of travel arrangements and packing. The same was true of Kensuke, and since their honeymoon in Thailand, the two of them hadn't been anywhere very far from home. In a way, it was maybe a good thing that she'd been dragged along like this. She picked up a jar of mountain vegetables from the refrigerated compartment to check its price, although she didn't especially want it. She remembered that she'd taken something similar home as a souvenir for her family from a school trip in middle school. The jar seemed just as expensive to her now as it had then.

'Are you going to buy that?' Eriko asked, darting a glance at her hand gripping the jar. Since they'd arrived at Hakone, Eriko's gestures seemed to Shōko to have grown more performative than ever, and her demeanour more and more like that of a teenage girl.

*Everything's going fine. Eriko's very gung ho about it all.*

She'd already sent Kensuke three texts before getting off the Romancecar.

The explanation she'd offered him was that Eriko's strange behaviour in the past was the result of a mini-breakdown; that she'd not really had many friends in her life, so she'd got a bit overexcited when she met Shōko; and that Eriko's mother had requested that Shōko go along with her on holiday. Even then he'd been reluctant to give his blessing, but had eventually been won over by Shōko's persistence, and had agreed to let her go, on the condition that she texted him frequently with updates.

Shōko was confident that, so long as Eriko stayed quiet about the Hashimoto thing, her husband wouldn't figure it out. For better or worse, Kensuke wasn't the type to harbour suspicions. He accepted what was in front of him at face value, and was unlikely to seize upon the shadow that had passed through their life and recognise it for what it was.

Across the wide road outside the station were two shopping arcades running parallel to one another, lined with an endless stretch of restaurants and shops selling traditional handicrafts. The soba restaurant Eriko had found in the guidebook lay at the corner of one of those. When they slid aside the latticed door of well-loved dark wood, the smell of warm bonito dashi came drifting out. The two sat facing each other at seats by the wall. Shōko soon located her beloved sardine soba on the menu, and Eriko, after deliberating endlessly, ordered what was apparently a local speciality of brothless soba with tempura and dipping sauce.

The sound of Eriko chirping on about this and that receded, and seemed to dissolve into the steam rising from the large bowl of soba noodles carried over and set down in front of her. Maybe this was how things were, Shōko thought as she used her chopsticks to break into the large sardine laid out flat across the top of the bowl, moving a piece to her mouth along with some noodles. Maybe many of the women who appeared so close to one another were actually only putting on a show of listening to what the other said, making half-hearted responses to a stream of conversation they didn't really care about. Her eyes landed on other pairs or groups of not-so-young women in the restaurant. She imagined they were all probably stay-at-home wives, or else colleagues, working professionals who had weekdays off. She couldn't see what looked like a single couple.

She remembered something that Hashimoto had told her: that these days, you saw more groups of women than you did couples at Tokyo Disneyland. She hadn't thought much about it at the time, but the fact that he knew this presumably meant he'd been to Disneyland with someone not that long ago.

Most bloggers would show off about their female friendships, their frenzied battle to demonstrate the depth of their connections with other women a clear sign that they believed this was where their value lay.

But a battle fought for what purpose? Because they didn't want to be lonely? Because they wanted to prove to themselves and to society that they were doing something meaningful? Everyone knew that romance between men and women often didn't go well, and even when it did, it would be submerged beneath the realities of daily life. Did these people want to protect the illusion that female friendship, alone, could continue to endure and sparkle?

The sardine soba was not only reasonably priced but thoroughly delicious. The sardine wasn't overly fishy in its taste, and the noodles had been boiled to perfection. As far as their hotel went, where they would head to next, it sounded as though Eriko had come up with a price that she thought would be manageable for Shōko. Shōko had stopped finding that kind of consideration either welcome or troublesome. She drank down the hot, sweet-sour broth. Her throat quivered all the way down to her chest, her body rejoicing at its flavour.

Somewhat flustered by the realisation that she was managing to feel perfectly at peace in this scenario, Shōko swallowed a fishy burp. As the buildings outside the train window had grown progressively lower, and the amount of visible greenery increased, she'd felt the truth about her connection to the woman next to her blurring in her mind. Losing sight of the fact that she was being blackmailed into coming along, Shōko had started to feel as though maybe they really were friends, and she was travelling on the train of her own volition.

Maybe I'm the kind of person who's just fine whoever they're with, Shōko articulated to herself. Which meant, anyone would do for her as a companion. Wasn't that why everyone ended up leaving her in the end?

In order to get rid of this thought, she shook a healthy sprinkling of shichimi over her noodles.

But no, she was wrong. Kensuke was different. Kensuke, she would not lose. At the very least, she was in a far better position than the woman sitting opposite her.

'Oh, no! I forgot to take a photo of your sardine soba for the blog!' Shōko looked up to see Eriko holding her phone in her hands, a guilty expression on her face. In front of her sat the tempura and noodles that had been brought over, as yet untouched.

Shōko looked down at her bowl, which was more or less empty.

'That's okay. I've eaten most of mine. Just take the one that looks better.'

'But then it'll look like Hallie B had the tempura, and that's not true.'

Eriko cocked her head, frowning inflexibly. Here was a person who was incapable of phoning it in, Shōko thought – a person who had likely never skived off from anything.

'That's okay. I like tempura. Just say that's mine.'

Eriko shook her hair and nodded. She began making minor adjustments to the food, setting straight the bamboo tray on which the noodles were piled, and using her chopsticks to reposition the tail of the tempura prawn. As Shōko watched her manipulate her phone camera with a nervous expression, endlessly retaking the photo, it struck her how tense she looked. Shōko's nerves, meanwhile, seemed to have been soothed by her soba.

Given that they were stuck in this situation, they might as well at least have a decent conversation. With this thought, Shōko decided to bring up a topic she thought Eriko might like. Yet almost immediately she bumped her head against a wall: she didn't know what such a topic would be. She had no idea of Eriko's tastes and preferences. Ultimately, she didn't know anything at all about Eriko.

'Are you watching anything on TV at the moment? I'm really into the drama screening at ten o'clock on Thursday.'

It was a slapstick comedy, the lead role was played by a famous young actor. The storyline was tame enough – a selfish, arrogant woman ends up having to fake a marriage to the son of her father's servant – but the dialogue was great, as were the women's outfits. She and Kensuke looked forward to watching it every week. Eriko, who had finally finished photographing her noodles and was gazing in satisfaction at the shots, now lifted her face in pleasure.

'Oh, that one! You wrote about it on your blog, so I watched one episode. I wasn't sure about it ...'

'You didn't like it?'

Eriko gave a troubled smile. 'I didn't dislike it, I just felt like I couldn't really relate to the main character.'

'Relate to her?'

'Yeah. I can't get into something if I can't relate to the people in it.'

Shōko had never watched light entertainment of that kind through that lens, and looked bewildered, rolling the unfamiliar-tasting candy that Eriko had fed her around her mouth. Eriko immediately grew loquacious.

'It's impossible to identify with a girl that young, beautiful and selfish. Also, I don't care what the circumstances are, I feel like living with a man you don't even love and then contemplating staging a kidnapping is messed-up behaviour. I don't like the kinds of women who are oblivious to the burden they're placing on everyone around them. And the worst part was when …'

On and on she went, as if a dam had burst. There was no room for Shōko to get a word in edgeways.

It appeared as though Eriko's assessment of TV programmes wasn't based on whether or not something was entertaining. No, Eriko imposed her own yardsticks even in the world of fiction, diligently measuring everything as though it were a professional assignment and finding it impossible to enjoy anything that didn't meet her standards. Feeling as if she'd discovered yet another troublesome aspect to Eriko, Shōko's warm, full stomach suddenly grew heavier. It was fine not to agree, surely? But all of a sudden the conversation had become a detailed takedown of the protagonist's actions.

If this was how Eriko felt, Shōko could understand why she might have become so protective over the blog. Since Hallie B's orientation had shifted, Eriko hadn't distanced herself from it, but rather, clung on even tighter. For Eriko, differences in values between her and others were something to be exorcised. Elements that caused her loneliness had to be corrected. Shōko had no doubt that, even as they sat here now, Eriko was judging her every move. How stifling it was! The idea that she'd ever attempted to be close to Eriko now seemed ridiculous. This woman saw only what she wanted to see. She had been born with a disposition that didn't require friends; Eriko herself was the only one who couldn't see it. Maybe Shōko should tell her.

'But you actually like those kinds of crappy dramas? You can let those kinds of women off the hook? That comes as a bit of a shock, honestly. It's disappointing.'

Saying this, Eriko gave an exaggerated frown, then leaned in and nudged Shōko's shoulder. Shōko was itching to be done with this topic already but Eriko was clearly not prepared to let it drop.

'Watching selfish women like that, who know nothing about how the world works, getting carried away, I want to reach out and give them a really good slapping. I guess I've got a bit of a big-sister streak in me like that. I can't rest until I've said what I want to say.'

With bold gestures, Eriko reached her hands out into the space in front of her, wringing the neck of an imaginary figure, then slapping them. Her elbow knocked over the bottle of shichimi, and a burst of citrus aroma rose up across the table. Eriko leaned in to scoop up the bottle, darting a glance over to the next table along as she did so. A group of four middle-aged women who had all ordered different items from the menu were sampling each other's noodles. They were enjoying themselves, paying no attention to Eriko and Shōko. Eriko immediately returned her gaze to their table and recommenced her diatribe on the TV series. Shōko felt a cold sweat film her body. Her vicarious embarrassment was greater than if she'd messed something up herself. She understood that for Eriko, what had just happened represented a moment where she'd got so into talking about TV with her best friend that she'd lost track of herself. She was doubtless ecstatic that, from a bystander's perspective, they looked like they got on fantastically. What Eriko wanted more than anything wasn't friends per se, but to be seen as a person who had friends.

'I get it. Relatability is important to you.'

'Isn't it important to everyone? Is that weird?'

'It's not weird. But it makes me wonder why you started reading my blog. You and I are so different.'

Looking down at her empty bowl, the words came slipping out. Eriko finally reached out her chopsticks towards the now thoroughly cold tempura, as if she'd finally remembered its existence, and took a bite.

'What? We're the same! Our interests and personalities are polar opposites, but at the root we're the same. That's why I felt we could become friends. If we were there to support each other, we could become an invincible duo.'

'An invincible duo?' Shōko repeated, hesitantly. 'Are you planning to go into battle with a vast evil organisation or something?'

'I want to go into battle.' Eriko slurped her noodles and swallowed, then looked dead seriously at Shōko as she said this. 'I want to build up my energy by talking with you and enjoying our shared interests, and then use it to take on something big.'

'What kind of "something" is that?'

'The thing that sets us against one another.'

'The thing that sets us against one another …?'

Not understanding what she was getting at, Shōko cocked her head. Eriko put her chopsticks politely down with both hands. 'It's not only Lake Victoria. Even in waters across Japan, ecosystems are being destroyed by the unregulated influx of invasive species. The creatures have to compete over food, ecosystems, mating periods. It doesn't end until one of the species is wiped out. The result? The creation of a monster. The invasive species have been set against each other by humans. It's not that they want to fight. They should by rights be pitied. It's the same with us. You know the things that people always say about women – that they can never get on, that female friendships are catty and emotional, that women always end up competing with each other. Since I joined my company, it's been ingrained in me by the men there that women are stupid and don't know how to collaborate. Gradually, without realising, I came to believe what they were saying. In my desperation to be treated as their equal, I did my best to become someone who was different to ordinary women. To be strong and straightforward, rational and not overly fussy … Now I wonder why I tried so hard to change who I was for the sake of the judgements imposed on women by men who are jealous of their closeness – or else, by women allying themselves with men. The reason that women's competitiveness over minor issues like marriage, or kids, or looks, stops them from getting along, even now, isn't through any desire of their own. It's because society foists all these standards on us. The world we live in is specifically designed to make us compete.'

Kensuke's face flitted into Shōko's mind. Now she thought about it, she realised that it was thanks to his pronouncement that 'women can be scary' that she'd come to feel afraid of Eriko's behaviour, and keep her distance. Maybe if she hadn't taken such a dramatic step back, Eriko's reaction might not have been this extreme.

Next she thought of Satoko – her face full of mirth as she discussed the catty interactions between the mummy bloggers from her safe position on the sidelines. She thought of all those women who had started out as regular amateur bloggers. Hadn't they only begun sizing each other up and competing that way after Satoko had reached out to them and encouraged them to make their identities public? She'd drawn them away from their privacy into the public sphere, introduced rankings in her magazines, allowing people to easily compare their looks and their level of fame, then fanned their sense of competition still further by sharing rumours with each of them individually. Back in Shōko's former job in the apparel industry, maybe the tension on the shop floor hadn't been all about the competition over sales – maybe it had been exacerbated by the divisive favouritism of the area manager and other staff members.

Eriko was selecting her words carefully. The expression on her face looked positively wise. 'Men are scared of women coming together. That's what I reckon, anyway. They're scared of women who trust each other and live lives of fulfillment in a way they can't access, which has nothing to do with sex or power. They're scared that women will stop treating them nicely. Women joining forces feels to them like a negation of their way of life, which is reliant on power and the judgements that come from it, and where they cling on to their hatred and their loneliness because they're too scared to let go of the rails.'

What Eriko was saying was abstract, but to her surprise Shōko found that she understood it. It actually made a lot of sense. It would scarcely be an exaggeration to say that she had opted for her current way of life because she loathed the competition that Eriko was speaking of. She could also understand the logic that to leave this tedious jostling behind, women needed to come together and understand each other better.

But although she knew that much intellectually, she couldn't bring herself to grasp the hand that was being proffered to her now. Shōko couldn't remember ever feeling relaxed in another woman's company, and she certainly didn't enjoy her time with Eriko. She felt far more comfortable around men, most of all around Kensuke. Ultimately, she didn't think she was capable of loving anybody who wouldn't protect her. Why would she want to become caught up in a larger struggle as Eriko was suggesting? She didn't want to fight anyone, man or woman. God, she missed Kensuke, she thought. How much more fun and relaxing it would be if he were here.

'Wow, you sure come out with some brainy stuff, don't you?' Shōko said with a deliberately flippant laugh. She saw Eriko pull a wounded face, before focusing on finishing her noodles. Shōko was certain that she was disappointed in her. Good, she thought. I don't have what it takes to become an accomplice in your great mission. She dropped down silently into her small world shrouded in darkness and waited for Eriko to finish eating.

When they came out of the soba restaurant they headed straight for the large resort hotel by the riverside. The sun was already beginning to set. They were already a quarter of the way through their trip. This realisation came as a relief, but the idea that she'd come all this way to Hakone simply to wait for time to elapse was intensely depressing. It was all her own fault. As she whiled away her time like this, her youth and physical strength would pass her by, with nothing left to show for it. Shōko was suddenly filled with a powerful desire to have a baby with Kensuke, and bring them both here. If only she had a child, she'd be able to forget the banality of her own existence – to see things through her baby's untainted eyes. She realised for the first time that she was utterly sick of herself.

When she looked down at the river from the bridge that led to the main entrance of the hotel, the water was so clear that she could make out the pebbles lining the bottom. Watching the movement of the water, she remembered the river that ran through her hometown. Was there really the kind of fierce competition for existence that Eriko had spoken of occurring even in water this calm and clear?

Next to her, Eriko leaned in her head and immediately started photographing the water's surface. The jarring sound of the flash ruptured Shōko's meditation. Everything was blog material to Eriko, Shōko realised, her irritation growing. When it struck her that Kensuke had likely had the same feeling about her, she felt both embarrassed and angry with herself. Maybe it was a good thing that Eriko had stolen her blog from her. She would leave it to Eriko and concentrate on making her life with Kensuke more secure. She couldn't wait for this trip to be over.

Finally they entered the hotel. In the giant, high-ceilinged lobby, they could see right up to the seventh floor. They made their way across the red-carpeted entranceway and Shōko waited behind while Eriko checked them in. A female employee took them into the elevator with its patterned glass and showed them to their room on the third floor. The exterior of the building was modern and Western-looking, but the room itself was rustic in feel. Onsen manjū sat atop the low table on the tatami. On top of the butterfly-patterned yukata piled up in the corner were beauty kits containing moisturiser and toner, wrapped up in matching hair scrunchies. To go by the price of the hotel, she imagined that most of the guests were university students. The room was spacious enough, and yet the thought of sharing it with Eriko left her feeling stifled. The silence, so profound that they could hear each other's breathing, felt unbearable.

'Shall we get straight in the baths, since we're here?' Eriko immediately said in a bright voice, the moment she'd set down her bags. 'There won't be many people yet at this time.'

'I think I'll pass on the baths, if that's okay,' said Shōko. This was a line she'd prepared. Shōko didn't want to get naked in front of Eriko, and neither did she want to see Eriko naked.

'What!? You don't want to get in together? You're kidding, right? I can't believe you'd come all the way to Hakone and then not get in the baths.'

Confronted with Eriko's flabbergasted expression, Shōko was close to bursting out laughing. Eriko was clearly bright, and yet she responded to even slightly unexpected developments with such risible panic. Maybe if Shōko could start up a new blog called *Diary of E-ko the Cringy Businesswoman* and record Eriko's behaviour in a way that the outside world would find amusing, then this time wouldn't have been totally wasted.

'But I've been thinking this whole time that we'd get in the baths together! That's what the whole plan hinges on! I've made so many preparations for this trip …'

'Yeah, sorry. I'm on my period,' Shōko cut her off in a tone that broached no objections. This was, naturally, a lie.

'Then use a tampon! I brought some with me, in case something like this happened.'

Shōko smiled, though she wanted to push the words that had just entered her ears right back out.

'Ah, I'm kind of scared of tampons. I've always hated them.'

'What? That's so weird, not to use tampons.' Eriko puffed out her cheeks, looking like she might burst into tears at any moment.

'They look painful.'

'They're not *painful*! You're a married woman, for heaven's sake! Don't go around acting the virgin on me. You're not a *schoolgirl* any more.' Letting out a peal of shrill laughter like a stick of chalk scraping the blackboard, Eriko took out a box of tampons from her shoulder bag and held it up high in the air.

'They're much easier to use now than they used to be. Shall I show you how to put it in?'

Was this woman in her right mind? Shōko stared at Eriko in astonishment. This didn't seem like the same person who had just been lecturing her on the importance of a world made up of women, unmediated by sex or power. She was a dangerous tapestry, where threads of wisdom were woven intricately together with those of utter delusion.

'I know how and I can do it myself. Okay, fine, I'll go to the baths.'

Saying this, Shōko took one of the tampons from the box, dived into the bathroom and locked the door, checking numerous times that it was truly fastened. She chucked the tampon into the bin and then sat down on top of the toilet seat. For a while, she sat with her head in her hands.

'Thanks,' she said to Eriko, who was waiting in front of the bathroom when she finally emerged, 'it didn't hurt.' The two of them left the room with their yukata in hand. When they reached the lobby again, they took the stairs that led to the basement and parted the noren curtain marking the entrance to the ladies' bath.

Seeing that there were no slippers on the boards, Eriko let out an excited screech.

'No way! It's just the two of us! Like a private onsen!'

Inside the changing room, Eriko began tearing off her clothes, lifting her sweater to reveal a bright white belly. Shōko quickly averted her eyes. In no time Eriko was naked. Only once she'd disappeared beyond the sliding glass door leading to the baths did Shōko begin to slowly remove her clothes.

Pulling back the frosted glass door, conscious of pressing her thighs together as she walked so the lack of tampon string wouldn't reveal itself, her body was softly enveloped by steam. Just as Eriko had said, the room contained just the two of them. Eriko was already sitting by the showers with her back to Shōko, scrubbing her body. The high-ceilinged room was large and spacious, and the window that filled one wall gave a view onto the mountains. The bathwater was clear. Turning around when she heard a gentle splash, she saw Eriko stepping into the baths. Circular ripples formed around her, expanding to fill the tub.

'Ahh, that's nice,' Eriko said. Narrowing her eyes in pleasure, she started swimming breaststroke through the water. Though the face poking above the water's surface had its eyes narrowed in a look of euphoria, her wet hair clung limply to her forehead, her legs were bent at a clumsy angle and opened wide as she swam so Shōko had to look away. She began to feel dizzy.

'I don't think you should swim. People might come in.'

She was so taken aback that she struggled to get even those words out. Had this person really graduated from a good university? Landed a job at a top-rate firm? Eriko was supremely critical of others but as soon as other people weren't looking, she behaved however she wanted. Was that how it was?

'Why not? There's nobody else around.'

Eriko seemed utterly unbothered.

'That's not the point. You're thirty years old! You can't swim in an onsen!'

Shōko's depth of feeling came as a surprise to her. What could she say to make Eriko understand – to make her see the weirdness of her actions?

'It's me and my best friend, which is basically the same as being on my own. Have you never wanted to swim naked in open water? Have you never longed to break free of the tank that you're in?'

Eriko began swimming backstroke now, directing her question up at the ceiling. The clump of dark pubic hair that appeared on the water's surface was sparkling in the water. Her nipples were the colour of café au lait.

'It feels great, swimming naked. So free! It makes you understand how much we're made to repress and endure as part of our daily lives.'

Eriko's pale body, like a giant white asparagus finger floating in the water, was less an erotic sight than it was a terrifying one. Shōko felt quite certain that, even if she were a young boy or a lecherous middle-aged man, she wouldn't have felt aroused by the sight of this woman. There was something off about it, as though the soft, contourless body of a young girl had been enlarged.

The revelation came to her unannounced: Eriko is actually a child. The person in front of her is not an adult. She's swimming simply because she feels like she wants to swim.

Swallowing back the words rising up in her throat, Shōko lowered herself into the corner of the tub and curled herself into a ball to shield the sight of her body.

I know what you're saying, but the truth is, you're not a little girl any more, Eriko. Things might be a bit different in Tokyo, but in the countryside, you'd already be thought of as middle-aged. Do your parents spoil you so badly that you've forgotten your real age? Or is it because you're still dragging around that event of all those years ago? Why don't you see how off-putting it is? It's bad enough when you do those things by yourself – why then seek someone to be your travelling companion? Yes, Shōko thought as she reached the end of her inner monologue – what Eriko was looking for was a travelling companion to accompany her inside her crazy world. That was why nobody wanted to be near her.

If she carried on hanging around with Eriko, Shōko would also end up going mad. That was a certainty. Just when she thought she'd got away from her father, she found herself tethered to a woman like this – it was too much to bear. Eriko made her way towards her now, parting the water and coming right up close to ogle Shōko's skin.

'You've got such nice elbows and heels. They're all smooth, like a child's. Do you have a special skincare routine?'

'Not particularly.'

Shōko couldn't sense the unique softness and fragrance of the water that the hotel was famed for at all. All she could think about was how much she wanted to push Eriko away and get out.

'I never really get build-ups or breakouts or anything on my skin. I've always been like that, since I was a child.'

'If I forget to apply cream I get dry as anything. I'm envious. Look, feel mine. They're like a man's.'

Eriko guided Shōko's hand through the water towards her knee. Swollen as it was in the water, it didn't feel hard or scaly. Shōko had the unpleasant feeling that she was being forced into the woman's role in some attempt at romance. Trying to change tack, she deliberately affected a bright tone as she asked, 'What are your parents like?'

Maybe if she heard Eriko talking about her family environment, Shōko thought, then she'd understand her a bit better.

'I guess they were somewhat on the strict side, but in general, I adore my parents.' Her cheeks seemed to flush slightly as she said this, and she looked quite beautiful.

'My mother's a real chatterbox, and a bit of a pushover, in certain ways. My father doesn't really talk, so sometimes you barely notice him. I don't think they get along too badly as a couple. I'm closer to my father, I guess. They've always been really supportive of my career, which has been a great help to me. Would you like to meet them one day?'

Shōko found herself on the verge of nodding. She felt, quite genuinely, that she'd like to sneak a look into Eriko's house. She felt certain that it wouldn't be in a state like hers. It would be immaculate, and smell delightful. There would be homemade cake, and amber-coloured tea. Shōko would be welcomed there.

She felt sure that Eriko had never experienced the sight of the lights from her own house on a dark street ripping her calm to shreds, making her stomach contract, as she had. Where, then, did this inconsistency that seemed to envelop Eriko originate from? She herself was inconsistent, and Shōko's assessment of her also swung around like a pendulum.

Sometimes she felt that Eriko was a sheltered little princess, brought up in a cocoon of love. She couldn't bring herself to ridicule her background. She guessed that her parents were temperate, good people. Their daughter's instability was doubtless a cause for concern for them, and they were probably sitting there right now, worrying about whether she was enjoying herself. The moment that Shōko stopped guarding over her thoughts, she would catch herself thinking that Eriko was probably simply incredibly bad at relationships, a feeling of sympathy unfolding inside her. She pictured the dark hollow filling Eriko's insides. Of course it came in different degrees, but this was in a way the same hunger and lack that everyone experienced. Eriko had surely turned out the way she had because, unable to develop the skills needed to make her relationships succeed, she had let the hollow expand until its growth was irreversible.

When it struck her that some simple twist of fate could have seen her, or indeed anybody at all, turning out like Eriko, she felt a heaviness form in her chest. Her sadness disappeared, and distress subsumed it. She wanted to run and hide from it all.

The idea that everything was Eriko's fault made her feel far more at ease, brought with it a pleasant feeling of superiority. She rubbed the bathwater into her upper arms and thighs.

It struck her that once again, she'd drawn one step closer to understanding her father. His slovenly way of life was his way of abandoning responsibility. Whatever happened to him, he could then blame his family. The reason that nobody wanted to go near him was that they could sense his dependence so keenly. Shōko tried now to recall her father's face, and found she was unable to. She didn't even know how long it had been since she'd seen him.

Why was she here, naked, with this woman, in a place she had no connection with? Who even was she? Without realising, her own sense of identity had grown weaker and weaker, and was on the verge of disappearing completely. Only now was she remembering that she actually hated holidays – and not because she couldn't be bothered with all the preparation or the travelling, either.

Apparently bored by Shōko and her lack of conversation, Eriko began swimming again.

# CHAPTER TWENTY-SIX

The noise of the river was ceaseless. If Eriko couldn't find a way to ignore it, or else to resign herself to it, then she looked set to spend a sleepless night.

Suspended in the darkness, Shōko's sleeping face was flat and without eyebrows, composed of simple lines. It seemed lacking in any kind of soul. It resembled not so much a Noh mask as the peculiar indentations on a ray's stomach, or a shadow falling across the folds in a sheet, which gave them the look of a human face. Why was Shōko so readily able to relax in front of another person? Eriko envied how quickly she'd fallen into sleep, despite the presence of someone else beside her.

Eriko struggled to get to sleep at the best of times, and she'd now been lying awake for almost three hours. Perturbed by the smell and feel of the cheap yukata fabric, and the stiff, starchy sheets and high pillow, she eventually sat up. She checked the time on her phone by her bed, and sighed as she thought of the hours she'd lost. When in another person's presence constantly, nothing went the way she hoped it would.

That said, she'd been on holiday with a boyfriend twice, and there hadn't been any major problems. Both of those had been overseas trips, and the man in question had planned it all ahead of time in a bid to please her. They'd decided in advance where they were going to go and what they were going to eat, and had moved according to the itinerary. In the evenings they'd have sex, and then fall asleep at roughly the same time.

Apart from her sleepovers at Keiko's house in primary school, Eriko had never spent this much time with a woman of her age, or slept alongside her.

When Eriko and Shōko had emerged from the baths, they'd found their dinner trays waiting for them in their rooms. The trays were clustered with tiny plates, each containing a different dish made with seasonal wild plants and mushrooms. Considering the price they'd paid, it seemed to Eriko like an excellent meal, but Shōko barely touched her tray. Eriko kept making suggestions – shall we explore the hotel? Shall we walk around the town? – but, complaining of bad period pain, Shōko changed into an old sweatshirt, got into bed and shut her eyes. As a result, Eriko had seen less than half of what she wanted to see.

Why was she so fixated on someone this mediocre, this inscrutable? Why did it have to be Shōko, of all people? Shōko, who had no ideas about what she wanted to see or do? Nor had she uttered one word of thanks to Eriko for planning the trip so conscientiously. She simply traipsed around after her, a bored look on her face, not reacting to anything that she put in her mouth. As a result, Eriko ended up scrutinising her expression the entire time, as if she were some kind of tour guide or servant. Shōko hadn't seemed particularly impressed by the baths, and when Eriko spoke about the art museum they were due to visit tomorrow, she only nodded. It had taken Eriko a while to work out that it wasn't that she had an inexpressive face, but that she genuinely had very little reaction to anything.

How much Eriko had liked the elusive quality of the prose on Shōko's blog! That Shōko didn't give away as much as other stay-at-home wife bloggers had given Eriko an impression of her rich interior world, studded with precious nuggets truly worth listening to. It was only now that Eriko understood the truth: this woman really had nothing to say. The scope of her interests was remarkably narrow. She lived out her everyday life in a sphere a few metres in diameter, and had no concern for anything that existed beyond that.

Recalling her failure to perceive the truth about this woman, the euphoria she'd felt at the simple fact of exchanging a few words with Shōko made Eriko tremble with embarrassment.

All day she'd been so tense that her body still felt stiff and tight to its core. What if she made some kind of mistake? That was all she'd been able to think about. Seeking reassurance, she now pictured her fridge at home. She imagined taking out the milk that lived inside the door, pouring it into a mug, adding in honey and rum, and warming it up in the microwave for a minute and a half. That was what she most wanted now: the drink that her mother had made for her when she couldn't sleep as a young girl. She wanted to let the hot, sweet milk loosen her body, then curl up in her old blanket and sleep. She remembered this longing to be at home from summer school and school trips as a girl.

There she'd been, thinking that if she went on holiday with her best friend she'd be released from the heaviness that clung to her. That as she was chatting with Shōko, taking in the changing scenery and enjoying the regional delicacies, she'd be freed from the circularity of her thoughts, and would return to the healthy version of herself, to the way she was supposed to be. Instead, she felt even less able to escape than ever, confronted by everything that she lacked as a person.

She wanted to change. Eriko wanted to change so badly the thought made tears prick her eyes. She wanted to become a stable person who approached life with a free and easy spirit, who could adapt to whatever environment she was in. Sure, she had grown more knowledgeable throughout her life, but at heart she remained that self that Keiko had turned her back on. It was strange – it wasn't how it was supposed to be. Experience was supposed to change people. There had to be something wrong with her that some minor event in her adolescence, the kind that everyone endured in some form, had affected her this badly. Even now, the notion that the cells in her body were dying terrified her. The idea of getting old, when she was still so immature, when she still hadn't understood anything, petrified her so much it made her want to curl up into a ball.

Was she really going to be like this her entire life?

Did her inability to become an adult have something to do with how she still lived with her parents in the same apartment she'd lived in since she was a girl? Was it because she'd never experienced the loneliness, the dissatisfaction, of being alone in the world, as Shōko and Maori had?

But the idea of changing her environment at this age was as bewildering as being asked to create a flower garden in the middle of the desert. To start a new job with no connection to her father, to live without the help of her mother, in a place where her background meant nothing – just the idea of it brought certain fears bubbling up in her head. That she wasn't young, for instance. That she was bad with people. That she didn't actually have very good life-management skills. She understood better than anyone that the reason she was able to pass judgement on those who didn't make enough effort was because she herself received plentiful support, and was in a position of privilege.

Eriko wanted to change herself without changing everything surrounding her. Changing her environment felt tantamount to rejecting the entirety of her life up until now: her choice of firm, her school education, her rupture with Keiko, the time she'd spent with her mother as a baby, even her parents' lives before they got married. It was far preferable to set about changing herself while still living in that same neighbourhood.

Eriko felt that this could happen if she could only spend more time with Shōko. Having arrived in that neighbourhood from outside of it, Shōko symbolised a world that was unknown to Eriko. Today, Eriko had succeeded in revealing herself to another woman for the first time since Keiko. She and Shōko had discussed their upbringings, talked enthusiastically about their favourite TV programmes and got in the baths together naked.

Her role was to tether the unfeeling, lackadaisical Shōko to this world, and foster in her a dose of common sense and a desire for self-improvement. Thanks to Eriko's help, Shōko's blog would be successful, and she'd release a book. Eriko would return to work, but rather than reverting to her former ways, she'd use her time after work and at the weekends to support Shōko. To do things for others, and have them do things for her – this was her dream. If she and Shōko could make up for each other's shortcomings, success was within their grasp. They would become an invincible duo. The story she'd taken the time to stitch together inside her heart was without cracks or contradictions. This was the ultimate happy ending, uniquely possible to Eriko and Shōko.

Such a narrative should in theory have been good news for Shōko. So why, then, did Shōko refuse to act as Eriko hoped she would? She had thought so far ahead, laid the groundwork for it all. Why did she always end up feeling as though she were in it alone?

Eriko let the tears fill her eyes before she began to think of the swelling that would await her the following morning, and got up.

Standing in front of the sink, she soaked a towel with hot water, wrung it out, and applied it to her eyes. Then she returned to bed. This was supposed to be her time off, and yet she couldn't seem to shake off the habits she'd had when she was working. Her mind was so filled with thoughts of the future that she couldn't enjoy the present. There was simply no way for her to immerse herself in the now. The inescapable feeling that the woman lying asleep next to her would never understand her formed the same register as the burbling of the river, saturating the darkened room.

# CHAPTER TWENTY-SEVEN

The photos that Eriko took looked like the pictures on postcards, Shōko thought. Their composition was immaculate, and the balance of the colours and the angle of light carefully considered. The crisp look of the mountains and river revived her memories of that clear, cool air, and all the food looked exquisite. The images were so perfect that they left no impression at all.

She and Eriko had been seeing different realities. Eriko had taken in a huge amount over the course of their short trip, endeavouring to imprint the scenery into her mind and make it her own, opening her eyes wide so as not to miss a single detail. Shōko wasn't like that. She had gone along reluctantly after she'd been ordered to do so, and the goal she'd forced herself to come up with was to while away her time in a similar manner to how she did at home. Until reading over the blog, she hadn't grasped even that basic difference between them. Opening up her laptop in the living room at home, she looked at Hallie B's blog about the past two days as if it were something written about someone other than her:

> *I took a little overnight trip to Hakone with my best friend who lives nearby. It was a pretty momentous trip – if you count top-quality girlchats as momentous events, which I obviously do!*

*We talked the whole time in the Romancecar and in the baths, and it still felt like I could go on talking to her forever ... Time alone with a girlfriend is indispensable, whatever age you are.*

The blog didn't really touch on the soba restaurant, which represented Shōko's most vivid memory of the trip. The majority of the word count went on describing the Pola Museum of Art, which in the end Shōko hadn't visited. It seemed as though, in her enthusiasm for explaining about the Impressionists, Eriko had forgotten about the task of becoming Hallie B. When Shōko checked the site traffic, it was at its lowest yet. That checked out, thought Shōko. People who were interested in art museums didn't read *The Diary of Hallie B, The World's Worst Wife*.

As her eyes scanned Eriko's cheerful, perfectly illuminated prose, Shōko felt as though she could hear its writer's screams of desperation. Eriko would almost certainly be on her own her whole life, kicking reality out of the way so as to see solely what she wanted, and being avoided by others as a result. Shōko didn't want to be like that. Breathing a sigh of relief that she was not Eriko, she lit a cigarette.

In her other hand she held a cup of instant coffee, which she accompanied with a product sample of a caramel cookie that Kensuke had brought home from work, and an apple. From the bathroom she could hear the splashing noise of Kensuke in the bath. Dinner had been rice with sardines and umeboshi with simmered greens and pork soup, a relatively elaborate affair by Shōko's standards, and she'd already done the washing-up. She had continued to make more of an effort around the house, while still being careful not to take it too far. The feeling of desolation that had come over her while away, which she found impossible to put into words, had vanished entirely by now. Shōko narrowed her eyes and stretched. Knowing that this was merely a temporary respite, that she'd soon have to meet up with Eriko locally, every inch of the apartment seemed precious to her. So long as she was here she was protected, wrapped snugly in a blanket that warmed her right to the tips of her fingers. However insignificant it might be in the grand scheme of things, this was her castle that she'd built herself, which she had no intention of ceding to anyone.

As soon as she woke on the second day of their trip, Shōko had complained of period pain again, telling Eriko that she wanted to go home ahead of her. It felt impossible for her to spend any more time with Eriko. At first Eriko had dug her heels in, adopting a concerned expression and offering to nurse Shōko there in the hotel room, but when Shōko had curled up and started groaning, her eyes filled with tears, Eriko had reluctantly agreed to let her go.

'Will you be all right? Text me when you get home, okay?' Eriko had repeated when they got to the platform of the station. It seemed that cutting the trip short simply wasn't an option for her, and she didn't offer to accompany Shōko. Naturally Shōko had no desire for Eriko to join her, but she mused to herself that it was this part of Eriko that rendered her incapable of making friends. She pretended to be attentive to what the other person was feeling, but when it came to the important things, she had no consideration for others. Just before the train doors shut, Eriko cupped her hands to her mouth like a megaphone and said, 'I've got to finish the trip alone, or we won't have anything to write on the blog! Good job we came together, isn't it? Take it easy today. Leave Hakone to me!'

Watching Eriko's figure receding, it occurred to Shōko that perhaps Eriko also craved some alone time. When the sight of her saluting, her bag over her shoulder like some military sash, finally disappeared from sight, Shōko had breathed a sigh of relief.

She wished that this was it, and she had now lost Eriko for good, but she also knew that this was a vain hope. This was a fight she had no chance of winning. Her opponent was blessed with far greater wisdom and fighting power than she. The best thing would be for Eriko to gradually lose interest, and naturally move away of her own accord.

An idea suddenly occurred to Shōko, and she almost dropped her cigarette. What about Nori? Wouldn't Nori, so smart and so well versed in the ways of the world, be able to rescue her from this situation? Recalling Nori's trustworthy, smiling face as she said, 'Be in touch whenever you like, I'm always happy to help!' Shōko was seized by an intense feeling of urgency. She reached for the empty bottle she used in place of an ashtray and stubbed out her cigarette. Bringing up the new message screen on her laptop, she immediately began typing at full force.

'Hi, Nori! How are things with you? I've got myself in a bit of a fix. I'm sorry to ask this when I know you're so busy, but could I pick your brains sometime? I'm being threatened by that obsessive fan I told you about, and she's even seized control of my blog …'

Shōko heard the bathroom door open. The smell of the bath salts she'd brought back from Hakone as a present came drifting out. She hurriedly saved her draft and shut her laptop. Kensuke appeared, naked from the waist up, his skin shining red and sweat on his forehead.

'Wow, your stomach! You look like you're pregnant or something,' Shōko said smiling, slapping his round belly. 'Speaking of which … it'd be nice to have a baby soon, no?'

Embarrassed by the cloying tone of her own voice, she wrapped her arms around her husband's warm stomach. The soft resistance it offered felt good and she pressed her face closer to it.

'Yeah, we need to think about that, don't we? I don't feel exactly brimming with confidence about it, though. The financials and stuff.'

With each word he spoke, she could hear his voice echoing through his stomach. It was fun.

'I'll get a job. I'll work part-time until the baby comes. Washing dishes or cleaning, I don't care. I'll do whatever.'

Shōko didn't have any special skills or areas of expertise. Given that, she might as well do whatever she could get – the thought suddenly made the world seem much larger.

'What happened to all the book stuff?'

'Mmm, I'm still not convinced about it. There are these mummy bloggers who write all about their kids and the childcare, but I don't feel great about that idea. I wonder if becoming a mum is a good time to stop.'

'It seems a bit of a waste, though, when you're just starting to get famous. I know what you mean, though. I do wonder about those parents who expose all the details of their kids' lives online. Maybe rather than getting rid of it completely, you could only write the blog when you felt like it? I'm sure your editor would be happy to discuss the best approach with you. You've been much less irritable recently. It seems like you're finding a good balance with it.'

She felt grateful for Kensuke's approach to conversation, which consisted in presenting the other person with new ideas, letting them understand that they had choices. She brought her husband's face closer to hers and kissed him. He wrapped his hands around her.

These days Kensuke would never initiate sex of his own accord, but if she reached out to him like this, he would respond. To Shōko, he was her father, her big brother and her only friend. His mouth tasted of sardine rice. This was the first time they'd kissed in a while. When was the last time they'd had sex? Just as she was wondering this, Hashimoto's face popped into her mind. The incident in the aquarium rushed back to her, and then the flash of fear that she'd experienced when Eriko came running up returned with full force, so that she had to stop herself from screaming. She lurched away from Kensuke's chest.

'Sorry. I think I'm a bit tired.'

'Whaaaaat! That's not fair, when you're the one who started it!' Kensuke blew out his cheeks sullenly, and walked away.

Shōko had thought that she could simply keep that stuff hidden away. If she didn't say anything to anyone, then it was as if it hadn't happened. Before meeting Kensuke she had cheated several times on the people she was dating, but had managed to wipe her hands of it, to carry on with the relationship as if nothing had happened. Those men were different to Kensuke, though. Kensuke was her rock, her family, whom she would never leave. She couldn't hide things from him.

'I, um …' she began. Her lips felt dry. Kensuke turned around, scratching his head. She wanted to tell him about what had happened with Hashimoto and get it over with. To tell him, too, about how she was being blackmailed by Eriko, while she was at it. She wanted him on her side. She didn't want to hide her darkest sides from him.

Staying as calm as possible, Shōko swallowed back the words.

In her heart of hearts, she wanted Kensuke to forgive her everything, wanted to depend upon him so completely that she lost her contours entirely. Surely she could be forgiven that much, when she had no other place to go home to? But this was far too childish, too self-centred a way of thinking, she told herself. This impulse to confess what she'd done was wrong-headed. She'd spent too much time around Eriko, and now she herself was losing it.

'No, forget it.' She'd brought this murky element into her peaceful relationship with her husband and there was no taking it back. The small stain would spread, and eventually engulf their whole apartment. This warm place, which was her only sanctuary, would someday become an empty box that served no function, like her dad's house. The ceiling seemed to be falling in on her. Kensuke shrugged. He padded over to the kitchen and took a can of chūhai out of the fridge.

# CHAPTER TWENTY-EIGHT

'What's wrong?! You've barely touched your food!'

Eriko's voice came out so sharp that even she recoiled from the sound of it. This only intensified her feelings of anger, and her tone grew still more reproachful. 'Is your stomach still not better? We travelled all that way to help you recuperate, and it was all for nothing! I've been thinking for a while that your self-management skills are sorely lacking.'

Shōko and Eriko had met up, as arranged, at the same Denny's that they'd visited before. Eriko had been dizzy with excitement at the thought that tonight, finally, they would reconstruct that same ambience that had existed between them that first evening, but observing that Shōko was as detached as usual, she couldn't hold back her irritation. From the bland music-box covers that they played as background music to the overly commonplace use of colour in the imitation Kandinsky paintings on the wall behind her, every detail seemed to grate on her nerves.

'Sorr—'

'I've told you, you're not allowed to apologise!' Eriko half screeched as she leaned in close. Her arm struck the parfait glass, knocking it over. Luckily, she'd eaten most of the huge fruit parfait, but the melted ice cream at the bottom came spilling out, creating a white, vanilla-scented puddle on the table.

As Eriko grabbed a wad of paper napkins and pressed them on top, Shōko blurted out, 'You know the blog has fallen down the popularity ranking?'

Eriko froze. The paper napkins swelled heavily as they soaked up the ice cream.

It was now a week since Eriko had taken over the blog. She felt that she was faithfully reproducing Shōko's style, but the blog had been sinking down the rankings, and as of today had dropped off completely. Criticising from a reader's standpoint was easy enough, but being on the side of the person writing, she'd appreciated for the first time the difficulty of creating original content. Whatever she wrote, she would be beset by worries that Hallie B had written something similar in the past, or that it wasn't the kind of thing that Hallie B would write. As a result, her progress was incredibly slow. The prose that she arrived at after deleting numerous drafts was exquisitely mediocre, the type of writing that as a reader she would want to declare formulaic.

'But listen, it's not your fault. Don't worry about it. People are just getting bored of me.'

There was nothing heavy-hearted about Shōko's tone. She lit another cigarette. The moment the filter touched her lips she moved it away, perching it on the rim of the ashtray.

'People liked it at first because my no-effort lifestyle gave them a sense of relief. But ultimately, I'm quite conservative in my choices. I don't have a strong sense of individuality, and I'm the type never to stray far from the beaten track. There's no danger there, so people start to find it tedious. Everyone's sick of me.'

'Then you've got to spice things up a bit to ensure they don't get bored. We can brainstorm ways to do that together.'

'No. At the point you start making stuff up and being "creative", it stops being a blog and starts being something else. I think it might be time to call it quits.'

Eriko couldn't believe the way Shōko was speaking – as though the blog was something totally detached from her. At the same time as she found it intolerable, she felt so envious of this stance that her body grew hot all over. How much easier would her life be if only she could wash her hands so readily of the things that didn't suit her!

'You're going to quit the blog? You're not being serious?'

'Yeah, I figure the time has come. It started out as a way of passing the hours, but then it ballooned, and honestly I've always been a bit conflicted about it. I couldn't get used to this feeling of being something for all these invisible people to consume. I don't think I'm made for it.' This is the problem with you housewives, Eriko felt like tutting, and kicking at Shōko's chair. Shōko was releasing a creation into the world, which bore her own name. It stood to reason that she would be consumed, feel worn down, find it hard – it stood to reason that sometimes she would feel so ashamed and so lonely she wanted to die. That was what going out to work in society meant! How could she pummel her friend's softness into something harder, more resilient? If she dragged Shōko to the floor, wrung her neck until she lost consciousness, would that precipitate a change of heart? Eriko felt like it was fair game to go that far. She was the representative of the blog readers, and had been Hallie B's supporter from the very beginning. In her vexation, Eriko clenched her thighs firmly together.

'Are you actually stupid? Can't you see what a terrible waste that is? It's not every day that blogs get made into books, you know! Most people can't do things like that! You're too soft on yourself. It's offensive to all the readers who have supported you up until now.'

'I don't care if I'm soft on myself, or if that makes me a failure in the eyes of the world. I don't need to be in the right any more. Why do I have to be in the right? I'm not planning to go places. These readers you're talking about are mostly reading my blog for something to do, without paying a single yen for the privilege. People I've never met. People whose faces I've never seen. And what is this support you're talking about, anyway? If I was in trouble, they wouldn't help me out. Why should I care about them?'

Though her delivery was slow, this was the most words that Shōko had ever spouted in a single stream. As Eriko looked on, astonished, Shōko finally met her gaze.

'I never really cared about other people. I don't get other people's feelings. Especially women's feelings. Maybe that's why I couldn't make any friends. But lately I've figured out that what matters most to me is my life with my husband. I don't want to parcel up and sell off my personal life any more.'

Her tone was gentle, but her steadfastness came through well enough. Sensing that a door had been closed in front of her, Eriko bit her lip. She had an urge to say the kinds of cruel things that she knew would make Shōko run out of the restaurant: to ask what on earth was so precious about a mediocre man like hers. But she understood that whatever kind of insults she threw at Shōko, she'd be unable to sever the bond that existed between her and her husband. The Shōko with a man all of her own seemed unreachably remote to Eriko. Eriko was gifted at figuring out and responding to men's needs, at sizing up their worth from their possessions and job performance, but she was somehow incapable of making a single one her own. It seemed to Eriko a cruel betrayal that, while she only had Shōko, Shōko had secured for herself someone who would always be on her side.

'That's rich, coming from a woman who goes around snogging younger men in public …! You can't go round playing the good little wifey now!'

She stuffed the napkins she'd used to soak up the ice cream roughly into the parfait glass, then glared at Shōko. Shōko's cheeks seemed to twitch slightly, but still she replied, although her voice was trembling.

'You're right … I know that it sounds strange. But I think that everyone has a place that suits them. I also think it's a waste for someone as talented as you to be pouring your efforts into a blog like that. Do you not need to go back to work? If you keep taking time off, will there still be a position for you when you want to go back?'

'Huh? What are you implying about our blog? We … we …'

Tears had filled Eriko's eyes. She knew very well that there were any number of people at work to replace her. When people quit with depression, the company went on, unaffected. Eriko had felt wounded by this knowledge the entire time, and now she found herself unspeakably exhausted by it. As concerned her best friend, though, it was the blog that had brought the two of them together – it was their history, their daughter. She couldn't forgive Shōko for trying to put it to bed so peremptorily. Why couldn't Shōko understand, despite all she'd said?

'Who is that "we", though? You don't feel like you can relate to me any more, do you? You said yourself that things that are unrelatable to you are bad. So why don't we let bygones be bygones? Leave me to my own devices. Put the time you spend on me to another use.'

Shōko's tone was cool and steady. Her disposition was that of a man ending a love affair, of someone so sick of the current situation that she was willing to become the bad guy in order to bring it to a close. That, at least, Eriko was determined to avoid. Her eyes and the insides of her nostrils grew hot. Just the act of opening her eyes sent a pain shooting down her throat.

'How fortunate for you, to have been raised in an unusual family environment! To have no academic record or employment history to speak of! You can blame everything on your environment, your parents, your hometown so far away. With me, everything is my fault, and I have to live here clinging on to all this shame. How convenient for you, to get to put everything on other people!'

Blinking hard so as not to cry, Eriko removed her phone from the pocket of her sweater dress. She understood that someone with a proper education like herself shouldn't be coming out with this kind of thing. She knew, too, that Shōko was right – that she no longer had any grasp on what Shōko was feeling. Try as she might to reach out a hand towards Shōko's interior world, which she'd once felt that she understood, it slipped out of her grasp. How did you bridge a gap like that? Eriko was sure there must be some kind of solution, but however hard she looked, she saw no light on the path ahead. Her breathing grew ragged. Managing to get the photo she'd taken in the aquarium up on her screen, she held it beneath Shōko's nose.

'Look at this. Anyone who sees it will know it's you. I don't need to tell you how easy it would be to post this to your blog. So don't go against me. You've got to do exactly as I say. I'm going to continue writing your blog. I'll send it back up the rankings again. You're my …'

*Best friend*, Eriko made to say, and shut her mouth. She felt as though the contradiction inherent in her words had been stuck on a knife edge and held up to her throat. Best friends were supposed to exchange their opinions readily with one another. Wasn't that the kind of warm, breezy relationship that she'd been so hungrily craving? But the eyes of the woman sitting in front of her had become the same as Keiko's back on that fateful day: gripped by terror and a violent desire to escape this situation unharmed as soon as possible. Eriko tried to reset the mood. She crinkled up her eyes, and attempted a gentle tone. She could feel the strain across her cheeks.

'Sorry for being harsh. I'm just worried about you. I'm doing this for your sake …'

She trailed off, realising not only how false her words sounded, but that it was these same words that had so infuriated Maori. She recalled the shock of Maori telling her that she made her want to puke, that she was the worst kind of woman, when she had been doing her utmost not to seem like the villain. Why were female relationships so filled with taboos? She'd finally found a best friend who she knew wouldn't betray her, and yet she still found herself trapped in a cold, hopeless place.

Their conversation trailed off, and half an hour later, the two left the restaurant in silence. The night air was now freezing, and seemed to slice right through Eriko's skin. Spotting the men's bike affixed to the railing with a chain, though, her despondency flew away.

'Ah, great! You can give me a backie again, like you promised! You remembered our agreement!'

Shōko straddled the saddle compliantly, and Eriko promptly sat herself down sideways behind her, wrapping her hands around her waist. Maybe all the bad feeling between them was simply a figment of her imagination.

'Off we go!' she called out cheerily. She remembered that she'd been startled last time by how slender Shōko's waist was, but it seemed to Eriko as if her friend had grown even smaller in the intervening time. The air was crisp now, and the evening darker, but otherwise everything was exactly the same as that night when everything had seemed miraculous. Shōko's body rose up and down softly inside Eriko's arms.

The bike moved off, veering left then right. The feeling, though, was that of proceeding slowly through the stagnant air: there was none of the rush of the previous time.

'Can't you go faster? It doesn't feel like it did before. Come on, pedal! You're not making any effort!'

Eriko remembered how back then, the lights from the convenience stores and chainstores had formed a bright ribbon that had trailed alongside her. The wind had ruffled her hair and set her skirt billowing. One after another, Eriko enunciated her complaints, the things she wanted Shōko to change. She knew that if she didn't speak them aloud, Shōko would never understand. In place of a reply, Shōko lifted her small buttocks from the seat. Why did she need to stand up to pedal? A trickle of sweat shone on her neck. The trains moving across the overpass ruthlessly overtook them.

'Are you pedalling properly? Last time it felt more ... Hey, are you listening?'

In the attempt to get her friend's attention, Eriko tapped Shōko's back. It was then that the bike lurched to one side. Shōko's toes touched the ground and she dug in, but Eriko lost her balance and was thrown off. The scenery tilted, the night sky flipped, and her vision was suddenly filled with the uneven grain of the asphalt. She knocked her knees and arms hard, and there was a ringing at the back of her nose. On the verge of tears, she cried out in pain. When she reached a hand towards her kneecap, she found the skin raw as if it had been rubbed by a grater, and she was bleeding enough that she could tell as much in the dark. She hadn't had such a bad fall since primary school. Shōko rested the bike on its side, then trepidatiously knelt down on the floor and touched Eriko's shoulder.

'I'm so sorry. Are you hurt?'

'Shut up! I told you not to apologise!'

In her anger Eriko brushed Shōko off, and Shōko fell to the floor beside her. Rolling her eyes at this show of melodrama, Eriko reached out a hand in her direction, but Shōko shielded her body with both her arms. Eriko inhaled sharply. Shōko squeezed her eyes shut, curling up in the foetal position and protecting herself with both hands to prevent Eriko getting any closer. Then Eriko heard the sound of voices from above. A couple passing by were looking down at them.

'What are those women doing?'

'Dunno. A couple of weird lezzers,' they said, their voices purposefully loud, and then snickered.

It was at this moment that Eriko realised she could see her and Shōko's reflection in the window of an estate agency, its lights turned off. In the darkness, the well-polished glass drank in the scenery like a mirror. At last Eriko understood. It wasn't that Shōko had got thinner; it was that she had got bigger. It wasn't that Shōko hadn't been pedalling properly; it was that she'd been struggling with the heaviness of the load. Looming over the delicate Shōko was a stocky, frizzy-haired woman so different to the Eriko Shimura that existed in her imagination that all she could do was stare. The woman stared right back. When Eriko moved a hand up to her cheek, the plain woman lifted a plump white hand up to hers.

When had she put on all this weight? When had she stopped paying attention to her appearance? Was it when she'd stopped going into work? Or did it date back to before then, when she'd got so obsessed by Hallie B's blog that she'd started staying overnight at the office? She could think of numerous possible answers. Now she understood why people's behaviour towards her had changed so definitively. Of late, she barely looked in the mirror. Naturally she hadn't been going to the gym – she'd barely been leaving her room. Unsatisfied by the meals her mother had been preparing her, she had been bingeing on the shrink-wrapped bakery items and instant noodles she'd bought in bulk instead.

Eriko felt an ant crawling up her thigh. She remembered how as a young girl, she and Keiko had often followed ant trails to the hole at the end, then stuck bamboo skewers or poured water inside. What a cruel pastime, she thought now. She could remember the twitchy joy she'd experienced at feeling the weight of another life in her hands like that. She was no different now to how she was back then.

Shōko still sat with her arms wrapped around herself, quivering.

Why didn't you tell me, she was on the verge of saying to her. Why didn't you warn me? We went to the onsen together! Couldn't you have said, you've put on weight, shouldn't you think about going on a diet? Why hadn't Shōko come out with the kinds of things that friends said to each other all the time? Was it because she was frightened? Or was it in fact that Shōko simply hadn't noticed. The thought sent the blood draining from Eriko's head. Maybe she'd noticed that something about Eriko seemed different, and that was as far as her understanding went. The notion seemed quite possible. She was, after all, stunningly uninterested in others.

Finally, Eriko understood. Whatever hopes she harboured, being best friends with this woman was no longer possible. She had tried profusely, in all the ways she could think of, to get across to Shōko that she wasn't some deranged person, that she wasn't a stalker, that she was on Shōko's side. But the harder she tried, the more the warmth between them bled away. However much effort she made in the future, the result would be the same. The distance between them couldn't be shrunk.

The Eriko of back then was different to the Eriko of now – the reflection in the shop window was all the proof she needed of this. Shōko had likely changed too, as Keiko had said. The pair as they were on that glorious evening when they rode together on Shōko's bicycle now existed in memory alone.

'Okay, I get it. I don't need you any more,' Eriko spat out, taking her phone from her pocket. She got up on screen the photo she'd shown Shōko less than an hour before, and after hesitating for a moment, pressed delete. 'I've erased the photos. Look, see? They're gone. I haven't got them in my deleted folder or my computer either.'

Shōko watched; her eyes filled with tears. Then she lowered her hands to her knees timorously and asked, 'Are you sure? You're going to free me?'

Shōko's expression was flooded with hope. Eriko had never seen her expression so invested with meaning before. Her lungs hurt so much she could barely breathe.

'Do what you want. Go home to that boring husband of yours. You and I weren't designed to have friends.' Eriko got to her feet, brushed off the front of her dress and set off walking. When it occurred to her that she'd most likely never see Shōko again, her vision grew blurry and a tear ran down her cheek. Now she would have to live all by herself once more. The asphalt road stretched mercilessly ahead to the apartment in which she'd grown up.

'Thank you,' said Shōko behind her, through her sobs. The road beneath the underpass was cast in shadow so intense that it seemed unthinkable that it was connected with anywhere else. Resolving not to turn back, Eriko gritted her teeth, and continued her progress through the dark. Up in the bright window of the passing train, she thought she saw a girl wearing her old school uniform.

# CHAPTER TWENTY-NINE

Despite the long train journey and her lack of sleep, Shōko didn't remotely feel like napping. She didn't want to look out at the scenery, she didn't have sufficient appetite to enjoy one of the special bentos from the station, and nor was she in the mood for reading. She spent the whole journey scrolling on her phone.

Her eyes grew sore and scratchy, and her head was tired. Her skin felt parched. The skin on her lips was peeling off, and when she licked it, she tasted salty meat.

She was reading over the blog entries that she'd written in her glory days, and the comments they'd accumulated. Then she moved on to Nori's blog and Twitter account, wondering as she scanned through what Nori was doing right now. How alluring her daily life was! From between the lines of her prose, Shōko could smell the rich aroma of baking cakes, hear the sound of mothers laughing together. Peeling itself from the mountains and fields passing by the window, Shōko's consciousness flew to Nori's side. She resolved that when she got to her final station, she'd read through her saved draft again, and then send it:

*Hi Nori. Sorry for messaging again! I know you're busy, and I hope you don't think I'm being pushy, but I can't think of anyone else I can turn to ... I've had to go back to my family home, and it's looking possible that I'll end up divorcing my husband. I can't really update my blog under these circumstances ... Please let me know your thoughts. You're the only one I can rely on.*

Reading the message over and over, Shōko began to feel embarrassed about how grovelling it sounded. But it also seemed to her that, without sounding desperate, she had no chance of pulling on the heartstrings of someone as high-flying as Nori. Summoning her courage, she finally pressed the send button at the station before hers.

Shōko had learned at her own expense that her real life was more valuable than her online one, but she also knew that to be true only when her real life contained people who were there for her. It wasn't only Kensuke who wasn't speaking to her; she'd heard nothing back from Satoko or Nori, either. She was entirely on her own. It was as if she'd gone back to the starting line.

As Shōko stepped down onto the platform, two girls dressed in her old school uniform got on the now largely empty train. Shōko exited through the ticket barriers. It was a relatively large station for this region, directly connected with the city hall, the library and a building containing various food shops, but seeing it for the first time in a while it seemed like a long, empty residential terrace, and it felt impossible to believe that somewhere like this could serve all the needs of the local populace. The place was steeped in the smell of the pickles that were a regional speciality. A few youngsters with apparently nothing better to do leaned up against the wall, staring absently at the people coming out of the ticket gates.

Outside the station Shōko took out her phone and called home, letting it ring on and on, but there was no answer. Tutting, she stuffed her phone back in her pocket. Her father didn't have a mobile, so she had no other way of getting in touch with him. He'd always had a propensity to go out wandering since she'd been young, so Shōko wasn't worried. He was probably out on a bar crawl, or else he and Urumi had made up, and the two of them had gone out somewhere. The idea of being on her own was far more appealing to her than the prospect of living under the same roof as her dad, who was always grinning but whose real feelings were impossible to gauge. The problem was that she couldn't think of where else to go. She hadn't yet touched the income she'd raised from her blog adverts, so she could in theory have lived in a hotel for a spell, but while she didn't know what the future held for her, it seemed better not to put her money to such reckless use.

The outlines of the autumn leaves blurred hazily into the backdrop of the cloudy white sky. The chill struck her skin, and she regretted not bringing another layer. She had hardly any clothes remaining in her dad's house, either. If she wanted to buy anything, she'd have to go as far as the shopping mall two stations away – a far cry from Setagaya, where you could get everything you needed without ever leaving.

This place really did have the same sweet smell as Hakone Yumoto. It seemed hard to believe that Shōko's trip with Eriko had been just a few days prior. Never before had her life shifted so dramatically in the space of merely a few days.

'What!? You're coming here? Why now? No, I've no idea where Dad is. I've not seen him this whole time. I guess he'll come back sooner or later.'

Before leaving Tokyo, she'd called up her brother Yōhei, who lived locally with his girlfriend, but his response had been perfectly detached. Maybe he was still resentful about how coldly she'd rebuffed him when he'd called her asking for help.

Walking down one side of the wide road, Shōko felt eager to get back to Tokyo. She was already beginning to regret her decision. A string of trucks passed her. On one of them she saw the logo for a famous dairy brand. She had the powerful urge not to go any further.

After deleting the photos she had been blackmailing Shōko with, Eriko had promptly stopped following Shōko around. It was less joy that Shōko felt at this sudden piece of luck and more a kind of bewilderment. She had no idea what kind of change had occurred in Eriko, but she knew what it signalled: if she could only keep her mouth shut about her indiscretion, everything would resolve itself. She would be able to return to her life with her husband, exactly as it had been before.

So why, then, had she gone and done what she'd done? Returning home after that night with Eriko at Denny's, she'd been overtaken by a feeling of enormous freedom, which had brought with it a sense of elated clarity. Suddenly, she found herself longing to tell somebody about how she had dealt with that dangerous situation with such self-possession – how she had got through it on her own. Finally, thirty years into her life, she felt there was nothing left to be scared of. And so, driven on by her heady exhilaration, she'd told Kensuke about Eriko's blackmail attempt, and about the kiss too. At first he'd smiled, apparently thinking it a bad joke, but when he read over her texts with Hashimoto, his expression clouded over. 'I'm so sorry,' Shōko apologised numerous times, sincerely.

Given her realisation that her marriage to Kensuke was the most important thing in her life, it had struck Shōko as cowardly to keep quiet and return to him as though nothing whatsoever had happened. It had seemed to her that telling him everything was a way of making it up to him – a form of fidelity. If Kensuke were to forgive her, everything really would go back to how it had been before, and their foundations would grow even stronger … So her hopeful thinking had run.

'I'm sorry. I can't live with you any more.' Kensuke's tone was clipped. He looked down at the floor so she couldn't see his face, but his shaking shoulders betrayed that he was crying. She could tell that he wouldn't tolerate excuses or emotional displays from her. He sank into silence, and didn't move. She'd never seen him like that before.

'I guess it makes sense if I go to my dad's, then. You should stay here, so you can go to work,' Shōko had said – in part because she'd simply wanted to escape, but she also felt that if she gave him a little time, then matters might resolve themselves. The situation with her dad had also been niggling at her. Above all, though, she couldn't bear the weight of the sin she'd committed in hurting her husband so definitively. She'd quickly packed up her possessions, and had spent the previous night in a manga café.

Of course she hadn't expected him to simply smile her infidelity off, or forgive her immediately, but neither had it occurred to her that he'd be this shocked by it. It hadn't even crossed her mind that she'd be rejected by this husband of hers, who shrugged everything off with a cheery 'it is what it is, I guess'.

She'd had no word from him since; he'd ignored both her texts and her calls. Was he eating properly? Was he going into work? Suddenly his physical health, which she'd previously been largely indifferent to, was all she could think about. The optimistic hope that he'd forgive her someday steadily dwindled with the passing of time. Kensuke hadn't had much experience with women before dating Shōko. Though he seemed generous, there was a fastidious side to his nature. What would she do if he filed for divorce? The image of this all-too-plausible future left her frozen. Why, oh why, had she told him?

She walked down the shopping street, lined with businesses with their shutters now permanently down, and then across the fields. As ever, the air here felt stagnant. This was not a place to stay for long. *You've got to make things better and then hurry back to Tokyo*, Shōko implored herself as she trudged on. Spotting from a distance the logo of a big supermarket chain to be found anywhere in Japan, she breathed a sigh of relief.

'Shōko …? It's Shōko, right?'

Hearing a voice pronouncing her name, Shōko spun around. Her eyes met those of a young woman slamming shut the back door of a small white car that had pulled up alongside her. The woman wore her brown hair up in a wispy bun, and the thin legs extending from her dark purple down jacket were clothed in flowery leggings.

'You remember me, right? Miwa. You're back in town? How long's it been since you were last here?'

The woman's small, lithe figure and the slightly proud point to the tip of her nose seemed familiar to Shōko. As she drew closer, Shōko suddenly let out a gasp. This was the only daughter of her aunt and uncle, who lived about ten kilometres away from here. Her uncle worked as a civil servant, while also managing a farm on the side. Though something of an introvert, he had incomparably more common sense than Shōko's father, and was the only relative of hers that could be relied upon in times of trouble. When she was younger, she'd spent a lot of time with this cousin of hers, who was separated from her by four years in age. They'd done their homework side by side, and bathed together. After middle school, they'd grown naturally apart, but when Shōko's mother had run off with another man, her aunt had been a great help. It came to her now that she had never properly thanked her for that.

'Wow, look at you! So grown up! I didn't recognise you at first. I'm going to be here for a while. I don't know how long yet.'

She wondered briefly what she'd do if Miwa started grilling her, but her cousin seemed as unpresuming as she'd always been. She smiled gently as she spoke.

'Oh, really! Is your dad doing all right? I haven't seen him recently. He used to be so sweet to me when I was younger. I got divorced and I'm back living with my parents, along with my son, so we should hang out!'

As Shōko was wondering how to respond, she spotted a young boy in the passenger seat of the car. He was engrossed in his games console, but seeming to sense her eyes on him, he turned and bowed his head at her before resuming his game. Shōko thought of Miwa as someone roughly of her own age, and she was struggling now to process the reality that she had a child. Without thinking, she reached out and touched the car. It seemed not to have been washed in a while and her fingertips acquired a faint layer of dust. Not only did Shōko not have kids, but she didn't even have a driving licence.

'What do you think, shall we go for dinner sometime? Although really the only place to go is the family restaurant on the other side of the station …'

Shōko knew the place: a Denny's, the same chain as the one she'd been to with Eriko that last time. Hah, she thought. In a way maybe this place wasn't that different to Tokyo after all. She felt a knot of tension in her chest gently loosening. She hadn't been sent away to a remote island; she was just getting some distance from her husband. Maybe she should try to see the move in a positive light – time for both of them to re-examine their relationship afresh. She felt genuinely grateful for Miwa's cheerful smile. The two exchanged contact details. A plastic model of the same cartoon character displayed on her son's console screen dangled from her phone.

'Thanks. I'll look forward to it.'

It was a long time since Shōko had had a proper conversation with anyone other than Kensuke or Eriko. Watching Miwa's car drive away, she felt the blood tingling in her fingertips. She was already excited about the next time she'd see Miwa. It was funny to think that she could feel this redeemed by the simple knowledge that she had a childhood friend in a similar situation to her whom she could meet up with. Her step growing lighter, she arrived at her house sooner than she thought. The door was unlocked.

'Hi, I'm home!'

Shōko's voice echoed up to the high ceiling. No sooner were the words out of her mouth than they seemed hollow to her – like the least appropriate words for this place, in fact. She frowned at the musty smell that greeted her. The shutters lay open, presumably still unfixed.

Shōko had been anticipating the place to be a mess, but when she stepped over the threshold, the extent of the disarray brought bile rising up in her throat. This was another order of magnitude to the previous time. There was something violent about the level of disrepair that her father had let the house fall into. To Shōko's eyes, it seemed like a punishment doled out to her family for their coldness towards him. The large entranceway was overflowing with bags of rubbish, littered with so many empty liquor bottles that she had to watch her step carefully when navigating them. Moving into the living room, she saw heaps of dust on the tatami. The flowers on the altar had withered, their water brown. The sink in the kitchen was piled high with dirty plates, and when she opened the rice cooker, what looked like fish scales went dancing up into the air. How on earth had he continued living in this state? The ashtray was heaped with cigarette butts, the walls yellow with resin. There was no doubting that things with Urumi really had come to an end. A horrible fear gripped Shōko that maybe her father was going senile. Where on earth had he gone? In normal circumstances, she would have called the police, but the thought of what the neighbours might think gave her pause. In this part of the world, rumours could be the death of you.

Her skin felt itchy. She wanted to scratch and scratch until she bled.

Where was she supposed to start? First of all, she thought, she had to fix the shutters. Thinking this, she sank down onto the tatami. A sea of dust absorbed her lower half like a cushion. She had no idea how to make an inroad into this mess. More to the point, she didn't understand why this task had to fall on her. She wanted someone to help her, but she didn't know who that someone was.

A cockroach went scurrying past, picking its way between the dirty noodle pots.

She thought of her father living in this huge house all alone, stubbornly waiting for his family to get in touch. The fathomless loneliness he must have been feeling pressed in on her mercilessly, and in no time, Shōko found herself incapable of getting up. Had she succumbed to her father's resentment? That was the fate she was most afraid of. She would stay here doing nothing, incapable of doing anything, but waiting for Kensuke to be in touch, for her father to come home. She would become one with the dust and rubbish, be consumed by the house and disappear entirely. Such was her destiny – it had been written for her from her birth. She had struggled against it, but now, eventually, she had given herself over to its grasp. Its power was irresistible.

She didn't know how long she'd been lying there when she noticed, peeping through the crack in the sliding screen, what looked like a human head.

'Dad …?'

She caught hold of the column and hauled herself up, took a few steps forward, and tugged open the sliding doors.

Her father lay face-down – a grey sweatsuit she recognised, and a head of messy, salt-and-pepper hair. His arms and legs were bent in different directions, like a swastika. There was liquid seeping from his head and the lower half of his body. He looked surprisingly small.

Shōko didn't feel surprised. She didn't even feel scared. She went up to him and shook his shoulder to find him hard and cold. The feel of his worn-out sweatshirt closely resembled the touch of her own favourite sweatshirt. Good, she thought, he's dead.

Her first sensation was that of the fog stretching before her clearing, a bright, wide plain opening out in front of her – a feeling of liberation so intense it made her want to cry out. This was what everyone had wanted, she thought – everyone around him, and her father himself. He had died without causing anyone any bother, here at home.

'Ding-Dong! The Witch Is Dead.' Hadn't she heard somewhere that that song had been number one in the UK charts after Margaret Thatcher had died? Shōko felt in that moment that she understood the British music fans. Just the fact that Thatcher was still alive gave them a sick feeling in their chests. Her father had died. The Wizard was dead!

Shōko was finally free. She spread her hands wide to see that the skin on her fingertips that had touched her father just now had broken out in a rash.

# CHAPTER THIRTY

It was nearly evening when her mother came to knock on her door, her eyes red and wet from crying.

'Someone from your company's come to see you.'

Eriko knew, instinctively, that this wasn't a visit from a caring colleague. She lifted her face, swollen from sobbing, and hauled herself up from the bed. She could only imagine it was the manager. After her excruciating performance in the love hotel, she was no longer worried about how she looked to him. She put a thick cardigan over her tracksuit, quickly tied up her hair with a hairband, and trod across the floor littered with empty ramen containers and half-eaten bags of snacks in the direction of the front door. The person standing there awkwardly with his smart coat in his hand was Sugishita.

'Can we go outside?' Eriko asked, wanting to be away from the eyes of her parents, and the two of them stepped out of the door.

The lunch that her mother had brought to her room earlier that day was brown rice pilaf, cream soup and hijiki salad. It had been colourful and excellently nutritionally balanced, but Eriko had felt, upon laying eyes on it, that she couldn't eat it. That wasn't what she wanted. When she turned away, saying she'd go and get something from the convenience store instead, her mother had finally flipped.

'Give me a break, will you!' she'd howled. 'How much do you have to hurt me before you're satisfied? I'm not your and your father's maid, you know! I'm not here to serve you, as a couple!' Picking up Eriko's lunch tray, her mother hurled it at the wall. The orange soup splattered across the duvet cover and curtains. It had never even crossed Eriko's mind that her mother might be feeling this way. Her mother was the most sociable person in their household, who served as their point of contact with the outside world. She had thought of her mother as a fully complete person, who didn't need any kind of support at all. A couple? Come to think of it, though, she and her father were very well matched as man and woman. They were the most compatible of anybody she knew. 'What is it that you hate so much about me? Do you have any idea how much I've given up for your sake? I wanted to work!'

Even her father, who rarely spoke up, had put his arm around her mother's shoulder as he mumbled tearily, 'Why can't you grow up, Eriko? What was it that we did wrong?'

Overcome, Eriko had shut herself in her room, where she had been sobbing ever since.

'It's been a while. You've … um … you've put on weight, huh?' As they walked along, Sugishita ran his eyes around Eriko's body, apparently unable to restrain his fascination. It was a simple fact, and she didn't feel angry with him for coming out with it. She kept on walking, leading him to a narrow park not far from her building. The park contained a playground, complete with a heap of tyres and a swing. How many years had it been since she'd set foot inside? As a young kid, she'd often played here all day with Keiko. There seemed to be far fewer children playing here these days than there used to be. The two of them sat down on a bench.

'I have gained weight, but this is really my original size. I was restricting myself before and now I am not.'

Eriko had never been good at managing her relationship with food. At university, when she'd got her first boyfriend, she'd got into dieting, and started making herself sick. This was the first time she'd admitted this to anybody other than her family, she realised as she spoke. 'You've had your wedding already, right? Congratulations!'

'No, it's actually been postponed. I mean, you told Maori about ... you know.'

For a moment, Eriko didn't actually know what he was referring to. Everything seemed so far away. The idea that she had slept with this man now sitting next to her seemed like a plot twist from a film or TV programme she'd watched long ago.

'Yeah, I'm sorry about that. I don't know what was going on with me.'

'Well, I'm glad you're taking responsibility for it. Although you weren't the only one I cheated on her with. But it seems like she has a resigned attitude to that stuff, and doesn't really seem to mind.' Sugishita laughed and fixed his eyes on the ground. He brought his hands together, twirling his index fingers as if searching for the right words. Eriko finally noticed that Sugishita, who was renowned for taking good care of his appearance, had grimy cuffs and a dusting of stubble.

'I never thought she'd be this much trouble. Honestly, the deeper she gets into wedding preparations, the more it's like her female friends are more important than me. She's out virtually every night having meetings with her friends about it, so I barely get to see her. She hasn't even made me dinner recently. She's obsessed with the seating plan and the wedding list, but when I try to talk about the honeymoon, it's like she's suddenly not interested any more. I've started feeling like she doesn't even like me that much ...'

Sugishita's voice had an extremely babyish ring. His face now crumpled in distress.

Had he only just realised, Eriko mused in amazement. She understood, instinctively, that he'd come to see her so as to regain his sense of pride. He wanted to meet a woman he'd once slept with and air his grievances to her, then return to his relationship and become Maori's priority once again. That was all it was. But finding Eriko unrecognisable from her former self, he was at a loss. His white teeth bared in a look of desperation, he shot Eriko a glance tinged with indignation.

'Women are scary! Everything's so messy and complicated with them. It's true what they say: a woman's worst enemy is other women!' he practically yelled.

It's not only women, though, Eriko thought. In the way that he was determined not to get caught in the complications he derided but watched on in delight, and in the way he saw the consideration and kindness of women as his divine right, Sugishita also struck her as somehow fundamentally broken. She didn't think he was a bad person deep down; she imagined he'd been brought up being given everything he wanted, and couldn't stop himself from expecting unconditional affection from others in the same way. Just like Eriko herself, he seemed to suffer from a strong, fixed idea of the way that things ought to be.

The five o'clock melody, the very same as when she was a child, now flowed from the speakers, and the children began leaving the park.

'Oh, yeah, I've got a message for you from the manager. Do you remember Naomi, the local coordinator in Tanzania?'

An image of Naomi's tanned skin and humble smile rose up in Eriko's head. She nodded, and Sugishita got to his feet disinterestedly.

'Apparently, when they told her you were off work, she seemed really concerned. Were you and her that close?'

The fact that the short time she'd spent with Naomi Akagi already seemed like a dream to Eriko made her concern even more touching. For a moment, a vision flashed into her mind of the sandy beach and blue ocean of Dar es Salaam, but it soon dissolved into the surrounding sunset air, hazy with the fumes of the city.

# CHAPTER THIRTY-ONE

Shōko picked up almost the second her phone started ringing. She didn't recognise the number, but the idea that someone she knew might be on the other end of the line took away her hesitation.

She rushed out of the room, her feet squeaking on the linoleum as she ran towards one of the three spaces in the hospital where phone calls were permitted. By now she had ascertained the location of all of them.

These days, her phone was as indispensable to her as back in the days when she'd been a popular blogger – or even more so. The small device now felt like the sole proof that Shōko was alive, the cord that kept her tethered to existence itself. It was still only a few days since she'd arrived back home, but she felt as though she'd been living alone for years on a remote island. Her Tokyo life as a married woman with a popular blog now seemed like it had happened to someone else. Whether because she wasn't speaking to anyone, or else because the heating was cranked up high for the patients, her throat was permanently scratchy and dry, and her lips had grown so chapped that no matter how much lip balm she applied, it was never enough.

The rest area was decorated with a plastic tree, whose flashing fairy lights only stirred up Shōko's sense of agitation. It was Christmas in just two weeks.

'Hello?'

She could tell that the person on the other end of the line was taken aback by the urgency in her voice. She didn't care who it was – Kensuke, Nori, Hashimoto, even Satoko. She wanted to exchange words with someone that she'd once stood in the same room as, so as to be reminded of her own existence.

An unfamiliar young woman's voice hesitantly named the library that Shōko had often visited in Tokyo, and informed her that the book she'd reserved was now available. Shōko's disappointment robbed her of speech. Her tongue lolled heavily at the bottom of her mouth.

'We can hold it for you for one week.'

Was there any chance that this situation would be resolved in a week? That she'd be back living with Kensuke in that same part of Tokyo by then, and could go to pick up the book? That routine act, which until five days ago she'd taken entirely for granted, now seemed unreachably removed from her current reality. There was no way that she'd be able to get there, not within a week. How much time would she need, then? Just the question made her want to toss everything here aside and run off to a place where nobody knew her.

'Could you cancel the reservation, in that case? I'm sorry for the trouble.'

After Shōko found her voice, she ended the call. She wanted to cry out and curl up on the floor right then and there, but instead she issued the appropriate commands to her body, and turned slowly on her heels. The corridor leading back to the room in question seemed so short, and the mountain she could see in its entirety through the long, thin window seemed to press in on her. The idea of returning to the private room where her father was waiting was unbearable. Even here, she found facing her father too much. The smell of the sweet-and-sour pork that had been cleared away an hour ago still lingered on in his room, making her chest feel heavy.

Investigating more thoroughly, she had realised that her father was in fact still alive. It had only been about an hour since he'd collapsed. The numbness and dizziness were the early signs of a stroke and he had passed out, ending up lying face-down. She'd called an ambulance, and they'd rushed him to the nearest hospital. After rummaging through the cupboard to find her father's address book, Shōko had called up her uncle for the first time in years, and he'd come into the hospital. The last time she'd seen him was when she was at university, and he'd since dyed his grey hair an unnatural-looking shade of brown.

The doctor had declared what a great piece of luck it was that Shōko had found her father when she did, praising her over and over.

'The dutiful daughter!' her uncle had said several times. Shōko, though, was unable to feel that this outcome was for the best. When her father had regained consciousness, he'd begun shouting out meaningless nonsense, struggling so much that they'd had to move him into a private room, where his hands and feet were now restrained.

Her father was supine, connected up to a drip, but when she slid back the door and entered, she saw him look at her. His brown eyes, reddened by years of drinking, were sunken deep into his face, and yet they appeared open, clear and wide, like one of the Seven Dwarfs.

'Wherzou go?'

He was still having trouble speaking.

'I was just on the phone.'

'Oh,' her father murmured. He clicked his tongue against the roof of his mouth and then shut his eyes. His legs moved restlessly, chafing against the straps. Was this, also, one of the symptoms of a stroke? Maybe her father didn't know what to talk to her about either.

The hospital gown he'd been given hung open, exposing the legs extending from his diaper. The hairlessness of his thin, white legs gave them the look of a woman's. Quite possibly, they were more delicate-looking than Shōko's own. The soles of his feet illuminated by the fluorescent lights were in such a bad condition that she couldn't help but stare at them. It was obvious that he'd spent years barefoot, his feet chafed at continually by the tufting tatami. The skin was thick, coated in a whitish-yellow scaly layer that looked almost like a plastic cover. The nurses must have cleaned them, but Shōko thought they exuded the same simmered smell as the house. In the places where his wrists and ankles were secured by straps, they had been rubbed red and raw.

Shōko sat down on the stool positioned by the bedside. She didn't feel sorry for her father. The only time he was this subdued was when it was the two of them. The person who directed a slurred stream of curses and sexist abuse at the nurses was a man that she didn't know – and yet she also felt that somewhere in her heart she had known this whole time that this was how her father truly was. He was ignorant and coarse, incapable of having a decent conversation with anybody. Some part of her felt relieved to glimpse the flashes of contempt passing over the faces of the doctors and nurses, which they hadn't quite managed to conceal. Antipathy towards her father was a feeling shared by many. Over time the doctors' and nurses' attitude towards Shōko, who watched her father's terrible behaviour with detachment, had grown increasingly perplexed.

Observing her father's high-handed behaviour with the young nurses, Shōko had a feeling that a long-standing mystery had been solved. Regardless of whether it was members of his own family or strangers, this was a man who took it for granted that women would serve him and act in his interest. His inheritance had made him intolerably arrogant. Even after regaining consciousness, he hadn't once thanked Shōko and seemed to show no awareness of the fact that she was currently away from her home in Tokyo.

'Wannagohome' – that was the phrase he kept repeating.

Distressingly, his behaviour, which he seemed to think totally reasonable, reminded her of her own attitude towards Kensuke.

Shōko remembered the stories she'd heard about her grandparents, now dead, who had spoiled her father – their son and heir – something rotten, buying him whatever he wanted and always letting him stay off school when he asked. He dropped out of the local university he was attending and drove around in his parents' car, hopping between the local drinking spots. The stories of his daring feats that he'd endlessly regale his drinking buddies with, to laughter and choruses of 'here we go again', were the same ones that Shōko had heard numerous times from his mouth. Of course, with his future being determined from such an early age, being tied to the house, and nursing both his parents through to their death, he must have had his own struggles. She supposed that was to blame for his recklessness, for his sense that he would live it up in the domain that had been granted him.

All that being so, though, she felt that it would have been better for him to have breathed his last breath alone in that huge house, undiscovered by anybody. She should have at least arrived home a few hours later – or not at all. She regretted each one of her actions. Why couldn't she get away from her father?

'What did you spend it on?' Shōko mumbled to him, now that his breathing informed her that he was asleep. After his hospitalisation, she had rifled through his crammed drawers in search of his bank book to pay the medical fees with. Alarmed to discover how little he had in his account, she had enquired with the family scrivener, whereby the details of her father's dissolute existence over the past few years began to assume concrete reality for her.

The divorce had already gone through, it transpired, and Urumi had returned to Niigata. She discovered that the scrivener in his sixties, whom her father had been relying on for years, was just a trainee. As she learned for the first time of her father's long-standing lack of money, and of how he'd sold off his apartment block, parking lot and fields a long time ago, she had felt a chill spread across her body. The decision had apparently caused rifts with some of his relatives, to whom he'd since stopped speaking. Even her uncle had hinted at how his money had almost certainly gone on alcohol and going out.

When Shōko had said impetuously that all that remained was to sell the mountain, her uncle had raised his furry eyebrows like a Shiba Inu's.

'That's easy enough to say, but who would you sell it to? You'd struggle to find a buyer for a spot in the middle of nowhere like this. Even company dorms and factories are being built in more accessible locations these days.'

Her uncle's tone was placid enough, but it was tainted with an ineffable vexation towards those, like her, who had got away. The kind, caring face that she knew from her childhood had vanished behind layers of wrinkles and exhaustion. She had imagined that her uncle's family would support her and her father while he was in hospital, but her uncle hadn't come back, and neither her aunt nor Miwa had called in once.

'It's a relief to know you'll be here for a while,' her brother Yōhei had said when he'd come in to see her father, but he, too, had stayed away since.

'He'll be let out eventually, right? I'll pop in now and then to see how he's doing. If there's anything I can do let me know,' he'd said with a peaceable expression.

There was not a single person concerned about her father's condition. Would the same be true of Shōko herself, one day?

The doctor had said that, though her father's stroke had only been minor, the real rehabilitation would happen once her father was discharged. There were any number of tasks his family would now be responsible for: helping him about his daily life, preparing special meals, helping him with his mobility and motor-skill exercises. When she thought about the circumstances in which she found herself, it seemed as if the gods had determined that Shōko should live with her father – that she was unable to get out of it. She had neither the energy reserves needed to push him away nor the financial assets needed to live alone in Tokyo.

Her behaviour that had caused the rift in her marriage was definitely not praiseworthy, and yet she couldn't quite believe that she deserved a punishment of this nature. She scrabbled around for a nice, heartwarming memory with her father from her childhood, but she couldn't recall a single one. All she could think was that she wanted him to hurry up and die. She could only surmise that her father knew that. She would sometimes glimpse flashes of fear and a pleading, almost coquettish expression in his eyes when he looked at her. This hard-heartedness – was this why she couldn't make friends? And did it come from being her father's daughter?

Shōko wanted a friend. She found herself yearning for someone she could talk to. She wanted, from the very bottom of her heart, someone to laugh about this situation with. She didn't care if it was someone she didn't connect with on a more meaningful level – someone with whom she could distract herself by chatting about TV programmes and food would be plenty. Now, it occurred to her, she could have tolerated even Eriko's exhausting conversation.

Why hadn't Miwa come to see her dad once? She didn't want to think that the smile on her face that time had been fake. She guessed that Nori had forgotten all about her by now too. She hadn't had so much as a single reply to her messages. Was she even visible to other people? Did she really even exist?

Please, I'm begging you all, will someone just remember me? Why are you all so cold, when I'm this lonely?

The resentment lapped through her body like a wave. She felt less and less able to move.

In that moment, perhaps waking from a nightmare, her father let out a girlish shriek and opened his eyes wide in fear.

# CHAPTER THIRTY-TWO

Eriko took out the pack of sanitising wipes. Their cool, wet texture pushed into the grooves in her fingerprints, sinking inside her flesh. Thinking that she would start off by reclaiming her old habits, she set about wiping down every inch of her desk. She even flipped her keyboard over and fastidiously removed the eraser shavings that had embedded themselves inside. She'd worried about the mass of documents that would have accumulated during her absence, but in fact, with the manager taking over much of her workload, all that awaited her was two small piles of circulars and post.

She'd been off work for over three weeks. Upon returning to the office, she found it chilly and smaller than she remembered, its ceiling lower. It's only a room, she'd intoned to herself several times when making her entrance. There's nothing to be scared of.

She was no longer that bothered by the glances darted in her direction, or the whispers that she could just about hear. Still, there were moments when she would wonder how far the rumours about her had spread, and would want to bury her head in her desk. At these times, she'd focus on taking deep breaths, and then try to involve herself in some task or other. If she could only immerse herself in her private world, she was no longer so bothered about other people. Protecting herself in this way would be her only chance to make it through her time here.

At some point, it had hit Eriko that the only route to getting her former self back was by going into work as if nothing had happened, and so she'd talked her worried parents round, and made her decision known. Before heading into the office, she'd bathed, tied back her hair, applied BB cream, and pencilled in her eyebrows for the first time in an age. She put on the baggy jumper and coat her mother had bought her. Most of her old clothes no longer fitted her. The crush of people around her on the morning commute left her reeling, and by the time she stepped into the company building she was already exhausted. Yet her desperation to return to the pace of life that she'd had before she met Shōko remained unaffected.

The manager had been kind to her, showing none of the harshness she'd seen that night in Shinsen. They'd met in his office before working hours commenced, and he'd talked at length, as if to prevent her from saying too much.

'Are you sure you're okay to come back? In any case, I won't be expecting you to return to how you were straight away. You can come back in once every few days, ease back into it gradually. We can also think about a change of position.'

Eriko could no longer fathom that she had attempted to sleep with this man. Her diagnosis of the situation now was that she had wanted to reach out and touch something that ran deeper than merely superficial interactions, something real and raw like magma. Yet what she'd found her way to instead was even more superficial, more fake than what had existed before. She imagined he was only being this supportive because she was the daughter of his former boss. His broad smiles formed dark creases in his face and seemed designed to warn her off trying to come any closer. Behind these smiles lay his wife and his daughters. He could guard his feelings because he had things in his life he wished to protect. Never before had he seemed so remote to her.

As Eriko set about opening her post and replying to the huge volume of emails she'd received, the time flew by. The manager had told her that the Nile perch account had been passed on to Tashiro, a colleague three years her junior in the adjacent division. When Eriko went to see him, he gave her a matter-of-fact update.

'Oh, the factory in Tanzania? That's on hold for the moment. I'm sorry, I know you went all the way out there and stuff, but right as we were about to sign, the processing company started issuing all kinds of unreasonable demands. Our expectations were too high. There was no way we were going to see any return on our investment in the facilities for years in the future, and there was no workaround for the issue of the funds being blocked during transit, either.'

As Tashiro handed back the materials, he explained that the market for fish imports from Africa was likely to keep shrinking.

Eriko drifted back to her desk, gritting her teeth as she reflected that if she'd only examined the facilities in Tanzania with a more exacting gaze, and hadn't given up responsibility of the job midway, then things might have turned out differently. The faces of the people who'd helped her out in Tanzania – Naomi, the managers and employees of the processing factories – flashed one by one before her eyes. There was no doubt that there would be people who'd lose their jobs thanks to her.

Above anyone else, though, she felt sorry for the Nile perch. The destruction of the ecosystem in Lake Victoria had caused an overabundance of algae and plankton, and the water was polluted. The Nile perch had been forced to battle for their survival, had fought bitterly to wipe out other species, and now, as a result, their own habitat was becoming uninhabitable …

Eriko raised her eyes to see that it was past two. She didn't feel like going outside, and so she decided to head for the canteen, which she hadn't set foot in since first joining the company. Raising her bottom from the desk chair, she spotted several men out of the corner of her eye pretending to step back in terror, and laughing.

Past peak lunchtime, the office canteen was largely deserted. Eriko purchased a ticket for Lunch Set A, which comprised white fish in batter with tomato sauce, rice, miso soup, potato salad and stewed hijiki. With tray in hand, she moved along the counter that ran alongside the kitchen picking up the individual dishes and bowls in turn, before taking a seat by the window. She felt grateful for being able to eat warm food that she could tell had been made with care without even having to step outside the building. Maybe she should have come here before. The fish in its thick batter seemed to be black cod.

Before, loathing the idea that people would see her eating alone, Eriko had either sat at her desk chowing down the food she'd brought in from outside while staring at her computer screen, or else eaten out at a restaurant far enough from the company that there was scant chance anybody would see her there. Now, though, she barely cared that she didn't have a single friend in the company, or that people were gossiping about her appearance and her behaviour. The rumours were true, and there was no point denying them. Nothing much had really changed from before, when everything had seemed superficially to be going well, but people had kept their distance regardless. The one thing she struggled to bear was the thought that her actions were sullying the reputation her father had built up in the company. For that reason, she was determined not to look scruffy, or make sloppy mistakes. It didn't matter if it took a while – she had to learn to swim in this place again.

The fish had perhaps been refried, as it felt heavy in her stomach. Suspecting that a cold drink would only make the oil harden, Eriko went for the first time in many months to the kitchen on the sales division floor, and made a cup of hot hojicha from the pot, which she drank standing up. As the warmth spread down her body from her neck, she felt the tension of the last few hours dissolving away. She caught sight of a bag of imo-kempi – long sweet-potato French fries with a hard sugared coating – fastened with a clip on the trolley by the wall. The message on the whiteboard read:

*I visited Kawagoe at the weekend, and brought these back for you guys! I thought I was going for the healthy option but then I looked at the calorie count (sob). If I keep them to myself I'll only get even fatter, so ta-da!*

*Maori*

At the end of Maori's message in its rounded, right-slanting letters was a drawing of a piglet. This central note was surrounded by subsidiary messages in assorted handwriting: *Thank you, Maori! Good luck with the bridal beauty treatments!* and *How many times do I have to tell you, you're not fat!* and *Omg these are so crunchy and delicious! Thanks.* Eriko found herself smiling, and reached out a hand to the board. The ink bled onto her fingers, staining them indigo. This humble interaction seemed wonderful to her, and it struck her that this board was the only place in the office that was alive with the warmth of human feeling.

Going to Kawagoe must mean a visit to Sugishita's parents' house, Eriko figured. He'd told her that the wedding had been postponed, but it seemed as though their relationship was still progressing, celebrated by the people around them. She felt relieved that she'd not taken what he'd said too seriously. It seemed a very Maori way of going on to declare that there was no love between them, but still waste no time in moving things in the direction she wanted them to go.

Just then, Eriko felt someone at her back. She knew, without having to turn, who it was.

'Stop! Get off.' She squirmed furiously, but Sugishita seemed to have mistaken her resistance for embarrassment. 'Things are going well with you and Maori! She went to see your parents! Someone will come in, you've got to stop.'

Eriko twisted round, trying to direct his gaze to the whiteboard, yet the hands grabbing her from behind only tightened their grip. She wanted to scream, but she knew that if someone came running in, she'd be in trouble. His arms, which could once have enveloped her with plenty of room to spare, now fitted snugly around her waist.

'It's okay, I don't mind that you've put on all that weight. The thing is, Shimura, I get you. I think I might actually *love* you. Since I saw you this morning I haven't been able to take my eyes off you.'

Eriko turned her head and looked at him from short range. From a distance he seemed so well presented, but up close she saw that his skin was rough and his breath smelt terrible. Doing her best to externalise her revulsion, she frowned.

'You ate lunch by yourself, didn't you? You've got no friends, and none of the women can stand you, but I think I really do love you. Just as you are. You've got so much pride, and yet you're always watching to see what other women make of you, and you're so quick to feel rejected. It's so cute. You're cute. I feel soothed watching you.'

His strength was sufficient that after a while Eriko gave up fighting back. They'd already seen each other naked – she felt like anything she tried to do now would be futile. It came to her with a shiver that all the men who had ever got close to her in the past had probably felt something similar to what Sugishita had articulated. Why else would they have chosen someone as closed-off as her?

'I want to get away from her. I've tried so hard, but I've reached my limit. She's going funny in the head. Ever since we've postponed the wedding ceremony, she's been totally different. Her mother pestered us into signing the marriage papers, but that was a mistake. She's just become … so …'

Sugishita's voice began to tremble, and then changed to a low sob. It's not only Maori that's going funny in the head, Eriko thought. It's you, as well. The very idea that you'd still not realise that you take it for granted that you'll be babied by the women in your life.

'The thing with Maori is that she's not got a lot going for her. This week she's not made me a single meal. She's left me on my own while she trots out every night to see her girlfriends and discuss bridesmaid shit or whatever. It's messed up! She seems very confident, but at heart she's scared of how she measures up to others.'

'She doesn't seem that way to me.'

'She needs the people around her to wait on her, to support her. She wants to believe that she's still a girl, not a woman, that her future's spread out limitlessly in front of her. Which is why she gets so excited about all this girly get-together stuff. People don't even like her.'

'Really? I get the sense they really *do* like her.'

This was the truth. Her eyes hovered across Maori's writing adorning the whiteboard in front of her. However vicious the side that Maori concealed inside, she never forgot to bring in presents for her colleagues, and this added touch of leaving a humorous, pitch-perfect message also struck Eriko as a rarity. Had it occurred to her, even for a split-second, to buy souvenirs and bring them into the staff kitchen? She had been on so many work trips and yet she'd never once thought to do it.

'Women don't like other women. A woman would never truly have another woman's back. You're such a coddled little princess, you've no idea how the world really works. But that's what I love about you.' His voice sugary with something like affection, Sugishita breathed right inside her ear, making all the hair on her body stand on end. He finally released his hands from his waist, and instead wrapped an arm around her shoulder in a gesture of apparent tenderness.

'It's just that other women don't feel threatened by her, because she's beneath them. She really believes in these flimsy bonds made up of lunches and teas and shit. But women are cruel, and unbelievably shady. I feel bad for her. She's disposable to them, like a clown …'

Sugishita trailed off suddenly. Catching the scent of something metallic, Eriko looked down to see a ribbon of red dribbling down her chest. It took her a moment to realise that the ribbon was originating from Sugishita's right hand on her shoulder. Jutting out at a right angle from the pale skin on the back of his hand was a particularly large and sharp imo-kempi, its hard surface glistening with honey. Unable to believe her eyes, a faint smile floated on her lips.

Maori was standing right behind her. She smoothly withdrew the imo-kempi from Sugishita's limp hand as he let out a stifled yelp and released his grip on Eriko. He fell to the floor, writhing at their feet. The blood oozed out from between the fingers of his left hand pressed to his mouth, and began pooling on the floor.

'Oh God … We better take him to the medical room!' Eriko said, although nowhere in her finally liberated body did she feel the desire to go anywhere. Never again, she thought, did she want a man touching her without permission.

'It's okay,' Maori said, with total calm, kicking Sugishita's lower back lightly with one of the sandals she wore in the office. Of the three of them, Maori seemed to Eriko the strongest, the best adapted to society.

'What will you do if he dies?'

In the time that Eriko hadn't seen her, Maori's body had grown thicker, assuming the stateliness of a mother. She looked eminently reliable. Maybe it wouldn't be so bad if Sugishita were to die now, she thought. She and Maori could dispose of the body and run away together.

'It's all right, I made sure not to do it too deep. He's so dumb that these are the lengths you have to go to, to get him to understand. I have to teach him this stuff, or else more women will suffer.'

Maori seemed so chipper that it was hard to believe she belonged to the same scene as this bleeding man. She swept up her hair, which she'd dyed back to her original black. Sugishita trembled, whimpering on the floor. Eriko wondered if the odd-looking scar on his neck was a bite mark from Maori.

'But if you do this kind of stuff at work, you'll not be able to stay here long, surely? You don't know who's watching.'

'Ummm, I don't really need that kind of advice from a deranged office slut. It's fine, though. If someone finds out, I'll blame it all on you. Nobody will ever doubt me. People like me and they don't like you. Now you've put on weight and stopped bothering about your appearance, you don't even have any male fans. This is why I hate men. If someone doesn't register on their attractiveness radar, they can't muster the slightest empathy for them.'

Saying this, Maori brandished the imo-kempi stained with her husband's blood and laughed. Eriko found herself smiling along with her. Her concern for Sugishita, who still lay between them on the floor, ebbed away.

Even in this situation, Eriko found herself drawn to Maori's curvy body, taken by a strong urge to be inside it. As different as they were, she couldn't help but conflate Maori and Sugishita with her parents in their younger days: the clerical worker from junior college who'd outdone all her rivals to marry the spoiled rich salesman, and then left the company. Maybe, as they got older, these two really would turn out like her parents. If that was so, then Eriko wanted to be born as their child and live her life over again. The new home would be similar to her original one, but she'd grow up with a better understanding of her parents as people. From Maori she'd learn how to make friends with other girls, and would bring classmates home every day. Maori would greet her friends cheerily and feed them shop-bought snacks. She'd be proud of her fun mum. The tremulous voice at her feet pulled Eriko back to reality.

'Why are you so obsessed with your female friends! Are you a lezzer or what? It's gross. If your friendships were as tight as you say, do you really think that your language would be this filthy, that you'd be this violent to your husband? You're so fucked up. In your heart of hearts, you're unfulfilled and resentful.'

'Hm? What's that?' Maori snorted and without hesitation drove the toe of her sandal into Sugishita's lower back. 'You think that having friends goes hand in hand with being a nice, well-rounded person? Well, let me spell it out for you: the fact that

I'm violent and obsessed with money, and the fact that I have loads of friends that I enjoy hanging out with, are Totally Un-Fucking-Related! Man, you're unbelievable. You really don't get anything.'

She narrowed her eyes and stared into Sugishita's face, which was twisted in pain.

'Look at you! You hate women, you can't get by without looking down on them, and yet you've been carrying around these overly high expectations of female friendship this whole time! I bet you picture it as some kind of female paradise, some glorious flower garden! And then when there's even the tiniest hint of difficulty between friends, you point your finger and laugh. Say, look, see, a woman's enemy is other women, that proves that men are better. Fucking moron.'

Maori tugged the back of Sugishita's hair with a jerk, and he fell into a violent coughing fit. 'You're a piece of shit. It's not me who can't grow up, it's you. You feel like it's only right and natural that you're handled with kid gloves. A squib like you. Before you start berating me, maybe do something about your lack of skills in the bedroom? Come on, get up. You've been so spoiled by your pushover of a mother that all the screws in your head have fallen out. You go around saying all this shit, and yet you don't have a single male friend. Do you know what they call you behind your back?'

'Women are scary, man. I can't take it any more. I'm begging you, please call me an ambulance,' Sugishita began sobbing. Maori picked up the wet cloth sitting by the sink and lobbed it at him. It bounced off his torso and fell to the floor with a splat, spraying water across the floor.

'And it looks like it's your fate to marry the scariest of them all! Do you really think I'd miss out on this opportunity to elevate my social standing in a single leap? You know that if word gets out that you got a temp pregnant and married her, only to dump her shortly after, you'll be relocated to some backwater branch? No question about it.'

Oddly enough, Eriko felt rather sorry for Maori: someone with this level of insight and resilience could easily get by on their own, and yet the only approach to life she understood was clinging to a man. At the same time, though, it occurred to her that Maori was the only person who could manage to be with Sugishita – Sugishita, who so urgently needed to be enveloped in maternal love and validation, while holding on to his loathing of women.

'You can go,' said Maori, turning to her. Eriko felt grateful that Maori had remembered her presence. She felt incapable of moving without Maori's permission. More than that, though, she wanted to remain here. Whatever tension it might contain, this kitchen had soul. It had a human warmth, which was free of superficial posturing. She found even the mouldy scent of the sink and the metallic smell emanating from Sugishita's wound comforting. Maori was munching on the remaining imo-kempi, with an expression that said this was a perfectly normal way to behave in this situation. There was a cute quality to her gestures that put Eriko in mind of a baby squirrel.

'Don't come back to the office. You've got to resign right away. Just the sight of Eriko Shimura back at her desk this morning gave me a heavy feeling in the pit of my stomach. It's like there's suddenly less oxygen when you're around. You make it hard to breathe. It's painful for me to look at you. I'm guessing everyone feels the same. It's less that they hate you, and more like everyone feels like they're having their most embarrassing, shameful parts revealed. That must be why you can't make friends.'

'But …'

Eriko couldn't give up. She couldn't relinquish the pursuit of becoming the good daughter, esteemed at the same company her father worked at; of changing herself without changing her circumstances. She just didn't know how to do it yet. It seemed that Maori intercepted her thoughts immediately.

'You're not still thinking that you can grow as a person simply by gritting your teeth and digging your nails in, are you? Trust me, you need a change of tank. Forget what your beloved ma and pa have taught you. You've been trying hard for God knows how long and it's not been working for you, has it? So you need to let go. Put some space between you and this place.'

Maori suddenly stuck the imo-kempi she'd been chewing into Eriko's mouth. Its blade-like tip made to pierce her throat, and she hurriedly bit down on it. She heard the snap ring in her ears, and then the gentle taste of sweet potato spread through her mouth. It made her think of the little sweet-potato cakes she'd baked with her mother and Keiko. She remembered scooping up the warm sweet cream in the pan with a spatula and licking it off – it was that same taste. Her eyes filled with tears and she murmured, 'That's so good.'

'Hah,' Maori cocked an eyebrow and smiled.

The pool of blood at their feet was edging towards their toes.

# CHAPTER THIRTY-THREE

The clock read eight-thirty – time for Shōko to leave for the hospital. The bus that took her there only came once an hour, and if she missed it, she'd have to stand there at the stop for what felt like an eternity, staring at the mountain. Her feeling of resignation far outweighed any exhaustion or misery. The choice was now out of her hands. That had been the case until now, and it now looked set to be the case into the future. Just when she thought she'd shaken herself free of Eriko's control, she found herself back in her father's thrall.

As her father had stopped paying his electricity and gas bills, the only heat generated in the house came from a single paraffin stove. With the shutters wedged open, the old Japanese-style house was only protected from the elements by single-paned windows, and so it was freezing cold. The air striking her cheeks was so frigid it made her bones hurt. The futon Shōko slept on was a heavy, dusty old thing that smelled of camphor, and yet she still felt reluctant to get up from it. The year was drawing to a close. Wanting to avert her eyes from the room and its all-too-potent reminder of her clichéd tastes in high school, Shōko gazed up at the wooden ceiling.

How was Kensuke getting on, she wondered. She texted him at least twice a day, but he'd never once replied. She imagined he was very busy, with the end-of-year sale and preparing New Year's gift bags and so on. Was he struggling without her? But no, she felt sure everything was exactly as it had always been. She had barely done anything for him in the first place.

Since they'd been married, she'd never once made New Year's osechi or done a big New Year clean, as was traditional. They watched the Kōhaku New Year's Song Contest together, then ate the toshikoshi soba that Shōko made with instant noodles. When the New Year's Sale at Kensuke's supermarket had finished, they went to see his parents. That was the sum total of their New Year's traditions together as a couple. Even that, though, had been more than enough to fill her with the quiet astonishment of another year passing, and the excited anticipation of a new one arriving. It occurred to her that this was surely because Kensuke had been by her side, and her eyelids grew hot.

The New Year's periods she'd spent in this house had always bristled with tension. Every nook and cranny of the house was polished until it sparkled, the dinner table had been piled high with delicious food, and yet Shōko had spent the entire time wishing it was over so that she could see her boyfriend. She didn't want to sit and watch her father and brothers treating her mother even more like a servant than usual. Her father, who would pretend to be engrossed in the TV when he was actually monitoring her mother's every move, would occasionally hurl words like sharpened knives. Once, when the family had been making to set out for the nearby temple to hear the tolling of the bell, they hadn't been able to find her mother. Shōko had gone to look for her and found her weeping in a corner of the hallway. When the first of January came around and her relatives came over, her father would suddenly act like a different person, becoming comical and amiable. Shōko had found this transformation horrifying.

Visiting her father in hospital gave Shōko little choice but to stay over in the house. She wasn't helping much with his rehabilitation exercises or bathing him, instead simply watching on as the nurses did it all, and yet she felt permanently physically and mentally exhausted. She felt hesitant to draw close to her father's withered skin, which she hadn't touched in years. Each time the young nurses' faces twitched in response to her father's behaviour, which was becoming more high-handed by the day, her stomach would clench.

Shōko finally dragged herself up from the bed.

She had no impetus to clean. On her first day she'd felt like crying at the prospect of spending time in a place this cold and dirty, but there were neither any capsule hotels nor manga cafés in the vicinity. She'd use the showers in the hospital, buy a beer and a bento at the convenience store without even properly checking the ingredients, and stay holed up in her bedroom until the following morning, relying on the paraffin stove and a torch. She'd shut the doors to the other rooms tight, and do her best to forget what lay inside them. She was determined not to think about the fact that just one wall away, all kinds of insects were probably crawling around, eating away at the rotting garbage. Instead she would snuggle under the duvet, and look at the phone she'd sneakily charged in the hospital, a cigarette in one hand. Her sole source of joy was following Nori's movements, messaging Nori to tell her what was going on with her, and checking every half-hour whether she had a reply.

According to her blog, Nori was currently caught up in decorating her house for Christmas and baking a new variety of pie, cookie or other confection on a daily basis. Her elder daughter, who was preparing for her entrance exams, had come down with a cold, and Nori was trying to get her to rest and ingest plenty of vitamins. The rice gratin that she'd produced in tandem with a convenience store had gone on sale in Tokyo. From the pictures Shōko could see on the website, with its golden cheese topping, it looked very appealing. For the winter vacation, Nori was taking her family to New York. Shōko admired how well she utilised her time, how she seemed to be capable of generating little bits of income here, there and everywhere. Comparing herself with this friend of hers, Shōko only grew more despondent. If only Nori were here to help her with cleaning the house, or even just to give her some advice, she felt as though her stress would lift in a second. Every part of her cried out to see her. These were the feelings that she poured out into her emails.

Her father would be discharged from hospital next week. That meant she had to get ahead with sorting the house, making it an appropriate place for him to be cared for, but she couldn't bring herself to do it. She had no idea where to start.

She craved a cigarette. The three boxes of Camels she'd bought yesterday were already gone. Her dad's Mevius were normally too strong for her, but as long as they contained nicotine, she no longer cared. She figured they must be in the drawer, along with his bank book and personal seal. If possible she wanted to avoid setting eyes on that room, but the prospect of getting ready and leaving the house seemed beyond her without a cigarette, and she shuffled from her room wrapped in her duvet. Even in socks, she almost jumped in shock at the coldness of the hall floor underfoot. The morning light cut through the hazy darkness in strips, as tiny motes of dust went dancing. Maybe she'd been blowing it up in her mind, or else it was a case of seeing it lit up rather than cast in darkness, but in either case, the main room didn't look as bad as she'd remembered. There was just rubbish everywhere.

She tugged several times at the drawer that was stuffed to bursting before it opened, and then tipped the contents onto the floor. Out spilled unopened letters, documents about the land and four sets of keys. However much she rummaged, though, she couldn't find the cigarettes. Instead, her eyes landed on some pills in a Ziploc bag. As if captivated, she stayed staring down at the blue pills in their foil sheets for what seemed like a while.

Finally she stood up and went over to the altar, and laid her grandparents' photos face-down. She picked up the vases, and tipped out the browning water onto the dirt floor in the entranceway. Taking that small step made her feel a lot better. She went down into the entranceway, despite how freezing it was, and rinsed out the vases. After filling them with water so cold she felt it might cut her hands open, she returned to the altar and set the vases down roughly. Droplets of water went flying, speckling the backs of the photo frames. She went back to her room with the Ziploc bag in hand, did a Google Images search for Viagra, and compared the splay of images to the tablets sitting before her.

Should she tell the doctor? While she deliberated, Shōko stepped into the same clothes as yesterday, put on a down jacket she'd worn as a schoolgirl with its stuffing coming out, and finally stepped outside. It was a clear day, but the air was so cold her fingers grew numb. By now she was thoroughly accustomed to the sweet, rotting smell of the mountain, and it didn't elicit any particular feelings in her. She walked down the narrow path by the rice fields without encountering anyone. The bus came on time, and she got on.

Was it possible that those tablets had been responsible for her father's stroke? Had he used them with Urumi? Or on his nighttime excursions? But no, it didn't matter who he'd used them with. It seemed to Shōko as though the three-storey hospital drawing nearer outside the window was her father himself. The idea that inside that violent, emotionless man resided the same murky desire as she herself housed made him even more repellent to her. He didn't want to do anything for anyone else, and yet he wanted other people to expend extraordinary amounts of energy on his behalf. She felt that she couldn't forgive her father for using medication like that to fulfil his utterly selfish desires.

She wanted to run away, right this second. She didn't want to see her father. She felt, once again, that she loathed him. Mercilessly, the bus pulled up at the hospital bus stop. Shōko was spat out of its door slowly, along with a few elderly people.

She entered the hospital via the same entrance as usual, for visitors and emergency patients. She got out of the elevator at the third floor and was about to walk past the glass-fronted lounge when she came to a standstill instead.

'Ken-chan!' said the falsetto voice that shot from her chapped lips. It was the first time she'd spoken in over ten hours. The gentle figure sitting in front of the TV raised a hand and then came over.

She hadn't seen him in two weeks, but he looked unchanged, with the same glistening, round face as ever. In his Uniqlo fleece, he looked somehow contented, fulfilled. He wasn't like her father, who couldn't go on living without women. She realised once again that the reason she'd fallen for him in the first place was his self-sufficiency. She felt embarrassed about her own appearance, scruffier than ever. She wanted to cry and fall into his arms, but the broad smile that she knew to be his work smile held her back.

The two of them sat on a sofa by the vending machine in a corner of the lounge. Here, too, the lights of a cheap Christmas tree twinkled relentlessly.

'I came on the night bus, and went to visit your dad. I hadn't seen him since our wedding, but he remembered me. He's in better shape than I was expecting. I was worried about him, so I thought I'd better come see him before the New Year.'

'Where will you stay tonight?' Shōko was sure that she was making a needy face. Kensuke averted his eyes in a manner that managed not to be cruel.

'I'm getting the bullet train back to Tokyo now. I've got to work this afternoon. Things are busy at the moment.'

He had most likely come here as a friend, Shōko judged dejectedly after studying his face for a while. She recalled how he'd always stepped in to help when any of his colleagues had a problem with their families. It was best that she didn't get her hopes up too much.

In a deliberately flippant tone, she narrated the events of the past few days, insulting her father and her stay in this part of the town with every swear word she had at her disposal. When a wry smile finally appeared on Kensuke's face, she was so delighted she ended up presenting him with the Ziploc bag.

'Can you believe it? Viagra, of all things! You'd think there'd be a limit to how fricking shameless someone can be! Still a lech, even at that age. Although I guess I'm hardly one to talk …'

She'd only intended to make a self-deprecating joke, but seeing that the smile had vanished from Kensuke's face, Shōko quickly pursed her lips.

'You should probably tell the doctors. I'm not an expert in this stuff, but I imagine that was one of the factors behind his change in blood pressure.'

Saying this, Kensuke slowly reached inside his rucksack. The five or so pills that emerged from the wallet that she'd once given him were the same as those in the Ziploc bag. Shōko found herself hardly able to process this development.

'What are those?'

'I got given them as a joke when I went out for drinks with a bunch of guys once. I've somehow never quite managed to throw them away.'

'You're not that old yet!' Shōko said jokily, but Kensuke didn't smile.

'I guess I don't really have any right to blame you for being unfaithful.'

'You mean you carried them around in case something happened with someone who wasn't me? Yeah, that figures.' She'd intended to smile, but she could feel the corners of her mouth twitching. Shōko never even once considered the possibility of Kensuke being with other women. The idea of it made her feel even more isolated. Was there really nothing in this world that she could rely on? Was this the effect that being betrayed by one's partner had – that one stopped trusting not only that person, but everything in sight? Her feelings of guilt towards Kensuke grew heavier. In the morning quiet of the lounge, his words seemed to echo.

'No ... I've never wanted to do it with anybody else. But they're like a talisman. For a man approaching middle age.'

'A talisman?'

'I think lots of people have talismans, in different forms. I always thought your blog served as one for you. A lifeline that enables you to remain connected to yourself. That was why I never told you to stop, even when you seemed to get caught up in it.'

Kensuke bought a can of coffee from the vending machine, pulled the tab and took a sip. Shōko carefully observed his movements, reluctant to let anything pass her by. Despite all the time they'd spent together, she'd barely been looking at him.

'Getting old is scary, isn't it? Every day I feel like I'm becoming less of a man. Unlike you, I'm not someone who can keep on discovering new worlds for myself. If we got divorced, I'm sure you'd find someone new in the blink of an eye, whereas I don't know if there'd be anyone else for me. It's not that I'm unhappy, but sensing your range of possibilities drying up in front of you isn't a nice feeling. I think the best thing would be to go on feeling that you'd actively chosen a good foundation for your life, but there aren't many people who actually manage that.'

The two of them had started out as a boss and a part-timer who got on well. For Shōko, who had no other friends, having someone like Kensuke that she could talk to about anything had been indispensable for her, even if it had taken her a long time to view their connection in a romantic light. They had often sat talking in the back of the supermarket with a drink in hand. When she'd realised that his kindness was directed at everybody, she had felt that she wanted to possess it for herself alone, and had laid a trap to make Kensuke hers. What would have happened if they'd stayed as friends, she now wondered. It seemed possible that they'd have maintained a friendship that felt better, more open, than the relationship they'd had as husband and wife.

'I think I understand a bit what you were thinking. It wasn't that you loved him and wanted to get rid of me. You just wanted to feel a sense of the possibilities available to you. I know that it wasn't serious, and yet in a way that makes it even harder for me to forgive you right now. In any case, you shouldn't be too ashamed of your dad. Forgive him, for my sake.'

Kensuke got to his feet. His denim-wrapped hips hovered at her eyeline. She wanted to grab onto them and bury her face there. She wanted to feel the heat of his body.

'I ... um ...'

She couldn't bring herself to ask him whether they could start over. She didn't want to see him looking pained, and she was also scared that he'd say no.

'Okay, keep well. Sorry for not being more help.'

'No, thanks for coming.' She was on the verge of offering to see him to the bus stop, but he walked away before she could get the words out. He stepped into the elevator, waved, and then disappeared from her sight.

For a while, she couldn't take her eyes from the elevator doors that lay beyond the glass. She felt as though she were dreaming. She stroked the seat of the sofa where he'd been sitting until just before, which still bore the impression of his body. Feeling how warm it was, tears spilled from her eyes – the first she'd cried since coming here.

If the tables were turned, she thought, there would be no way that she could go and visit a member of Kensuke's family. She wanted Kensuke to know that there were all kinds of possibilities open to him that she lacked. But how was she to do that?

Sensing eyes on her, she lifted her head. She hurriedly wiped away her tears, took her phone from her pocket and pretended to be engrossed in it. To her surprise, she'd had a missed call in the last few minutes: Satoko. This alone was a big event. Shōko dashed into the phone area and pressed her mobile to her ear. She no longer minded who it was – talking to anybody was better than sitting there snivelling by herself.

'Shōko, it's been a while. It's Satoko.' Shōko recalled that clipped tone, that husky voice. Before, she'd found the seamlessness of Satoko's interactions lacking in authenticity, had even avoided her as a result, but now this woman was her sole bridge to society. A feeling of elation blossomed in her.

'It has been a while! Sorry I didn't pick up before. I guess you're calling about the book. I'll do it. Please let me do it. I really want to work. Though I'm actually back home at my parents' at the moment, and haven't been able to update the blog for a bit.'

Filled with the joy of speaking to someone other than her family, Shōko felt like she could go on and on, but Satoko cut her off flatly.

'That's not why I was calling. I am getting in touch to ask if you could please stop contacting Noriko Ikeda.'

'Noriko Ikeda …? Who's that?' she asked, marvelling to herself how imbecilic her voice sounded.

'Do you really not know? That's Nori's real name.'

'Is it!' The idea that someone like Nori had such a regular sort of name, like a local schoolteacher, suddenly made Shōko want to burst out laughing. The true identity of that glamorous blogger invited to the opening reception of a new pancake restaurant on Omotesandō, who'd been selected as the face of a huge outlet mall was … Noriko Ikeda.

'She's been quite distressed by the number of messages she's receiving from you. It seems as though this morning's message came as a particular shock …'

Shōko frowned. Her text this morning had simply said, quite honestly, how much she wished that she was spending Christmas with Nori and her family.

'Wait a minute, please. Nori and I are friends!' Shōko made a spirited attempt to fight back, but was once again cut off with indomitable momentum.

'I'm imagining that you're back at your parents' house because there's some sort of family situation, and I suspect that you're tired. I think it's best to think of this as a time to get some rest. Oh, yes, and I'll transfer the money for the interview and panel the other month, maybe you can buy a treat for your family. I'll be in touch when the time is right.'

Shōko felt as though Satoko placed a lot of emphasis on the 'I'll', then ended the call. For a while Shōko stared at her phone, and then buried her face in her lap. She felt laughter bubbling up slowly from inside her.

It was too funny. Nori was thinking that she, Shōko, was a stalker.

So it had happened, at last: Shōko finally understood the behaviour of the woman that she'd found so terrifying and incomprehensible.

Shōko had happened to appear in front of Eriko when she was frantically searching for something to cling onto. It seemed unfathomable to her that Eriko, who lived in central Tokyo not wanting for anything, could feel the same way as Shōko, living alone without money or a job with her father out in the sticks. Maybe that was the extent to which living without someone in whom you could confide meant losing yourself as you had existed up until then. You lost sight of yourself and how you appeared to others. Shōko realised she'd had no grasp of the severity of the appeal she'd waged on Nori. She guessed that if she were to go through each of her actions one by one, she'd find the spectre of Eriko rising up before her, staring her down.

How ridiculous she'd been, she thought, for loathing Eriko that intensely, and distancing herself.

She started laughing out loud, and then found that she couldn't stop. An elderly woman in pyjamas walking past shot her a pitying look. Her long, kind-looking face with its bluish-white skin somehow resembled Shōko's grandmother. At that moment, something inside Shōko began to whir, something that felt like it didn't belong to her. Some part of her that was focused on the feelings of others had begun to function.

Why had her caring uncle and Miwa with her straightforward kindness not reached out to help her? Why had her aunt not come to visit the hospital?

Shōko's fingers moved across her phone. In a few moments, she heard her uncle's dry voice.

'Shōko, it's you.'

'Listen, uncle …' Hearing his tired sigh, Shōko's sense of conviction grew. 'There's something I want to ask you. Is Auntie ill?'

For a few moments, she listened to her uncle breathing. Then she heard him swallow. 'I'm sorry I didn't tell you. I thought it was better not to, when you were going through so much.'

Shōko let out a stifled cry. She felt a lump go falling from her throat into her insides.

'She's been bed-bound since last year, with bronchitis. Miwa's looking after her. It's a full-time caring responsibility, and she's virtually housebound. Her son's only little, still … It sounds as if that was in part the reason for the separation. She and her husband didn't see eye to eye about her caring for her mother. It's a real shame.'

When Shōko had seen Miwa, she'd not got the slightest hint of her suffering. So that invitation to go to dinner had been a mere pleasantry, she thought now.

The same as Nori's exhortation: *Be in touch whenever you like, I'm always happy to help!* She'd taken them at their word, had been waiting impatiently for them to contact her. Shōko could hardly laugh at Eriko when she herself was no better.

She knew now why she'd treated Eriko so cruelly – it was because the two of them were so similar. The unsightly way they misjudged distances with others, and were left spinning round, going nowhere. That was what had made Eriko's behaviour so hard to watch.

'Would it be okay to come and see her?'

Shōko had been miffed that Miwa hadn't texted, but it had never occurred to her to think that maybe she had a good reason. Now she felt that, if at all possible, she wanted to help Miwa. That was perhaps the first time she'd had that thought, about anybody. Miwa most likely needed someone to talk to, if anyone did. Above all, she wondered how her aunt was doing.

'Thank you. She'd like that, and so would Miwa. We've hardly seen anyone, so we could do with a change of scene. But I know it's a hard time for you too. Don't push yourself.'

'I won't. I'd really like to see her.'

After putting the phone down, Shōko went over to the vending machine, inserted some coins, and selected the same coffee that Kensuke had bought. She took out her phone once more and brought up the familiar number. Kensuke was apparently on the move, and it went straight to his voicemail. She made sure to speak fast, in a bid to say all she had to say in the allotted time.

'I'm guessing you're at the station already. The thing is, Ken-chan, I've always been afraid of having nothing to show for my life, for myself. That's not an excuse for what I did, but I think it's also true that when that guy showed an interest in me, I felt a form of relief, like I wasn't a lost cause after all. The same went for people praising my blog. I wanted to create some record that I'd been alive. Like you said, I think I wanted to feel like I had possibilities open to me. But by letting other people determine my own worth like that, I lost the thing that was most important to me. What I love about you is that you would never do anything like that. That was why I felt so relaxed around you. I'm not going to do that any more, let other people decide my worth. I know that sounds easy to say.'

Her mouth grew dry and she struggled to get the words out. She took a sip of coffee and swallowed. When she spoke again, her voice came out far smoother.

'I want to start over with you, Ken-chan. I want to try to become the kind of person who makes you feel that so much is possible, that the whole world is open to you, just by being by your side.'

After hanging up, Shōko blinked slowly. Her eyes scanned the room, taking in the linoleum floor and the patient in pyjamas hooked up to a drip, desperately trying to locate some ray of light imbuing everything with hope, and failing.

She'd said it. That was all that she could do – tell him the truth. There was a significant possibility she'd never see him again. This was only one step. Even if she did eventually manage to return to the place she'd once been, the road leading there was mind-bogglingly long. Yet Shōko wasn't thinking about turning back.

She had to go and see her father. Today had only just begun. She stood up, and threw back her coffee in one, then crushed the can, and threw it in the bin. Her body was now thoroughly warmed.

It was then that Shōko realised something. She was no longer so frightened of spending time alone with the father she'd so disliked.

# CHAPTER THIRTY-FOUR

Back when Eriko was a girl, it would always reassure her to catch a distant glimpse of the block of apartments where she and Keiko lived when rising to the top of the playground seesaw or when flying high into the air on the swing. Even when playing with her closest friends, it was by her parents' side that Eriko felt the most at ease. Now she could see her apartment block even from the bench – presumably because the building that used to stand in front of the park had been knocked down, and a car park created in its place.

'Did you never think about moving away?'

'I did think about it, but I didn't have the right to decide. Your father had taken the decision to keep on living there, based on various calculations he'd made around his job and the mortgage, so I just went along with it.'

The white air around them was chilly. The year was almost at an end. The biting wind felt somehow refreshing to Eriko, honing all her senses.

It was a long time since she'd come on a walk with her mother like this. She was still going into the office, but despite not making any mistakes, the only work she was being entrusted with were basic administrative tasks. As a result, she didn't feel exhausted at the weekend, and had the energy for things like this. Her mother had been frosty towards her since their argument, so Eriko had invited her out for a stroll.

In the clear light of the day, Eriko saw that her mother's face was covered in lines and liver spots – that nothing about her seemed young any more. Looking at her amicable, slightly drooped eyes and the corners of her mouth, which pressed downwards into a faintly troubled expression, it struck Eriko once again that she and her mother really didn't resemble each other.

'I knew from the start that someone like your father was too good for me, really. I won out against all the other women at the company, despite being no great beauty. I was punching above my weight.'

She was like Maori, Eriko thought. Maybe Eriko found herself drawn to Maori precisely because of that similarity.

'But then you were born, and you seemed a far better match for your father. That was why I tried to give you everything you wanted. I thought my whole role as mother lay in supporting you. I'm still a bit afraid of you, you know. There's a part of me that always wanted to be more like you.'

'Even now I've put on all this weight?' Eriko responded instinctively.

'You're still beautiful to me,' her mother smiled, and placed her soft, cold hand on top of Eriko's. It seemed she understood everything that Eriko was thinking.

'It was all my fault, I think. I became like your and your dad's slave, and never found my own voice. I'm not blaming you two. I wanted to look at the pair of you and find you perfect. I didn't have a very good relationship with my father, so I'd always admired girls who got on with their dads. You don't really know about the unsavoury parts of your father, right? That's because I always stepped in and hid them from your view. I guess you grew up thinking that all women were like me.'

Her tone was calm, but Eriko sensed in her mother a reserve she'd never encountered in her before. It wasn't born of coldness, but consideration. She knew that her mother was trying to gently break free of Eriko's grasp. Eriko felt she finally understood a little better why she had turned out the way that she had. She hadn't even understood her mother, the closest woman to her in her life. The reason that she couldn't make friends with other women wasn't that there'd been a problem with how she was raised, but because she'd never tried to imagine how anyone else was feeling, not even her parents. She tried picturing her father. Just as her mother said, she could only bring to mind his peaceful, considerate side. For a start, he hadn't been around that much when she was younger. When Eriko lost her cool, he would stand there watching on – it was always her mother who'd borne the brunt of her attacks.

'What about leaving home? Did you ever think about that?'

'I considered it several times, yes. It's thanks to Keiko's mum that I never went through with it.'

'Huh?' said Eriko, staring wide-eyed at her mother. It was as though several mysteries had been resolved at once. No wonder Keiko had known so well what was going on with Eriko.

'I'd go round to her house and talk over the various problems I was having. Keiko was often there too. I never told you, I know.'

Once her initial surprise had passed, a sense of betrayal began to blossom in Eriko. She knew that her mother needed friends, but the thought that, unbeknown to her, her mother had been discussing her shortcomings with other people cowed her with shame. She felt her voice grow sulky.

'I wonder if Keiko and her mother understood how you felt? I don't think they've forgiven me …'

After a while, her mother adjusted her scarf and then spoke slowly.

'You might be right, maybe they didn't really understand. But having someone listen quietly to what I was saying, simply the fact of not having to pretend things were better than they were – that saved me. That house was my place of refuge.'

It didn't matter if they didn't understand? Just having someone listen quietly was enough? The words crowded into Eriko's throat, but she swallowed them back, knowing that there was no point asking. She could only suppose that these reactions were available to her mother because at her root she was a kind person who fundamentally liked other people. These were quite possibly things that Eriko would never be able to feel.

'I can't understand other people's feelings. I always get irritated and misread them. I can't even *pretend* to understand them. I don't know what to do about it.' However hard she tried to squeeze her words out, the most that Eriko could muster was an embarrassingly small, squeaky voice. She'd never before felt embarrassed in front of her mother. She wasn't a little girl any more – and yet here she was. Eriko felt she wouldn't even know the right path if she saw it.

'Understanding other people's feelings is really hard. But you need to know that you won't find other women like me in the world, who'll always smile and do all the work for you. Who'll understand everything about you without you having to explain anything. I should have taught you that. Friends aren't like family.'

The wind blew even colder. Eriko had always believed that friends were somehow superior to family – even though, when she thought about it, there was no way that she could have experienced anything better when she was incapable of relating to the family that she had.

If she couldn't become friends with her mother, then Eriko could likely never have any friends at all. What she needed, in order to do that, was distance.

She noticed then that a cluster of five primary school girls had appeared by the entrance to the park. Eriko recognised a couple of them – she guessed they must live in the same apartment building as her. As she watched, the girls dived into the sandpit and began sumo wrestling each other, apparently unfazed by the prospect of dirtying their skirts. Their shrill cries echoed through the white sky, and the plumes of dust eventually reached the bench where Eriko and her mother were sitting.

Surprised, the crows lurking by the rubbish bins took flight.

# CHAPTER THIRTY-FIVE

There was a big moth on the other side of the frosted window glass, its brown wings dotted with violet. Shōko remembered seeing one similar as a young girl, while in the bath with her mother. She'd been frightened of it then, and her mother had comforted her, but hadn't chased it away.

'It's come to see you because it got bored and lonely up in the mountain,' she said, scooping water onto Shōko's back. The water here, in this town where she'd been born, was good for Shōko's skin. The hot water that twinkled clearly in the morning light was soft, sliding smoothly across her body. Now she'd paid the utility bills, the gas and electricity were working again. She stretched out her legs as far as they could go. Cleaning the mould-covered bathroom had meant several hours' labour with bleach and a scourer in a room as cold as any fridge, but her work had paid off. Just the simple act of bathing in hot water helped to wash away the day's exhaustion.

Glancing in the mirror when she got out of the bath, Shōko noticed how dry the skin around her eyes and mouth was, and decided to pop into the chemist before visiting the hospital. The sum of her skincare routine of late was applying Nivea cream and a haphazard coating of beauty liquid from a spray bottle she'd brought with her, so it figured that her skin wouldn't be looking at its best.

She dried her hair, tugged on all the clothes she could find and stuck a beanie on her head. She used both hands to drag out the heavy plastic bag stuffed full of empty cans and liquor bottles that she'd left in the corner of the entranceway.

She dragged the bag along the side of the rice field to the collection point, where she sorted the cans and bottles into the appropriate containers. Throwing her head from right to left, she attempted to loosen her stiff neck. Little by little, she had made a start on disposing of the rubbish littering the house. It was impossible to do it all at once, but with each dent she made, a tiny sliver of confidence opened up in her that maybe she wasn't as lazy as she thought.

The bus was pulling up to the stop as she ran for it, and the elderly driver waited patiently for her to get there. She nodded at the now-familiar face, and took her seat at the very back, as usual. The mountain that her father owned slipped by in the bus window. This run of days seemed without exit, but there wasn't a total absence of light in the distance. Since her message, she'd had only one text from Kensuke:

*How long has the udon in the freezer been in there? It's okay to eat, right?*

Despite the banality of the subject matter, her body had flushed with pleasure on receiving it.

Tonight Shōko had arranged to visit her uncle's house, and was planning to take Yōhei along. Dumb and inconsiderate her brother may have been, but he didn't defy her when she was forceful with him. She needed as many people on her side as she could get. It would be her first time seeing Miwa since that day on the roadside. What's more, she would be meeting her aunt for the first time in over ten years. Shōko had never known that having things to accomplish could make you feel so invigorated and full of purpose.

The hospital appeared in the distance, just as it always did.

Yesterday, when she'd finally told her dad that she had separated from Kensuke, she'd detected no trace of concern for his daughter on his face.

'In that case, you can come home. It's good in the countryside.'

Even now, Shōko couldn't quite throw away the hope that maybe her father did actually love his family. She would also end up thinking that maybe the fault lay with her, for failing to express herself properly. So she would keep on observing her father's gestures and disaffected looks, finding herself disappointed again and again.

Sad as it was, humans were not psychic. It wasn't possible to read a person who revealed nothing about what was going on in their head. Not for the first time, Shōko resolved that today she would express all the rage and sadness she'd been keeping inside to her father. Tomorrow, he was being discharged from hospital.

There was nothing so arrogant as the belief that people would understand you if you said nothing. Maybe she was the only person that could explain to her father how much simply opting out of the act of communication hurt and confused the people around him. She was past the point where she could let herself off on the grounds that she was scared or embarrassed. Sitting there on the seat of the bus, she pushed the buzzer hard.

After alighting at the stop before the hospital, Shōko headed for the big pharmacy. It had only just opened for the day, and there were no other customers inside. In the cosmetics section, she picked up moisturiser, skin lotion and face packs. Feeling the items dropping into her basket, however cheap they were, sent

Shōko's heart leaping like a pinball. This was a feeling she'd forgotten. Even if it was only small amounts, spending your own money was fun.

She caught sight of a promotional sign reading *Kiss Goodbye to Scaly Winter Skin!* The rack beside it was filled with files and pumice stones, corn-removal sticks and creams. The idea suddenly hit her to give her father a pedicure. She would file away the scaly skin and cut and varnish his blackened nails. It was a silly idea, but it also struck her as a good one, and she smiled. If she was going to go to the hospital anyway, she might as well find a way to enjoy her time there at least a tiny bit. Just the thought of getting rid of all of those corns and hardened skin made her fingers quiver in anticipation. She dropped a selection of footcare items into her basket, and headed for the cash register.

Because she had to walk one stop's worth, she arrived at the hospital half an hour later than usual. Her father said nothing but the glance he shot her seemed somehow reproachful.

'Morning. Listen, I was thinking about what we were talking about yesterday …'

Her father cocked his head, a blank, unserious expression on his face. She could still just say nothing, and act like she usually did. Even now, the idea of wounding him was terrifying to her. And yet, Shōko marshalled all of her energy, and sat down on the stool by the bed.

'I'm not going to come back to live here. Because … I don't want to.'

With his eyes like brown-sugar candies, her father was trying to drink her in. Terror rose up in her, and Shōko reached for her father's foot. His ankle, so thin that it looked like it could have snapped in two at any moment, was no longer that of the intimidating man she had grown up with. So long as she was touching his feet, she didn't have to look at his face – for that she was grateful. She began by wiping her father's feet clean with a hot wet towel from the nursing station, then took out the cream for softening keratinous skin that she'd bought and rubbed it in. The soles of his feet were even harder than she'd thought, and so ice-cold it was hard to believe they belonged to a human.

'You think that people should look after you as a matter of course, without you even asking for it.'

'Have I ever said anything to that effect, Shōko?' he snapped immediately. She had always hated how aggressive her father was in his turns of phrase, his tone of voice. When it occurred to her now that he'd likely be the same until he died, she suddenly felt sorry for him. She was still better off than him. At the very least, she had more potential to change than he did. As she massaged the soles of his feet, Shōko went on.

'We don't have any money left. I don't have any of my own, either. So we have to sell the house, and the mountain. I know you've been protecting them all this time, but that's how precarious our finances are. We can't even be sure we'll find a buyer. If we manage to sell them, we'll be doing well. We need all the money we can get.'

Shōko parted her father's toes and smoothed the cream in. So long as she was moving her hands, the awkward moments passed by, and she was connected to her father, effortlessly. This stopped her from making herself small or over-apologising. Quite possibly, Shōko would be well suited for a job like this: a profession where she didn't have to speak to people. Would it be possible to train as something new, at this stage in life?

'It's not my fault that you're unhappy or lonely, just as it's not your fault how unhappy I am, how little I have in my life.'

Shōko spread a towel beneath her father's feet, took out the footfile and held it to her father's right heel. Just a single stroke produced a comically large shower of white powder. Shōko didn't have the courage either to accept or reject her father in his entirety. She was scared of this father of hers who flaunted his unhappiness to curse those around him. If it wasn't for the file in her hand, she would have been running away. From the ankles down, this person wasn't her father, she told herself keenly.

'It's your fault, Dad. It's your fault for valuing booze and all those one-off fun times where you feel special for a moment above anything else. You got yourself into this mess. You act all mysterious, but actually everything you do is a bid to get other people to pay you attention. But you never attempted to change the situation yourself. Saying that you can't be bothered is, in effect, saying that you care about yourself most of all. I'm grateful to you, though. You've taught me what comes when you see that way of life through to its endpoint. As a parent, that's a great service. But, I can't do anything else to help you.'

Her father's big toes twitched. The scaly keratin layer was peeling off in Shōko's hands.

Her mother had cracked in the process of trying to make her father feel complete. She wondered if he had done nothing precisely because Shōko and Yōhei had fled the situation, without ever telling him what they thought. Don't expect anything of us, Shōko thought as she brandished the file with extra vigour. There's no longer anybody left in this world who will save you from your solitude. Just as there was nobody like that for Shōko any more, either.

His voice reached her, from a place far removed from the feet she was staring at.

'I don't understand what you're going on about. Why do you have to make everything so difficult? I guess you've got all progressive now you've gone to Tokyo. Well, I'm just a dumb country man, remember?' Her father's tone was jokey, but the soles of his feet were trembling. It was then that Shōko understood: deep down, her father was broken beyond repair. Whatever Shōko said, it wouldn't reach him. She understood for the first time, and with her whole self, that there were people in this world that you simply couldn't get through to.

She'd been so resistant to confronting him all these years. Just as she had been incapable of accepting Eriko for who she actually was. She couldn't stop believing somewhere that a miracle would occur, they would be bonded together, and the affection she'd felt for her on the first day would return. Now she felt the hope definitively vanish. What of it, though? It was in losing this hazy image of a future convenient to her that Shōko had finally seen what it was that she had to do. She licked her lips and brandished the file again.

'You don't want to lift a finger, do you? Okay, I get it. I'm not up to much, either. What I can do, though, is clean that house, and sort your stuff. I don't know how long it'll take to sell that and the mountain, but when it's done, I'll leave. I'll find a job and a place to live where I can send you money. That definitely won't be enough, so we'll have to get Yōhei to help out too. As for what happens after that ...'

She'd put her father in a home, she thought. There was no way that she could deal with him alone, without the involvement of third parties. The idea that it would be her making all the decisions gave her the feeling that her stomach was being gouged out. She didn't need to look up to know that her father was shooting her a testing look, as if to say: You're going to cut me out, aren't you, like your mother did ...

She recalled Eriko's phrase: *the thing that sets us against one another* ...

Back then Shōko had laughed, thinking her overly dramatic, but maybe the truth was that it wasn't only about society and other big structures. Maybe it all started out with the individuals closest to you.

Though he would never admit it, her father was currently challenging his daughter to a battle on which his life was staked. He was thrusting a binary choice on Shōko: would she cast him out and become the ultimate bad guy, or would she forsake her freedom in its entirety and become his slave? Just like he'd done to her mother. What a pointless waste of an existence, Shōko thought coldly.

That was why she mustn't let herself become embroiled. She mustn't rise to his provocation. She was neither going to win nor to lose, but rather to attempt, with everything she had, to find the middle path – even while knowing that that was the most troublesome solution. She had given up on her father's approach to living, which meant avoiding bother wherever possible.

She breathed in, and bore down even harder with the file. Keeping her hands moving meant she didn't get stuck in her head.

She would have to find a place that would take her father in. She would leave here, find a job, live alone and send him money. Her ideal scenario would of course be to return to Tokyo, but when she thought about the price of rent and the commute, it seemed like that might be tricky. She didn't know what was going to become of her and Kensuke, and she knew that for the moment, it was important that she didn't depend on him. He hadn't cut off contact with her; he seemed intent on visiting her father once a month. She had to wait patiently, to play the long game. To move forward, trusting the dim beacon she could make out in the distance.

Shōko figured that the reason that people studied and learned skills at work was to enable them to act with tenacity in dire situations like this one. Shōko had always avoided these kinds of studies, and she wasn't sure she could suddenly summon up the abilities she now needed. But she did know that she couldn't afford to behave with Eriko-style rashness. She would list up the tasks that had to be done and go through them one by one. Rather than relying on her younger brother, she'd seek out her elder brother with whom she was out of touch, and ask for his help. Then there was her mother, who she hadn't seen all these years. She knew that she couldn't expect support from her, but she still wanted to speak to her. She'd turned a blind eye to her mother's difficulties, right to the end, but now there were endless things she wanted to say to her and consult her about.

'Well, anyway. For the moment, let's see to these feet. I'll have a think about the other stuff.'

There was a small, glistening mountain of rough skin on the towel. Now Shōko started on the left foot.

Eriko had once said that women needed to join forces with other women to avoid becoming embroiled in fruitless competition; now, finally, Shōko recognised that she was right. If she had just one female friend around whom she felt at ease, to whom she could air her complaints and ask for advice, her current stress would surely be halved.

And yet there were people for whom that was simply impossible. For the time being, Shōko hardly stood any chance of making new friends. The same was surely true of Miwa, who'd seemed so relaxed when she'd bumped into her.

'I don't have the skills it takes to clean that house. So I've searched online, and I'm going to ask a cheap handyman to do it. I can cover that. I've got a bit of money from the affiliate ads from my blog and the publisher. Although I'm guessing that doesn't mean much to you.'

Shōko channelled her force into the hands gripping her father's left foot. The thought that so long as she didn't leave, nobody would blame her was a source of courage to her. To an onlooker, she could be nothing but a woman caring for her father. She didn't need to be worrying about overlooking some crucial sign that she was in fact a bad daughter.

She gazed intently at the soles of her father's feet, which were finally regaining their softness. The wrinkles tracing their surface looked to her like a smiling face, and Shōko smiled back at them. Maybe she'd be able to unearth something similarly unterrifying from that godawful house. If she only put in the time, maybe something unsullied would emerge.

'Dad, your feet are in such bad shape! There's so much hard skin there. Look at this! It's like a fossil!'

The thought suddenly occurred to Shōko that she wanted to post a picture of this skin on her blog. Rather than keeping this small occurrence to herself, the desire rose up in her to broadcast it to the world, and entertain people with it. Soon, though, she set herself right. It was interesting to her because it belonged to someone close to her. From a stranger's perspective it was only scaly skin. People would say how disgusting it was. She was glad she'd experienced the trouble that the internet could bring in the early days of the blog. How much more careful she'd become since.

Then it struck her that she'd just thought of her dad as someone close to her. Maybe the very fact that she was touching his scaly fossil skin was already a sign that she thought of him as family.

Shōko chuckled, and took out a nail file in a bid to sort out her father's toenails, which had turned black and formed multiple layers like a mille feuille. She remembered being a young girl and finding her dad cutting his nails on the porch. That innocent astonishment she'd felt then at how big and thick they were wasn't that different to what she felt now.

# CHAPTER THIRTY-SIX

Eriko had been dozing for a while, but she woke with a start and sat up in bed. She drew her phone by her pillow towards her and checked the screen to see that it was a little after half three in the morning.

Roused by something akin to a premonition, she checked through her bookmarks to find that, sure enough, Hallie B's blog had disappeared.

Now all the links between them had truly been cut. For a while Eriko stared at the chaotic interior of her room, illuminated by the streetlight outside her curtain. How many minutes went by like that?

Her body informed her that she wanted to breathe the outside air, to stretch her stiff legs. She put on a coat over her pyjamas, and crept outside, taking care not to wake her parents.

The cool air felt pleasant on her skin. In the entrance to the building she paused, asking herself if it was a bad idea to be out walking alone at this time, but then told herself that very little was likely to happen to an average-looking woman over thirty. The loss of her beauty had made Eriko feel ever so free.

The clear blue night extended all around her. Even when she passed out of the residential area and onto the main road, she encountered no one. Only the waste collection van passed her by, leaving a foetid smell in its wake. She felt like a fish, drifting around the bottom of a lake. It even seemed as if she were the only person in this part of town – maybe the only person still alive in the world. Maybe her parents, her colleagues and Shōko had never really existed.

It occurred to Eriko now that this was possibly what she'd been wanting to do for a long time. She'd wanted to live unattached to anything, to be able to pop outside for a walk whenever she felt like it. So preoccupied had she been by other people's expectations that she'd never really asked herself what she liked to do. Walks, eating out, travel – the things that Eriko longed for were all pursuits that she could ultimately manage even without any friends. If she'd been to Hakone alone, she'd have seen the exact same scenes as she had done with Shōko. Which surely meant that it was better to go alone, without involving other people. How great it would be, she thought, if she could see the things she wanted at her own pace, without having to worry about other people, or getting upset about this and that.

The halo of bright yellow light under the overpass welcomed her in. She had only bitter memories of this Denny's, but it was also the only place that would receive her at this time of night. She pushed open the door with the tinkle of a bell, and then heard a familiar low voice.

'Irasshaimase! Would you like a non-smoking seat?'

The oddly shaped hat, apron and dress in its bright peach-and-white stripes made for a strange combination with the puffy, unsmiling face of a jaded thirty-year-old.

'Why are you looking at me like that?' Keiko now said flatly. 'I've started working here. The night shifts pay well, and as you can see it's deserted, so I can get away with doing basically nothing.'

'How come?'

Eriko sat down in the window seat that Keiko steered her to, and looked up wide-eyed at her friend. Taking advantage of the absence of other customers, Keiko sat down opposite her.

'I dunno ... I guess I realised that it wasn't so great being in the house doing nothing the whole time. I think seeing you and Shōko had something to do with it.'

'Right ... It's hard for women to be fully independent when their parents live in Tokyo, eh?' she said, and Keiko snorted.

Ever since Eriko's childhood, the sorts of sought-after shops and restaurants that were featured in magazines had always been a walk or a quick train ride away. People at both her university and her company were envious when they found out that she commuted in from home. She had no aspiration to live in other places, and no insalubrious background she wanted to forget. She had none of the nostalgia or the bittersweetness of having to leave home; instead, time passed by with perfect flatness. With no need to change anything about herself, her choices had grown more conservative, and she had gradually lost her powers of imagination, become ever more frightened of the unknown. Though she hadn't seen most of her schoolmates since graduating, she knew that they were the same. All of them were getting incrementally older in the same part of town, and before they knew it, they would come to perfectly resemble their mothers. Maybe Tokyo wasn't a special place that had everything, after all. There were similar places to this all over Japan. The independent bookshop she'd loved as a girl was now a chain pachinko parlour. The local station building was indistinguishable from all the other stations on this line. Last week, an old artisan cake shop that had been here for generations had closed down. Tokyo was gradually losing its distinctive features, the individuality that made it feel alive.

There was a rumbling sound, and the ashtray shuddered. A train had passed over their heads. At this time of the morning, it had to be out of service – maybe on its way back to the depot. Eriko prayed that it would carry this sense of constriction she felt far away, that it would take her to a distant, unknown place, where nobody knew her. Would it be possible to start over again as a new person? She'd dreamt of going somewhere else as a young girl, throwing everything away and starting afresh. Why, then, had she never left this place?

Wherever she went, though, Eriko now thought composedly, the world would still be divided into men and women, and she would likely run up against the exact same problem. Now that she was approaching thirty, she could no longer picture a perfect future in the way she used to be able to.

Keiko glanced up at the ceiling.

'We had to take such a stupid roundabout route to school on the train, didn't we?'

'Yeah, when you look on a map it's so close by! It'd take, what, fifteen minutes in a taxi? Even by bike, it's less than half an hour.'

'My mum got up at six-thirty every day to make my lunchbox.'

'The lunches your mum made were so fancy.'

The two of them were talking totally normally, just like they used to. Yet Eriko didn't find herself getting excited, as she had when she and Shōko had got along. On some level, she understood that this was a passing thing.

'We both went to such a good school, and our parents were so devoted, and look where we've both ended up. We're both single at the age of thirty, and struggling with work, and still living at home. We don't even have friends, let alone relationships. Our parents basically threw their money down the drain.' Keiko smiled.

Eriko's mouth, too, loosened. Eriko wanted to start her life over again, right here. She wanted to make friends in this part of town, where her parents and Keiko could see.

'Maybe my life would have gone better if I'd been allowed to cycle into school,' Eriko said.

Then she wouldn't have had to get on the same train and feel envious of Keiko surrounded by her new friends. She wouldn't have got so excited at the experience of her first backie at the age of thirty that she'd have lost herself entirely. When Keiko said nothing in reply Eriko began to feel embarrassed, and changed the subject.

'Why weren't we allowed to cycle into school, do you know?'

'Because there were those girls who got into an accident riding on the same bike, remember? They both died on the spot. I think it was a few years before we joined the school. I remember everyone saying they were really close, and they were always giving each other rides on the backs of their bikes, even though the school had banned it. They would talk the whole time they were cycling. I remember people at school saying that they bet they didn't even notice when the truck ran into them because they were so involved in their conversation.'

'Maybe that's a good way to go. I'm kind of envious.'

'Why?'

'I mean, it's difficult to be friends with other girls! Everyone goes on about girls' nights and all this stuff, but for me friendship is only ever a momentary flash. Friendships that last forever only really exist in stories. I feel like the only way of vacuum-packing that moment when friendship shines its brightest and preserving it would be …'

But Eriko couldn't finish her thought. To come out and say, *the only way of doing that probably would be for the two of you to die simultaneously at the high point of your friendship*, seemed too tragic and too alarming a conclusion to draw.

'I don't see it that way.' When Eriko looked up, Keiko was staring at her with a more serious look than she'd ever seen her adopt before. 'I think all relationships reach a peak. If those two schoolgirls had lived, then by the time the next term rolled around, one of them would probably have found someone they got on with better, and the other one would feel abandoned. Eventually they'd leave school, go to different universities, stop remembering the other's name. But then, as adults, there's a chance they'd bump into each other on the street, and have a nice chat for a few minutes. I feel like that's enough.'

'A nice chat on the street!? That's it?'

A short, superficial exchange of pleasantries. Even if they smiled at one another, they wouldn't make plans to meet again. They would only pretend to understand one another. Eriko couldn't see how such an interaction could deliver the salvation that her mother seemed to think it did. Eriko felt that she'd rather be curtly rejected than on the receiving end of fake kindness.

'You've got it wrong, Eriko.'

Eriko had no memory of Keiko ever being anything other than dispassionate about the world around her, but she now saw that she'd flushed red to her neck. Eriko stared, disbelieving. The scar that rose up there was the wound she'd sustained on account of Eriko.

'I think it's when two people separate that the things they've learned through their friendship can really blossom. It's all very well to stand on the sidelines and laugh at women for gossiping, and complaining, and comforting each other in a shallow, superficial way. But who's to say that the ruthless urge to get at the truth, regardless of whether it breaks the other person's heart, is more virtuous than phrasing your words carefully, out of consideration for another person? I understand now what a talent it is to show care for other people. I've always ridiculed it, could never be bothered with it, and that's why I'm where I am now, with nothing.'

Keiko's hands resting on the table were clasped together tightly. Her blue veins protruded so much it was hard to look at them.

'I feel as though women's optimism, cheerfulness, all the skills they have to make the little moments enjoyable, make them sparkle like fireworks – even if those qualities don't solve anything, they still bring salvation for a lot of people who encounter them. To go back to what we were saying before: what if, while those two girls who were once friends were chatting to each other on the street, two schoolgirls went past on one bike. They'd see it, and laugh. I feel like that one moment is enough, to make it all worthwhile.'

Eriko was thinking of the last backie that Shōko had given her. She still had the graze from that day on her knee. The image of Shōko crying endlessly came back to her. She couldn't erase it from her memory.

'That's why I don't think it's better for them to die. You shouldn't think that either. You've got to live. However hurt and embarrassed you are. Even if you don't have any friends.'

Was it for her sake that Keiko was getting so ardent about this? Was she trying, even temporarily, to repair her relationship with Eriko? Trying to prevent her old friend, who'd fallen as low as she could go, from becoming any more messed up? They would never confide in one another again, or make plans to meet – and yet, in this moment, Keiko and Eriko were connected by an invisible thread. What about Shōko – would Eriko ever be able to meet her again in this way? If she bumped into her, by chance, would they be able to have an enjoyable conversation there on the street, without Eriko trying to squeeze her for more?

'I'm sorry for ignoring you back then,' Keiko said, apropos of nothing. 'For avoiding you, and for lying. I'd started to enjoy the other girls' company more than yours. It wasn't that you did anything wrong. It was just that I'd changed. Maybe, if I'd been able to say that to you, things wouldn't have turned out the way they did.'

It occurred to Eriko that these would most likely be their parting words. Eriko felt fairly sure that she would be leaving this area soon. She had come to understand that something in her meant she ended up hurting the people she cared about when she was with them. She wasn't sure what she would do, but she knew that her time had come to fly the nest. She should doubtless have done it already. Still, she couldn't change the past. The only things that Eriko could exercise freedom over were those beginning tomorrow.

What was Shōko thinking about, in her apartment not far from here?

*You'll remember me sometimes, won't you? We'll see each other again, won't we?*

As if in answer to Eriko's questions to her old friend, another train passed over their heads, and the tremors spread through the whole restaurant like ripples. Possibly it was the first train already. Keiko got slowly to her feet and walked over to the cash register. When she returned, she had a stack of breakfast menus clasped to her chest, which she went around tossing onto the tables with a carelessness that was so very her. Were any of the ingredients there the kind that her mother thought of as real food? Eriko wondered. But right now, that didn't matter.

Eriko took out her phone, held her breath and deleted Shōko Maruo from her contacts. The whole thing took a matter of seconds. She exhaled, sat up straight and looked out of the window.

What really counted was having somewhere brightly lit that would receive solo customers at this time of the morning. Even if this fake food, high in salt and calories, was rotting people's bodies, and would in the future steal away this city's signature culture and flavour, that wasn't important in this moment. This family restaurant had given work to Keiko, who was neither young nor had any skills to speak of, and given a moment of something like warmth to Eriko, who had no friends now, and probably never would. She prayed from the bottom of her heart that Shōko had a similar place accessible to her.

The night was slowly fading into day.

A cumulonimbus cloud flooded with the light of the rising sun stretched through the sky like an enormous hand, blotting out the darkness. If only the night were a little longer, Eriko sighed, and reached a hand out towards the breakfast menu.